T5-DIG-345

DARK MOON

DARK
MOON

J.H.BRENNAN

 Holt, Rinehart and Winston / New York

First published in the United States in 1981 by Holt,
Rinehart and Winston, 383 Madison Avenue, New
York, New York 10017.

Library of Congress Cataloging in Publication Data

Brennan, J.H.
  Dark moon.

  1. Mary Magdalene, Saint—Fiction. I. Title.
PR6052.R412D3   1981   823'.914   80–20034

ISBN 0–03–058013–7

FIRST AMERICAN EDITION

Designer: Lucy Castelluccio

Printed in the United States of America
10 9 8 7 6 5 4 3 2 1

DARK
MOON

ONE

1

The horror was coming again, as it always did on nights without a moon.

It scratched, like a dog at a door, on the outer edges of her awareness. Miriam shivered. She had long since accepted the inevitable, but each time it occurred, her body trembled, her bowels turned to water. There was a disgust beyond describing, a loathing outside reason, a terror that grew until it filled the whole horizon and left her a child again, mewling and quaking and wanting to hide . . . or die.

Would even death release her?

The room was richer than anything her parents had ever known, just as the house itself was larger, brighter, more luxurious. There was not a brick of it she did not own, not an ornament mortgaged to the moneylenders. It was comfortable and welcoming, tastefully furnished, without ostentation, for her clients were mainly sophisticated Romans with a sprinkling of respectable elders from among her own people, and discretion was demanded. But on nights of the waning moon, it became a pit of writhing maggots.

She took no clients on such nights as this.

It always began with the scratching. Such an innocuous little sound, and not even a sound, for the scratching was within her mind, inaudible to all but her. She went to a chair and sat.

3

Although her own people squatted, the Romans preferred to sit when they were not reclining, and Miriam had taken up the habit. She stared before her blankly, waiting. There was no defense.

Was this a punishment for sin? She knew she was a sinner, for even the elders who came to lie with her had told her so. And the Lord was terrible in His punishments. The rabbis told how He had stricken men dumb and blind, tortured them with boils, starved them, maimed them, struck them down, consumed them with fire as He had with Nadab and Abihu. But this? Was her sin so great that she deserved this?

Behind the scratching, something was singing, a high-pitched discordant song devoid of joy.

Her eyes alighted on the bed. This was always what they meant by sin, those pompous, rigid elders so anxious to help her commit it. Before the act they talked of love, but in their satisfaction they railed against her fornication. And she knew they were right. It was a grievous sin for a woman to tempt so many men to lust, accepting payment for the service. But she also knew this could not be the sin which provoked such anger in the Lord, for the thing had first come for her when she was still a virgin.

She remembered the terror of that time, the confusion, the bewilderment. It had come barely days after the smaller fear, confusion, and bewilderment of her first monthly issue. While her body bled, her mother reassured her it was simply a sign that she was becoming a woman, but Miriam did not like the sensations she felt, did not like the moods they engendered. It had passed over, exactly as her mother had predicted, and in the relief of the passing, she was ill prepared for what came next.

There had been no scratching then—or at least she had not noticed it. Instead, in the night, a dark shape had entered her mind. It was a shape without form, and it stank of putrefaction, a shrilling void that pushed her small thoughts to one side and squatted, brooding, on the throne of consciousness within her skull.

At first, and for a long time afterward, it did no more than that. Each time it left her, Miriam lay sobbing with relief. Each time it returned, she shrank back into the darkest corners of her mind in loathing.

She never lost the loathing, never lost the fear. But while she never learned to understand it, she could not stop herself from

4

observing it. Eventually, it occurred to her that it fed on physical sensation: any physical sensation.

Strangely, it was almost two years before anyone noticed the change in her. Perhaps this was because the creature only came at night, when her family was sleeping. But one night, for no reason, it made her cut her body. She used a piece of sharpened flint to gouge flesh from her breasts and belly, buttocks and thighs. She inserted the point in her rectum and vagina, twisting fiercely. The pain was appalling, but the presence in her mind would not permit her to stop. She hacked at the tendons between her toes and prized off three fingernails in mind-wracking flares of agony. The flint was moving up toward her eyes when she lost consciousness.

There was no hiding the signs of that night. Her bedding was saturated with her blood, her hands were black and swollen, her skin was so bruised and lacerated that scarcely an inch anywhere remained free from damage. She was too weak to move. Her mother's screams when she found her scarcely impinged on her awareness.

The women of the family cleaned her carefully and nursed her. Throughout the convalescent period, the creature did not come again, and for a time she even came to believe it had left her for good. But then, when she had almost recovered, once again she heard the scratching and the joyless singing and it entered her. For the first time she was not alone. Her father was with her, and her pious uncle. The creature knew them and disliked them so that after a moment it shouted obscenities at them in Miriam's voice. Their shock amused it—she could feel the black pulsations of amusement crawling through her skull—and it began to blaspheme. When it used the Forbidden Name of God, her father struck her violently, and the creature laughed at him out of Miriam's mouth.

She watched in horror as her body moved to take off her robe, exposing her nakedness to her father and her uncle. She saw their faces as her body writhed, legs spread, and began to pump itself toward a peak of pleasure, then as alien to her as the creature squatting deep inside her mind.

After that they took her to a rabbi—not one of the village rabbis, but a venerable teacher in Tiberias. He listened to their story, nodding quietly, darting an occasional glance in her direction. When they had finished, he asked to be left alone with her.

5

"When did it come to you?" he asked her gravely.

She was sitting at his feet, head bowed, as Hebrew women were taught to do in formal audience with a venerable rabbi. But though he was old and undoubtedly very wise, she had little hope that he would relieve her burden. There was too much fat on his bones and his eyes had no compassion. Nevertheless, she said, "Two years ago."

"Speak up, child!"

She was no longer a child, not by her own measure or the measure of her tribe, but she repeated meekly, "Two years ago."

"And you told no one?"

"No."

The compassionless eyes bored into her. "Why not?"

Why not? Whom could she tell? Who could help her when she did not even know herself what was happening to her. She remembered the things the creature had made her do, both alone and later before her father and her uncle. In remembering she flushed and said softly, "I was ashamed."

"Ashamed?" His plump features contorted into a sneer. "What did you do, woman, to bring this abomination upon you?"

"Do?"

"What was your sin? Were you pure, it could not fasten on you!"

She knew of no sin, at least none grave enough. Helplessly she whispered, "What is it, rabbi? What comes into me?"

"You don't know? After two years, you don't know?" He actually spat. "You are infested! Your soul crawls like rotting meat."

"With what, rabbi?" Miriam gasped. "With what?"

"Demons!" roared the rabbi, eyes ablaze.

§2

Pontius ascended to the first subdivision of the tiers, carrying his cushion. There was a stubborn ulcer on his right leg—some three weeks old now and still without the slightest sign of healing—which affected his mood as did his financial problems. But he maintained a brave front, as befitted a patrician, and took his place with sober dignity. He appeared to have arrived a little early, for there was scarcely a face he recognized on the tiers reserved for equestrians like himself—and few enough on the tier above, reserved for citizens and tribunes.

It was a very different story in the remainder of the stadium. Behind the third partition, the poor swarmed like ants, jostling and sometimes even fighting for what they considered the prime positions on the benches. Having nothing better to do, he turned to watch them for a while, since it was always amusing to try to judge the tenor of the crowd before the Games began. Today they seemed an even more raggle-taggle lot than usual, sporting patched mantles and badly cobbled footwear. But he noticed with interest the outbreak of another of those wholly unpredictable fashions which seized plebeian imagination from time to time: quite literally hundreds of them were wearing felt *pilei*, the brimless hats modeled on (of all things!) the headgear of Greek sailors.

He turned again and glanced down toward the podium. The Emperor's box was still empty, which might mean nothing at all, or could mean that Tiberius was preparing to ignore the Games altogether. It would be a radical step if he did. The Ludi Magni were a far cry in importance above the Ludi Plebeii, which he had failed to attend last year, or even the Floralia in April, of which he had missed five full days. It was all very well for an emperor to disdain the Circus, all very well for him to cut back on the *munera*, abandon the special games Augustus had instituted, all very well to reduce the number of gladiator matches permitted in any given spectacle, and even to reduce the budget for the major games themselves. But to ignore the Ludi Magni altogether would be taking things a shade too far, even for a Caesar. Pontius shrugged inwardly. In all probability Tiberius would simply arrive late, or very late. One of the more pleasing prospects of the purple was that the Games would scarcely begin without him, unless he sent word.

There was a sudden outburst of applause as two of the more popular Senate representatives entered the podium, which changed abruptly to whistles as attention switched to a considerably more spectacular sight than the pristine togas of these worthies. Unlike the common women, who had a covered gallery so high above the arena it was a miracle they could see men slaughtered at all, the wives of important dignitaries were permitted to sit near the vestals, where the view was infinitely better. One was entering now, preceded by Nubian runners, and riding in the most ornate litter Pontius had seen for many a year, its uprights intricately carved with animal reliefs and its support finished in gold leaf which flashed and sparkled in the sun. The carriage was borne by no fewer than eight liveried Syrians (who on earth would choose to dress her slaves in scarlet?), and had a muslin half-veil to protect the occupant from the glances of the vulgar, as if this were not precisely what the ostentation was designed to provoke.

Since he considered himself as vulgar as the next knight, Pontius watched unashamedly. The litter stopped, surrounded by its entourage—maids, friends, even a nurse—and there emerged from it Portia, wife of the noble Gaius. The gold leaf, if nothing else, would have given her away, since Gaius was the only man in Rome with sufficient wealth, allied to sufficient stupidity, to permit indulgence in such frivolity. She had, he noticed, dyed her hair bright yellow, in some fearful imitation of the current Germanic fashion. But since her skin was so naturally dark that no amount of powder could lighten it, the contrast merely gave her the appearance of a clown. Rings glinted from each finger, jeweled bracelets hung heavily from her wrists and—dear gods, had Gaius no control?—her ankles. A movement among the multitude of necklaces attracted his attention and he saw that she was wearing a small snake draped around her neck. Knowing Portia, Pontius was sure the reptile would be both exotic and deadly—with the fangs drawn, of course.

"The wife of Gaius excels herself today."

Pontius glanced up to discover that he had been joined by Corax, one of the city's more amusing ne'er-do-wells, a man at once famed for his wicked tongue and totally impassive features. "My very thought," said Pontius warmly. "Am I to have the pleasure of your

8

company today?" They were not close friends, but close enough. With Corax by his side, even the dullest bout might be enlivened. Anything to distract the mind from ulcerated legs and empty purses.

"Indeed you shall, dear Pontius," said Corax easily. He placed his cushion on the bench and sat, a tall, slightly stooping figure, slim as a reed despite the prodigious quantities of food he consumed. Pontius noticed he carried a small basket as well as the cushion. It would certainly contain several well-boiled eggs, bread, perhaps a little honey, fruit, and at least one, more probably two, cold roast guinea-fowl. Since Corax was nothing if not generous, the day seemed brighter already. Pontius himself had neglected to bring a snack, a lunatic token to the gods of economy which he had regretted the instant he entered the Circus.

As Pontius had done, Corax glanced around him. Following his gaze, Pontius noticed that the stadium was filling fast. Despite the appearance of anarchy, it was apparent that the plebeians were once again arranging themselves in the familiar tribal blocs. Later, of course, these loose subdivisions would diminish in importance and the crowd would become a single animal, speaking, by and large, with a single voice.

"A respectful mob," Corax remarked. "Have you noticed they seldom jeer at us nowadays?"

"They never jeered at me," Pontius told him wryly. "I've never been important enough to merit their attention."

"Is that what it is?" Corax asked, his face immobile. "I often wondered why my entrance was greeted with disdain while someone like Portia can have them whistling at the twinkle of a diamond." He looked back toward Portia, who was handing her little snake to a serving maid. "Do you imagine it's true that she lies with those Nubians?"

"Does she?" Pontius asked. "I thought they were eunuchs."

"Oh, indeed not. Every one is virile as a bull."

"Doesn't Gaius object?"

Corax shrugged. "I expect he's quite relieved. By the time he counts his gold each night he must be utterly exhausted." The blue eyes flickered sideways. "I understand you have few problems in that department nowadays."

"My virility or counting my gold?" Pontius inquired smoothly.

"I should never dream to question your virility, dear boy."

9

A sudden roar informed them that the Emperor had arrived. The spectators were rising, row upon row, as the clamor swelled to a crescendo. Pontius and Corax both stood up and began to applaud with the necessary enthusiasm. (One never knew when such things might be noticed.)

Tiberius had the height of his father, but not the bulk. Despite his vaunted dislike of the Games, he seemed pleased enough at his ovation. And there was little reason why he should not be, of course, since he had purchased it so cheaply. Poor old Augustus had emptied his coffers financing new Games, every second week it seemed. He believed the money well spent, since the people had loved him for it. But here was Tiberius, drawing back from almost every entertainment, replenishing his treasury with the savings, and if his welcome was no more enthusiastic than that granted to his father, it was certainly no less.

He stood for a moment, a vivid splash of purple among the white togas of his retainers, then sat and stared out across the arena toward the empty box of the editor. Was he, Pontius wondered, bemoaning the fact that the box was empty? The editor organized and financed the Games. The special box remained empty only on those occasions when editor and Emperor were one and the same person. Even with all his economies, the Ludi Magni must have cost Tiberius a pretty penny.

"Now," said Corax, "we may sit and enjoy the show." He opened the basket. "Can I tempt you to a little fruit?"

"Thank you," Pontius said.

Together they sat peeling oranges.

The heralds struck up to renewed cheering from the crowd and the procession began. Below them, doors opened in the arena and the first priests in their gold-embroidered *chlamides* stepped out to lead the grand parade. Censers swung and even from that distance, Pontius caught a whiff of incense.

"I wonder," Corax remarked, "if the gods will be satisfied with the celebrations? They say Tiberius has arranged that the hunt will consist entirely of rabbits." He looked directly at Pontius, face impassive. "To save money, you appreciate."

"Perhaps he will have the priests fight to make up for it," Pontius suggested. The orange was delicious.

"It certainly costs much less to train a priest than a gladiator.

Speaking of which, have you heard of Gaius's other obscenity —apart from his wife, that is?"

"No," Pontius admitted, intrigued.

"He has given Tiberius a dwarf to fight in the arena."

"A dwarf?"

"Perhaps the word is too strong," Corax admitted. "The creature comes from an island near Cathay. Imported at great personal expense, as you may imagine. The men of the island race are all small, if one can credit the reports, so perhaps he is a giant among them. But by our standards, he is scarcely more than a dwarf."

"And Gaius proposes to fight him? A clown's match?"

But Corax was shaking his head. "No indeed. A clown's match would be an amusement, possibly. Gaius wishes him matched in the main events."

Still puzzled, Pontius said, "Against a trained gladiator of normal size? Where is the sport in that?"

"No sport, merely slaughter. So few people can tell the difference these days."

"And Tiberius has agreed?"

"He has the creature free," Corax said impassively. "He will hardly bring himself to waste it."

Which was true enough. And a man so disdainful of the Games could scarcely be expected to appreciate the centuries of sporting tradition which lay behind them. "Perhaps," Pontius suggested, "they can even out the balance by the weapons chosen."

"Do you really think so?" Corax asked him blandly. "Perhaps if they gave the gladiator a dagger and the dwarf a very long spear . . ."

An obscenity indeed for anyone with the best interests of the Games at heart. Although he was not by nature an emotional man, Pontius bridled. There was no doubt in his mind that the real cause of degeneration was the execution of criminal elements as part of the overall spectacle. Unquestionably, any society must rid itself of criminal elements. Unquestionably, any necessary executions must be public as a warning to those tempted to do wrong themselves. But all that was a far cry from making them part of the Games, which were, after all, a religious and a sporting spectacle —rather more sporting than religious, however many priests took part in the opening ceremonies. He had once argued the point in

11

public, advocating the setting aside of special days for mass executions (which might then be made as dramatic or amusing as the authorities chose). But these would not be the days of the Games. The two would be entirely separate and seen to be entirely separate. No one had listened, of course—at least, no one in authority. So criminals continued to be executed as part of the Games and the tradition of fine sportsmanship continued to be eroded. Now, it seemed, it had been eroded to such an extent that the Emperor himself would conspire to turn a noble contest into a bloody farce.

"Well," Pontius said, "it really is too bad of him."

"Perhaps we can spot the dwarf in the parade," said Corax.

As it happened, they did not, although this was probably because of his size. But when the matchmaking draw began, there, unmistakably, he was: toward the right of one loose group to the far side of the arena. Once spotted, there could be no possible mistaking of his identity. Not quite a dwarf, as Corax had admitted, but certainly very small indeed: he scarcely reached the shoulders of the men on either side of him. Like everyone else in the ring at that time, he was almost naked and unarmed. From a distance, the body seemed undernourished and distinctly frail, like that of an old man, but it was quite impossible to judge age from his features. They were, Pontius thought idly, almost demonic —high cheekbones, slitted eyes, prominent ears, all set beneath a shaven skull. But the most noticeable thing of all was his coloring.

"Is he ill?" Pontius asked. "He seems to suffer an infection of the liver." Bad enough that a clown be sent to fight, but a sick clown . . . !

"Ill?" Corax frowned. Then his brow cleared. "Oh, the color! No, I'm told that is the natural pigment of his race, as Africans are brown or black."

"Are you sure? It looks like liver trouble to me."

"Reasonably sure," Corax told him.

A surge of wild enthusiasm from the crowd greeted the imperial party as it entered the arena. The Praetorians came first, of course, forming an avenue for their Emperor, but Tiberius strode out at the head of his entourage, relaxed, smiling, and apparently content, as if he had never expressed disapproval of such occasions. In a moment the stewards were swarming around him like obsequious flies; and like flies he brushed them aside, to walk—quite alone—to the nearest group of gladiators, where he stopped and briefly chatted.

It was a superbly calculated gesture and the crowd was lavish in its appreciation. Perhaps, despite all, there was more to Tiberius than Augustus. The father had only tried to buy goodwill. The son used his head and had it free. The Emperor's patrician gaze swung around.

"I'll wager he's looking for his latest toy," Corax suggested quietly.

And so he was, for he left the group and walked directly to where the dwarf was standing. This time, however, the Praetorians had caught up to flank him. Sporting gestures were all very well, but even an unarmed gladiator could be dangerous, especially when he had nothing to lose. Not that Tiberius seemed to lack popularity among the fighters either, by the look of them.

A gesture from the Emperor, and the little yellow man stepped forth. For a moment there was silence, then the crowd began to clap and cheer, interspersing their enthusiasm with a great deal of laughter—and not all of it derisive.

It was too far to hear, but Tiberius seemed to say something and the dwarf first bowed deeply and appeared to answer.

Pontius allowed one eyebrow to drift upward. "The creature has command of civilized language?"

"Even a raven may be taught to speak," said Corax blankly.

Now Tiberius was returning to the temporary stand set up beneath the royal box. As editor he had two tasks: to draw the lots and to inspect the weapons. Then, as Emperor, he had only one: to give the signal that would start the Games.

The drawing of the lots was not all luck, since leaving the matchmaking entirely to chance would produce too great a risk of uneven contests, hence poor sport. Advised by the trainers of the gladiatorial schools, the marshals had already made the preliminary subdivision, segregating the fighters into two main groups, each with a balanced complement of *thracians, thraxes, provacators, secutors, retiarii, mirmillos,* and other gladiator types. One group then paraded, man by man, before the Emperor, who drew lots from the marked container in accordance with the gladiator's type. There was no real reason, Pontius supposed, why a *scissor* should not fight a *scissor*, but the crowd traditionally considered such contests to be poor sport, so arrangements were made that it should not happen.

For some reason, the plebeians heartily enjoyed the drawing of the lots. But Pontius found it a bore, at least until the Emperor's dwarf stepped forward. Since the creature was closer now, Pontius could see that what he had previously taken for frailty was a type of wiriness, although if there was stamina in those slim muscles, there could be little strength.

"I wonder how he has been classed," he murmured. It had occurred to him that if the creature was a *sagittarius*—a gladiator armed with a bow—the ensuing contest might not be so ill matched, particularly if the dwarf had skill.

"No doubt we shall discover shortly," Corax said.

With no more than a passing glance at his dwarf, the Emperor drew the lot. A marshal stepped forward to announce the result.

"Trajan!" Pontius echoed, appalled. "He's been matched with Trajan." He forgot himself so far as to grip Corax's arm in momentary emotion. "It will be slaughter in minutes!" Minutes? Seconds, more like. In the two years he had been fighting, Trajan had fast become a legend in the arena. He had the build of an ox and the stamina of a mule. In the early days, this had been enough—if only just—to carry him through his initial fights. Later, his swordplay improved. Now, although he was far from being Rome's most skillful gladiator, he was one of the most feared. His list of kills grew longer with each event. Oddly enough, the crowd did not like him greatly. His brute crudity, his savage bloodymindedness, seemed too much, even for them.

Some of that feeling showed now, when the draw was announced. At first silence, then a growing sound eerily reminiscent of a growl. It appeared that more than Pontius disapproved, so perhaps sportsmanship was not altogether dead in Rome. But Tiberius ignored the crowd and the draw continued, so that the attention of the fickle mob was soon swallowed up by other interests.

The displeasure revived, however, when the moment came for arms inspection. Strictly, as editor, Tiberius should have carried this out himself. But after a token glance at the first three swords and a trident, he retired, leaving the remainder—and the bulk—of the inspection to a senior marshal. The plebs accepted it, as they accepted so much from Tiberius. Or perhaps they were simply too interested in how the fighters would be armed to care overly much for tradition and the niceties of etiquette. Certainly Pontius could not have given a broken *denarius* who made the inspection. He wanted only to see how the dwarf and Trajan would be armed.

"They've classed him as a *thracian*, by the gods!" For the first time, Corax actually sounded surprised.

So it was to be slaughter without even the pretense of a fight. As a *thracian*, the dwarf would be unshielded. His only protection would be the metal leg guards and the leather sleeve on his left arm. His only weapon would be the *sica*, a short, curved saber which was deadly enough in the hands of an expert; but what would this tiny, yellow island-savage know of swordplay?

Trajan, on the other hand, was a *hoplomachus*, which meant he not only carried a long sword but also a shield large enough to cover the vital areas of his massive body. As a contest, the match had all the uncertainty of the fate of a beast in a butcher's shop.

"Why do they do it?" Pontius moaned. "Tiberius loathes the Games, of course, but Gaius . . . Whatever his faults—and they were legion—Gaius had some reputation as a sportsman.

"Ah, but Gaius thinks he will win," Corax answered quietly.

"Trajan? Of course he will win! They might as well have him fight a sheep!"

"Not Trajan—the dwarf!"

"The dwarf?" Pontius turned, but could read nothing in those immobile features.

Corax shrugged. "Such is his belief. The dwarf, you see, is a magician."

Pontius smiled uncertainly. Corax sounded serious enough, but it was always difficult to tell.

Catching the expression, Corax added, "Don't take my word for it, dear boy. Ask anyone who knows him. He makes no secret of the fact."

Pontius stared down at the dwarf, now half-hidden as he took his place for the second parade. The creature certainly looked strange enough to be a wonderworker, but Pontius had little faith in the effectiveness of magic when it was faced by the keen edge of a well-tempered sword. Especially a sword wielded by a bull like

Trajan. "Well, well," he murmured, and turned to Corax. "You must excuse me for a little while, dear friend. It occurs to me I have some urgent business I must attend to."

In fact, as he abandoned his cushion and left the *maenianum*, Pontius was convinced the gods had granted him an answer to his most frequent prayer.

∫3

The singing stopped, which meant that the creature would soon enter her. The fear pushed her mind into limbo, so that she sat in an aching void, thoughts sluggish, fighting off a desire to sleep—or die. Sometimes when it came she fought it fiercely. Sometimes she resisted it with listless resignation. Neither made any difference at all. The thing went on its own way, using her precisely as it pleased.

Always, always she remembered how the world had been before.

How the world had shattered that day in Tiberias. . . .

"Demons, rabbi?" her mother had whispered. Miriam remembered her as a sad creature, gray-haired and weary from too many years of hardship, but never so sad as at that moment. Her eyes had grown large and luminous with sorrow, huge despairing orbs that stared out on the ultimate disaster too full of tears to weep.

The plump rabbi nodded sagely. "At least one, possibly a host. It is difficult to tell. Infestation comes in many forms." He spoke so calmly, like one voicing an opinion on the weather.

"But why?" This from Miriam's father.

The rabbi shrugged. "The girl has obviously sinned."

"She is a good girl," her mother whispered.

"She may have seemed a good girl," the rabbi corrected her firmly, "but possession follows definite laws. Like attracts like. This thing has found in the child a quality sympathetic to its own nature. Such a quality is always the result of sin." He moved his

16

head so that his words included Miriam's father as well. "You must not blame yourselves. No parents can watch over children all the time. This child strayed from the paths of righteousness when your eyes were not upon her. Perhaps only a momentary matter, but the demon was watching and seized its chance."

It had not been like that, Miriam thought. It had not been like that in the slightest. She had only been relieved to be done with her first monthly issue. She had worked as she always worked and thought as she always thought. She had made the necessary observances laid down for women. Yet it had come to her in the night.

"What's to be done?" asked her father. He was a strong man, always practical, always willing to face up to necessity.

And her mother, almost simultaneously, asked, "Can it be driven out?"

The rabbi, with his bald head and his long gray beard, chose to answer the woman's question. "Exorcism? A possibility, of course. Certainly a possibility. But I should not advise it. No, not in the smallest degree. A skilled exorcist is difficult to find—and costly. There are many charlatans, of course, but their interference invariably makes the matter worse: the demon entrenches itself, so to speak. And even if you should be fortunate enough to find someone with sufficient power, there is always the question of where the demon will go. These entities cannot be destroyed, of course, only driven out. It might find a new home elsewhere: in the exorcist, perhaps, or in another member of your family, or it can even return again to the girl at some future time and then your efforts and your money would have been completely wasted." He shook his head firmly. "No, I should not recommend exorcism, not in the least."

"Then what's to be done?" her father repeated.

An expression of professional concern settled on the rabbi's features. "There are certain diseases which, by the Lord's will, cannot be cured—plague, for example, or leprosy. When we discover such a case, our concern cannot be for the unfortunate who has contracted the disease, but for those around him, who might contract it from him in their turn. The Lord is merciful, so we do not put a leper to death. But we cast him out, to find his own way in the world, so that his foulness may not contaminate the good health of others."

They were speaking about her as if she did not exist, as if she were not present here and listening. Her father stared at the rabbi, eyes wide, but jaw set and grimly fixed. "We must drive her out?"

"For the sake of your wife and your other children and yourself. Since we cannot cure demonic infestation, we can only ensure it does not spread among those that we love."

But she was one of those they loved! Miriam protested in her mind. She looked from her father's grim face to her mother's sorrowing face and read fear in both of them. Fear. Only fear; no longer love.

They took her home after that and for a day and a night she sat by a wall in the main room of their home and listened while they discussed the matter endlessly She grew more weary than a child had any right to be and eventually their words no longer concerned her. It was as if they were discussing someone else. It was as if the world had somehow grown less real.

She felt nothing, nothing at all, when they drove her from her home.

Magdala was a small town, little more than a village really, built around a communal wall and market square. Even before she was driven out, the news of her infestation had spread like wildfire. She walked along a short, familiar street and neighbors pressed themselves against the walls until she was past. No one would speak to her. No one would give her food. A group of children, several of her friends among them, stoned her until she ran bruised and bleeding from the market square and hid from them behind a low stone wall. She was lost and frightened and did not know what to do. Her mother had pressed a small sum of money into her hand as her father drove her out, a few copper coins —enough, perhaps, to buy some goat's milk and a loaf of bread. But no baker would sell to her. For all the copper coins in Magdala, no baker would sell to her. She wept a little and stared at the coins, the final, useless token of a mother's love. They were stamped on one side with the portrait of Augustus Caesar. She would go, she thought, to Tiberias, the city. They would not know her there, so she could spend the coins.

She rose from her hiding place behind the wall and discovered that the crowd of children who had stoned her was now gone. She left Magdala and set out, walking, on the dusty road to Tiberias.

That first night she almost died. She was tired and hungry, her feet raw and bleeding, and since she did not know about such things, she lay down by the roadside when night fell.

She slept, and as she slept, her body chilled. Her robe was of thin cotton, suitable for the day, but no protection from the cold night wind that swept down from the mountains. She awoke in darkness, numb. It was not an unpleasant sensation, for her feet no longer pained her, and she was sorely tempted to sink into the numbness, to let it wrap around her, carry her away from the hunger and the sorrow and the fear. But somehow she did not sink into it. Instead, she forced herself upright. Her feet burned in protest, but she walked again, backward and forward in the darkness, backward and forward, backward and forward, her thin arms clutched across her abdomen, keeping the cold at bay until the dawn, when she collapsed where she stood and slept again beneath a warming sun.

She awoke to an agony of aching muscles, but her mind at least was clear. And she learned quickly, this little Miriam. She knew she could not survive another night in the open without a heavy cloak to keep her warm. She knew she must find water to drink and food to eat. She knew she must fight to survive.

She walked for two more miles before she found a farmhouse where she stole a small cheese from the storehouse in the yard. She would have taken more, but the farmer kept geese and she was frightened that the noise the birds made would lead to her discovery. She ate the cheese and found a hollow stone from which the sun had not yet evaporated the morning dew. She drank from the hollow and licked the cool surface of the stone. It was not enough, but it was something.

A carter with a load of roots took her a full five miles further on toward Tiberias. She stole a handful of the vegetables as she left him and ate them raw by the roadside, scraping off as much of the mud as she could with a flat stone. She still had no cloak, but before sunset she searched out a sheltered place to sleep and managed to survive the night.

Events from that point lost their clarity, became a blur and a blood-haze of pain that turned to agony. Her mind set like stone into a single knot of hard determination. She walked and she stole and she ate and she slept. Images blended like the shifting landscapes of a dream. Eventually, while passing through a tiny hamlet, she bought a woolen cloak with stolen money, then

19

doubled back to steal some food. The chill wind plucked at her toes and fingers in the night. The fierce sun sucked her moisture in the day. The road to Tiberias wound endlessly before her.

One day, incredibly, she reached the city. She no longer knew why she had journeyed there, only that she had arrived. It pained her to walk and it pained her to breathe. She staggered through the streets, not knowing where to go. The people did not shy away from her, but somehow that no longer mattered. Nothing mattered really. She had reached Tiberias and it seemed she should rest. Yet where could she rest? Where could she go?

She reached the city's Temple to the Lord and sat down with the beggars on the broad stone steps. Long before nightfall she stretched out and passed into a deep, exhausted, dreamless sleep.

"Child . . . ?"

Miriam awoke. A man was bending over her, his face illuminated by the torchlight of a flaming brand he carried in one hand. He had soft eyes and kindly features and was plump and clean-shaven. All the same, she started away from him like a frightened animal.

"It's all right, child. I shan't harm you." He looked wealthy. Even in the torchlight she could see that his robe was nearly new.

She licked her lips and said nothing, watching him warily.

"You can't sleep here, child. The Temple is closed for the night."

"Are . . . are you a priest of the Temple?" Miriam asked. She had heard that priests sometimes give alms to the needy.

"Me?" He smiled. "Dear me, no. I'm not a holy man, not in the least degree. I'm a merchant. My name is Talmon. This is my manservant, Joed." She noticed for the first time that another man stood close behind him on the edge of the circle of torchlight. "What's your name, child?"

"Miriam," she told him. "Miriam of—" She stopped, unwilling to let him know her town of origin. "Miriam," she said again. "Just Miriam."

"Why were you sleeping on the Temple steps, Miriam?"

"I was tired," she told him simply.

"Don't you have anywhere else to go?"

She shook her head dumbly.

"Where is your home, Miriam?"

"I do not have a home." It was true, of course. Magdala was no longer her home.

20

"No home? Dear, dear! Your feet are swollen. Have you come far?"

"Far enough."

"Too far by the looks of it," Talmon said in an aside to Joed. He turned back to Miriam. "How long is it since you've eaten?"

She shook her head. She could not exactly remember.

"A long time?"

She nodded. "Yes."

"I think if you have nowhere else to go, you should come home with me, Miriam," Talmon said kindly. "My wife can give you food."

She stared at him, not really comprehending or caring. "I have nowhere to stay," she said dully.

"Then you must stay with us," said Talmon firmly. "You can rest and recover and when you are feeling better, you may like to help my wife with the housework." He held out his hand and she took it instinctively. "I think we'd better carry her, Joed," Talmon remarked. "I doubt if she can stand on those feet."

They carried her easily and set her gently in the merchant's carriage.

From that time of nightmare, from that confusion of sorrow, fear, and pain, the Miriam who sat waiting for her demon retained vivid, pleasant memories: hot food upon a scrubbed pine table, and clean, fresh sheets on a soft, inviting bed.

4

It did not last. It did not last.

She rested and ate and recovered her strength. Shimrith, wife of Talmon, was a fat, maternal woman who took to Miriam instantly, treating her more like a daughter than a servant. Talmon and Shimrith had produced no children of their own, despite frequent Temple offerings, and this may have explained a great deal of their attitude toward her. Once, Miriam overheard

Talmon say he believed the Lord might have guided him to her on the Temple steps. Miriam doubted it: her faith in the Lord had waned a great deal since the demon entered her.

The merchant's home was unlike anything she had previously experienced. Now, looking back, she realized it was no more than an average city house of a member of the trading class. But then, with nothing to compare it to except the poverty of her own small home in Magdala, it had seemed a veritable palace. She had a room of her own to sleep in, and there was a separate room for washing. It was unlike any other house she had known: she had always drawn water from the well and washed outside, summer and winter. There were two house servants apart from Joed, a maid with goiter called Rebecca and a sullen ancient by the name of Adab. Neither they nor Joed paid a great deal of attention to Miriam, as if they recognized instinctively that her status was somehow different from their own. Which, in effect, it was, for although she carried out simple household tasks when she recovered her strength, they were the same tasks she had carried out at home in Magdala and no one ordered her to do them.

Since Talmon was generally away most of the day—and very tired in the evening when he returned home—and the house-proud Shimrith spent a great deal of her time cooking, Miriam found she was often alone. Once she discovered that Shimrith did not mind, she sometimes walked about the city, admiring the tall buildings and visiting the colorful bazaars. She was fascinated by the goods the traders had to offer—ointments and unguents, vessels of brass, jewels and beads, foodstuffs and sweetmeats by, it seemed, the ton. But more than that, she was fascinated by the Romans. Tiberias was a garrison town and the proud, strong soldiers seemed to be everywhere, their armor glinting in the sunlight. Miriam had never seen a Roman before, although she knew Augustus ruled Judaea, as Augustus ruled the entire world.

In the early evenings, she would sometimes walk in Talmon's walled garden, enjoying the scent of herbs that the sullen Adab cultivated so assiduously. Her enjoyment of these strolls ended when Talmon returned, for then he would release his guard dog Keilah, a savage brute which prowled the grounds and thus assured the safety of the house.

The days slipped into weeks, the weeks into a month, then two. Miriam entered a timeless cocoon, half forgetting the village of

22

Magdala, half forgetting her mother and her father, her brothers and her sister, half forgetting the horror that had brought her to this comforting house in this fascinating city.

Then, one night without a moon, the demon took her.

It entered her while she slept, so that she awoke in darkness with the creature already pulsing in her skull. She sat up, and though there was no light whatsoever in her room, the demon enabled her to see. She stepped from her bed, naked, and walked unerringly toward the door.

The house was quiet. It was difficult to judge the lateness of the hour, but certainly she had been asleep for some time, certainly the servants and the master and the mistress should all be asleep by now as well.

Although she was not hungry, Miriam went to the kitchens. There she found a long-bladed knife. She drew the edge across her palm to test its sharpness and watched with interest as the blood welled up from the thin, red line. She stabbed the point into her wrist and found that it entered easily, painfully. In her skull, the demon giggled at her pain.

She carried the knife outside.

The vision of the world the demon granted her was flat and listless, lacking depth and color, lacking life. She smelled the herb scents and they revolted her, although they had not changed from anything she remembered. A part of her mind felt fear because she knew that Keilah would be loose, but the demon told her the dog slept.

Miriam went searching for the sleeping dog.

She found it curled beneath a tree beside the boundary wall. It was a black dog, vigorous and muscular, standing—when it stood—the height of a man's thigh. There was much power in Keilah, an elemental savagery which shone from the sleek coat.

Miriam stabbed him neatly, slipping the knife blade between the ribs into the heart. He jerked slightly as he died, but did not cry out. She smiled.

She knelt and turned the body, then took up the knife again and slit the belly open. She plunged both her hands into the entrails and began to anoint herself with Keilah's blood, daubing it liberally across her face and along her naked breasts and loins, and rubbing it into her hair. Then she rolled across the open corpse to smear blood on her buttocks and her back.

Keilah's blood was warm.

Miriam walked to the little wooden shed where Adab kept the garden implements. The door was secured by a sturdy wooden latch, and at the moment she discovered she had forgotten utterly how to use it. She attacked the door savagely and though she was only a girl with a girl's strength, it burst open with a splintering of wood. She found a small hand ax inside and carried it back to the bloody corpse.

Judging precisely so that seven blows were needed, she hacked off Keilah's head and carried it, dripping, to the gate, where she impaled it on a stake so it could still stand guard.

She returned to the corpse and found the kitchen knife. With rising excitement, she cut off the genital organs, piece by piece, and ate them raw.

The power of Keilah, the raw lusts and angers of the huge dog, flowed into her. She threw her head back and howled loudly for sheer joy.

It was thus—naked, bloody, howling like a fiend toward the sky—that Talmon and the servants found her.

5

Sejanus had been difficult to convince. In a mood of desperation that carried him beyond the habit of dignity, Pontius recalled their friendship, evoked past favors, even groveled a little—at least as much as a patrician ever groveled. The ploys were successful, for Sejanus agreed to let him have the money—agreed reluctantly, but agreed. It was a staggering sum for Pontius and substantial even for Sejanus, who insisted it would take him more than a day to raise. But that would not matter. The dwarf was drawn to fight late in the Games, so there was time enough. Besides which, in certain circumstances, the promise of gold was as valuable as gold itself.

Now, back at the Ludi, he was about to discover how valuable. The matter, he felt, must be handled with delicacy.

It was past midday and the sun had grown hot. Sailors of the fleet were busily manipulating the *veles*, those bands of white linen roped and flown like sails from their masts. But the purpose of these sheets was not motive power, but shade for the spectators. Clever manipulation could even produce wind currents on an airless day. Stewards, more harassed than the gladiators, passed among the crowd with perfumed sprays. Though Tiberius had banned the *sparsio*, he could not ban this. The plebeians could live without the excitement of a lucky counter which might win them pigeons or a lucrative estate, but cooling breezes and perfumed sprays were a necessity of the Games. Except, of course, for the fighters, who were trained to ignore the heat.

The vulgarity of Portia's carriage was missing from the podium, and it was equally unlikely that Gaius would be anywhere within the Circus at this time of day. His wealth put him far beyond the need to observe tradition. Not for him the packed lunch of Corax, nor, since he was fond enough of his belly, the spartan resolve of Pontius. He would be eating in comfort somewhere. The problem was where.

Portia, of course, was well known to favor picnics in the Pontine parkland during the period of the Games. They provided her with further opportunities for public ostentation. Until a year ago she had actually used golden platters for these luncheons, but some ungrateful pauper had stolen seven of them—too great a wastage even for Gaius to stomach phlegmatically. Now she used silver, on the pretext of devotion to the lunar goddess Diana, and contented herself with the flamboyance of her food, pets, and general retinue. Would Gaius involve himself in this nonsense? He had little personal interest in display. The wits said his talent was strictly confined to accumulating wealth and he had been forced to marry Portia to show him how to spend it. But whether he played his own part in the spending depended on his current relationship with Portia; and that varied like the seasons.

Would he be with her now?

It was, Pontius realized, an academic question. If Gaius was not with Portia, he would, presumably, have returned to his villa. Since Pontius could no longer afford to maintain a carriage and was scarcely dressed for riding, there seemed little point in trying to follow Gaius to his home. On the other hand, the park was within walking distance. Pontius left the stadium by the northwestern gate, passing the marble statue of Augustus in the process. Would it, he wondered fleetingly, survive the whole of Tiberius's reign? Images of past emperors were notoriously short-lived in Rome: even filial respect had its limitations.

The drawback with walking distance was that it depended largely on the capabilities of the walker. With his ulcerated leg, Pontius found himself wilting by the time he reached the entrance to the park and actually limping before he caught the first glimpse of Portia's party. But the thought of a solution to his financial ills spurred him on. If his plan succeeded, it would be an enormous coup, something to be talked about in society for years—not that that excited him overly much: he would willingly settle for release from his debts.

Portia had excelled herself. She had chosen a site within easy reach of the path, shaded, but not obscured, by a clump of overhanging limes. Her uncastrated Nubians (could it really be true?) were posted in a dramatic semicircle around a linen cloth, threaded in gold, which was spread upon the grass and already weighted down by a feast that would have done justice to an emperor's banquet. Reclining beside it was Portia herself, resplendent in a light blue robe which would have matched her coloring to perfection had she not changed her hair to that repulsive blond. Thankfully, she had abandoned some of her jewelry, presumably because of its weight in the heat. To compensate, she was now flanked by two leopards, obviously well fed since they were ignoring the food. All the same, they were securely staked with silver chains and an armed guard from Gaius's private legion stood next to each. A striking display; and how boorish it would be to ignore it.

Pontius, who had rested just enough to rid himself of that infernal limp, strolled toward the party, his features composed into a look of vacant irresponsibility which was sometimes taken as the hallmark of the idle rich. He half hoped Portia might call out to him, but when she did not, he pretended to catch sight of her suddenly, stopped, and smiled disarmingly. "Why, Portia, what a delightfully wicked touch!" he exclaimed.

She glanced at him suspiciously. They had been lovers once,

briefly, although that was something she had obviously taken pains to forget. Nevertheless, his remark intrigued her, as it was intended to. "Wicked touch, noble Pontius?"

"The leopards," Pontius said. He glanced at them affectionately, thinking what vicious brutes they looked, more than a little thankful for the thickness of their chains.

The look of suspicion deepened. She had obviously heard malicious rumors of his impecunious situation—all of them too true. Such things weighed heavily with her. "My pets?"

Pontius shrugged lightly. "Since they're saying Tiberius plans to hunt rabbits to save money, only Portia could have the wit to provide wildcats to amuse the disappointed." It sounded feeble, even as he was saying it, but he watched her closely, knowing her susceptibility to anything that smacked of flattery. And sure enough, her expression lightened.

In a moment she was actually smiling. "You were always such excellent company, Pontius. Will you join me and allow my maids to tempt your palate?"

Pontius would have accepted even if he had not been planning to salt her husband. Ostentatious or not, her cuisine was always excellent and the orange donated by Corax, while most welcome, had been less than filling. All the same he said, "For a moment, perhaps. Business matters press hard on me."

"Ah, business," Portia murmured. "Men seem always in pursuit of business. I sometimes wonder how dear Gaius has time to fit in everything he must do."

It was the opening he had been waiting for, and far sooner than expected. "The dedication of the noble Gaius is an example to us all." He glanced around him. Portia's maid had the look of a lively little filly. "Is he not with us? I'm afraid I was so taken by your looks, Portia, I did not notice."

"He will be joining us presently. If your business allows you to stay long enough to meet him, that is."

Oh, it will, it will, thought Pontius. He smiled at Portia and allowed that lively little maid to help him to a sweetmeat.

They were engaged, Portia and himself, in an excruciatingly boring conversation about the merits of Greek musicians—a hobbyhorse of Portia's since she had slept with one—when Gaius arrived. Pontius scrambled respectfully to his feet. As an equestrian himself, Gaius held no higher social rank, but he had the

27

advantage of age and, more to the point, quite limitless coffers. Wealth was power, in Rome as everywhere, and while Pontius might joke with Corax about Gaius behind his back, his habit was to keep a civil tongue while face to face. Besides, Gaius had an uncertain temper, the Emperor's ear, and, Pontius suspected, a shrewd suspicion his wife and Pontius had once been lovers. In such situations, an easy politeness was the keynote.

But as it happened, Gaius seemed in excellent humor. "Noble Pontius," he exclaimed, using the honorific without an apparent hint of sarcasm. "How good of you to keep my little Portia amused in my absence. Please sit. This is no occasion for ceremony." He leaned across to kiss Portia, who offered her cheek with no discernible warmth. "And how are your little pets behaving? Have they created a great stir?"

"They bore me," Portia said. "Like the Games." Pontius remembered that petulant look well. It was the first hint of an impending demand for a new toy. Gaius must have known the sign by now, but he did not react. Perhaps the cost of new toys—even the incredible new toys Portia's appetite demanded—was not sufficiently large to ruffle the feathers of the richest man in Rome. Was it literally true? Pontius wondered. Richer than any member of the Senate? Richer than the parsimonious Emperor? If he was the richest man in Rome, arguably he was the richest man in the world. Could such a one be tempted to gamble? Experience, of course, said yes. But for what motive? Not, surely, the accumulation of more wealth when he already had so much that even Portia could not squander it. Not for the first time, Pontius found himself musing on the peculiarities of humanity.

"The Games will provide tolerable entertainment when my man fights," Gaius said cheerfully. In an odd way, he was still a handsome man. Or perhaps the better word was *interesting.* He must have been nearing sixty—substantially older than Portia, or Pontius, for that matter—but his skin was still sound and the gray of his hair merely added to the distinction of his features. The trick was partly in the aura of gold that wafted round him like a perfumed cloud. His toga was cut from the finest material, his sandals superbly made by master craftsmen, his personal adornment vastly more tasteful than the garish baubles Portia wore, but no less costly. Yet Gaius cut an impressive figure even in the baths, where—if nowhere else—all men were equal. He had, Pontius decided, a confident bearing. He had also eyes as hard as diamonds. For the first time Pontius felt a flowering of unease. Was he really planning to cross swords with this man? He remembered the eyes of his creditors and the unease vanished, swamped by a greater fear.

"Your man?" he asked innocently. "Have you entered a gladiator?" Gaius could afford to enter a thousand, but, oddly, had sponsored few fighters in the past, despite his love of the sport. He was really a man of the *missa*, doting on chariots and a violent partisan of the Green Faction.

"A gladiator in a million," Gaius confirmed bluffly. He sat down on the grass and helped himself to some grapes without waiting for the slaves. "A wonder-worker from the East."

"Not the dwa—small fighter with the yellow skin?" Pontius concluded, frowning. "I thought he was a curio from the Emperor's stable."

"Indeed he is," Portia cut in. "But who put him there? Why, Pontius, my generous husband." Her tone dripped disapproval, although he could not quite understand why.

Gaius seemed in no way disturbed, or inclined to take up the point. He merely said, "He will fight for the glory of Tiberius and carry the Emperor's colors, but the man is mine." With an unusual note of pride, he added, "Bought by me and brought by me to Rome."

"But not trained by you, my dear," said Portia silkily. It was obviously some private disagreement—and a bitter one by the sound of it.

Nevertheless, Gaius said calmly enough, "No, indeed, not trained by me. He has his own way of fighting." He gave a secretive smile.

It was time, thought Pontius, to dangle bait before the fish. As the maid presented him with a bowl of water for his fingers, he remarked, "He seems a little . . . small for a gladiator."

"Small?" Portia sniffed loudly. "The creature's a dwarf! And an ugly one at that!"

"Size hardly comes into it," Gaius said. He was echoing an old saw at the Circus: Size hardly comes into it, it's skill and stamina that count.

Pontius allowed himself just the hint of a cynical smile. "Even drawn against Trajan?"

"Even drawn against Hercules," said Gaius softly.

"I'll wager you're wrong," Pontius told him casually, hopefully not too casually.

"If you did, you would lose." There was a smug note in Gaius's voice, enough to make the next move believable.

Pontius pretended to bristle slightly and said coolly, "I think not, sir. Would you consider a small bet?"

"Have a care, Pontius," Portia put in surprisingly. There was a hint of genuine concern in her voice. "The dwarf is a magician."

Pontius turned to her, trying to strike the right note of gratitude combined with total disbelief. "So I have heard. But I have seen magicians die in the arena and not all the spirits of the underworld could help them."

Gaius sighed. "Not a magician, Pontius. Merely a priest."

It stopped Pontius short. He blinked. "A priest?" His joke to Corax came back to him. But it had only been a joke.

"Not one of our gods, of course," Gaius said hastily. "Nor one we're likely to adopt either, since he forbids the carrying of arms."

Intrigued, Pontius said, "Forbids arms? How do his followers defend themselves?"

Gaius shrugged. "Perhaps their god protects them. I really couldn't say."

"But the priesthood is exempt from this ruling?"

"Oh, no." Gaius shook his head.

It grew more ludicrous by the minute. "This one will have to carry arms in the arena," Pontius said, smiling openly.

Gaius answered the smile, eyes hard. "Perhaps there are special dispensations in certain contingencies."

One could hardly suppose otherwise. Nonetheless, the information was useful. If the creature was forbidden to carry arms by his religion, then however much he armed himself for his forthcoming encounter, the skill would be lacking. The last vestige of doubt, already shrunk to small proportions by the dwarf's fighting classification as a *thracian*, now disappeared altogether. Pontius said, "So he will carry a saber and rely on his god to protect him?"

"Perhaps." Gaius nodded.

"What's his repute as a runner?" Pontius asked casually. It was one of the worst insults one could toss at a gladiator, and by extension toward his sponsor.

Gaius was still smiling, coldly. "You said something of a wager, noble Pontius. What a pity your—" he hesitated just long enough to make the unspoken point "—financial commitments make it impracticable."

The fish was on the hook! With a great deal more calm than he felt, Pontius said airily, "Not entirely. I am in a position to back Trajan to the tune of—" He swallowed and named the monumental sum he had borrowed from Sejanus. If Gaius did not bat an eyelid, there was at least the satisfaction of a startled look from Portia.

"Are you serious, Pontius?" Gaius asked him soberly.

Heart pounding, Pontius said, "Of course." Then, to nail it home, added, "If you prefer not to accept the wager, I shall understand perfectly. Your fighter is very small. . . ."

A new voice said, "He shall accept all right, but only half. And I shall cover the remainder."

Pontius spun around with a sudden feeling of leaden doom. The regal tones were unmistakable. He stared up into the amused, cool eyes of Tiberius Caesar, Emperor of Rome.

6

Miriam remembered.

In the stillness, Miriam remembered, for memory was all there was left to her.

When Talmon drove her out in horror, she reverted for a time to her old ways on the road to Tiberias. But now, in Tiberias itself, the going was a little easier: at least she no longer clung on the edge of death each night. There was always shelter, of a sort—archways in dark alleys, disused buildings, on cold nights a pigsty, where the heat of the sleeping animals compensated for their smell. And there was always food of a sort. She stole from the bazaars, less often from the houses. On bad days, when the traders were too wary, she searched among refuse for a crust of bread, or that portion of the fruit which frequently remains ripe when the rest

31

has all but rotted. Often she had to fight the rats and stray dogs for these scraps.

For a time she tried her hand at begging, but found she had no talent for it. The beggars of Tiberias were legion—and professional. They had a staggering persistence that might well have been praiseworthy in some other field. They feared nothing, neither scorn, insults, nor floggings, beatings or stonings. Most of them highlighted their deformities, mutilated their bodies, or exaggerated their illnesses in an effort to generate pity. Miriam could manage none of these things. Had she been prepared only to beg, she would have starved.

As it was, she grew thin and was often weak and listless. She dreaded the nights of the dark moon, for then the demon came and gibbered in her skull.

One winter night, it came as she huddled in a goathouse. The thing liked goats and gloried in filth, but that night, for some reason, the surroundings offended it. And so, Miriam discovered, did her body. It felt through her hands as she stroked the wasted flesh of her legs, felt the bloated, empty pot of a half-starved belly. It touched her sunken cheeks and, though it had always delighted in her suffering, now it was offended.

It took control of her body as it had often done before, bloating itself, swelling to send tendrils into every vein and fiber. Then, though she was tired, it marched her from the goathouse and made her walk.

At first she thought the walk was aimless, for the demon's own delight. Of all things, aimlessness was what it most enjoyed, above pain, above blood, above filth. It absorbed itself in chaos and frequently forced her into silly, random movements for no purpose whatsoever. But that night was different—she found eventually the walking carried her to the edge of the city and beyond.

Miriam had no control over what she did. The thing was massive in her now, so that she herself was squeezed into a single corner of her brain, lonely and frightened, surrounded by foulness and slime. Yet the real horror was always that she remained aware. She knew what her body did, experienced its exhaustion, its pain, and its emotions. But while she knew, she could not influence it in the slightest degree.

The demon in her body walked her toward the Legion encampment.

This was Roman territory, plain and simple, set out like every other Legion outpost in the world. It was established on a plain, to guard against surprise attack, set near a river as a water source, within easy reach of the capital, yet sufficiently divorced from it to prevent complete absorption.

The ground plan had been laid down rigidly centuries ago. First the perimeter fence, guarded by patrolling soldiers day and night. Then the stockade, with its inner ring of bowmen. Then the open campfires, more for light than heat in this season. In the dancing firelight could be seen the tents of the men, the permanent barracks buildings, the administration buildings, the officers' quarters, the wooden mess hall. All there, all waiting in the darkness, shapes against a skyline, visible reminder of the heart of Roman might.

At a great distance, the demon smelled the male smell of the soldiers and grew strangely excited. Miriam did not know why.

Before they reached the fence, the demon halted. It held her body still and stretched out its perceptions as a hound might sniff the air. Eventually it moved again, walking her body parallel to the fence. Some three hundred or more yards from the main gates, well out of sight and earshot of the guards, they came upon a body huddled in the brush.

Miriam stopped, then impelled by the demon, knelt beside it. The man was a soldier for sure, one of the thickly built, beetle-browed Sicilians too stupid for anything but fighting. He was not dead, but drunk. His tunic was torn and smelled of vomit. His penis was exposed and he lay in a pool of urine as if he had stopped to urinate and tumbled where he stood. Saliva dribbled steadily from one side of his mouth. He snored, his breath smelling heavily of wine.

Miriam leaned forward and licked the flaccid penis.

In the depths of her mind, Miriam cringed. She was accustomed to demon-driven abomination, to pain, to filth and foulness. But until now these things had involved her and her alone. Her father and uncle had witnessed her shame. Talmon and Joed and Adab had witnessed her shame. But none had partaken of it, and for that she had always been strangely thankful.

Now, it seemed, the demon brought her company.

The Sicilian stirred, then woke. "What are you doing, girl?" he murmured in his heavily accented Latin.

She looked up at him and placed a finger to her lips, then bent once more to take his member in her mouth. It stiffened instantly. The soldier groaned. She slid one slim hand underneath his scrotum and worked a single finger deep into his anus, searching for the trigger nerves. She found them at last and he convulsed, spending his male fluid copiously into her throat. She released him then, and the demon smiled. Miriam smiled. She fumbled with her robe and took it off. Her body was wasted and displeased the demon, but this Sicilian was too drunk to care for niceties of form. Bacchus had presented him with the gift of a willing woman and a man did not question a gift of the gods. He sat up unsteadily, then fell upon her and took her with an animal moan.

He was strong.

Miriam lay with his weight upon her, feeling him within her in the ultimate invasion. Her soul was cold as he used her, but her body, demon-driven, responded with spastic convulsions of desire. She scratched and bit and hissed obscenities into his ear. She begged, she pleaded, she arched until he filled her. After he came and rolled away, she crawled after him and rubbed his member in her hands until he hardened again, and took her again. She drained him.

Strong though he was, she drained him.

And afterward, immediately afterward, the demon left her. Miriam sat naked, shivering, aflame with shame. She felt used and abused and ravished, body, soul, and spirit. The soldier's breath reeked in her nostrils. Her thighs oozed with his fluids . . . and worse, with her own. For the first time in a year she wept, convulsive sobs that shook her meager frame. The Sicilian fumbled in his pouch, threw something at her which struck her face stingingly, then stumbled off into the darkness.

After a long time, Miriam noticed what he had thrown. Silver coins. Like a sleepwalker, she gathered them up and walked away toward the city.

7

She awoke cold, aching in her abdomen and full of nameless fears. For a time she could not think precisely where she was. Then gradually the bitter memories returned.

The silver coins—three Roman *sestertii*—were still clasped in one numb hand. She stared at them for a long time, her mind numb too. She had passed beyond sorrow, beyond shame.

In the nearest bazaar, the coins bought her food, a new robe, and a phial of herbal medicine to still the pain in her loins; with money left over for more food next day and the next. It was greater security than she had ever had—greater than her home in Magdala, where the family had always lived on the edge of poverty, greater than at the house of Talmon, where she had been treated well, but retained no control over her destiny.

The actuality of security interested her, but just barely, for she was consumed by a coldness, a calculating anger. She recalled the first time she had experienced the coldness, and now, remembering, Miriam realized that it had never left her. It had been first her protection, then ultimately her strength. It defeated so many negative emotions: loneliness, compassion, fear, pity. The coldness enabled her to survive, had almost proved strong enough to permit her to cope with the demon. Almost. But the demon stood far beyond those normal things which humans fear, and when it entered her, nothing proved a protection.

It would enter her again soon, very soon.

As she waited, Miriam remembered that girl she had once been, that child in a woman's body who had woken to find an icy diamond in her heart. She had eaten well of the food she bought from the bazaar, had washed in a stream near the city's edge, and had worn the new robe, which was softer than anything she had ever worn before. The potion for her pain worked well, so that by noon there was no more than an occasional discomfort. She examined herself where he had entered her and found no worse damage than slight bruising on the inner thigh.

She returned to the bazaar and bought a phial of perfume, the first she had ever worn. Since she was young, her taste was poor, but it pleased her, and she anointed herself perhaps too liberally.

That night, even though the demon presence was not in her, she returned to the soldiers' encampment.

There were two sentries at the gate, big men who looked alike in their armor, grasping spears and standing stiffly, eyes alert. They saw her approach, of course, but called no challenge, probably recognizing her for what she was, or perhaps mistaking her for a young boy in the half-light. But when she made to enter, one stepped directly in front of her, barring her way.

"Just a minute, young one. Where do you think you're going then?"

Miriam stared up at him coolly. "Into the camp."

"Into the camp, is it? Have you business in the camp?" She judged him to be about her father's age, but more muscular and better fed.

"I've come to entertain the soldiers." She knew prostitution was permitted in the camp. The officers considered it a necessity when men were far from home.

"What, all of them?" The sentry grinned.

"Just those who can pay."

The arrogance amused him. "Hear that, Sextus," he called to his companion. "Only those who pay, she says." He turned back to her. "You're a Hebrew, aren't you?"

"Yes."

"But you don't mind lying with Romans so long as you're treated right, is that it?"

"Yes."

"What age are you?"

"Twenty," Miriam lied.

"In my eye!" the sentry remarked. "You run along now before your parents miss you."

Innocently, she had not expected to be turned away. But now that she was here, she did not intend to accept defeat so easily. "I want to talk to your commanding officer," she said.

The sentry chuckled. "You do, do you? The trouble is he doesn't want to talk to you—does he, Sextus? Now run along. I can't stand here all night talking to the likes of you."

"You have no right to turn me away," Miriam said obstinately.

"No right? That's a good one! Let me tell you something, my girl: I have every right. Every woman who comes here to entertain the lads needs a certificate from the administration officer, and she can't get that without examination from the medical officer. Can't have a lot of silly little sluts spreading disease through the Legions, can we?"

"Very well," said Miriam. "Take me to the medical officer."

"Oh gods!" the sentry groaned. "Don't you ever give up?"

Miriam stared at him. "If you don't do as I ask, I shall tear my robe and scream and tell your officers you raped me."

He snorted. "And Sextus here will back you up, will he?"

But Sextus himself was moving over, staring at her intently. "Let her through, Cato," he growled quietly. "I know this one."

Without emotion, Miriam stared into the coarse features of the Sicilian who had taken her the night before. She waited.

"Can't let her in without a certificate, Sextus—you know that," the sentry protested.

"Can't get one if you don't let her in, can she?" Sextus remarked reasonably.

"She can get it the same damn way every other Hebrew whore gets it—by making application in the usual way at a normal time, not in the middle of the night." He glanced again at Miriam. "Besides, she's too young."

"She's a goer, that one," Sextus said. "My word on it. The boys will love her. You let her in, Cato, if she promises to get a certificate tomorrow."

After a grumbling moment, Cato said, "Oh, all right. But it's your responsibility. I'm not taking the blame for this if anything goes wrong."

"What's to go wrong?" Sextus shrugged. "You think the lads are going to turn her in? Half the whores in the camp don't have a certificate most of the time. This one's all right."

"Oh, all right," Cato said again, and stepped aside.

She had earned seven further silver pieces that night, from four different soldiers. (All four had been sober, and consequently less generous than the brutish Sextus.) The following day she underwent a cursory medical examination by a bored officer who commented on slight malnutrition and told her various methods of avoiding pregnancy. The administration officer accepted her lie about her age without even a pretense of interest and issued her the official certificate on payment of five of the silver pieces she had earned the night before. She felt no resentment. After the abominations forced upon her by the demon, this work was simple, the men easily satisfied. When she returned again, she could quickly make up the five *sestertii* and more.

Miriam did return again, and again and again. The coldness in her solidified until it became a part of her, no longer alien. She rented rooms in the city, bought herself clothes, and, most important, ate well. Gradually the skeletal look faded and though she never became fat she filled out and lost her childlike appearance.

She met with many of the other camp followers and though she liked none of them, she pretended well enough and they taught her much she needed to know. Within a year, she no longer confined her professional activities to the camp. She quickly learned how to please men, and more slowly how to groom, dress, carry, and conduct herself so that they paid more for the privilege of lying with her. Although she soon abandoned the common soldiers, who only had real money on pay night, she kept her attentions firmly fixed on the Romans. The creature that controlled her approved of her profession, or at least did not interfere. Sometimes when a Roman used her, she was aware of its presence on the borders of her mind, watching. Occasionally it possessed her fully in the act, drinking the sensations of her body. On such occasions she would writhe in orgasm after orgasm—the only time such a thing ever happened to her. Her reaction seemed to please men greatly. Her reputation increased, and so did her fees. Incredibly, she grew wealthy.

With no ambition, but an awesome relentlessness, she bought herself a house and set her sights on richer, more powerful clients. These were still Romans in the main, members of the imperial administration, but eventually—for the power of choice still did not lie solely in her own hands—she accepted a man of her own race. He was overweight and elderly and easily pleased. Gratitude made him even more generous in his payment than the Romans. But the sight of his penis disturbed her profoundly, for it carried the mark of the covenant between her people and the Lord. She no longer liked to think of the Lord now, having placed herself so far beyond the bounds of His salvation.

Something in the experience worked deep within her mind, so that she found herself longing to go home to Magdala. When the pressure became unbearable, she did go, richly dressed and driven in a carriage, veiled so that none of the villagers would recognize

38

her. She avoided contact with her family, even avoided those places where she might meet any of them accidentally. Would they have recognized her now in any case? Would they have seen the frightened, demon-ridden child within the sophisticated courtesan? The child and the demon were still there.

Strange how different demons seemed from everything she had been taught. When the rabbis talked and she had listened as a child, she thought of devils as real enough. But they were like dangerous animals, rarely seen. She could picture them as little men—or big men, as the fancy took her—spiteful, malevolent, perhaps deformed. What was lacking in the picture was the utter *otherness* of the thing that now possessed her. It was not a little man or a big man. It was not an animal, however strange and dangerous. It was maggots in meat, the slime of a snail, the void between the stars, it was filth and oozing corruption, it was nothing, it was putrefaction of the mind, it was vast, yet it could squeeze into her skull.

And it was frightening. Nobody could ever understand how frightening it was.

Though she avoided her family, she made a point of seeking out one childhood friend. She was in need of a servant: one she could trust, one strong enough to help her should the need arise—men did strange things in their passion—one who kept his own counsel, saw nothing, heard nothing, said nothing. Above all, she needed one who would not run from her, horrified, if he chanced to discover her affliction.

She found Benjamin in the hills. He had grown a few more inches since she had last seen him, but the impressive change was in his build. He had always been squat and strong, but now his muscles had filled out in knotted cords, his back had broadened, his legs thickened so, that it seemed he might crush rock with a single blow. His movements were as she remembered them, slow and deliberate. And when he turned his head, his expression was as vacant as ever, his eyes brown and warm, but strangely blank.

"Do you know me, Benjamin?" As she asked, she was suddenly, stupidly, afraid that he would not.

It took him a long time to answer, as it always had done. Then, "You are Miriam. You went away."

She nodded. "That's right, Benjamin. I've come back now."

He said nothing.

Miriam said, "Would you like to come with me, Benjamin? Would you like to come and work for me?"

The brown eyes stared at her blankly.

"I would buy you fine clothes," Miriam said. "You could stay with me always in my house in the great city."

There was no change in the blankness.

"I would feed you well, Benjamin, and keep you strong. You would never have to tend to goats again."

Still nothing.

"Will you come with me?" Miriam asked him softly.

"Yes," said Benjamin dully.

She called on his parents. They were a simple couple, in old age now—much older than her own parents. As sometimes happens, they had lived together long enough to look alike: the same soft eyes, so like the eyes of Benjamin, the same slim, hard bodies, even in old age, the same wrinkles and skin tone. Most of all, the same habitual expression. Sorrow had touched them, the sorrow of a single child without a mind, the sorrow that the Lord's touch brings.

They did not know her and when she told them her name, they were frightened and did not bother to conceal it. They were simple people who had heard the talk and so could smell the demon, who was not then in her. But when she told them what she wanted, the fear was edged out by surprise, and then relief. Whatever love they had once had for Benjamin must long since have died, crushed under the burden of caring for an idiot. She offered them money and they took it gratefully. They smiled as they waved good-bye to their son.

He made a fine servant. He did exactly what she told him, no more, no less. His presence was a reassurance to her. Once, long after she had gone to bed—alone—a noise aroused her and she found that two thieves had entered her house. They did not flee, but turned on her. One covered her mouth so that she could not scream. The other was searching round for a weapon when Benjamin burst in. Oddly enough he seemed to know exactly what to do. In only seconds, it seemed, one of the men was unconscious, the other running for his life. With the crisis over, Benjamin reverted to his usual blankness, but that was no matter. He had proved he could act on his own initiative when the need arose. She wondered, though, what had alerted him. Perhaps it was the same sound that had aroused her.

He made no noise about the house and seemed to stay hidden when clients visited. She wondered what he thought of these men who came to see her. It struck her as unlikely that he knew the reason, for his mindlessness left him innocent of the way of men and women. . . .

The thing had oozed into the room. She could feel the change of atmosphere, as if the very air had become sullen and slimy-cold. She sat and waited passively as it began to invade her in the most intimate, most loathsome way imaginable. It crawled like a bloated leech between her legs, slid coldly into her body, then climbed with slow deliberation up the spine to squat, pulsating, in her brain.

After a time, Miriam rose and rang the bell. When Benjamin appeared, dressed in the deep blue livery she had had made up for him, she ordered him to stand before her in the room. She removed her robe. He watched her without expression. She walked to him naked and began to undress him. He permitted the actions without resistance. When he too was naked, she knelt before him, eyes locked in black fascination on the circumcised penis, token of this man's covenant with the Lord.

Her tongue slid out and licked her dry lips once in a long, slow, unhurried movement.

§8

"Pontius, dear boy," exclaimed Corax solicitously, "you look white as a sheet! Another orange?" He began to fish in his basket.

Pontius shook his head and sat down heavily. He was experiencing a curious mixture of fear and relief, and had just enough self-interest left to wonder why that relief did not wash the fear away. He also felt excited, a delightful tension that made images appear sharper, colors brighter. "Has the dwarf fought yet?" he asked. He did not think he could possibly have missed it, but what a tragedy if he had!

"Quite soon, I believe." He gave a desultory glance toward the arena, where two *essedarii* hacked clumsily at one another from the comparative safety of their badly driven chariots. Dramatic chords erupting from the organ attempted to inject excitement into their maneuvering, without much success. "I must confess I'm almost looking forward to it now. The standard so far has been quite execrable." He looked back at Pontius. "Your business mission has caused you to miss very little, let me assure you."

"Corax," Pontius asked hesitantly, "how well do you know the Emperor?" Of all things now, he needed reliable information on Tiberius, especially on his humor in defeat.

"I, sir?" There was exaggerated surprise in Corax's voice, although the face remained as blank as ever. "Why, not at all from personal experience. But how flattering that you should suppose I might."

"Not from personal experience. But hearsay, from those who do have personal experience. A great many people talk to you, Corax. You must have heard many opinions of the Emperor."

"As have you, dear boy. He hates the Games, but you know that, as does everybody, since he announces the fact on all possible occasions. He is mean, but you know that too. There is some talk his sexual preferences are Greek, but I can scarcely credit it. He has a taste for asparagus, as his father had before him. He can handle a sword, but prefers a javelin and seldom uses either. He eats well, though sparingly, gets drunk occasionally—"

Pontius shook his head. "Is he spiteful?"

"Spiteful? We are speaking of an emperor, Pontius. It is bred into their bones."

It was no more than a confirmation of his own opinion; nonetheless, Pontius chilled inwardly. It was one thing to win a wager against Gaius, who had so much money that the loss of a little—or even a lot—scarcely mattered. It was quite another to win against the parsimonious Tiberius, who would resent every copper *denarius*.

42

"May I ask why this sudden interest in the Emperor's spite?" Corax inquired politely. "You are surely not about to make him your enemy."

Pontius frowned. "I might be. I've wagered against his man."

"The dwarf? I imagine half the audience must have done the same. It's a miracle you found anyone to match your money."

Still frowning, Pontius said, "I didn't just find anyone, I wagered with the Emperor himself."

It was too much, even for Corax. A flicker of surprise actually crossed his face. "Tiberius is backing the dwarf? He must be mad! How much did you wager?" He remembered himself abruptly. "Forgive me, I did not mean to pry—I was taken aback."

"No matter." Pontius shrugged. He named the sum and added, "It's borrowed money, of course."

Corax nodded sympathetically. "Some hint of your financial difficulties had reached me. Still, if Tiberius is mad enough to gamble against Trajan, you will have a handsome profit when you repay the loan."

"That's what worries me," Pontius admitted. "Do you think he will hold it against me when he loses?"

"Most assuredly, but what can he do? Even an emperor must appear to be a good sport. If he does not, who will gamble with him? Tiberius enjoys a little bet now and then." Corax pursed his lips. "Although this is rather more than a little bet, is it not? I wonder why he thinks the dwarf can win."

"Gaius thinks so too: he has covered the same amount with me."

"Has he, by Jove! You have been able to borrow a substantial sum." Corax shifted his position. Even with a cushion, the wooden tiers were never comfortable for long. "Well, now, I can understand it in Gaius. What else has he to do with so much gold except squander it foolishly? Anything else would be utterly unfashionable."

"But he doesn't think he's throwing it away. He thinks the dwarf will win."

"Obviously he must say so," Corax observed thoughtfully, "and perhaps it is even the truth. I think I mentioned earlier that Gaius believes the dwarf to be a magician. A superstitious fancy, of course—you need have no fear of your wager—but superstitious fancies have led good men into grotesqueries before now."

Something between a groan and a growl from the watching

crowd heralded the sudden downfall of one *essedarius*. In dodging a blow, he had apparently lost his balance completely and fallen from his chariot. With distinct lack of finesse, the opponent promptly drove his chariot over the man's head, crushing the skull with a metal-rimmed wheel. It was a poor conclusion to a poorer fight.

"He told me the dwarf was a priest rather than a magician," Pontius remarked.

"Much the same thing, isn't it, when you're dealing with these foreign gods?"

"Yes, I suppose so," Pontius agreed.

They watched as a steward appeared to drag the body of the vanquished *essedarius* into the *spoliarium*. A roar went up when the steward was abruptly recognized as a confector. Confectors had the task of cleaning up after the animals.

"At least someone has a sense of humor," Corax murmured appreciatively.

After a moment, Pontius said, "What is your opinion, Corax, of the power of these foreign gods?"

Corax glanced across at him. "That question is unlike you, Pontius." He sighed. "Still, I suppose in your position I might have moments of doubt." He contrived to sound thoughtful, although there was no change in the masklike features. "As a philosophical point, with no bearing on your wager, one must allow a certain degree of potency to foreign gods—otherwise their adoption into our pantheon would be quite pointless. Yet we have, from time to time, made such adoptions. But if you talk to a priest—assuming you can believe a word he would swear—he will tell you a god's power is strongest in his own territory and weakens the further away one moves from it. Oddly enough the followers of a foreign god will tell you substantially the same thing. With one notable exception, of course."

"Really?" Pontius asked politely. His attention was wandering. The arena was being prepared for the next combat and he was fairly certain it would be the match between Trajan and the dwarf.

"The Hebrews," Corax said. "They consider their god—they have only one, you know—the most powerful in the world."

"Really?" asked Pontius again, intrigued despite himself. "More powerful than Jupiter?"

"More powerful than Jupiter and every other Roman god put together. Do you know any Hebrews?"

"No."

"They're quite mad," Corax said. "Every one of them. The men hack off a portion of their penis as an offering."

"Are you serious?" Pontius asked.

"Perfectly, although I can think of few less suitable gifts to a god." He blinked, face impassive. "Perhaps he uses the pieces to form a godlike penis of his own."

Pontius smiled, then commented seriously, "Even if they're right about their god—the extent of his power, I mean, not the extent of his penis—it will not make any difference here. The dwarf is not a Hebrew priest."

"I know," Corax said. "He's the wrong color."

Tiberius was back in the royal box! Pontius glanced around hurriedly and found that Gaius had also taken his seat in the podium, a sullen Portia by his side. It must mean the dwarf was to fight next.

Corax seemed to have the same idea, for he said casually, "At any rate we shall soon see the extent of the dwarf's magic. I believe he is about to fight."

The stewards left the arena and the organ struck up a ludicrously lighthearted piece, then died abruptly as the heralds sounded their trumpets to announce the next contest. Not every gladiatorial pair received such a fanfare, but then not every gladiator was sponsored by the Emperor.

The last note died and even before the official announcement was made, word was passing through the stands that Trajan and the foreign dwarf were next. The news was met with pockets of laughter and more than a passing glimmer of anticipation. Sheer novelty might compensate for what the fight would lack in sportsmanship, and the plebs always welcomed novelty. Or perhaps they had heard the stories that the dwarf was a magician. Gods only knew what they expected: Trajan struck down by a thunderbolt, no doubt.

"Intriguing to consider," Corax said seriously, "that I shall be seated next to a wealthy man in only a few moments."

"Hardly wealthy. Most of the winnings will go to pay my debts."

"Won't you have even a little left over?" asked Corax blandly.

Pontius smiled. "Perhaps a little."

Trajan entered the arena. Someone had been teaching him the elements of showmanship, for he walked beyond the shadow of the *balteus* and paused dramatically, legs spread like tree trunks and head thrown back in a gesture of defiant arrogance. Sections of the crowd began to hiss.

"Still not overpopular," Pontius remarked. He himself was experiencing a distinct feeling of warmth toward Trajan, as men do when they see their salvation in the flesh. He really was a bull of a man, much taller than average and immensely strong. Like most men of his bulk, he lacked agility. But Trajan made up for it in stamina, and, of late, in vastly improved swordsmanship. The lengthy broadsword weighed several pounds and tended to drain the strength from a fighter's arm over an extended bout, but Trajan handled it like a feather. He was one of the few fighters who really benefited from the *hoplomachus* shield, which gave superb protection, but only so long as one had the energy to lift it. It was the basic theory of the Games that heavy armament only gave a fighter the advantage at the beginning of a contest. As its use began to tire him, the greater agility of his lighter-armed opponent then came into play. But as his opponents had found to their cost, heavy armor never seemed to tire out Trajan.

He stumped to the Emperor's box and gave a brief salute, right arm extended. The hissing grew more general. Trajan spun to salute the crowd, but this time the hand at the end of the extended arm was curled into a fist, with thumb poked out between the first two fingers. It was the sign of the peach stone in the anus of the donkey (which an ancient king had once commanded his subjects to remove with their teeth). The crowd responded with a burst of fury, jeering and booing as Trajan, grinning broadly, shook the fist and wiggled the thumb.

"How they hate him," Pontius smiled delightedly. He liked a man of spirit, even when his money was not laid on him.

"On the contrary," said Corax mildly, "they are beginning to love him. He stirs their emotions, and is that not why they come?"

A few members of the crowd expressed their affection with missiles of rotting fruit as Trajan lumbered to his chosen spot. But, in the main, the jeering died, and was replaced by a hum of expectation as the entrance of the dwarf was awaited.

"You don't think there's any chance he really can work magic?" Pontius asked in a sudden, irrational upsurge of alarm.

"Against that?" Corax nodded toward the brute form of the massive Trajan now poised in the center of the ring. Pontius followed his gaze and relaxed. No other comment was needed.

The dwarf emerged, ludicrously framed for a moment by the massive double doors of the gladiators' enclosure. The crowd promptly split itself three ways: those who found the sight funny giggled, those touched by the pathos of it sighed, but the majority—still incensed by Trajan—actually cheered.

"They've given him a shield!" Pontius exclaimed with a hint of alarm. He glanced toward the smiling figure of Tiberius and felt a surge of anger. A *thracian* might sometimes fight with a shield by special dispensation. And certainly in this case it was a token gesture toward evening up the contest. But for the Emperor to grant the dispensation to his own man was the very worst of sportsmanship, especially when a wager was involved.

"It is only a small shield," Corax pointed out.

Which was true. The shield was tiny, an elongated oval which could only protect one vital area at a time. And the dwarf was unhelmeted. Despite his priestly vows, he carried the saber.

Pontius noticed the curiously rolling, bowlegged gait as the dwarf walked toward the royal box, and wondered briefly if the man had ever been a sailor. Instead of saluting in the Roman manner, the dwarf bowed deeply once, then walked away.

And dropped his sword!

The crowd went silent in an instant. There was no doubt that the gesture was deliberate. But what did it mean? Was the dwarf refusing to fight?

Pontius leaned forward, bewildered, as the dwarf threw away his shield. A puzzled hum, like a swarm of bees, arose over the stadium. It grew as the dwarf clumsily removed the metal leg guards and tore away the leather protection over his right arm. He was refusing to fight! It was the only possible explanation, damn his priestly vows! The hum took on an ugly note. However unpopular Trajan might be, the crowd could never back a coward against him. Pontius felt disturbed for a different reason. If the dwarf did not fight, would his wager become void? The little yellow man would be killed, of course, swiftly dispatched by Trajan, or left to the attendants to brand and execute. But would either really count as any more than a technical win for Trajan? Would Tiberius, too mean to pay, use the excuse to weasel out?

With no more protection than his loincloth now, the dwarf moved to his spot and stood, face perfectly still, his calm eyes regarding Trajan. For some reason he did not look like a man about to sacrifice himself. Certainly there was no hint of fear in his features.

Trajan glanced up at the Emperor, quite obviously at a loss. This was, after all, the Emperor's man. Tiberius gazed back at him impassively. From where Pontius was sitting, he thought he could even catch the barest hint of a smile on the royal face. What in Hades was going on?

Trajan raised his sword uncertainly, then shook it at the dwarf. The little man did not move. Trajan began to walk toward him, then must have realized he looked idiotic bearing a huge metal shield against an unarmed man, for he stopped abruptly and cast the thing away. He waved the sword again, a half-comic, half-threatening gesture. Evidently he hoped the dwarf might run, for that at least would give the crowd some entertainment. Trajan roared suddenly, like an animal, and stamped one foot heavily. But the dwarf did not run.

"What on earth is he doing?" Pontius asked breathlessly. He was as bewildered by the dwarf now as was his opponent in the ring. And behind the bewilderment was a gnawing feeling of unease. Was it possible that this ugly little foreigner really did have magic to protect him?

"I don't know," Corax said, his voice puzzled.

They leaned forward together.

Trajan stopped only a yard or so away from the immobile dwarf. They locked eyes and for a moment nothing happened. Then Trajan gave another roar and swung his sword up in a vicious arc which should have ended in the dwarf's throat, half decapitating him. But with superb control, the sword blade stopped so close that it actually pressed into the skin, but drew no blood and made no mark.

Incredibly, the dwarf still had not moved.

The crowd gasped, then went wild. It was like nothing they had ever seen before, yet it was what they always sought to see: precision swordsmanship and fearlessness in the face of death. At once the figures in the ring took on a new aura. Trajan was no longer the unpopular brute—had he not proved his skill? The dwarf was no longer a coward or a clown—had he not shown his mettle in the teeth of hell? The crowd divided and began to cheer, some for Trajan, some for the little yellow man.

Encouraged, Trajan swung again, this time at the unprotected body. There was not so much as a twitch from the dwarf. The sword edge came to rest across his belly.

Trajan stepped back, shook his sword, then swung again and again, always stopping the blows at the last conceivable second. But the tone of the crowd was changing subtly, as admiration for the totally immobile dwarf began to swamp appreciation of the finer points of Trajan's skill.

And Trajan caught the smell of the change.

"Strange," murmured Corax, "how one man can make such a fool of another without moving a muscle."

It seemed Trajan had come to the same conclusion, for he stopped his brilliant swinging and prodded the dwarf with his sword tip, just above the navel. Still no movement. Trajan prodded harder. The dwarf remained as still as stone. Trajan frowned.

"I do believe he's losing his temper now," said Corax.

"That will be the end of it," Pontius remarked confidently. Although behind his tone a curious unease remained, and now it was forming itself into a monstrous suspicion. Was it possible —was it remotely possible—that Tiberius had conspired to arrange this match as a special display? That Trajan was following imperial orders and the dwarf remained calm because he knew it? Tiberius could always justify the ruse on the premise that it had produced some novel entertainment. Which was true, except that if it was all arranged, the end would be arranged as well. And Tiberius would hardly throw away his dwarf.

It was not arranged. Trajan was no actor; and even if he was, no actor could counterfeit that rush of blood to the face as it dawned on him eventually that this little yellow clown had absorbed all the crowd's attention and transformed Trajan into a buffoon in the process. With an ear-piercing yell, Trajan leaped, the full weight of his massive body behind the swing of his sword. There could be no stopping it this time. Not even the master swordsman of the world could halt that blow.

The dwarf moved.

He came in beneath the swing of the sword and turned. It

seemed he actually reached up for Trajan's wrist, but the action was too fast for anyone to be sure. Then Trajan was flying in an arc over his back to land with a heavy thud on the arena sand.

For a moment, there was stunned silence. Then, in one voice, the crowd began to laugh. The monstrous Trajan had actually tripped over his tiny opponent! It was unheard of, but it had happened! New supplies of rotting fruit began to fall into the ring.

But Pontius was quick to notice something the other spectators seemed momentarily to have missed. Trajan's right hand was now hanging uselessly by his side: the bone of the arm appeared to have been broken.

Broken arm or not, Trajan was retrieving his sword. He hefted it once in his left hand and came at the dwarf again, enraged both by the humiliation and the unexpected pain. It was like the charge of a bull.

"I fear," said Corax, "this is indeed the end."

But the dwarf was inside Trajan's guard, his arm stretched stiff to jab a single finger in a point on Trajan's chest. Trajan screamed in agony and dropped his sword. The dwarf chopped like an ax with the side of his hand across the giant's throat. Trajan's eyes glazed and he toppled. Incredibly, he toppled.

The dwarf stepped forward and kicked him once with great precision in the rib cage, driving a bone fragment inward to the heart. Then before the crowd could catch its breath, he turned and walked away, leaving the corpse where it lay on the sand.

"Sorcery!" breathed Pontius wildly. In his own special agony, there was nothing else he could think of to say.

TWO

9

It was like a lingering illness or a slow-acting poison.

Even when the demon was not in her, the fear of it, the memory of it, twisted her moods, distorted her actions. There was no joy in her and little rest. But her profession prospered.

"The centurion Longinus," Sara announced and withdrew, softly closing the door behind her, like the servant on some great estate.

Miriam turned slowly. As was the custom, he had removed his armor in the vestibule and was dressed now in a simple tunic and leather sandals. But his size and bearing still marked him as a soldier. She raised a single eyebrow. "I had not heard you were returned from Rome."

"Two weeks since," he told her gruffly. She was aware that she made him uncomfortable, as she made most men uncomfortable. They reacted to her cold patrician posture, the aristocratic hauteur of her voice, the steady chill of her gaze. She was, to them, the supreme bitch goddess—and what black joy they felt when the time came to take her.

"You must tell me the news." She waved him languidly toward a couch and he moved obediently to sit. And he did sit, rather than recline in the Roman manner. She smiled inwardly. It would be some time before she permitted this one to relax.

53

He coughed. "It's changed. Soldiers' rations are actually worse than they are here."

She chose a chair some distance from him. "Soldiers' rations?" she echoed, managing to make it sound as if he was talking of manure.

Longinus moved uneasily. But he had not risen through the Legion ranks without some degree of backbone. "Even the Games have gone to hell."

"Ah yes, tell me of the Games. Was there great slaughter?"

He ignored the question. "Tiberius has abolished the *sparsio*."

"Really? But what is *sparsio*?"

"They used to throw lucky counters into the crowd. If you got one, it entitled you to a prize." He relaxed a little at the memory. "Some damn good prizes too—I once knew a cobbler who won himself a country house."

"How quaint," said Miriam. "Did he know what to do with it?"

He ignored that question too and only said sourly, "Tiberius has stopped the whole thing now."

"But why? It sounds amusing."

Longinus shrugged. "Meanness. Although he claims it was because the custom started fights in the stadium."

"And did it?"

"All the time. Broken heads all over the place."

"Then perhaps his decision was wise, even though it must have annoyed the cobblers."

She did not, she knew, enjoy the company of men. Their minds were too simple: little better, really, than the mind of Benjamin. And their desires were too obvious, which made them utterly predictable. Long ago, she had discovered it was all too easy to manipulate a man, and the discovery bred contempt.

She stared at this man now. Longinus was a Roman by nationality, not by birth. Those broad shoulders and strong arms were the product of Sicilian stock, and there were still hints of the shrewd peasant in his nature. He had come to Rome and joined the Legion and clawed his way into the officer ranks by courage, toughness, and determination. What's more, he had had the intelligence to put a gloss over the rude peasant manners, to force his tongue away from the rolling bewilderment of his original Sicilian accent. Now he looked like an officer, behaved like an officer, even sounded like an officer. A man among men who had

54

reached his present station through effort and intelligence, not an accident of birth. He had the respect of his peers, the admiration of his inferiors.

And yet a Hebrew country girl could make him lick her feet.

Strange how not one of them ever noticed her contempt. Or, if they noticed, how not one of them ever took it seriously. It was as though their lust for her made them blind.

She moved, as if to ease a cramp, and saw how his eyes fell hungrily on her breasts. This was the key to controlling a man. That restless snake between their legs could be relied upon to lead them as effectively as the ring through the nose of a bull. However she belittled him, however uncomfortable and insecure she made him feel, however she sneered and paraded her airs and graces, he would still be pathetically grateful when she satisfied that rampant urge within his loins.

Indeed, the colder she was beforehand, the more grateful he would eventually be, returning again and again for more of the same, as they all did.

Perhaps, Miriam thought, it was the power of contrast. If that accursed demon had done nothing else, it had at least taught her how to please a man. In the bedroom, all pretense of coldness vanished. She was a wanton, a harlot, an animal that tore and scratched and pumped, permitting every indignity and suggesting more. How they loved that contrast, these brutish males. And how they strove to please her, even then. She had learned early that if she did not simulate orgasm, they remained vaguely discontent —sometimes grew actively depressed. But they were easy to fool, every one of them. She moaned and jerked and sighed and the heavy weight of their conceit did all the rest. Would they be angry, she wondered, if they learned she never did reach climax with a client?

Unless the demon entered her. . . .

Miriam pushed the thought aside. "And on your return, Longinus, did you find matters much changed here under the new administration?"

"The new Governor, you mean?" He shrugged. "That makes no difference to the army unless he starts a war."

"And Pilate is scarcely of that vein," Miriam murmured.

"Do you know him?" Longinus asked unwarily.

She stared at him and he reddened, well aware of her rule that clients' names must never be divulged. To cover his embarrassment, he went on hurriedly, "He may have his hands full with this bloody rabbi stirring up trouble."

"The Baptist?" Miriam asked, frowning. She had heard that the man was dead.

"No, the new one. Any fool could see the Baptist was just a lunatic. Joshua, or some such name."

She cast a look of boredom toward the window. "I'm afraid I haven't heard of him." Which was true enough, although she wondered why. All talk filtered back to her eventually, it was one burden of her profession.

"I suppose he's a Zealot," Longinus said. "Most of them are. Although there's some talk this one was an Essene."

"Monk or lay?"

"Monk."

Miriam shrugged. "He can't be. They never leave their communities." She stood up. "May I offer you a little wine?"

"Thank you," Longinus said. There was no hint of it in his voice, but she knew his anger was building. The real art was to hold him at a peak of irritation before permitting him to use her. That way he could feel he had tamed a bitch. Men were always prepared to pay a heavy price for that.

She rang the bell for Ruth, then came back to her seat. She was wearing, quite deliberately, a Roman toga cut from the finest cloth in the patrician style. The pristine whiteness accentuated her own sultry beauty, became another symbol of her assumed station as a highborn lady. As she sat, she asked, "Don't you think Pilate is capable of handling this rabble-rouser?"

The question embarrassed him further, as it was meant to do. His conflicting emotions were really so easy to read. Eventually he said, "Depends how far it goes. Leave them alone and most of these men overreach themselves eventually. Like the Baptist. Herod had his head fast enough and we didn't have to raise a finger. Junius knew how to let things sort themselves out."

Junius had been the last Governor, a client of Miriam's when his gout permitted. Age and experience had brought him a little wisdom and he was famed for his policy of minimal interference.

"And you don't think Pilate does?" Miriam asked blandly.

The question obviously touched a chord, for Longinus said quite heatedly, "Pilate's a younger man."

"And young men are sometimes rash?" She allowed a note of sympathy to creep into her voice to make him unwary. The selfsame Pilate had an appointment with her—his first, as it happened—in two days' time. She was curious to learn his character in advance.

"Sometimes," Longinus said tightly. But he added, "Pilate has a horror of magicians."

It was so unexpected that her mask slipped. "Magicians?"

Longinus shifted uncomfortably. "It's the talk of Rome. There was a match in the Games between the gladiator Trajan and a foreign dwarf. Pilate borrowed money to wager on Trajan—it was certain he would win. But the dwarf was a magician and killed Trajan with a touch, so Pilate lost."

"How much money was involved?"

"They say twenty thousand *libra*."

Despite herself, her eyes widened. It was a staggering sum. "Who took a wager of that size?"

"Half was covered by a rich man named Gaius. The other half by the Emperor himself, Tiberius."

"He bet against the Emperor?" Miriam asked incredulously. This Pilate would be well worth meeting.

"And lost," Longinus nodded. "Worse still, he couldn't pay."

"Why not? You said he borrowed the money."

"Well, he tried to. They say it was promised him, but in the event the sum could not be raised."

The story was ceasing to make sense. Miriam said, "But if he could not pay the Emperor, was he not cast into prison?"

Longinus snorted. "He's an equestrian—a knight. That sort can always pull strings. He was friendly with the senator Sejanus and Sejanus convinced the Emperor the only way he would ever see his winnings was to give Pilate a rich appointment. So he made him Governor of Judaea."

"Good God!" Miriam breathed. Was there no end to the folly of men? And this imbecile was Emperor of Rome!

Longinus must have caught something of her thought, for he said apologetically, "It's not as silly as it sounds. Tiberius insisted half the stipend goes back directly into the imperial purse."

Not so silly indeed. But what a fate for poor Pilate. Condemned to an imperial backwater on half pay, with all the expenses of a governor's position. No wonder he had a horror of magicians.

"And this rabbi," she asked, "he too is a magician?"

"A healer anyway," Longinus confirmed. "He cures the sick and casts out demons."

§10

Herod belched, not altogether delicately. His stomach had been acting up for weeks, and even the new Greek physician insisted it was nerves. As it was, as assuredly it was. No one realized the strain of a Tetrarch's position: running the realm, pleasing the priests, pleasing the people, pleasing the Romans . . . dear God, pleasing the Romans! Old Junius at least had the good sense to keep his nose out of affairs he did not understand. But this new man, this Pilatus, he had the smell of a different horse. He was younger, for one thing. And bitter, if the stories were true. Lost all his money at the Games, they said—and to Tiberius, to boot. It hardly bore thinking about.

He reached for his potion, a noxious brew of wild mint, elderflower, and valerian root. The mint to settle his stomach and cut the wind, the Greek said; the elder and valerian to steady his nerves. All of it tasted foul and none of it worked. The problem was that the Greek insisted on a diet to go along with it. No rich food, no exotic food, no spices, no acid fruit. No pulses which created gas. Less poultry, less meat, less vegetables. No wine, no desserts. How could a man steady his nerves if he was not permitted to eat? And yet it was a vicious circle. All the doctors agreed the nerves caused the stomach upset and the stomach upset exaggerated the nervous condition. If he ate sufficiently to calm his nerves, his stomach protested and agitated the nerves again. And if he did not eat, all they could offer were foul potions.

"I don't like it," Herod said.

"No, Tetrarch," Zephaniah agreed.

There existed a strange relationship between them and consequently they were hiding from the women—particularly Herodias

58

—in Herod's secret chamber. Word had been spread abroad that it was a private temple where the King might communicate in peace with the Lord. In actuality it was a massive bedroom, with leopardskin covers on the bed and a heady atmosphere of musk which clung to every stone block of the walls. The chamber had been decorated specifically to Herod's taste, so that erotic tapestries predominated. There were sheepskin rugs and cushions on the floor. There were heavy purple curtains on the windows. There was a secret exit through a tunnel in the floor and another behind the massive fireplace. There were three doors: one, with heavy locks, led out into a palace corridor, little used, but well guarded at a respectable distance; one led into a bathroom and chamber of relief; and one led into a well-stocked larder.

The two men had abandoned the bed and were seated, more or less naked, at some distance from one another, on cushions. The Tetrarch's cushion was naturally the higher of the two.

"You tell me he heals lepers?" Herod asked.

Zephaniah nodded. "So it is said."

"And cures blindness?"

"I believe so."

"And helps deaf men hear again?"

"Yes."

Herod's frown deepened. "No good will come of it."

Zephaniah was quite a handsome young man, slim, small, lithe and athletic in build if not in inclination. But he had a shifty look about the eyes as a result of his constant search for information. Strictly speaking, he was a professional spy. His odd relationship with the Tetrarch interfered somewhat with his duties, but did not stop them altogether.

Herod himself provided something of a contrast, especially when nude. He was not a particularly tall man either, but he tended to make up for that in bulk. A heavy beard hid the jowls of his jaw, but rolls of fat transformed his chest into breasts and his stomach hung so massively that it totally obscured his genitals. He had nice eyes, deep, black, and liquid. Zephaniah, in a rare poetic moment, had once described them as tranquil pools of Gideon. But much of their tranquillity had vanished since his stomach upset started.

"You know what this is, don't you?" Herod asked abruptly.

"No, Tetrarch," Zephaniah said politely. He was always polite to

Herod, except for those moments when they were in close physical proximity. Experience had taught him it was the safest course.

"It's a reincarnation," Herod told him grimly. He chewed the word and spat it out a second time. "A reincarnation." He had a powerful voice, deep and masculine, with a hint of gravel in the timbre.

"A reincarnation, Tetrarch?" Zephaniah echoed, frowning.

"It has to be. Look at the things he does. Healing. Calming storms. Levitation. You don't get power like that this side of the grave. That rabbi's twice-born, take my word for it. He's been here before and now he's back again, up to his tricks in another body."

"There's been some talk he might be Esaias come again," said Zephaniah uncertainly. "Or Elias, or even Elijah. A lot of people do believe prophets can be reincarnated, but I can't say I've put much credence in that personally."

But Herod was shaking his massive head, the black eyebrows knotted high above the bristling beard. "Not those men, you fool. John. It's John back from the grave."

"John the Baptist?" Zephaniah sucked in his breath involuntarily.

"Yes," Herod growled thoughtfully. The insight, now that it had dawned on him, was proving far from comfortable. In fact, it was downright frightening.

Zephaniah, who was intelligent enough to see the implications instantly, said, "Oh, surely not, Tetrarch. The man was a great nuisance for a time, but he's dead now. Well and truly dead, buried and rotted, most of him." A thought struck him like a revelation and he added cheerfully, "Besides, this new rabbi can't be his reincarnation. I mean, even if I believed in reincarnation—which I don't—this new one, this Joshua, can't be John."

"Why not?" Herod asked suspiciously. He was in no mood for empty reassurance, but something in the other's tone suggested there might be more to it than that.

"If reincarnation works at all, Tetrarch," Zephaniah explained carefully, "it works because the soul released at death eventually enters a fertile womb and is born again as a baby."

Herod nodded. "Yes." It was his own understanding of the process.

"Well," said Zephaniah, "how long is it since you—since John the Baptist died?"

60

Herod shrugged. "Not long. Weeks. A month or two." He did not really want to think about it. The whole Baptist business had been a horrendous mistake, even if the man had been a damned nuisance. But for all his sanctimonious cant, he hadn't deserved what happened to him. It was that little bitch Salome, of course —all her fault, really.

"Well then," said Zephaniah triumphantly, "there you are, Tetrarch. If John had reincarnated, he would be at most a month or two old by now. Still a baby, you see. But this new rabbi is thirty if he's a day. So he can't be John."

"He can't?"

"No, Tetrarch, he can't."

"Then how does he do these tricks you've been telling me about? This healing business, for example. And this levitation on water."

"I don't know," Zephaniah admitted.

"Could you do them?"

"No, Tetrarch."

"Neither could I—and I'm the King."

"Yes, Tetrarch."

Herod belched again. "I'm hungry," he said.

"Shall I bring you some mutton, Tetrarch?"

Zephaniah was halfway to his feet as Herod waved him down again. "No, if I eat anything now my stomach will play up. God knows it's bad enough when it's empty." He scowled heavily. "You don't get power like that this side of the grave," he repeated.

"But if he isn't reincarnated, Tetrarch—"

"Not reincarnated, risen! Back from the grave!" Such things happened. The priests were always warning about necromancy, an art which involved the reanimation of corpses. Lord God Jehovah, it was a terrifying prospect.

"But men can't rise from the grave," Zephaniah protested. He was not particularly happy with the turn of the conversation either. He had watched Herod sink into this sort of mood all too often before. He would start out with some simple little bit of nonsense and worry at it until it grew to enormous proportions, getting himself more and more upset in the process. Which was bad enough in isolation, but when Herod—Tetrarch of Galilee— got upset, nasty things happened, especially to those nearest to him.

"Witches can," Herod said. "That's why we stake them through the heart. It's the only thing that keeps them six feet under, according to the priests. We didn't stake John, did we?"

"No, Tetrarch. But then we didn't think he was a witch. The worst anyone ever called him was a prophet."

"He was a witch all right," said Herod gloomily. He too was aware he was digging a trap for himself. The habit sometimes made him suspect a flaw in his own character. If he dwelt on anything long enough—especially anything unpleasant—he ended up believing it. The trouble was, his beliefs usually turned out to be true, which made a repetition of the process easier. At this moment, at this precise moment, he did not believe John the Baptist had been a witch. But he would believe soon. That was inevitable, now the thought had occurred to him. In five minutes' time, he would be convinced of the Baptist's witchcraft. It was a daunting realization. Dear God, how had he ever become involved with that lunatic in the first place? Why hadn't he simply ignored him, examined his prancing at a distance, from royal heights, with a faint touch of regal amusement? That would have been the best way. But too late now. Although John, admittedly, had been hard to ignore. The wild men from the desert always were. And when he'd started to rant about Herod's relations with Herodias, the situation had become impossible, intolerable. Beyond ignoring. It was a poor thing when a king couldn't indulge in a bit of incest when he felt like it. The Egyptians did it all the time, at least the Pharaohs did. And they with their own sisters. All he'd done was take up with his brother's wife. No blood relationship, so it was hardly incest at all. Now the business with Salome was different. She *had* his brother's blood in her veins. That was real incest all right, and very nice too. But the Baptist never knew about that, so he had no cause to complain.

Unless, Herod thought suddenly, that was why he had returned from the grave.

"What's the matter, Tetrarch? You've turned quite white."

"You don't think he's coming after me again, do you, Zephaniah?"

"Coming after you, Tetrarch? Why should he want to do that?"

"I had him executed, damn it! Some men never appreciate the necessities of these things." He preferred not to mention the matter of Salome. Zephaniah could be very unreasonable about certain other relationships. He sighed and felt a tightness in his

62

chest, as if all the threatening aspects of the world were closing in around him.

Zephaniah licked his lips nervously. "He used to preach forgiveness, Tetrarch."

"Would you forgive a man who took your head off? I wouldn't."

"But, Tetrarch," Zephaniah said carefully, "if you consider the matter fully, it seems to me that even if he could—which I don't admit for a moment, of course—but even if he could, had the power, that is, it's doubtful to me that John could actually manage to rise from the grave, given the circumstances."

"I didn't understand a word of that," Herod said in irritation. "Why can't you speak plainly, Zephaniah?"

"Well, plainly, Tetrarch," said Zephaniah even more carefully, "plainly, sir, the fact is his disciples—John's disciples, that is—took his body off to be buried. I mean we didn't bury it here at the palace—they took it off for burial."

"Yes, I know that. What's that got to do with anything?"

"No head," Zephaniah said simply.

"No head?"

"They only buried the body. If you remember, you ordered the head brought to Salome on—"

"I know, I know! I know what I ordered!"

"But that's the point, Tetrarch. When the disciples came for the body, that's all they got. The head remained here in the palace. So even if he had the power of resurrection—which I would not admit for a moment—he would logically have to resurrect without his head. And having—"

"It's not still here, is it?" Herod asked stiffly.

"What's not still here, Tetrarch?"

"The head, you blithering fool! The Baptist's head!"

"Well, yes, Tetrarch," Zephaniah said uncertainly. "At least I should assume so. Salome gave it to her mother, of course, the lady Herodias, but—"

From the depths of his pallor, Herod groaned. His stomach had begun to churn like a farrow beneath the first cut of a cruel plow. "That's what he's after!" he exclaimed hollowly. "The head! That damned head!" He rose and began to waddle aimlessly around the room. "The head!" he muttered. "He must have come back for his head! That damned head is what it's all about. That head." He opened up a door and disappeared into the larder, his eyes

63

completely glazed. From within, his voice still reached Zephaniah clearly. "The head," he murmured, again and again. "The head. The Baptist's head."

11

Pontius approached the house under cover of darkness, his face half-hidden by the hood of a heavy woolen cloak. (The garment was not entirely for disguise: the evenings grew chill in these latitudes.) His formal retinue had shrunk to three: two armed guards for protection and Corax for companionship.

It was odd, he thought, how events had thrown them together. He had never felt Corax to be a really close friend before; but now, in this godsforsaken backwoods his urbane wit made him something of a savior. The puzzle was why he had volunteered to come, and as a private secretary, of all things. Admittedly he was superbly qualified for the post, but in Rome Corax had never been known to do an honest day's work in his life.

The woman's house was in an expensive quarter of the city, not far from the imperial administration—a deliberate choice, possibly. Junius had assured him she made a speciality of entertaining Romans, but only the best Romans. Externally, the architecture was Hebrew, a barbaric white-walled styling set within a walled courtyard which had not changed appreciably for centuries. But this one was rather larger than most and the woman could obviously afford a complement of servants, for there was one stationed at the gate, a squat, ugly brute in blue livery who looked capable of cutting your throat for a coin. He emerged out of the darkness as they reined in their horses and stood watching them silently.

"Is this the house of Miriam the Magdalene?" one of the guards called down to him.

The man stared back, his face expressionless in the torchlight.

"You there," the guard repeated sharply. "Is this the house of Miriam?"

Pontius glanced around him uneasily. The last thing he wanted was to draw attention to himself. Bad enough to be the Emperor's buffoon in the outback without the gossips having it that he had started to go native with a Hebrew whore—although Junius claimed she was quite an exceptional whore, and he should certainly have known, the lecherous old goat. All the same, he hissed at the guard, "Quiet, man. Do you want to wake the neighborhood?" Then, less angrily to Corax, "Do you think the man's deranged? He has a strange look about him."

"He certainly does not appear to be the most intelligent of mortals. Perhaps if I spoke softly to him. . . ." He started to dismount. "You will see my dependents are cared for should he decide to strangle me?"

The servant did indeed look something of a strangler: his arms were long and his hands very large and broad. Perhaps the woman needed someone such as this to keep out undesirable elements.

The creature moved sideways to block the doorway as Corax approached. They made an odd contrast, the one squat and powerful, the other tall and stooped. But at least they shared one thing: the blankness of their faces. Despite himself, Pontius found he was deriving some amusement from the encounter. Not that it lasted long, as it happened.

Corax stopped a foot or two away. "Is your mistress called Miriam?" he asked softly. Then, as an afterthought, repeated the question in Hebrew, a language he had picked up a great deal faster than Pontius.

The servant stared at him for a moment, then nodded.

Corax half turned. "This is Pontius Pilate, Governor of Judaea. He has come to see your mistress. Do you understand that?"

Was everyone determined to broadcast his identity? There was some excuse for the guard, who was marked as a fool both by his station in life and his chosen occupation. But Corax had no such excuse. Pontius sighed. It seemed entirely possible that the dwarf who had killed Trajan had also cast a spell over Pilate. Since that fateful day at the Games, he had not had a moment's good luck.

The creature at the gate looked up toward him. As their eyes met, Pontius was suddenly taken by the depth and warmth in those great orbs. They were brown and wide, like the eyes of cattle, yet somehow they lacked life. Pontius felt a curious stirring in himself, almost like a tickling of his mind. Then, without a word, the servant opened the gate and stepped aside.

They rode in and two grooms appeared to take their horses. At the same time, the main door opened and Pontius could see the shapely figure of a woman silhouetted in the lamplight. Was this the famous courtesan? Was this Miriam of Magdala? As he approached, he could see she was certainly an Israelite: black-haired, slender, sloe-eyed, and with that lengthy nose so many of the women seemed to have here. But she bowed and said, "Welcome, lord. My mistress is expecting you." She moved aside politely. "Your men will be entertained in the servants' quarters." She glanced uncertainly at Corax, whose dress and bearing clearly marked him as something other than a servant.

"My secretary, Corax," Pontius explained.

"I accompany him everywhere," Corax said with that blank expression so many people found disturbing. "The Governor sometimes requires me to compose letters."

Pontius grinned inwardly at the girl's expression. She must be wondering what sort of lunatic would require letters written in a brothel. But to her credit she merely nodded and gestured them both to enter. "If you are armed, sirs, I must ask you to leave your weapons in the hall. It is the rule of the house."

"We are not armed," Pontius told her.

Corax coughed. "I fear I invariably carry a dagger strapped to my left leg." He glanced at Pontius apologetically and hitched up his toga. Incredibly, there really was a dagger there. He handed it across. "One never knows when one might be the subject of an attack by wild animals or maddened women—something of that sort."

If the architecture was barbaric, the interior furnishings were strictly Roman, and in exceptionally good taste. The floor of the hallway was inlaid with polished marble tiles, covered by a scattering of the Egyptian rugs so popular in the capital. There was even a niche in the wall, of the type usually filled by statues of the household gods, although here, he noticed, it contained nothing of greater religious significance than a vase of cut flowers. The woman—a maid, presumably—led them to a doorway which

66

opened into a heavily curtained and well-lighted room. "My mistress will join you presently," she said.

"A veritable home from home," Corax remarked, staring around him.

It was, in fact, considerably more opulent than the Governor's quarters in the imperial administration. The imperial buildings totally lacked a woman's touch. Junius had been unmarried, and no civil-service wife had ever yet achieved enough stature to leave her mark on the place. As a result, a certain austerity reigned, although it was clean and comfortable enough in its fashion, impressive enough for visiting dignitaries, and expensive enough in its upkeep—especially for a governor on half pay. But this room certainly had a richness his own quarters lacked. Here again the pillars and the drapes were strictly Roman, as were the couches, cushions, and rugs. There was even a wall ornament of Germanic basketwork, an intriguing touch. He had not seen anything like it since his arrival in Judaea, but with the current fad in Rome for German artifacts and styles, it was exactly the sort of display he would have expected in any patrician house at home. It seemed, then, that the harlot had pretensions.

Pontius found himself a couch and sat. There was just the faintest scent of musk from the cushions and for the first time he felt a stirring of excitement. On his arrival, over wine, Junius had told him of this place. After a lifetime in the imperial service, the old Governor had been put out to graze in Judaea, an easy, unimportant station blessed by perpetual good weather. The expectation was that he would pass the years until retirement in avoiding work (thus causing no one any trouble) and drinking wine. He had disappointed no one on either score, but despite his age and the ravages of wine-induced gout, he had added a third vice of his own: womanizing. When administration wives had proved too virtuous—or perhaps just too disinterested in the balding, potbellied old warrior—and since the Hebrew women, by and large, shunned contact with the Roman male, he had turned, with enormous enthusiasm, to the country's professional court-esans. The gods alone knew where he found the strength to service them—and so many of them, if the rumors, and his own boasting, could be believed. The women themselves must have assumed that his infrequent visits were due to his illness or declining years, whereas, in point of fact, his net was spread so wide that in calling on them all, he saw each one perhaps no more often than at six-month intervals.

And with such experience, the one he talked about—the only one he talked about—was Miriam. On such recommendation, who could deny that the woman was worth meeting, at least once? Although Pontius had been a little taken aback by her cool insistence that he should visit her. Emperor's buffoon or not, a governor was surely entitled to have people call on him. Especially whores. Not that he would necessarily have entertained her in the administration, but still. Nevertheless, as he thought about it, her attitude engendered a smoldering sensation of respect. He had dispatched three emissaries and she had returned each one with a flea in his ear. If the Governor wished to avail himself of her services, then the Governor was very welcome to call on her. He would be guaranteed the same discretion as any other client, and perhaps a little extra in the way of entertainment. The touch of diplomacy did nothing to soften her stance. She might be a whore, but she was her own whore.

"Have you seen this, dear boy?" Corax asked abruptly. When they were alone together he reverted to an easy informality of address. He had been exploring the room with an open curiosity his blank features did nothing to mask and was now bent over a small table tucked beneath a wall lamp in one corner.

Pontius walked over to join him. On the table was a hefty parchment scroll, in many ways similar to the books so prized by Roman historians, except that the paper had the sheen and texture which marked its manufacture as Egyptian. But as Corax began to unroll it, the resemblance to any historical tome ended abruptly. The scroll told a story all right, but in pictures, not in words, each one exquisitely drawn in finest detail, line, shading, and perspective all indicating the hand of a master artist. The story featured a slim, black-haired beauty, dressed—at least at first—in softly flowing robes, and a tall man, broad, curly-haired and with, as became very evident in the second picture of the series, the largest penile erection a human being was ever likely to produce.

Despite the overt erotica, with basic sexual positions giving way to increasingly complex and perverse couplings, Pontius found his attention drawn quite irresistibly to the woman's face. It was not merely the exotic beauty of her features. There was something in the eyes, subtly caught—or instilled—by the artist: a haunted, almost fearful look, buried deep, but quite definitely there. How very curious.

"Good evening, gentlemen. Which of you is my lord Pilate, Governor of Judaea?"

Pontius set the scroll down hastily and turned, gripped by exactly the same sensation of guilt he used to experience as a child when his mother caught him stealing cakes. It was ludicrous, but there it was.

Corax, whose frozen features may also have covered embarrassment (there was no telling), said politely, "This is the Governor, Pontius Pilate. I am his private secretary and companion. My name is not important." No one would have the opportunity of learning that noble Corax was prepared to consort with Hebrew harlots!

But the woman said, "Your name, sir, is Corax and your fame has preceded you." She came forward and bowed coolly to Pontius. "I am Miriam of Magdala."

He was looking at the woman in the scroll! The same arrogant tilt of the head, the same upright stance, the same long, dark hair, the same high breasts, the same long legs, the same slim hands. And most of all, the same haunted eyes. The reality of those eyes was even more peculiar than the representation. They were a deep brown, almost black, like so many eyes one saw among these Israelites, but they were larger, rounder than usual, with a luminosity that could drown a man. This made them beautiful, but what made them peculiar was something swimming in their depths. In the drawing it had seemed like fear; and certainly fear was a part of it, well disguised, carefully hidden—so carefully hidden he doubted many another man would ever have noticed it.

But it was not just fear. He stared, enraptured for a timeless moment, trying to explain, but failed. The quality (expression? trick of light?) was so entirely alien that it baffled him. For some reason he remembered the sensation he had had outside when that idiot servant stared at him and he fancied that his mind itched. The woman's eyes gave him substantially the same feeling, but in the spine and heart, rather than the head.

He forced his eyes away from hers. "I am very pleased to meet you, Miriam of Magdala." He turned and strolled casually back to his seat on the couch. The scroll had not been left accidentally. She was wearing exactly the same flowing robe in which the artist had depicted her. Beneath it, her feet were encased in jeweled sandals, exactly as shown in the first picture. Even the bracelet on her wrist, the pendant at her throat, the ring on her left hand—a tiny silver serpent biting on what seemed to be an apple—were all as shown in the scroll. An intriguing, imaginative ploy. Her manner was as cold as snow, yet she had obviously gone to pains to ensure that she was immediately identified with the woman in the scroll, the woman who had accepted that grotesque, gigantic penis in every orifice available.

She walked to a chair and sat with dignity, for all the world like some senator's matron entertaining guests from the Capitol. "I have instructed my maids to bring us some refreshment. No doubt your journey has left you hungry."

That short ride from the administration? Whether from the smell of musk, the pictures in the scroll, the vivid descriptions of the lecherous Junius, or the breathing reality so cool and calm before him, Pontius felt his animal excitement mounting. Hungry, perhaps, but hardly for food. "Perhaps," he suggested, smiling, "a little wine . . ."

"And meat," added Corax, who had eaten a full meal only half an hour before they left. "Perhaps some pulses and, of course, some bread. Indeed—"

She glanced across at him in some surprise. Pontius thought he caught the faintest, almost startled, hint of amusement around her mouth as she put in mildly, "I fear all I requested from them was some fruit." Her face went absolutely blank, as expressionless as Corax's own, but the tip of her tongue flicked out across her top lip in an intensely sensual gesture. "In my experience, a full stomach will often interfere with other pleasures."

"You think so?" Corax asked mildly, although Pontius knew him well enough to read the surprise in his voice. "I've always felt it adds to them."

"In Rome perhaps. Here the climate is hotter and the body must adjust." She turned gracefully to Pilate. "And speaking of Rome, how is that great city, Governor? I believe you have only lately come from there."

So well spoken (her Latin was flawless, without the hint of an accent), so formal. But not, perhaps, so well informed. His last adventures in Rome must be common gossip. She would scarcely have asked about Rome had she known of them. Unless, he

70

realized with a start, she knew and did not care. He had a sudden suspicion his moods might be in the process of manipulation. He was not sure he cared much for the discovery. Pontius shrugged. "Rome is, as Rome always has been. Nothing changes."

"Except the *sparsio*," said Miriam.

"Ah," Corax remarked blandly, "you are familiar with our Games?"

"Not personally," Miriam told him. "Like most Jews I prefer life to death. But naturally, the Games are a frequent topic among my Roman friends." She turned back with great deliberation toward Pontius and smiled. "I understand, my lord, that the Games have not always brought you good fortune."

For a moment he could not decide between anger and amusement. Was this what Junius had raved about? The woman was a bitch. Beautiful, admittedly, but if one wanted only beauty, one could admire a Greek marble. Behind the beauty nothing showed at all except chill arrogance. How pleasant it would be to break that arrogance! To rip away her gown and force her to—

Incredibly, against the rising tide of anger, amusement suddenly erupted and won out. The loose folds of his tunic hid the plain fact he was already mightily aroused. And was this not why he had come? And did the bitch not know this was why he had come? And did the clever bitch not make a substantial living from her ability to ensure arousal? The amusement reached his face and he smiled. "The Games have so far ruined me, Miriam Magdalene, that I have had to save pennies for weeks to afford your fee." He was gratified to see the flash of surprise—almost immediately hidden—at his honesty. She was a fascinating one all right, this Hebrew Miriam. What a pity she was a whore. She might have made an interesting companion.

She returned his smile, and for the very first time there was at least a hint of warmth. "You may find your evening worth the effort, Pontius," she told him softly.

The maids entered then, as if on some secret signal. Both carried silver trays, one with the promised fruit—melon, oranges, pomegranates, apples—the other with a large jug and several exquisite crystal goblets. But even Corax was not looking toward the food. Both girls were naked but for tiny linen loincloths. They set down the trays and stood like matched, contrasting, perfect statues; one an African so black her oiled skin shone with a hint of purple, the other a pale Jewess, her brown hair lightened with dye until, with her gray-green eyes, she might have been taken for a German. Their bodies were beautifully muscled and, apart from a slight heaviness in the white girl's breasts, almost flawless.

"Do you like my little servants?" Miriam asked ingenuously.

"Very much," breathed Corax, face expressionless as ever, but his color rising.

"I trained them myself," Miriam remarked. "They are really quite talented." She stood up and reached for a tray. "Let me help you to some wine while they entertain us."

The tones were still those of a Capitol matron, perhaps introducing a musical evening. But these attractive young women used no less interesting instruments than each other's bodies. They sank together on a pile of cushions, embraced, kissed fondly, then began a series of caresses orchestrated as much for the watchers' entertainment as their own amusement. Yet, their own passions were very soon aroused—aroused, but not quickly satisfied, even when the loincloths were removed and they writhed together in the delightful, riveting obscenity of a superbly imaginative carnal display.

Pontius, who had always recognized more than a passing hint of the voyeur in himself—with few enough opportunities to pander to it—watched with unashamed fascination until a soft touch on his arm drew his attention away.

"Shall we leave my little maids to pleasure your friend, dear Pontius?" Miriam whispered. She took his hand and led him gently from the room. He glanced back from the doorway to see that Corax's eyes had glazed into a sort of trance. His face remained impassive, but his body had begun to shake. The black girl, noticing the movement of her mistress, broke away from her companion and walked toward him, smiling, arms outstretched.

The room was smaller than the one they had left, more dimly lit and simply furnished, though still in the same exquisite taste. Miriam closed the door behind her and as she did so he could feel the change in her. The arrogant stance was the same, the tilt of the head was the same, but there was a smoldering fire in her eyes now, quite obliterating that earlier, alien expression. And like Corax's, the woman's body trembled slightly, then was still. "Do you want me, Pontius?" she asked hoarsely.

A harlot's world was full of pretense, but if this was pretense, he had never seen it done better. Even her body scent was that of a woman stirred. He stared at her in silent admiration, sending a mental word of thanks winging toward the absent Junius. "Yes," he breathed.

"Then take," she told him.

And he took, exactly as he had imagined it, ripping the gown in his haste, scarcely waiting to remove his own clothes, throwing her upon a pallet near the door, sinking deep inside her while her arms and legs came up to embrace him like a bear trap.

"Take!" she hissed again. "Take! Take! Take! Take!"

Afterward they lay together like old lovers in the gentle twilight of their (his?) satisfaction. He noticed for the first time that there were erotic carvings on the ceiling: a satyr, penis rampant, pursued a laughing, willing nymph. The flickering of the lamplight made the figures appear almost alive.

All the coldness and the arrogance had gone, or so at least it seemed. But even in his satisfaction, something made him wary. He decided he must see this whore again, but also decided he must never underestimate her. She was a skilled professional, as skilled—if not more skilled—than the finest courtesans of Rome.

But he could not quite see what lay behind the skill and the masks. It made him vaguely uneasy, but deeply fascinated. He touched her breast, quite gently, without passion, and thought he felt her body stiffen slightly. Thought, but could not be quite sure. "You're not asleep then?" she asked casually.

"Just quiet," Pontius told her. "You have drained me."

"What else is a woman for?"

Indeed, what else, although he had the oddest feeling this woman was good for a great deal more than the amusement of men. He thought about it, and thought about the alien fear in her eyes—which had returned now that their more violent antics were ended.

"Is it difficult to be a governor?" she asked seriously after a moment.

It was so unexpected, he chuckled and answered her with total honesty. "Never that. The civil service runs the country. The Governor could well be a trained ape." Which, in a way, was all he was.

"I had thought this new rabbi might be causing you some trouble."

It was said casually, yet every instinct rose up to inform him this was not a casual remark. She had an interest here that went beyond pretending, almost as if this, and not their loving, not his money for her fee, was the most important part of the evening.

Pontius, who trusted his instincts implicitly when they arose this strongly, said with equal ease, "New rabbi? Which new rabbi do you mean?"

And Miriam's voice caught just a little in her throat as she replied, "The one who casts out demons."

§12

The Tetrarch's palace was considerably larger and older than the Roman residency. These two characteristics were interlinked, since the massive spread of the building came from generations of additions and extensions. As a result, this seat of Jewish power looked like something grown organically on the barren hillsides of Judaea: cactus spires, cauliflower domes, cedar-tree pillars, flower-petal windows. An architect's nightmare, but home for Herod, King of the Jews in Galilee.

Except that it did not feel like home now, for home should be a haven and a comfort, while Herod felt threat oozing from the very walls. Where was Herodias?

The life of Herod's palace centered round two chambers: the throne room and the banquet hall. Herod was seated in the former, idly wishing it were the latter. He was a man of appetites, but not all of them for food, so the wish indeed was idle, a background fancy in a mind mainly concentrated on far more important things. Where was Herodias?

Since he knew the throne room would be as crowded as the throne room always was, the Tetrarch had clothed himself in stately robes, ornately worked in finely drawn threads of gold and silver. He had placed bracelets on his arms and hung a jeweled breastplate round his neck. Joachim, his chief body servant, had set the heavy mitre-crown upon his head and slipped gold sandals on his feet. Herodias would know what this was all about. Certainly the courtiers knew, for they moved about like ghosts, without their usual chatter. Even the court fool was subdued. He sat on the floor beneath the dais picking his toenails with abnormal concentration.

"Where is Herodias?" Herod roared abruptly.

The silent court became a still court. No one wished to answer, but someone obviously had to. Eventually Abrim ben Abrim, the only majordomo to survive the Tetrarch's rages for three years, said carefully, "She has been sent for, Tetrarch."

"I know she has been sent for!" Herod shouted. "She has been sent for *a long time ago!* Did I ask you if she had been sent for? I asked you where she was!"

"She is in her rooms, Tetrarch," said Abrim ben Abrim confidently, without the slightest notion where Herodias might be. "She prepares herself for the Tetrarch's presence."

Herod snorted. It was a slick reply, but then everything was oily in this damned palace. They weaseled around him like slime, every one of them, terrified to say a word out of place. Except Herodias. Preparing herself for the Tetrarch's presence, indeed! Since the bitch had gotten her claws in him, the only preparation she made for the Tetrarch's presence was opening up her legs. And that only when she felt like it. He should have left her to Philip. Philip knew how to handle her. She had seemed so desirable when she was his brother's wife, so full of dark, erotic arts. But even then the situation had been barely tolerable. The secret nights of passion and tureens of chicken soup to follow. But when Philip died, the whole thing crumbled. Herodias insisted on open recognition. Why, oh why, had he permitted himself to be persuaded on that point? A moment of weakness. A brief instant of sheer madness. But a secret once released can never be recalled. The scandal! Such scandal! And just as the court became accustomed to it, the Baptist came marching out of his damn desert raving on about blasphemy, incest, and abomination.

The Baptist. . . .

Herod was afraid. As Tetrarch, only Pilate stood above him. He should fear no man. He *did* fear no man. No living man, that is. But a man who rose from the grave . . . that was a horse of a very different color. What if the arisen Baptist was walking to the palace at this very instant? Walking? What if he was riding a horse, galloping full tilt toward the gates, cloak spread out like the wings of the Dark Angel? He would demand what was his, and Herod could not give it to him. Did she still have it, the bitch? Or had it rotted now? Did heads rot? Could they be preserved? How did one preserve a head? The Egyptians knew; they could preserve anything. Had she called in an Egyptian to preserve the head? Why would she want to keep a preserved head? Where had she put it? Would the arisen Baptist be satisfied with just the skull?

"Where is Herodias?" Herod bellowed.

"I'm here, you old fool! Keep your voice down!"

It was a whisper in his left ear. He swung round to find her glaring at him angrily. She had sneaked in through the side door, a typical maneuver. Why could she never approach him with respect, from the front, bowing and scraping and weaseling oilily like everybody else? But he had no control over her, none at all. "Did you have it preserved?" he hissed.

"Did I have what preserved, Herod?" She was a slim, dark woman with high cheekbones and a stately carriage. Her hair was showing gray now, for all her herbal lotions. But she would still be attractive if it wasn't for her tongue. God in heaven, but she had a sharp tongue, especially when she was angry. And by the look of her eyes, she was angry now.

But he would tame her. He would have to tame her. This matter was too important to allow himself to be browbeaten by his brother's wife. Why did you have to die, Philip? It was such a small dose of aconite. You could have fought it easily. "The head!" he hissed back. Whatever mistakes had been made in the past, there must be no mistake now. He had to have the head. He had to have it before this wonder-working wizard Baptist came to claim it.

"What head? You're making a fool of yourself again, Tetrarch. First this ridiculous summons when you know perfectly well I always have my hair dressed at this time. And now all you can do is mumble nonsense. Your courtiers are all looking at you."

He glanced around and discovered it was true. The entire court was staring at him, slack-mouthed and open-eyed, straining to catch his private conversation. "Out!" he screamed. "Get out of my sight! All of you! Every one! Guards, be sure that no one enters until I give the word."

"No one but my daughter!" Herodias called imperiously, unable to resist the smallest opportunity to contradict him in some measure.

He let it go. No sense in arguing when you knew you wouldn't win. Later he could always flog a slave girl to relieve his feelings, but at the moment there were more urgent matters at hand than squabbling with Herodias. When the chamber emptied and the brass doors shut with their usual impressive clang, he turned back to her, forcing himself to be calm. "I called you here for a purpose, my dear, something perhaps a little more important than your hair: the head of John the Baptist."

Although she was not the Queen, she moved and sat upon the Queen's throne, staring at him coldly. "What of the head of John the Baptist?"

"You have it?" he asked, leaning forward anxiously.

"I, sir? Why should I have the smelly thing? You gave it to Salome."

"Who in turn gave it to you."

Her eyes narrowed. "Where did you obtain that information?"

"From Zephaniah." It slipped out before he could stop it, although he realized, even as he spoke, that naming Zephaniah had been a mistake.

Herodias leaned back easily. "Ah, Zephaniah! Your mincing pretty little spy!"

"He does not mince!" said Herod hotly.

But she ignored him. "And where did he tell you this, Tetrarch? In your secret bedchamber while he tricked with your member to improve your potency?"

"There's nothing wrong with my potency!" Herod shrieked. Then, as an afterthought: "I don't have a secret bedchamber."

Her eyebrows rose. "In the east wing of the palace at the end of the blue corridor?"

"That's my temple!" Herod snapped.

She smiled.

"It is!" he shouted wildly. "It's my private Temple of the Lord!"

"Don't blaspheme," Herodias told him. "If you weren't such a perfect fool you would know everyone is well aware what goes on in your 'private Temple of the Lord.' First it was serving-wenches when you thought I might be jealous if you left my bed. Then it was sheep when you feared the serving-wenches might talk. Then that ridiculous business with the chickens because you imagined people would assume you were eating them. And now it is young men—the boy Jacob and that creature Zephaniah—when you are not trying to persuade your own niece, my daughter, into further filthy acts of incest."

"You sent her!" Herod hissed. "You encouraged her! You thought because your hair was graying and your breasts were sagging, you would trap me with your own daughter!" Why was he arguing about this? Why did he permit her to provoke him when one thing and one thing only was important?

Herodias shrugged, as if none of this was of any real concern to her. "Why are you so anxious to learn about the Baptist's head? You were happy enough to be rid of it when it was fresh."

"I want it back."

Her eyebrows arched again. "You want it back? The great Tetrarch recalls his gifts? What else shall you want back, Herod? My jewels which you gave me to buy my favors when my dear husband was alive?" She waved heavily ringed hands. "This gown you also gave me, so that I must walk naked on account of a king's meanness?"

"Just the head," Herod muttered. "I only want the head."

"But why," Herodias said coldly, "do you want the head?"

"I can't tell you."

She stood up abruptly. "Very well, Tetrarch, then our conversation is at an end."

In sudden chill he waved her back to the throne. If she became stubborn, he would never get the head. He took a deep breath to calm himself and forced a smile. "No need to upset yourself, my dear. I have no secrets from you—you know that. I only wished to save you worry." He coughed. "The fact is, John the Baptist seems—" he swallowed "—seems to, well, seems to have risen."

She frowned. "Risen?"

"From the grave," Herod explained.

"From the grave?"

"Risen from the grave," Herod said. "Risen from the dead."

Herodias was staring at him. "You are telling me the Baptist has come back to life?"

"Yes."

"He has resurrected?"

"Yes."

"He is walking around the kingdom?"

"Yes."

"*Without his head?*" She began to laugh. The laughter gripped her so, that she lay back helplessly in the Queen's throne, her body quivering with waves of mirth. "You're a fool, Herod! Oh, God help me, was there ever a greater fool!"

"This is serious, Herodias," Herod scowled. He fought to hold his temper. One had to appreciate that it was startling news the first time one heard it. She had not yet had time to consider the matter as he had. Patience was called for. "This is serious," he said again, more gently this time. He waited until the gale of laughter died down to an occasional intermittent gurgle, then went on earnestly. "Have you heard reports of this new rabbi?"

The laughter died completely and she frowned. "Joshua? The one associating with the Zealots?"

"Yes, Joshua." He had not heard about the Zealots and filed the information away in the back of his mind. "You know that he has been working miracles?"

"I had heard some fools consider him the latest Messiah. I assumed he must have learned a few party tricks to get that sort of reaction."

"More than party tricks, I think," Herod told her. "He heals lepers and walks on water and a great deal more besides, if only half my information is true. You don't get power like that this side of the grave. It is my belief the rabbi is really John the Baptist risen from the grave."

"But he does not look like John the Baptist," Herodias protested.

"You've seen him?" Herod asked excitedly. The bitch was everywhere, except where you wanted her when you needed her.

She shrugged. "In passing. My carriage chair happened on one of his meetings. I glanced out."

"What does he look like?"

"Not terribly impressive. About John's build and height—small and wiry. But you may take my word for it, he has a head on his shoulders. Not a very handsome one, admittedly, but serviceable enough."

About John's build and height! The woman did not even realize what she was saying! *About John's build and height!* "Of course he has a head on his shoulders," Herod told her patiently. "He could scarcely resurrect without one." He leaned forward, anxious she should understand. "But it's not his own head. That's why you failed to recognize him as John. The same build and height, you see. John's body, but a different head. It's the Baptist, all right: it has to be. And sooner or later he will want his own head back." He sat back on the throne. "Now do you see why I need it?"

"But this rabbi can't—" She stopped abruptly and her eyes narrowed. She stared at him for a moment, then said slowly, "Yes, I can see why you need it, all right."

Herod sighed with relief. "Then you'll give it back to me?" An earlier worry returned. "You did have it preserved, didn't you? I mean, it hasn't rotted away now or anything like that?"

Herodias licked her lips briefly. She had that shrewd look in her eye that always indicated trouble. But she only said, "You need have no fear of that, dear Herod. It would have rotted by now, of course, but when Salome showed it to me, the dear child was so delighted with her little trophy that I made arrangements to have it stuffed and mounted. An embalmer from Memphis did the job—I always think Egyptians are best for these things, don't you? So much practice."

"And it's all right? No decay?"

"None whatsoever. Of course, the man was a master craftsman, quite at the pinnacle of his art. He removed the brain through the nose. I was quite fascinated. I should have thought it would have been much easier to reach by working upward through the severed neck, but he explained that through the nose was the traditional way. It apparently prevents any damage to the skull casing. Then he packed the aperture with alum and preserving resins—quite pleasant-smelling, although one would not want them as a perfume. He had to remove the scalp and facial skin for tanning, of course, but when he sewed them back you could scarcely see the join. Masterly work. Quite beautiful in its own strange way. And not a sign of rot, not even a small fungus attack."

Would a head still work without a brain? Probably well enough. Since no one seemed to know the function of the organ, it probably was not all that important. He might feel a little light, a little dizzy perhaps, but he would soon get used to it. A more important point struck him and he asked, "Did he leave the teeth intact?"

"Oh, yes. Perfect teeth. He set the jaw so that the head was smiling slightly for a more aesthetic effect."

"So he will still be able to eat?"

It seemed Herodias paused for a second before she answered, "If he wants to."

"My dear," said Herod, "you have no idea how happy this makes me. So relieved. So very relieved. Shall we have it sent for now?"

"Sent for, Tetrarch?"

"The head. Shall we have it sent for so that I may see it and keep it safe until the rabbi arrives?"

That expression was back in her eyes again. "The preservation process was extremely costly, Tetrarch. To bring a man from Egypt is an expensive procedure. And he used only the finest materials. And his own fee, of course. . . ."

"I'll pay," said Herod promptly. "Whatever it cost, I'll pay."

But she was shaking her head. The bitch was shaking her head, slowly, from side to side! "Well, yes, there is the money, of course, but that is hardly the sole consideration." She pursed her lips. "This was a present for Salome, for my little baby."

"Your little—?"

"We can scarcely tear her plaything from her without so much as an explanation, now can we, Herod?"

"I want the head!" Herod roared, fear overcoming his caution.

Herodias leaned across to tickle his chin fondly through his beard. She smiled. "I shall have a word with Salome, my dear. I'm sure we can come to some arrangement."

13

The creature was a Zealot. Miriam was sure of it even before he spoke. He had the proper look of drawn rigidity. She disliked Zealots as a breed. Their hatred of Rome was understandable and she might even have considered it praiseworthy were it not for her suspicion that it was generated to fill a need in their own lives. The few she had met shared a characteristic with this one—they looked at the world with narrowed eyes, as if they felt themselves to be central characters in some vast, important drama. But despite their rabble-rousing and secret military forays, the real drama was played out in the privacy of their own skulls. How did he see himself, this Zealot? A warrior like King David, striding bravely out to meet the monolithic Goliath of Rome? The reality before her was less impressive: a straggle of a beard, emaciated features, filthy robe, and unwashed body. He smelled of grime, this Zealot; and the air of self-importance that hung around him like a cloud made all his boasted ruthlessness pathetic. Nonetheless she needed him.

"You are the one they call Simon?"

"Yes."

The name she had been given was Simon Zealotes—Simon the Zealot—for more, she suspected, than his political affiliations. The tavern was a little too crowded. Across the way, three Roman legionnaires were drinking wine. Why did he choose to sit so close to Romans? Did danger excite him, make him feel more real? There was a tightness in his voice when he spoke, as if he had been aroused by the sight of a woman. But it was not she who aroused him. His excitement grew from the contemplation of his own daring.

"May I speak with you?" Miriam asked politely.

His eyes flickered to Benjamin, a pace behind her right shoulder, squat and muscular as an African ape. "Who is your companion?"

"A good Hebrew like yourself," Miriam said. "He is my servant."

"Is he talkative?"

Miriam smiled inwardly. No man on earth was less talkative than Benjamin. But she only said, "No." Without waiting for an invitation, she sat beside him. She had no heart for the childish games of intrigue these men played. She only needed information, and when she received it, she would leave, hoping never to set eyes on Simon the Zealot again. Benjamin remained standing, so solidly immobile that people walked around him. His eyes were even more blank than usual, as if his mind had strayed back to the goatherds of his native hills. But if she needed him, he was there. And his hands were very strong.

"What do you want, woman?" Simon Zealotes asked sourly.

82

Despite the reassurance, he seemed disturbed by Benjamin's presence.

Miriam dropped her voice. "They tell me you are a follower of the rabbi Joshua."

He stood up abruptly and walked out into the sunlit courtyard, then stopped and stared at a rumbling cart taking produce to the market. After a moment of surprised hesitation, Miriam followed him.

"There are Romans in the tavern!" he hissed angrily. "Have you no intelligence?"

"I did not choose your drinking companions," Miriam told him mildly. She gave him the benefit of her coolest smile, well aware of the effect it would have. Behind her she could sense Benjamin's presence and knew, without having to look, that he was staring at the Zealot. The anger in the man's tone would have drawn him like a lodestone.

Simon sensed the menace too, for his eyes flickered beyond her, then back to her own, with the anger replaced by a hint of genuine fear. It was one thing to plot the overthrow of Rome; quite another, apparently, to face the immediate threat of a Hebrew goatherd. She allowed the tension to mount for a moment before saying briskly, "I ask you again—here where no one else may listen—are you a follower of the rabbi Joshua?"

"I have heard him speak at the Temple," Simon Zealotes admitted cautiously.

"And elsewhere?"

"Yes." Still reluctant. She suspected that were it not for Benjamin he might have stalked away.

"They say he is the Messiah," Miriam remarked casually.

He said nothing.

"They say he preaches sedition against Rome—is that why you were afraid of the Romans hearing?"

"I fear no Roman!" Simon spat. Oddly enough, she believed him. Something in his tone told her that behind the private self-aggrandizement there was a cord of courage that was real enough.

"I should like to meet this rabbi," Miriam said. "Can you tell me where I may find him?"

"No." Too quickly.

"That is strange, Simon Zealotes—" she pronounced the word with great emphasis and clarity "—for I know you to be one of his chosen."

"And I know you to be the Magdalene who takes the Roman scum into her bed!" His fury was open and obviously genuine since it had chased away his fear. Benjamin made a small movement forward, but Miriam stopped him with a gesture.

"It is true I number Romans among my friends," she said. "But why should your precious Joshua be troubled by that fact? Is he a Zealot too?"

"You are a harlot!" Simon hissed. "The rabbi does not consort with the likes of you!"

"A strange rabbi if he has no time for sinners," Miriam remarked easily.

"No time for a whore of Romans!"

"Shall he not be permitted to decide that for himself?"

"Send your Legion officers to find him, whore!" snapped Simon. He turned to walk away.

Miriam gestured lightly and Benjamin reached the man before he had taken two steps. The massive arms went round him, squeezed, and locked. Pain flared in the Zealot's eyes, but to his credit he neither struggled nor cried out. Miriam moved to face him. "I have spoken politely to you, sir. I require only that you speak to me politely in your turn."

"The soldiers will come if your man does not release me," Simon told her quietly. "It may go ill for me if they question me too closely."

Without being told, Benjamin released his arms. The Zealot stood very still, breathing heavily, watching Miriam.

"You see," said Miriam, "I do not choose to put you in any danger. And as you say, I have friends among the Legion officers, so the soldiers would certainly come if I should call them. Or, if I should order my servant to crush you to death, they would not interfere—especially if I told them of your politics. But I mean you no harm. And I mean no harm to your master."

"My master?"

"The rabbi Joshua. Where may I find him, Simon Zealotes?"

"What do you want of the rabbi?"

She hesitated, seized by a sudden feeling of unreality. The sun shone brightly from a cloudless sky, reflecting off the white walls of the houses. A woman passed with a clay pot balanced on her head, on the way to the well. A group of artisans gambled with dice on the baked earth of the courtyard in a corner just outside of earshot. From behind her, the clatter and the chatter of the tavern floated clearly through the open doorway. What did she want of the rabbi they were calling a Messiah? There were too many Messiahs in Israel, men like this Zealot, but with their brains afire with holy visions that made them doubly dangerous. Imbeciles made mad by too much contemplation of Jehovah. She had heard at least three of them at one time or another, babbling their lunacy in the market square while fools with nothing better to do had listened open-mouthed. What business had Miriam with another of these?

"Is it true," she asked, suddenly very much afraid of the answer, "that the rabbi Joshua has the power to cast out demons?"

Her words hung in the air, bathed by the warm sunlight. They had a life of their own, those words, a compulsion born of desperation that reached out to touch something in the soul. Simon Zealotes dropped his voice so that it was scarcely more than a whisper. "Demons, Magdalene?"

"Demons," Miriam echoed.

His head turned again to look at Benjamin. "He is infested?" All his former antagonism was suddenly gone.

"Not he," Miriam said.

For a moment it seemed he did not understand. Then: "You, lady?"

She turned away from him, utterly unable to speak. Did one speak of putrefaction and festering sores? Did one speak of corruption and abomination? Did one admit to foulness? This meeting had not gone as she had planned. She had wished only to talk to the rabbi, not expose her shame to this fanatic. Why had she mentioned demons? Why had she even asked the question? She might have threatened him until he told her where to find the rabbi, or pleaded, or cajoled. She knew the weaknesses of men and she might have played on his without a single mention of foulness. But it was done now. She tilted her head back and looked at him directly.

To her astonishment he reached for her, not in anger, not in horror, but with something that might well have been compassion. His hands gripped her arms. "You, lady?" he repeated.

85

Miriam nodded mutely.

"Forgive me," Simon whispered. "I did not understand."

Perhaps it was his words, perhaps relief at having openly admitted her affliction, but whatever the reason, a wild hope surged through Miriam's being. She was no longer aware of the tavern or the courtyard or the passersby, only of the face of the man who gripped her arms. "Your rabbi—can he cure me?"

"He has raised the dead, lady! What demon could withstand that power?"

"Can you take me to him?"

He hesitated, glanced around toward the tavern and the Roman soldiers within. "There are those who would do him harm. It might be better if you were not seen with him publicly." Then, mysteriously, "The Romans are not the worst of our enemies."

"I don't understand you," Miriam said.

He released her arms. The emaciated features reverted to their former grim rigidity. "Your profession, Magdalene," he said.

"My pro—?" Light dawned abruptly. "The priests do not approve of him?"

"They watch us constantly." He did indeed look at that moment like a man accustomed to being watched constantly, although she still felt it was part of a role he played. A role played constantly and with such conviction that he might have come to believe it himself, but a role nonetheless. Did his master, the rabbi Joshua, play at being holy? Did he perform simple tricks with such conviction that his followers believed him to be the Messiah—or at least a great magician who could raise the dead?

Miriam felt a rising panic stalk her thoughts. She could not afford the luxury of disbelief, for if the rabbi Joshua did not cure her, then who would? She remembered Pontius Pilate and his easy dismissal of the man as another Hebrew lunatic who drew support from the uncouth and desperate. But Pilate had heard of him. Could the rabbi be so unimportant when his fame had reached the ears of the Governor himself? And she remembered that there was something in Pilate's eyes when he spoke about the man—a wariness, not as obvious as the wariness in the eyes of Simon, but possibly more genuine for that. What was it Longinus had said? Pilate has a horror of magicians? Did the urbane Governor then believe that the rabbi could work miracles, could kill at a touch like the dwarf in the Roman arena?

Miriam was about to speak again when Simon said, "I will take you to him in secret, by night when no one will see."

"Yes," Miriam said. "Yes, I will go with you by night."

He stared at her, his eyes searching for some sign of demons. "Meet me by the well, three hours after sunset. Bring a donkey to ride on, it is a long way on foot." Then he turned and strode away abruptly. This time Benjamin did not move to stop him.

§14

The reception chamber of the Governor's palace was considerably more opulent than anything Pontius could have afforded in his Roman villa. No concession had been made to native custom or design. Both the architecture and furnishings were strictly Roman, a little conservative, perhaps, a little less fashionable than he might have chosen himself, a little grandiose for a sophisticated palate, but then it was always necessary, after all, to impress the natives. Not that Caiaphas appeared unduly impressed.

Pontius stared easily at the man, idly wondering about the diplomatic implications of spitting in his eye. If the High Priest had a single, overpowering trait, it was his total lack of humor. There was a dreadful intensity about him, a somber pomposity, a doom-laden earnestness that was reflected even in his facial characteristics. He was dark, of course, as all these Jews were dark—black hair, black ringlet beard glistening with some abominably sweet-smelling anointing oil—but the darkness extended to the rings around his eyes, the eyes themselves so deep a brown there was no telling where the iris left off and the pupil began. His eyebrows were bushy and black, yet strangely intrusive. His robes were black, embroidered with those ridiculous symbols that priests always seemed to sport in order to impress the superstitious. Even his teeth—and he had large teeth like a horse—tended toward blackness (or at least a dingy gray), a consequence of some herb he chewed constantly for, so he claimed, medicinal purposes.

Out of this gloomy, overpoweringly depressive presence, there emerged a high-pitched whining voice, as delicately melodious to the ear as a rasp on metal. Dear gods, why did these Hebrews choose such dreadful men to lead them? Their Tetrarch, Herod, was a pig, a man ruled entirely by his stomach. The type was not unknown in Rome, where gluttony ran second only to lust as the most popular preoccupation of the rich and powerful. But Herod carried gluttony to rare extremes, demanding even that viands be left by his bedside so that he might eat should he awaken in the night. Worse still, his table manners were appalling and his taste in food quite execrable. Pontius had been forced to dine with him on several state occasions, at one of which, single-handed, Herod consumed an entire sheep, including intestines and brains, not to mention marrow sucked from cracked bones. The intestines and brains were no surprise. The Tetrarch's craving for exotica was such that a persistent rumor had it he sometimes sampled human flesh. It was this, said the gossip, that accounted for his gargantuan appetite—an affliction sent by his god to punish him for sin. Pontius doubted it. He suspected Herod merely suffered from worms.

There was a wormy look about Caiaphas as well, as if he spent too much time in graveyards, ministering to the dead. Pontius sighed and reached out for a grape. At least the fruit was excellent in this appalling country. The fruit, and certain of the women.

He realized abruptly that Caiaphas had stopped his grating monologue and was looking expectantly in his direction. A comment or an answer was obviously expected. But how embarrassing, since he had not heard a single word. He glanced across to Corax, who was reclining on cushions near the official bust of Caesar, his frozen features masking who knew what depths of boredom or amusement.

Corax caught the look and read the difficulty, for he prompted gently, "The rabbi, Excellency. Our friend from the Sanhedrin wonders what action we propose to take, if any."

The rabbi? The rabbi? As far as Pontius could remember, Caiaphas had been whining about a hideously convoluted complaint concerning taxes levied on some prime ingredient of Temple incense. What was this about a rabbi? Pontius sighed inwardly and vowed to himself to concentrate harder. This was, after all, an official audience despite his attempts to create an informal atmosphere. Perhaps that was the trouble. Perhaps these people required a stern, seated Roman governor full of documents and edicts, not one who reclined and offered them fruit. (Fruit which Caiaphas had consistently refused, he noticed. Surely their ridiculous food laws did not extend to pears and oranges?)

"The . . . ah . . . rabbi?" Pontius murmured.

"The man Joshua," Corax prompted, obviously sensing his continuing difficulty. "The vagabond magician. You recall, sir, we were discussing him just the other evening." He glanced piously toward the ceiling. "Following our visit to the Temple of Venus."

"Ah yes," Pontius said. "Just so. The rabbi Joshua. He has a curious fascination for a—friend of mine." He wondered again about Miriam's interest. She seemed far too intelligent to have fallen for this Messiah nonsense, yet some profound interest was obviously there. Perhaps now was as good a time as any to learn something more about the man. At worst it would provide a little light relief from the moaning diatribe on taxes. He smiled at Caiaphas, who had not the political wit to smile back, and said, "You must tell us more about this man, High Priest."

"But I have just been telling you all about him, excellent sir," Caiaphas protested.

"Then you must tell me again," Pontius instructed him kindly. "This matter may have some importance to the state." There were, he thought, certain benefits to a governor's position, even in this godsforsaken backwater. One could utter the most inane banalities without the slightest danger of being called a fool. He smiled again at Caiaphas, partly to encourage the repetition, partly to discover if the man would smile back under constant provocation.

The former ploy, at least, succeeded, for Caiaphas said heatedly, "Indeed, sir, it may have serious implications for the stability of the state if some action is not soon taken. The man is becoming a menace. A serious menace."

"Is the man a true priest of your religion?" Pontius asked curiously. It was always intriguing to hear one priest call another a menace. If his experience was anything to go by, their differences would appear to be religious while in reality they would be purely political. Priests were always meddling in politics, even in Rome. Here their meddling seemed endemic.

"Oh no, excellent sir. Not a priest at all, in fact."

"Did I not hear you call him rabbi?"

To his amazement, Caiaphas smiled, an oily gesture at once sycophantic and patronizing which revealed only a little of his dingy teeth. "In our tongue, *rabbi* merely means 'teacher.' It is an honorific bestowed by the credulous on anyone with a little learning."

"Thus any fool may become a rabbi," Corax remarked. "Only provided he is surrounded by greater fools."

Caiaphas glanced at him suspiciously but, unable to read anything in those immobile features, eventually said, "That may be putting it a shade strongly, noble Corax, but what you say is essentially correct in this case. The man has no formal education. And let me assure you, he has certainly never been anointed into the priesthood."

"But he has a following," Corax murmured.

"Indeed. An increasing following—which is precisely where the danger lies."

"Tell me of his background," Pontius instructed, determined that Corax—who was manifestly bored—should not turn the affair into one of his ghastly private amusements.

"Excellency, he is the son of a carpenter. Or at least—" He stopped suddenly, a flicker of fear in his eyes.

Corax was on it immediately. "At least . . . ?" he asked.

Caiaphas shifted uncomfortably. Unlike both Pontius and Corax, he was not reclining, but had chosen a chair as more suited to the dignity of his office. His eyes moved away from Pontius, apparently to examine Caesar's marble nostril. He coughed. "We have reason to believe he may be illegitimate."

With his unerring instinct for the jugular, Corax asked blandly, "Who is the real father?"

Still obsessed by Caesar's fine patrician features, Caiaphas said nervously, "There is some talk he may be a soldier."

"A soldier?" Pontius asked.

"Surely not a Roman soldier?" This from Corax, his tone profoundly shocked as if he believed the Legions virtuous beyond a charge of bastardy.

"I believe so," Caiaphas told him seriously.

"Fathered on a Jewish woman?" Corax asked incredulously. It was so well done Pontius was forced to turn away to hide his smile.

"Sir," Caiaphas protested, "noble sir, it is not unknown for legionnaires to consort with Hebrew women. Of a certain type."

"The legionnaires or the women?"

"The women."

"So the mother of your rabbi was a woman of a certain type?" Pontius put in. Despite himself, he was enjoying the High Priest's discomfort and his unconscious humbug.

"Not as she should have been, Excellency. A God-fearing woman does not play the harlot."

Corax, who would never leave well enough alone, then asked, "Can you seriously expect us to believe a Roman would debase himself by lying with a Hebrew woman who was not as she should be?"

"I fear it happens, noble Corax," Caiaphas said piously.

Corax subsided. "Indeed?" He reached out for a bunch of grapes and began to eat them with intense concentration.

To put an end to the tomfoolery, Pontius said, "So there are suspicions our friend may be a Roman bastard, brought up as the son of a poor Jewish artisan?"

"Yes, Excellency."

"Does the man himself claim Roman blood?"

"No indeed, Excellency. He acts in every way like a Hebrew."

Corax glanced up from his grapes. "You have described him as a rabid troublemaker." He had the advantage of having actually listened to the High Priest's first whining diatribe. He blinked. "Is this Hebrew behavior?"

"Hardly, sir. This is precisely why I have taken the liberty of raising the matter before His Excellency. The man is more dangerous than you seem to imagine. With respect, good sirs. You see—" he leaned forward as if to impart an important secret "—he engages in the practice of necromancy."

Corax raised his eyebrows. "Necromancy?"

"Isn't that forbidden by your law?" Pontius frowned. If it was not, it ought to be. Far too many people were dabbling in the magical arts.

"Indeed it is, excellent sir. Expressly forbidden. But that does not stop him. We believe him to be in league with Shaitan."

"Shaitan?"

"The Evil One. The primal enemy of the Lord God Whose Name May Not Be Spoken."

"That is serious," Corax said solemnly.

Caiaphas shrugged. "An ecclesiastical matter, which will certainly be dealt with in good time. The important thing is he impresses the rabble with his tricks. They have begun to call him the Messiah."

"And that disturbs you?" Pontius asked.

"Does it not disturb you, Excellency?" Caiaphas blurted. "The Children of Israel are children indeed. They have dreams of a Messiah who will lead them to glory as Moses once led us out of Egypt. Naturally I do not disclaim the advent of the Messiah in a purely spiritual sense at some later time—nearing the end of the world, perhaps—but the unsophisticated seek a more immediate, more mundane Messiah. Many, in their foolishness, feel the country would be better off without a Roman presence and look for a soldier Messiah who will help them toward this end. You see the problem, Excellency?"

Pontius nodded. "Rebellion?" Perhaps it might become a serious problem. Heaven knew, there was hardly a sane Hebrew to be found in the whole of Judaea. And the Zealots had been making trouble for so many years now that people could scarcely remember when it all started. Perhaps this idiotic priest was right. Perhaps a spark might start a blaze. Besides which, if the rabbi was a necromancer, he was hardly to be trusted. "This Joshua has political pretensions? He preaches sedition against the lawful authority of Rome?"

Caiaphas hesitated. "Not directly, although certain of his remarks might be interpreted . . ." He gestured with one hand. "Frankly, Excellency, it does not matter what he preaches directly. The man may in fact concern himself largely with religious matters and still be a danger. It is what his followers believe him to be that is important—that and the number of his followers, of course. At present, the group around him is small enough to be contained, to be dealt with without fuss. But his following is growing. The lower classes are always impressed by wonder-workers, I'm afraid. And they believe him to be the Messiah—at least, many of them do. I fear they may force a political role upon him whether he wishes it or not."

"Yes," Pontius said. "I see." Under all the bumble and the obvious self-seeking manipulations, the man had a point of sorts. Or if not a point, at least a request. The priest was after something

92

and it was time to find out what. Otherwise the man would go on all night, which might prove amusing to Corax, but Pontius himself could think of better ways to pass the time. He looked directly at Caiaphas. "What exactly do you suggest we should do about him?"

The man's eyes grew immediately hard and even the whining note in his voice was replaced by an unexpected hint of steel. He did not avoid Pontius's eye. "Arrest him, Excellency. This very night if possible."

15

The seven Nubians were all quite naked, large, muscular men with shaven heads and Negro members, five of them already erect and the remaining two proceeding upward very satisfactorily. Salome watched, eyes glittering, as she began to fumble with the fastenings of her robe. It hissed to the ground, leaving her as naked as they were, although considerably paler despite her olive skin. She licked her lips and moved toward them.

Behind her, someone coughed.

Salome looked around. "Hello, Mother. Won't you join us?"

Herodias glanced at the Nubians with a look of expert interest, but shook her head. "I'm afraid your little party will have to wait, Salome. I have something to discuss with you."

"We could talk while we sported, darling. It's so long since we had any fun together; and Uncle Herod will never know—he thinks these are all castrati." At fifteen, Salome was still not fully grown, but her proportions were nonetheless splendid. Her hair, light for a Hebrew, streamed in torrents down her naked back; her breasts were high, with fine, small protruding nipples; her legs were long and slender, but without a hint of coltishness. But what made her really irresistible was her face. She had the face of an angel—a child angel, full of innocence and grace. Her eyes were wide, as if locked in an expression of perpetual surprise. Men saw her and wished instantly to corrupt her—at least Herod did, which was the important thing. Not that she had ever needed much corrupting. Seven Nubians! Not one, or two, but seven! What on earth had the child planned to do with them?

Herodias dismissed the question for later investigation. "The matter is private, my dear." She dismissed the Nubians with a gesture, noting with interest how quickly those magnificent erections faded at a hint of female coldness. As the last of them left, she turned back to her daughter. "I'm sorry to spoil your fun, my dear, but I imagine you will forgive me when I tell you my news."

"It's often so much nicer when one has to wait," Salome shrugged. "Would you care for a little wine?"

"Yes," Herodias said. "Perhaps I shall." The wine, she thought, would complement the glow she already felt inside.

With Salome robed again, they sat side by side together on a small divan, their hands curled round silver goblets brimming with the heavy, purple wine. "You really do look radiant, my dearest," Salome remarked. "What news has cheered your spirit?"

"Your uncle," Herodias said.

"My uncle. Always my uncle. What foolishness has gripped the Tetrarch now?" She had always been a precocious child, and now, at fifteen, often sounded positively world-weary. Although she always retained her capacity for innocent reactions when they suited her.

Herodias smiled slightly. "Foolishness is right, Salome my petal. But this time his foolishness will deliver him into our hands."

"Ah."

"Tell me, dearest child, do you still keep the Baptist's head?" Herodias glanced around the room. The trophy had once been displayed in a place of honor on the wall above the bed, but Salome had removed it during one of her more elaborate orgies and Herodias had not seen the thing since.

"Oh, yes—somewhere." Salome looked around vaguely. "Why do you ask, dearest Mother?"

"Herod wants it back."

The wide eyes swung on her, widening even further, but in anger rather than surprise. "He shan't have it! He gave it to me and it's mine! Every time I look at it, it reminds me of that arrogant peasant. Did you know John refused to pleasure me?"

Herodias nodded. She knew, of course. It had been the key to persuading Salome to ask for the head in the first place. Without her help, Herod would never have agreed. The man was hardly fit to be a king—locked in delusions, never prepared to take decisive action unless someone pushed him. For all Herod cared, the Baptist could have gone on preaching against incest until the Sanhedrin was forced to take action. Then where would their relationship have been, hers and Herod's? Aloud she said sympathetically, "That's all past now, fruit of my womb. We need to look to the future, you and I. You see—" she sipped some wine, staring at her daughter over the goblet's rim "—Herod wants the head very badly indeed."

"You mean," said Salome carefully, "badly enough to pay for it?"

Herodias nodded. "Badly enough to pay a great deal for it."

"How much?" Salome asked bluntly.

Herodias looked thoughtful. "I don't know, not precisely. He has already agreed to pay for the embalming."

"But that was only a few talents!"

"Herod doesn't know how much it was. And did not ask—that's the important fact. Have you ever known your uncle to agree to anything without asking the price?"

"Never," Salome said.

"Nor have I. I led him to believe we brought the Egyptian here specially. It never occurred to him the man might be living in Tiberias. Thus when he offered to pay, he imagined the cost far higher than it was. Yet he did not ask. He was so anxious for the head he did not ask."

"Interesting," Salome mused. "I wonder why he wants it."

Despite herself, Herodias began to giggle. "Now, that I *can* tell you precisely, heart of my heart. Your uncle is sometimes prey to . . . shall we say, flights of fancy—"

"He is a raving lunatic, Mother. We both know that."

"I should be hard put to disagree with you, my dear. However, his madness makes him vulnerable: especially in this instance. It is an opportunity I should not care to let slip."

Salome smiled. "And when did you ever let slip an opportunity, wonder of my world?"

"Perhaps not," Herodias agreed. "But you wished to know the reason for your uncle's current madness." Her smile returned. "Herod believes John the Baptist has risen from the dead!"

"He believes what?"

"Surprising, is it not? He has heard reports of the new Zealot rabbi, Joshua ben Joseph, and believes this man to be John risen."

Frowning, Salome said, "The new rabbi? That deformed little cripple? I thought he sounded interesting when I heard reports of his wizardry, but when I went to see, he turned out to be an ugly little brute with a twisted spine. And very dark skin—far too dark for a purebred Hebrew. I was dreadfully disappointed. I doubt if he can do any magic at all, and he certainly does not look a bit like John."

"Your uncle thinks the difference is because John is now wearing a different head."

Salome stared at her, smiled, then laughed. She had a sweet, child's laugh, like the tinkling of a mountain brook. "And does he fear the Baptist will come here to ask for his old head back?"

Herodias set down the goblet. "That is exactly what he thinks. And we must do everything in our power to foster the delusion. For so long as Herod believes that, he will want the head. He is very frightened, and so long as he wants the head and we have the head, he may be easily manipulated."

Salome stood up and walked around the room. It was a small chamber as palace apartments went, spotlessly clean and decorated in childish pastel shades. She stopped beside a vase of flowers and idly plucked a single petal from a pink dog-rose. She turned. "How far do you think he might be driven, sweetest light?"

"A considerable distance, if my instincts are correct," Herodias said bluntly. "He is frightened and so long as he remains frightened one may mold him as a potter molds his clay." She shrugged. "Oh, not just money, although there could be gold enough for both of us before this thing is finished." She leaned forward. "Power, Salome. That is what this really means. Real power. If only he remains sufficiently frightened. . . ."

Salome caught the nuance, for she said, "You think he may not?"

"It is difficult to be sure. The idea is so ludicrous, even for your uncle."

"He has clung to strange delusions before."

"He has, but in an odd way he never quite loses complete touch with reality. This is what worries me in the present case. Granted he now believes Joshua is John the Baptist risen. But if he should investigate too closely, he will find positive proof this cannot actually be so. I am afraid he might accept that proof and abandon his delusion."

"What proof is that, Mother?"

"Why, the fact that the new rabbi was alive and preaching long before John died. The two of them actually met once. I believe the Baptist immersed Joshua in the Jordan. Once your uncle realizes that, even he must see the one cannot be the other risen."

"Then he must be prevented from realizing it," Salome said simply. "It should not be too difficult provided we keep his mind on other things."

"Perhaps not."

After a thoughtful moment, Salome said, "You spoke of power. Of what were you thinking?"

Herodias picked up her goblet again. "I am your father's widow, sweetness. That is my position, my only official position. I have influence with the Tetrarch, to be sure. But it is in the nature of influence to wane with the years—the influence of a woman over a man, that is. I grow old—"

"Never, my golden peacock!" Salome cried.

"I grow old," Herodias repeated. "And soon not all the skills of my beauticians will keep the wrinkles from my face. I can excite your uncle now, but in a year or two at most, that power must desert me. What position shall I have then, my innocent? Or you either, for that matter." She stared dreamily into the middle distance. "No, my precious, the situation as it stands is too precarious. I have ambitions to become the legal Queen."

"To marry Uncle Herod? Will he agree?"

"At the moment," Herodias said, "he would agree to anything in order to obtain that head. If we move quickly, we might achieve our ends in a week."

"He will be very angry."

"Of course he will be very angry. He is always very angry about something. It means nothing. The woman who has the head can twist him around her little finger however angry he becomes." The dreamy look returned. "Queen Herodias. The name has a truly regal ring, don't you agree, my jewel? And Princess Salome—how does that sound to you?"

"I like Queen better," Salome said.

Something in her tone snapped Herodias's head round. "What do you mean by that, child?"

"You say you could force Uncle Herod to marry you and so become Queen. From what you say about his madness, that is true. But you also say you are growing old and that is also true. You might enjoy your power for a few years, but the enjoyment would be limited by the time left to you." Salome's eyes hardened. "Would it not make more sense, dearest mother, if I were to become Queen? I should have all my life to enjoy it."

"You?" Herodias gasped, outraged. "Herod would never marry you!"

Salome smiled her sweetest smile. "But, crown of my affection, it is I who have the head."

⟨16

The great doors swung closed in a flurry of salutes, salaams, and farewells. Pontius walked back to his divan and sank down gratefully. The man was an amazing bore, one of those rare individuals who could take what was intrinsically a fascinating subject and present it in such a manner that one fell instantly asleep. Or did not fall asleep if one was the Governor of Judaea with appearances to keep up, the dignity of Rome to preserve. Individuals like Caiaphas, wrapped in their mist of gray black gloom, were kin to the leech and the flea, except that they sucked away pleasure instead of blood. Even the disciplined Roman guard looked bored, and the young slave who kept offering the fruit which Caiaphas refused seemed positively enervated.

"Well," Pontius said, the cushions embracing him, "what did you think of that?"

"Interesting," said Corax.

Pontius sighed and waved away the formal guard. He felt like moving to a smaller room, but was momentarily too exhausted to bother. Were all principalities as draining as this? Or was it just

Judaea? Or was the problem just Pontius, the Emperor's ape? He had little real interest in politics and none at all in the techniques of diplomacy. There were, of course, enormous satisfactions in the exercise of power, but power in Judaea had somehow not quite the same flavor as power in Rome—not that Pontius had tasted much power in Rome, but he could imagine it. The essence of the satisfaction was, of course, one's ability to impose one's will on people. But the Judaeans were not people, any more than the Gauls or the Huns. They were more like talking animals, distinct in their own smells and customs. The servile among them one treated as pets, the dangerous as wild beasts. And those like Caiaphas, who had their own measure of power allied to the servility of a conquered race . . . well, they could only be endured. He sighed again, longing to be back in Rome. Despite all his financial problems, it had not been a bad life. Civilized friends, interesting women, and the Games. Gods, how he missed the Games. He wondered vaguely if he could establish some such institution in Judaea. He was Governor, after all, and could do what he damn well liked within reason. But the Jews would never live with it. He could hear Caiaphas quoting the endless list of Commandments they claimed to live by: thou shalt not kill . . . thou shalt not steal . . . thou shalt not commit adultery. All handed over personally to Moses by their gloomy old straitlaced god. Not that the Commandments stopped any of them from killing, stealing, or fornicating, but the priests loved hypocrisy far too much to miss the opportunity of quoting the Mosaic Law against the Games.

In a surge of annoyance, he turned on Corax. "What do you mean—'interesting'? The man's a crashing bore. If we had priests like that in Rome, they would be lion fodder in a month."

"I was thinking of the rabbi," Corax said. "I agree with you about Caiaphas—the man should be put down."

It was, Pontius thought, far too early to go to bed. And he had eaten so much fruit in an effort to amuse himself while burdened with the dreaded Caiaphas that he could not even look forward to a decent meal now. Perhaps he should order an entertainment. Surely the majordomo could round up a few jugglers or tumblers for the Governor's pleasure, although he would probably protest that he had not been given enough time and Pontius had not the energy to argue. Which really only left wine. Did everyone get roaring drunk after a visit by the High Priest?

"It strikes me, dear boy," Corax was saying, "that we should take a closer look at him."

"The rabbi? You don't take Caiaphas seriously, do you?"

"About the man being a danger to the state? Hardly."

Pontius, whose boredom had made him irritable and argumentative, said, "Not even if the mob thinks he is the Messiah?"

Corax handed another orange to his little hand-servant for peeling. "Messiahs have always been two a penny in this country. Have you read its history?"

"Not much," Pontius admitted. In his enfeebled state he felt faintly guilty. Should a governor not take care to educate himself about the background of his province?

"For as long as anyone can remember, there has been at least one Messiah in any given generation. Old Junius had three during his period of tenure—not counting John the Baptist—and you know how short that was. The Hebrews breed Messiahs the way a hound breeds fleas. Most of them have gathered their supporters and most of them have preached the overthrow of Rome. But we are still here, dear boy, you and I, both Romans, both safe in our administration buildings. The One God Whose Name May Not Be Spoken has not hurled a single thunderbolt in our direction, despite the prayers of all his Messiahs."

"What about the Zealots?" Pontius asked sourly.

Corax shrugged. "If we were in Gaul, we would be worrying about whole tribes. It is usually too much to expect that a people will enjoy being conquered. Frankly I feel the Zealots work greatly to our benefit."

"How?"

"They do little real damage, dear boy. Every now and then they kill a few of our soldiers, who are, after all, paid to be killed. But each time that happens, they drain away the accumulated resentment of the entire people so they become that much easier to manage."

The trouble was, you never knew when Corax was joking. But what he said made some sort of perverse sense, joking or not. Pontius frowned. "If you don't think this latest clown is dangerous, then why should we concern ourselves with him?"

"Because, dear Pontius, he could be our passport back to Rome."

Pontius blinked, staring at him. A wild hope surged, to be replaced almost instantly with an equally wild anger. If Corax was joking, he would have him publicly flogged. Or hanged. Or both. Reading nothing in that paralyzed expression, he asked cautiously, "What do you mean?"

"I mean that I am a little bored by this country and assume you are the same. Thank you." He took the peeled and quartered orange, split off a section, and popped it in his mouth. He had eaten some seventeen oranges throughout the course of the High Priest's audience, and yet, Pontius knew, he would tackle his next meal with the enthusiasm of a ravenous jackal.

"Yes, of course I'm bored with this country," Pontius told him irritably. "Apart from our adventure the other night—" he was thinking of Miriam the Magdalene "—I can hardly think of a single hour here I've really enjoyed. Too many flies. Too much heat. A population of lunatics and no Circus. Who wouldn't be bored?"

"Who wouldn't indeed? But the facts of the matter are that you cannot easily return to Rome because of your financial commitments to noble Caesar, while I—since my fate is linked with yours—cannot return until then either. It would seem to me this is an unacceptable situation to men of resource such as ourselves and the sooner it is changed the better." The blank face turned toward Pontius. "Unless, of course, you wish to preserve your appointment as Judaea's Governor."

Pontius smiled thinly.

"Well then," Corax went on, "this is what makes the rabbi so interesting. He is not, of course, the Messiah, but if we believe only half the reports, he is something of a wizard."

Pontius, who did not see the connection, said, "Do you think he can spirit us to Rome?"

"In a manner of speaking. What occurred to me, noble Pontius, was that you find yourself in your present situation because the Emperor—and Gaius, of course—purchased themselves the services of a magician."

Still at sea, Pontius said, "The dwarf? Do you mean the dwarf?"

"Yes, of course. The man killed Trajan with a touch. That is witchcraft in anyone's language. I seem to recall you remarked as much at the time—in somewhat stronger language, naturally." Corax finished the last section of this, his eighteenth, orange and reached out for another. The little hand-servant, a girl child who obviously doted on each immobile feature of his face, smiled and began to peel this one as well. "But that is not the point," Corax continued, using the edge of his toga to dab a spot of juice from the side of his mouth. "The point is you did not know the dwarf was a magician."

"No, of course not," Pontius said. "Otherwise I would not have bet against him, would I?"

"No, of course not," Corax echoed. "At least not so heavily as you did." He glanced at the little servant girl. "Do you think this child is too young to take into my bed?"

"Much too young," Pontius told him shortly, although the girl's look suggested she knew perfectly well why her master was considering a change in her sleeping arrangements. "Please get on with what you were saying."

"Perhaps in a year . . ." Corax murmured. He switched his gaze back to Pontius. "It seems to me, dear boy—if this is not a treasonable utterance—that both the Emperor and the disgustingly rich Gaius took unfair advantage of you when they neglected to tell you the dwarf was a magician, especially when it became clear such information was vital to your judgment of the wager."

"Grossly unfair," Pontius confirmed. The memory sent the old anger rising. He pushed it away with an effort. It was fruitless to rail against Caesar, for Caesar would always prevail, to quote the military proverb. It had been coined in the days of the mighty Julius, but held just as true of his successors.

"Worse than that," said Corax with as much feeling as he ever injected into his voice, "it was unsporting. When one wagers on a gladiator, one wagers on his fighting abilities, not his talent in the black arts. If this were not so, half the priests in Rome would be waving their wands in the arena and we should see nothing of the Games for the clouds of incense. Thus the wager against you was unfairly won." He stopped Pontius's comment with a movement of his hand. "But—" he said, emphasizing the word strongly "—there is one aspect of that whole sorry affair which may yet be turned to your benefit, noble Pontius."

"What is that?" the noble Pontius asked, thoroughly fascinated. There was one thing about Corax: he could drive away boredom with the flick of an idea.

"The prime fact that you wagered with the Emperor!" Corax said triumphantly.

Pontius did not understand. He sat waiting for some further

explanation; then, when Corax remained silent, he asked, "What has that got to do with it?"

"Is the Emperor not the final arbiter of our customs, our fashions, even our laws? Is it not the Emperor who decides the rules? It would seem to me apparent that the Emperor has decided it is perfectly sporting to conceal information about a fighter's mystical abilities when one wagers on his performance in the arena." He patted the girl lightly on the bottom. "Now run along out of earshot, my dear, for what I am about to say is surely treason." As she did so, he dropped his voice. "And that, Pontius, means the Emperor can hardly complain if someone were to play the same trick on him that he played so successfully on you."

After a moment's staggered silence, Pontius said, "Another wager?"

Corax nodded.

"As substantial as the first?"

Corax nodded again. "It would be necessary to match the first in order to recoup your losses. Ideally, of course, it should be higher in order to give you a profit."

"Let me see if I understand correctly what you are driving at," said Pontius carefully. "You are suggesting, are you not, that we examine this rabbi who is upsetting Caiaphas?"

"Yes."

"You are hoping we will find he is actually a magician as the gossip says?"

"Yes."

"Not a Messiah, but one well versed in the mystic arts?"

"Yes."

Pontius leaned forward. "You are also suggesting that if this rabbi is half the witch we hear he is, we should then transport him to Rome?" His voice was rising despite all he could do to keep it level. "We should transport him to Rome, enter him as a gladiator in the Games—a half-starved, long-nosed, prepuceless barbarian who looks as though he could not kill a squirrel, let alone a trained opponent. Then—" his voice had risen to the edge of hysteria, but he was now beyond caring "—then, Corax, you are suggesting that I should place another bet with Caesar, a larger bet even than twenty thousand *libra*, a bet that this oily, one-god Hebrew, this

103

half-caste Roman bastard, can win against the gods alone know who? And because he works magic, you are saying I should win that bet?"

"Yes!" exclaimed Corax triumphantly.

"You are mad," Pontius said with feeling.

If Corax was put off, he did not show it. "Dear boy," he said easily, "your sensitivity is quite amazing. I had thought my train of thought subtle, yet you followed it perfectly, even before I had expressed it in its entirety. But please do not dismiss it now without consideration."

"Consideration? Consideration? That damn priest's endless prattle has deranged you, Corax. Or perhaps it's from eating too many oranges. Can you seriously expect me to put a Jewish rabbi into the arena as a fighter?"

"Tiberius put in a dwarf."

"The dwarf was a sorcerer!" Pontius screamed.

"So is the rabbi, if what we hear is true."

In his agitated state, Pontius strode across to lean over him. "What have we heard, you frozen-faced lout? That this man heals the sick? That he makes the blind see and helps the lame walk? That on a good day he can raise the dead?" He sniffed suspiciously, wondering if Corax had been drinking, but there was no smell of wine. "What good are those tricks in the arena? Useless. Worse than useless! A gladiator is supposed to kill, not cure!"

"What do you know of the magical arts, noble Pontius?"

Taken aback, Pontius said, "Nothing, as you are well aware. What would an equestrian know about sorcery?"

"Precisely the level of my own knowledge, dear boy. But think on this: if a man has the magic to raise the dead, can he not reverse it to slaughter the living? If the spell that heals the sick is chanted backward, will it not strike down the healthy with a fever or a pox? Is that not logical, dear boy?"

Logical? Pontius hesitated. It had a mad logic, to be sure, the sort of logic a mind like Corax's would seize on and worry half to death. He began to walk back to his divan, stroking the first faint hint of stubble to emerge since his morning shave. Logical? There was no logic to a dwarf who could kill Trajan at a touch. No logic at all, only sorcery. And as Corax pointed out, the rabbi was also a sorcerer. Everybody said so, even the High Priest Caiaphas—and if anyone should know, he should. Could the healing magic be reversed?

By the gods, what a joy if it could! What a joy to take this Hebrew rabble-rouser and use him against Tiberius precisely as the Emperor had used the dwarf. What poetic justice! What delicious irony! The Emperor would never forgive him, of course, but as Corax said, he could scarcely complain. Had not the Emperor introduced magic into the Circus in the first place? He turned to look at the immobile features of his old companion. Corax had something, all right. A daring plan. A dangerous plan. A convoluted plan.

Above all, an exciting plan.

And what had Pontius to lose? Here he was the Emperor's ape. He looked forward to nothing but more and more years in this stinking Judaea until he was too old and sick to care. Was this so much to lose? What a glorious gamble it would be—the talk of Rome for years, perhaps centuries. It was the stuff of which the poets spun their epics.

"You think this rabbi can do all they say he can?"

Corax shrugged. "I doubt it. But there is seldom smoke without at least a little fire. I think we should take him and question him and force him to show us the extent of his powers. If we find he has enough magic to do as we require, why, then, Pontius, we shall make a Games the like of which Rome has never seen before!"

"Yes," Pontius breathed. "We shall!"

17

What dress did one choose when meeting with a rabbi?

She surveyed her wardrobe in a sudden panic. Roman silk *tunicas*, flowing robes of finest linen, gowns in blue and green and white, even red. A king's ransom in clothing, but each piece suffered from the same fault: it was cut to emphasize in some way an aspect of her physical attractions. Here a robe was slit along the thigh. There a gown dropped low to show a soft expanse of breast. A harlot's wardrobe. One that clients would appreciate, especially Roman clients. But was there anything suitable to greet a venerable rabbi?

Eventually she chose white, with a deep blue, fur-trimmed cloak to ward off the evening chill. It was a poor outfit for horseback, but she was completely torn between practicality and . . .

She stopped short as she drew the brush once more through her long, black hair. And what? The desire to make an impression? When had Miriam of Magdala ever concerned herself with the impression she might make on a man? She knew how men saw her—Romans, Jews, Syrians, Persians, Medes, Greeks: whatever their race, they all shared one reaction, a mixture of fear and fascination. She had always made men afraid, as long as she could remember. It was the secret of her success in her profession. They saw her and they feared her and since fear was one emotion men could not endure, they sought to banish it by vanquishing the source. How often had her little scene with Pontius Pilate been played out with other men. The initial nervousness—nervousness in the Governor himself!—the flickering fear, the welling anger, and the brutal conquest. How pleased they were when it was done. How smug and self-satisfied. How relaxed and confident in renewed reassurance of their strength.

Would a rabbi react any differently? She remembered her last meeting with a rabbi, the venerable ancient who had first diagnosed her condition in Tiberias. There had been no fear in him, admittedly, but she had been a child then, unskilled in the arts of lust. And even as a child she had seen that a rabbi was no different from other men. More learned perhaps in certain matters, but with a man's contempt for women—even child-women such as she had been. It was their contempt that rankled, their arrogant, mindless, all-assuming contempt which fed her own hatred to give her strength and power. Were all women filled with such hatred of their men? Or was it just harlots forced to meet so many of them in the way of business? No, she thought, for she had not been a whore when she met that first old rabbi. She had been a child, frightened and alone, afflicted with a horror that sucked on her mind as bloated ticks sucked on the body. Where was his pity, that learned old man? Where was his compassion for the suffering of a child? He had shown only loathing and disgust.

She was not so foolish as to imagine that this new wonder-working rabbi would react in any other way. But she was older now, and could work her own wonders. She could look past his veneer of piety and see the man's soul underneath. She could read his weaknesses, the petty lusts and longings others could not see. Rabbi or not, God still cursed him with the restless snake between his legs, and she could stir it for him. By God, how she could stir it! She could play with his emotions until he could not tell the Sabbath from a weekday. And then, however much the work disgusted him, she could lead him by the nose until he worked the magic to dismiss her demon.

Pray God he knew the spell!

She pushed the thought aside and returned to her wardrobe. The white gown was cast aside and another chosen, still white, but subtly cut for more erotic emphasis. It was no more suitable for riding than the other, but now she did not care. She hoped he would have opportunity to see her astride the horse, for she knew how the image would affect him: a fine, regal lady, virgin-white as a vestal, yet with her slim legs opened to embrace the powerful, rippling, sweating muscles of her stallion. He would see her thus and he would feel aroused and, poor fool, he would not even dimly suspect what stirred him.

She dressed quickly without the help of her maids—who were in any case busy easing the disappointment of those clients who would not see their mistress this night. When she had finished, she stood before the polished shield, inspecting the reflected image for some flaw. The gown clung to her—an Egyptian trick not even Roman seamstresses could match. Her hair shone from the brushing. Her breasts rose through the folds in subtle invitation. He would find her statuesque and beautiful. Her eyes would disturb him as they disturbed all men.

She went to the door to call for Benjamin and was only a little startled to discover he was already there. Lately he had developed the trick of anticipating her needs—although God alone knew how, since his mind, manifestly, still functioned at the level of a loyal dog, or lower than a dog's in some respects, for a dog had always purpose and curiosity. Benjamin had been standing immobile, staring at the blank wood of the doorway to her room. Perhaps he had been there only moments, but from experience she knew he might have been there, quite literally, for hours, his gaze fixed, his eyes blank and unthinking. Did he have any thoughts, this creature she had taken from her native hills to serve her? Did he have feelings? Did he have even simple plans? Feelings perhaps, for he protected her from harm. He could scarcely be moved to action of that sort without experiencing feelings. It was possible he even loved her, in his simple fashion. How strange if it were so. How strange to be loved.

The thought disturbed her so profoundly that she pushed it aside without examination. "Fetch the horses and a torch, Benjamin," she said. "We have a journey to make." As he turned to obey, she noticed that he was, coincidentally, dressed for riding in a short open jacket and rough peasant's breeches. Unlike his livery, which had been tailored with some thought of style, the dress accentuated his squat bulk. Did he love her, this creature of muscle, bone, and little brain? Whatever he felt, he was her creature without reservation.

It was a moonlit night, so the torch did not prove necessary. Miriam instructed him to store it, unlit, with the tinder and the kindling in his saddlebag, lest the moon set before they returned. She mounted her own horse, a gray stallion, and pulled the collar of the fur-trimmed cloak high about her neck. "Ride beside me, Benjamin," she ordered. She would have preferred him to lead, but was far from certain he could find the way even though he went often to the well on foot. But as he pulled obediently beside her, she felt a comforting reassurance. He had strapped around his waist a sword, similar in shape to those used in the Legions, but far shorter. It was the only weapon he ever wore, and he wore it infrequently, prompted by God alone knew what impulse or instinct of impending danger. She had no idea where he had got it, or even if he knew how to use it, but none of that mattered. What mattered about Benjamin was his brutal muscle strength, his willingness to use it in her service. In a sense—she hesitated, then admitted it—he was her only friend.

The ride was short, the streets almost deserted, so that they reached the well a little before the appointed time. The well had been there for a very long time indeed, a focal point of activity when the city was still a village. Women came to draw the water for their homes, and stayed awhile to exchange gossip. Men came too, mainly to gamble. A market square had grown up around the well. City traders set up their stalls, itinerant merchants spread their rugs. By day, this whole area was a bustle of activity. Now it was deserted in the moonlight, peopled by ghosts and memories. Miriam found herself staring out across the bleak, baked-earth expanse, enjoying the solitude. The oddest things, she thought, were beautiful when the people went away.

A shadow moved in the far corner of the square. Simon Zealotes? Miriam waited, still seated astride her stallion. It was certainly a man, well wrapped in the dark robes the Bedouin favored. Who else but the Zealot Simon in this place at this time of night? Yet there was something about the walk which told her this was not the Zealot. He moved too directly toward her. Simon would have crept, glancing ostentatiously over one shoulder to ensure that they were not observed by prying eyes. He stopped and threw back his hood, so that the moonlight fell across a pleasant, bearded face and soft brown eyes. "Mistress Miriam of Magdala?"

"I am she."

"My friend Simon has sent me to guide you. He is himself engaged in other matters." He smiled suddenly. "Plots and intrigues and such things." His eyes flickered to Benjamin. "Is this your manservant?"

"Yes."

"No wonder he frightened Simon." He drew his robes about him. "I see you are mounted on fine horses. I'm afraid I could only afford a donkey. She is tethered just beyond the square. Will you follow me?"

He was, she discovered, a friendly, easygoing soul, older than Simon the Zealot and with neither his aggression nor his need of self-dramatization. As his donkey plodded patiently along the moonlit street, she felt compelled to ask him, "Are you a Zealot?"

"Good heavens no."

"Simon is, isn't he?"

"Yes. It shows, don't you think? No, I work for the imperial administration. If Simon ever succeeds in overthrowing it, I shall be out of a job."

"I had thought you might all be Zealots," Miriam remarked.

"All of us? The rabbi's followers, you mean? Oh, no—we're a

motley crew: artisans, fishermen, civil servants . . . there's even a tax collector, although we pretend not to know him usually. There is a sprinkling of Zealots, of course, all trying to persuade the rabbi to go into politics. They make so much noise I'm not surprised you thought we were all of the same persuasion."

"Are there women among you?" Miriam asked curiously.

"A great many women come to hear him teach. He really is a remarkable speaker. But I don't think you'll find any women among his serious followers. His sister makes an appearance from time to time and I've met his mother once, but they don't really take him seriously—you know what relatives are like. To be honest, I think there is trouble in the family over him."

"What sort of trouble?"

"I gather his mother thinks he is insane."

There was a curious tightening in her chest as Miriam asked, "And is he?"

The man shrugged. "He's certainly very odd. I was quite put out the first time I met him. Very peculiar eyes. And, of course, his background upsets people. His father was a carpenter before he retired and a very good one, I believe."

Although she felt no great antagonism toward this man, something prompted Miriam to say quite bitingly, "I thought he was the illegitimate son of a Roman soldier."

If the remark offended him, he did not show it. "You've heard that rumor, have you? I've never actually asked him about it, but he looks Jewish enough to me. Too dark-skinned for much Roman blood, although I suppose it's possible. His mother had something of a reputation in her younger days. She's a Miriam too, like you."

She glanced at him suspiciously, wondering if this was an oblique reference to her profession. But his face and voice remained open, far more friendly than Simon Zealotes had been. She found herself speculating about which of the two the rabbi himself more closely resembled, although from what this man had said, he resembled neither very much.

"Soldier or carpenter," the man was saying, "he certainly hasn't followed in the father's footsteps. He ran away from home when he was twelve or thirteen and joined an Essene community."

"I had heard he was an Essene," Miriam said. The confirmation disappointed her. She had met a great many of the sect, both monastic and lay, and found them to be without exception an unpleasant mixture of prudishness and bigotry.

"You heard wrongly, Mistress Miriam. He ran away from the monastery as well. Somehow he made his way to Bengal. Walked the whole way, I believe. It took him three years. No wonder his mother thinks he is insane."

"Bengal? Is that in Syria?"

"A province of India, far to the east. A country full of spices and magicians. They say he met God there."

"Do you believe that?" Miriam asked curiously. She was interested in hearing his answer. This was no narrowed-eyed fanatic like Simon. He seemed instead a sober, thoughtful individual, educated and intelligent—one who would not be easily impressed or taken in.

"Do you know," he said, "I think I do."

They rode in silence for a time, moving at the donkey's pace into the outskirts of the city.

"Where are we going?" Miriam asked him eventually. "Or is that a secret?"

He turned to smile at her broadly. "You *have* been listening to Simon, haven't you? We could never keep the rabbi's whereabouts a secret—far too many people know him now. The Zealots try to make a mystery of everything, always playing silly games about security and plots. The rabbi and a little group of us are staying at the villa of his uncle. It isn't far from here, in fact."

They turned a corner and Miriam realized suddenly there were people in the street, a tight group of excited men milling around the gates to a large building, shouting and gesticulating wildly. One turned at their approach, then broke away to run toward them.

"Judas!" he called, and Miriam recognized the voice as that of Simon the Zealot. "Quickly, Judas!" He stopped, panting, by the man on the donkey, completely ignoring both Miriam and Benjamin. "They've taken him, Judas!" he screamed. "Not more than a moment ago!"

"Rabbi Joshua?" Judas asked in sudden alarm. "Who has taken him, Simon?"

"Pilate's men!" the Zealot told him. "A Roman detachment just a moment ago. Some of us wanted to fight but there were too many of them—big brutes armed to the teeth. There was nothing we could do, Judas! There was nothing we could do!"

⸂18

"Hear, O Israel, the Lord our God, the Lord is One, and you shall love the Lord your God with all your heart and with all your soul and with all your might." Caiaphas removed the *tefillin* thonging from his head and began to unwind the remainder from his left arm, wrapping it around the little leather boxes as he did so. "These words shall be upon your heart," the Scriptures said, "and you shall bind them upon your hand and they shall be as frontlets between your eyes." Which was all very well when a man had nothing else on his mind. But as things stood in the country, it was almost impossible to pray with any concentration. If only the Romans understood the situation better. A rumbling volcano. They were seated on top of a rumbling volcano and did not even hear the rumbles.

He entered the inner sanctum as was his right as High Priest, noticing instantly that the Ark of the Covenant was very slightly askew on its pedestal. Another sign of the pressures on him these days. He was usually absolutely meticulous—*absolutely meticulous*—in his handling of the Ark. He moved the ornate rosewood box to its proper position and removed the lid to ensure that the scrolls were intact. What a tragedy if the pressures upon him should cause him to neglect his duty to these precious documents. But they were untouched. A great relief. He lifted one reverently, setting its little silver bells atinkle. The words of Moses, the very words of Moses, laboriously copied century by century. He set it back in place. On the Sabbath he would take this scroll and parade it through the Temple while the congregation stood. And then an honored one would make the reading, so that the words of Moses might again be heard in the land. A ceremony hoary with the frost of time. That's what was wrong with the Romans: too short a cultural tradition. It left them with no real feel for history, no understanding of an older culture. He closed the lid and bowed, rocking from the waist. "Adonai," he intoned, "let them recognize the rumbles."

It was the Zealots, of course—young men with no respect for their elders, never content to leave well enough alone. And they had support. Half the population had a sneaking admiration for their ideals, if not their methods. He himself had a sneaking admiration for their ideals. A shocking admission, perhaps, but surely he was as good a patriot as the next man? The thing was, patriotism had to be tempered with reality. And the reality was that the Romans were here to stay. The worst Zealot outrage was no more than a pinprick to Rome, if indeed it was even felt in Rome at all. Sometimes he suspected the Emperor did not even know where Judaea was. Certainly he attached little importance to the country, judging by the quality of the governors he appointed.

Caiaphas thought of those governors now, as he stood locked in reverie before the Ark of the Covenant between his people and his Lord. He had known four of them in his time: the ludicrous Septimus, who arranged frog races (frog races!) on the residency lawn; Cassius Petronius, with his delusions of grandeur and literary pretensions, who died while composing the nine-hundredth line of the most execrable epic poem ever penned; the senile Junius, perpetually lusting after harlots without even the excuse of youthful passion; and now this young clown Pontius Pilate with his frozen-faced companion, banished to Judaea—if his information could be believed—to recoup a fortune gambled on the fighting abilities of a Chinese dwarf standing no more than a cubit high! Were there ever such fools in a position of authority? No wonder resentments smoldered. No wonder the country was going to the dogs.

But fools or not, they were fools with power. That was the reality of the situation. The power of Roman Legions stood behind Pilate as securely as it stood behind the Emperor himself. Thus it was necessary to ingratiate oneself with such men, for the good of the country. The welfare of Judaea could be furthered only with the help of Roman fools. That was the tragedy, but that was the reality.

Herod might strut and posture like a king—when he was not gorging himself or lying drunk—but he was a king on sufferance of Rome. Naturally, one kept on the right side of Herod, for he had a fearful temper like his father, but when anything important needed doing, one went to Rome—figuratively speaking, of course. Actually, one went to the Roman Governor, the ridiculous Pilate who bet on dwarfs.

Except that Pilate did not listen. Caiaphas still burned with humiliation at the memory of his last audience. The lout had actually received him lying down! Him, the High Priest of Jerusalem! Where were Roman manners? Where was Roman courtesy? Not vested in the person of Judaea's Governor, that was certain. And the initial insult had set the tone for the entire audience. Half the time the Governor had been miles away, not even attempting to disguise his disinterest. And he, Caiaphas, could not even speak without being perpetually interrupted by that stupid Greek boy-slave who kept trying to make him eat oranges. Oranges! On a state occasion at a time when vital matters were at hand! They seemed obsessed by oranges, these Romans. Pilate himself had dreamily eaten eight, while his peculiar companion, if Caiaphas counted correctly, had made his way through more than twice that number. They would sit well with Herod, these Romans. They might match themselves against him eating hard-boiled eggs—it was precisely the type of contest they would find amusing.

All the time they gorged on oranges, what was happening to the country? Did they ever stop to ask themselves that? Did they ever stop to ask themselves how many Roman soldiers had been slaughtered by the Zealots in the past three months alone? Did they ever pause to consider the temper of the people as a whole? Did they ever worry about a bloody revolution that could topple the administration (at least until Caesar sent in further Legions) and assuredly vent its spleen on those who, like Caiaphas himself, had loyally cooperated with Rome for years?

Now there was the nub. The danger of a revolution. You could no longer trust the young to behave with even minimal intelligence. The Zealots had widespread support among the young. All they really needed was a focal point, a leader, and the unrest could spread like wildfire. In the sanctum, Caiaphas was gripped by a vision of blood spilt, much of it draining from his own veins. He

114

had his supporters, of course, but a high priest was seldom popular with the rabble. It was the position rather than the person. A high priest was concerned with morality, observance of the Canon Law. That was never a popular position.

Would the rabbi prove a focal point for revolution?

It was always disturbing when the rabble started talking of a new Messiah. Not that many of them ever came to very much, of course. Caiaphas paused, remembering Messiahs as he had remembered governors. Except that with Messiahs he had more trouble recalling the names. There had been that redheaded throwback, hadn't there? The one who ate toadstools and eventually walked backward over a cliff? And the brute with the long black beard from the east shore of the Kinneret. The Romans jailed him eventually and he died of food poisoning. And wasn't there an Esau ben Joachim in the bunch? The astrologer with palsy? And the Zealot Messiah Josephus, with his Roman name and dreams of an organized army. He had looked very dangerous at first, but what a disappointment he had been to the Cause. It was a miracle the Zealot movement survived him. Four hundred men he marched into the desert on a training exercise and not one marched out again, including Josephus himself. There was talk of a Roman ambush, but the Governor—that had been Petronius, hadn't it?—the Governor himself denied it. So no one really knew what actually happened. Perhaps a sudden sandstorm. It was exactly the sort of situation where one might expect the Lord to take a hand and bury them. A sorry list, to be sure. But this new one was different. Or at least the time was different, even if Joshua was as big a fool as all the rest.

Caiaphas was no stargazer, but he believed implicitly in times. There would even, he half suspected, be a time for throwing off the yoke of Rome. Not now, of course, not for several hundred, perhaps several thousand years. But if the universal wheel spun long enough, it would produce a time for anything. Now, though, was a time for bloodshed, if the authorities were not very, very careful. He could smell it in the air, or, more accurately, overhear it in whispered conversations. A great deal of discontentment was abroad these days. The taxes were a shade too high, which probably accounted for most of it. But what could one do? The Romans demanded their tribute, Herod had a palace to maintain, and naturally the Temple required income so its priests might continue to do the Lord's work. But reason was wasted on the rabble. They saw no further than their noses and discontent festered. Drop a new Messiah in the middle of that mixture and he would blow it out of all proportion like strong yeast in a loaf of bread.

And this Joshua was clever. He carefully avoided any direct claim to be the Messiah. A subtle touch, one the others hadn't thought of. He could wander from town to town as if butter wouldn't melt in his mouth and let his followers take the risk of spreading the news. But it all amounted to the same thing in the end.

Of course, he'd made a mistake with the healing. That was witchcraft. You couldn't go around curing lepers without a knowledge of witchcraft. It was unnatural and unholy. Everyone knew leprosy was the Lord's punishment for sin. But, admittedly, the healing was impressive. Witchcraft always was in its own dark way. The rabble loved it, which was why his following had grown so large—not that Pilate realized it, sitting up there in his marble halls eating his oranges and practicing God alone knew what sort of Roman abominations with his tall thin friend.

Witchcraft. . . .

There was only one way to deal with a witch. The Scriptures were quite explicit: *Thou shalt not suffer a witch to live.* Not a Commandment, precisely, not one of the Decalogue, but clear enough all the same. What this rabbi needed was a few days hanging on a cross to give his followers the warning, then a quiet grave with a stake through the heart to keep him there. Unfortunately that was not about to happen without a word from Pilate, and judging by that last disgraceful audience, Pilate had as much interest in the rabbi as he had in Temple incense.

"Adonai," Caiaphas intoned again, "make him aware of the rumbles."

He adjusted the position of the Ark a fraction, then left the sanctum. As he passed through the veil, he caught a movement in the main body of the Temple. "Who's there?" he called out irritably. It was far too early for the congregation and he disliked having his Temple duties interrupted by some oaf of an insomniac who had nothing better to do in the mornings than pray.

"Only I, Caiaphas." The movement resolved itself into a shadow and the shadow into a priest.

116

"Oh, it's you, Anninaias." He felt instantly uneasy, as he always felt in the presence of this coldly scheming man. Ruthlessness was all very well in its place, quite necessary, in fact, in many circumstances. But there was so much ruthlessness in Anninaias that one never quite knew where it might end. They said he had ambitions to become High Priest—a rumor which had encouraged Caiaphas to employ a food-taster the moment he heard it. But at least Anninaias and he were at one about the rabbi. It was Anninaias, in fact, who had suggested he broach the matter with the Governor.

"I have come to congratulate you, holy sir," Anninaias said smoothly. He was the only human being known to Caiaphas who could make congratulations sound both threatening and sinister.

"Congratulate me?" Caiaphas asked. The man had heard something—but what?

"Indeed, holy sir. I was delighted to learn you had persuaded the Governor to our cause."

"Our cause?" Caiaphas echoed. He was aware he sounded foolish repeating everything Anninaias said, and the awareness annoyed him. But he had not the least idea what Anninaias was talking about, unless the man was being sarcastic—which was entirely possible despite the fact he was the High Priest's inferior in rank. It was not the rabbi, certainly. Pilate had looked as though years might elapse before he was persuaded to that cause. It was scarcely the matter of the Temple incense either, since the tax remained. What cause?

"The matter of the rabbi Joshua," Anninaias said. He smiled with no great warmth. "Pilate's men arrested him last night. But you were aware of that, of course, since the force of your arguments have obviously provoked the move."

Caiaphas realized abruptly that his mouth was hanging open and closed it as discreetly as he could manage. He coughed. "I was not aware exactly when the arrest would be made. Once I realized the Governor supported us entirely, I left the precise details to him. Timing and so forth. Such things are properly the Roman province."

"But does the Governor support us entirely, holy sir?" He was an exceedingly slim, upright man with brooding eyes. The Temple black hung round him like folded bat wings.

"Why do you think he does not?" Caiaphas asked quickly. "Have you heard something?"

Anninaias, who had spies placed everywhere, spread his hands. "Where should I hear anything, Holy Caiaphas? My Temple duties leave me little time for worldly affairs. I merely asked since it occurs to me our new Governor may not grasp the seriousness of the rabbi's activities to the same degree as a man of experience such as yourself."

The man had heard something. He always poured oil liberally when he was scheming. Cautiously, Caiaphas said, "I think he is aware of the seriousness of the situation, all right. Does the fact of the rabbi's arrest not prove it?"

"Not entirely," Anninaias said smoothly. "This rabble-rousing Joshua may be only taken for questioning, or a short term of imprisonment. You know how slack the Roman courts can be. Besides which, since the rabbi claims blasphemously to teach the Lord's word, is this not more properly a matter for the Temple than for Rome?"

"We've been through all this before," Caiaphas snapped. "Rome has the power to deal with him effectively, the Temple has not."

"But will Rome use the power?" Anninaias asked. "That is my point."

"What do you suggest we do?" Caiaphas asked, admitting defeat.

"First," said Anninaias, "we must discover the Governor's intentions—his exact intentions. If they do not fall in line with our own plans, we must take action to persuade him to amend them."

"Action?"

Anninaias shrugged delicately. "A little public pressure, perhaps. Who knows, it may not be necessary."

"No," Caiaphas murmured thoughtfully. They began to walk together out of the Temple. As they did so, Caiaphas tossed a thought back toward the inner sanctum, a word of thanks to the Lord of Creation for a prayer answered.

19

The residency of the Governor of Judaea paid no tribute, or even passing lip-service, to Hebrew taste or architectural style. It was pure, monumental Rome—granite and marble (with a little local sandstone where it did not actually show), transported, so it seemed, onto a site of two hundred and seventeen acres overlooking the main sweep of Jerusalem. The estate was walled and guarded, and though the Legion camp lay closer to the city, a little to the south, the Governor's own military elite—five hundred men in all—were quartered in permanent barracks near the residency itself.

The narrow road from barracks to residency meandered throughout its half-mile length. This departure from the prime rule of Roman civil engineering—*build roads straight*—had come about partly for aesthetic, partly for political reasons. An early governor had ordered the meander on a personal conviction that curved roads looked pretty, and justified it to a less than sympathetic military commander on the premise that the road could now be largely concealed by strategic trees and bushes. The decision was taken at a time when it was fashionable to pretend that the Hebrews welcomed their Roman overlords as a civilizing influence, so that military matters were frequently underemphasized. The present military commander, having inherited the folly, could do nothing about it. But he liked it no better than his predecessor.

Three hours and thirty minutes after sunrise, on orders from a civilian governor who liked to sleep late and considered even this time abominably early, he ranged the escort around the prisoner and marched him out of the barracks with as much precision as that idiotic road allowed.

The residency was flanked by a paved courtyard and approached up broad white steps that led through towering colonnades into a vast, tiled reception hall. From the internal gallery above it, Pontius watched the guard approach with that flowering of delight that never failed to accompany a well-drilled military display. Next to the Games, he enjoyed parades and processions more than any other public spectacle, and had since childhood.

There was something especially grand about armored men moving rigidly in step, wheeling as one, stopping as one, standing as one, grim-faced and vaguely threatening. This, he often felt, was the real purpose of an army, the purpose most pleasing to the military gods. Actual fighting was only a messy necessity.

If the guard was aware of his presence—which, of course, it was—not one man showed it by as much as the flicker of an eye. They entered the hall in a well-formed square, halted in the central position, then split at an order from their commander and parted to reveal the prisoner who, until then, had been entirely hidden by their bodies. As one they turned, raised their heads, and saluted. Pontius returned the salute regally, but could not quite suppress a childish smile. On occasions like this, it was easy to imagine himself Caesar, taking the Praetorian salute. It was a pleasant feeling, one of the few compensations available to the Emperor's ape. For a moment he basked. Then he looked at the prisoner.

And looked again.

"He's deformed!" He turned accusingly to Corax, who insisted on accompanying him on any important occasion. "You call that a sorcerer?" The man had a spinal curve that was almost a hump, twisting his body at an angle as he walked. And from this distance he looked hardly taller than the Chinese dwarf who had conquered Trajan. A wizard? A Roman half-breed? If that one had Roman blood in him it came from biting his captors when he was taken. The nose alone marked him as a Jewish thoroughbred, although his coloring was dark, even for a Hebrew.

Corax's face remained as expressionless as ever, but he still seemed at least a little taken aback. After a moment he said, "One cannot judge proficiency in the black arts on superficial appearances, noble Pilate." It was that "noble Pilate" which gave him away. The only time he ever used formal address in private conversation was when he was badly shaken.

"Damn it to Hades, man, he's supposed to be a healer!" Pontius snarled. "Look at him." He distorted his own spine in a parody of the prisoner below and began to shuffle along the gallery in imitation of the prisoner's walk, when he remembered the watchful eyes of the guards and straightened himself abruptly. He rounded on Corax angrily. "He can't even keep himself in shape. Would you walk the streets looking like that if you knew the healing magic?"

120

"Perhaps not," Corax admitted, "but I am a Roman. These Hebrews are different from you and me."

"Not that different, Corax! Not different enough to suffer a twisted spine if they knew how to help it!"

"I don't suppose the soldiers could have injured him last night?" Corax suggested.

Pontius stalked toward the doorway. How did he let himself be persuaded into these ridiculous positions? Put that thing into the arena? Wager another twenty thousand *libra?* He stopped and turned, staring down again at the little Jew, his robe streaked in mud, presumably from the struggle of the night before, his back twisted so that his body was thrown to one side, his stance a painful contrast to the upright posture of his guards. "Put that into the arena?" he shrieked at Corax. "Wager with the Emperor?"

"He is bigger than the dwarf," Corax said.

"He is not bigger than the dwarf!" Pontius swore. In fact, Corax was probably correct, but in his anger Pontius was prepared to concede nothing. Besides which, Corax was only right by a fraction of a technicality.

The trouble was, after his initial shock, Corax was regaining something of his usual self-assurance. He walked to the edge of the balcony and peered over like some huge, shortsighted bird. "You know," he said thoughtfully, "there may be some benefit to this yet." He turned back to Pontius. "You appreciate, dear boy, that the man's appearance will work for us?"

"Work for us in what?" Pontius snapped. "Shall we make him a clown? Shall we enter him in an amusement in the second interval of the Games? I doubt he'd even stand up to that. Look at him, you fool! Look at his condition! I can't even understand why he worries Caiaphas. Judging by appearances he will be dead within the year."

"You exaggerate, dear boy. But even if you did not, surely you can see the benefits?"

He was going to lecture again. Pontius wanted to tear himself away, to stride through the door before this man's tongue persuaded him to further folly. But he could not. Somehow he could never quite free himself from Corax soon enough to do the slightest good. Curiosity held him, as curiosity always held him. What could he possibly say, what could anyone possibly say, that would turn the creature below into a gladiator?

Corax said, "Look at the facts, noble Pontius. He does worry Caiaphas, and worries him a great deal, to judge by the time Caiaphas spent talking of him."

"Caiaphas would spend time talking of a moonbeam if he could find anyone to listen!"

But Corax waved this aside. "And he has a following—a very large following. A man does not gain a following without abilities of some sort. Think on that. Even your friend Miriam knew of him."

My friend Miriam? Was there no means of dealing with a man like Corax? He was outrageous. He spoke without any thought of consequence. Miriam the harlot a friend of the Governor himself? Discretion might have suggested a different phrasing, but when had Corax ever shown the slightest discretion in anything? Did Pontius have to endure this? But he heard himself asking, "What do you mean by that?"

"Only that we may be far too hasty in our judgments. The man excites the Jews, keeps the High Priest awake at night. That must mean something. Look at him again, Pontius. Does he not stand straighter now?"

Pontius looked despite himself. The Jew did indeed look a little straighter. Or was it his imagination? He scowled.

Corax moved across to stand beside him. "Remember our plan, Pontius," he whispered. "If this was a towering giant, a man of threatening face and bulging muscles, we could certainly enter him in the Games, but who would take our wagers? Is not the whole point that this man should look nothing like a fighter, as the Emperor's dwarf looked nothing like a fighter? As you can see, the rabbi does not seem immediately impressive. Would we be happy if he was? We would not, for our entire plan depends—"

"Your plan!" Pontius hissed. "Not our plan—*your* plan!"

"—on misleading the Emperor's judgment through superficial appearances." He turned to stare with great conviction into Pontius's eyes. "As we ourselves were momentarily misled by superficial appearances."

Pontius stared at him, then looked at the Jew, then looked back to stare at Corax again. He said nothing. He looked back at the Jew. Was his spine any straighter? A trick of the light? He looked at Corax, then pushed abruptly past him. But he strode toward the staircase, not the door.

The guards snapped to rigid attention as he reached the hall. He had always suspected Corax was half-mad, but half-mad or not, he might be right. A chance in a thousand, but he might be right. At ground level, the Jew looked a little taller. Not a great deal, but a little. Dear gods, he was beginning to think the way these Jews talked! Corax and the heat were addling his brains. "Are you a magician, Jew?" he shouted. He walked across and spun the man by the shoulder, jerking the head around so that they were face to face.

There was something very odd about the rabbi's eyes.

§20

"Uncle. Dearest Uncle," said Salome. She smiled, as the great cats smiled in the Roman arenas before they ate their victims.

Herod knew that smile of old. If anything, it made him even more nervous than her mother's smile. He drew a small hambone from the folds of his robe and gnawed on it absently. (Strange how the Ordinances forbade pork when pig's flesh was so succulent.) With his free hand he waved her to a chair set lower than his own. They were meeting in the small chamber of private audience—formal, yet very private. He was wearing his state robes, but not the crown: it struck just the right balance, he thought. And the right balance would be needed if he was to keep this brat under any sort of control.

Salome sat. She was wearing a light blue tunic, cut short at the hem and low at the neck. As she sat she contrived, despite his elevated position, to show him momentarily that she was wearing nothing underneath. He felt a stirring and suppressed it savagely. This time he was not going to be led around by the scrotum. That was how he found himself in this mess in the first place. "You sent for me, dearest Uncle?" Salome said, still smiling.

There was talk that she had poisoned three of her lovers.

Difficult to believe as she sat there with her long legs and wide, innocent eyes, but the rumors persisted and there was seldom smoke without fire; especially in this damn palace. How could any child look like that, yet be so ruthless? Her mother's daughter, he supposed.

"Yes," he said. "I did." He placed the bone in the side of his mouth and cracked it with his back teeth, then scooped up the marrow with a deft movement of his tongue. Delicious, quite delicious, whatever the Ordinances had to say. He dropped the bone on the floor for the servants to pick up and smiled back at her. "A small snack," he explained. "Now, are you well, Salome?"

"I am pregnant," Salome said.

For an instant he thought he could not have heard her correctly. "What?"

"I am carrying your child," Salome said.

"My—?" He stared at her. "You are carrying . . . ?" He spluttered. Not a dozen words into their conversation and already he felt as though the sky had fallen in! He steeled himself. "Rubbish!" he said clearly. As it was. As assuredly it was. There was no way a woman could get pregnant by accepting a man in her posterior passage. At least he did not think so. Could she be pregnant? He had always thought the Greek position was the perfect prophylactic. Of course, she might be pregnant by someone else, one of those buck Nubians, for example—the ones she kept pretending were castrated.

But Salome had leaped from her seat and was running toward him, arms outstretched, the picture of childlike enthusiasm. "It will be a son, dearest Uncle," she said as she climbed onto his knee. "Tall and strong and handsome like you. An heir to the throne. You can teach him to hunt and fight and—"

Herod managed to extricate himself from her embrace and stood up. The little bitch was wearing musk. He turned his head away. "You can't be pregnant," he said firmly. "I won't allow it." Nor would he. She was far too young to carry a child, even if she was old enough to engender one. Not that she had, of course. It was a trick. Everything she did was a trick, as everything her mother did was a trick. Dear God, why was he surrounded by so many scheming women?

"I'm afraid it's too late not to allow it now," Salome smiled.

"And I am definitely pregnant—I have missed two of my monthly seasons."

Two? He began to count backward silently, but lost track before he could decide whether his own small indiscretions were timed correctly to have caused the damage. All the same he said, "Not by me, niece. Not by me!"

"By you, dearest Uncle!" Salome gushed excitedly, or at least it appeared as if she gushed excitedly—she was such a fine actress it was impossible to be certain. "He will have your hair and your eyes and your big—"

"You can't get pregnant in the Greek position!" Herod hissed, hoping before God it was true.

"How then is it there are baby Greeks?" Salome asked ingenuously. She blinked at him with those innocent saucer eyes. "I know this is your child, dearest Uncle, for I was virgin when you seduced me and I have known no man since."

She was mad. It was the only answer. If she thought he would believe that, she had to be mad. Her lust was the talk of the palace, of the country. He doubted seriously she had been virgin since the age of four. And so far as other men were concerned . . . !

In an attempt to regain some semblance of control of the situation, he turned and said severely, "We shall discuss this at a later time. I sent for you on another matter."

"Yes, dearest Uncle," Salome said meekly. She sat down, once again briefly indicating her lack of underclothing.

Herod mopped an errant trickle of sweat from his brow. "Listen carefully, Salome. You may recall that some time ago we struck a silly bargain, you and I."

"Bargain, dearest Uncle?" Her eyelashes fluttered like wheat-stalks in a storm.

Herod coughed uncomfortably. "I required you to entertain me with a little dance—"

"And I stripped my body naked before you, dearest Uncle! I bared my breasts to you, my loins to you, my legs to—"

"Yes, yes—that occasion. We were both perhaps a little the worse for wine. But no matter." He coughed again. The hem of her skirt was riding up along her thighs, but she made no move to adjust it. He pulled his eyes away. "You may also recall that you, for your part, required, ah, shall we say, a little gift from me. In return, so to speak." He had rehearsed the words carefully before she arrived, but somehow they did not carry the same force now.

"A little gift, Uncle?" Salome echoed. She smiled again, probably at the memory.

"A little gift," said Herod firmly. He returned to his chair and sat down. From this position the tunic seemed even shorter, its neckline even deeper. She leaned forward the better to hear him and he found himself staring down on two perfectly formed, almost totally exposed, soft, voluptuous, and nubile breasts. He tore his eyes away, swallowing heavily. "I had thought," he said, "you might ask for some bauble—a sapphire necklace, a pair of golden sandals, something of that sort. But . . ."

"But instead I sought to please you, sweetest Uncle," Salome told him smugly. "I knew that smelly prophet from the desert had been causing you and dear Mother so very, very much embarrassment that I decided I must put aside my own desires and ask instead for his life. To please you," she repeated.

Herod seized on it. "Then you didn't really want his head? Not for yourself, I mean?"

She contrived to look shocked. "Wanted his head? Oh, Uncle, what would a woman want with a man's *head!*"

"That is all I needed to hear, my dear. All I wanted to hear." He smiled, silkily. "You see, a situation has arisen—" he waved one hand around vaguely, exactly as he had rehearsed "—an affair of state, a political matter which need be of no concern to you. This situation makes it imperative—*imperative*—" he stressed the word "—that the head be returned to John—to me, as soon as possible. Now I have no wish to deprive you of your plaything—"

"My *plaything?*" Salome asked, astonished.

"Your mother's word, not mine," Herod told her quickly. "As I was saying, no wish to deprive you of something you might value. But since it is imperative that the head be returned to me, and since you say you have no real need of it . . ." He was beginning to gibber: who ever had *need* of a human head? Except the Baptist, of course, which was what this business was all about. "Since you have no need of it," he repeated, "I should like it back."

"It has been embalmed," Salome said.

"Your mother mentioned that."

"An Egyptian from Memphis who commanded a very high fee." Her tunic had crept back so far now that just the merest hint of

126

pubic hair was showing curled gently at the top of her thigh. Herod felt himself beginning to sweat and stood up as she parted her knees slightly. He turned away. "I'll pay his damn fee!" he snapped savagely. Didn't she realize what she was doing to him? She realized, all right: that was the trouble. She knew what she was doing every inch of the way, as she had known what she was doing the last time and the time before. His member, with a will all its own, was erect now, but fortunately hidden from her by the folds of his state robes. If he gave in now he was finished. Pregnant indeed!

"Will you, Uncle?" she asked coyly.

"What's more," said Herod, playing his trump card, "since it was a present, a present to you, after all, I think it's only fair—yes, fair—that when you give me the head, I give you something in return. A silk tunic, from Cathay, for example." A *long* silk tunic. Dear God, his member ached. "Or a peacock, or—"

"But may I not name my present?" Salome asked innocently.

He was not going to fall for that one twice. "Within reason," he said. "What is it you want?"

"You, dearest Uncle," Salome said.

He was so surprised he turned (and found, Lord protect Israel, that the full dark triangle of her hair now showed). "Me?" he echoed foolishly.

"Marry me!" Salome exclaimed. "That is what I wish most in all the world. I shall give you the head and you shall make me your Queen. And I shall bear your son and hold my head up proudly now that you have made an honest woman of me. We shall be so good for one another, you and I, dearest Uncle. We—"

"Marry you!" Herod exploded. "*Marry* you?"

"But say the word, Uncle, and I am yours forever."

It was too much, too much for any man. She had spread her legs now, exposing the entire pubic area, and yet her face was innocent as an angel's. It was too much, too much! That childlike face, those innocent eyes, and that inviting—

As happened all too often, something inside Herod's willpower snapped and he launched himself toward her, hoisting up his robe; but the material wrapped itself malignantly around his erect member, so that his anxious tug came close to giving him a hernia. He closed his eyes to scream in pain and felt—too late—his foot catch on an ornamental stool. He tripped, staggered, and fell upon her like a tree. Salome squealed as her chair toppled backward, then gasped once and was quiet as his vast bulk pinned her to the floor. Herod moaned with pain and lust as he sought to free his aching member from the constrictive folding of his robe. Annoyingly, the garment had lifted perfectly at the rear.

"Tetrarch . . . ?"

"Out!" Herod roared. "I am engaged in a private audience!"

"But Tetrarch—"

He rolled off her, his member still strangled, a red haze of rage before his eyes. "Get out!" he screamed. "I gave orders not to be disturbed!" Too late—why was everything always too late?—he saw it was Zephaniah. It would have to be Zephaniah, who would sulk for weeks now and sigh endlessly about unfaithfulness and treachery. "This isn't how it looks!" Herod screamed, the real tragedy being that for once he told the truth. "We were discussing the blasted head and I tripped! I tripped, do you hear? Fell on the poor child." She looked as if she might be unconscious. But still deliciously exposed. She would have to be exposed. Was the Lord visiting punishments upon him for his sins? Nothing went right. Nothing ever went right. He had not had a moment's good fortune since the Baptist strode out of the desert. "This isn't how it looks!" he screamed again. "We were discussing the Baptist's head!" He began to struggle to his feet.

"Sir," said Zephaniah, "the Governor has arrested him."

"Arrested him?" Herod roared, his great voice reverberating through the room. "Arrested who, you—" He stopped. "Arrested him?" he asked again, very much more quietly.

"The rabbi, Tetrarch."

"They have him?"

"He is being held at the residency, Tetrarch. You realize what this means, sir?"

Herod realized, all right, realized well enough. Oh yes, yes indeed. Thank you, Lord. Thank you, thank you, Lord. "It means he can't come after me, Zephaniah. He can't come after me for his damned head!" He felt so elated he kissed Zephaniah fondly. "It really wasn't as it seemed," he said, nodding toward the supine Salome.

"No, Tetrarch."

"They're holding him?"

"Yes, Tetrarch."

"Well guarded?"

"They are Romans."

"Yes, of course he will be well guarded. No chance of his breaking free. None at all. You have to say that for the Romans —they really know how to jail a man." He frowned suddenly. "What have they arrested him for?"

"I don't know yet, Tetrarch. But the orders came direct from Pilate."

"You're sure of your information? There's no possibility of a mistake or a misunderstanding?"

"I'm quite sure, Tetrarch."

"Well, well, well," Herod remarked, grinning.

On the floor, Salome stirred. There was a glazed look in her eyes, but she was obviously recovering quickly. "You are so masterful, dear Uncle," she gasped softly. "It will be wonderful when we are man and wife, when you are King and I am Queen." She stared at him with a fine imitation of absolute devotion.

"That's what you think! Go to hell, Salome," Herod said.

$21

". . . mount an attack," the Zealot was saying. "Once we find out where they are holding him."

"The garrison?" a worried young man named Thomas suggested.

Judas frowned. "I can scarcely see us attacking the garrison, no matter how many men we can muster."

"He would be held in the guard barracks of the Governor's estate," Miriam said dryly. "There is a small cellblock mainly used to discipline the soldiers."

"You see?" Simon Zealotes seized on the information without

bothering to ask where she had obtained it. "There are only a handful of men in the guard—we could attack them easily."

"There are five hundred," Miriam said shortly. Longinus had mentioned the figure on the same occasion he had told her of the cellblock. She sighed inwardly. These men were fools. Did they seriously consider they could attack the Roman Legions? A raggle-taggle rabble against armed, trained, highly disciplined fighting men? There would not even be a hint of a contest, only slaughter.

They had gathered in the villa of the rabbi's uncle—a very wealthy man to judge by the surroundings. There was no sign of the uncle himself and the place, while luxuriously furnished and equipped, had the gloss of a second home not overly used. A fond uncle, presumably, since he had obviously placed the house at the disposal of his nephew and his nephew's followers. She looked around at those followers now, in small amazement that anyone could have gathered about himself such a painfully ineffectual group. And greater amazement at herself among them. How had she joined this tattle? And why had they accepted her when she might easily have been a Roman spy? Yet they were her only real link with the rabbi and they seemed to be so shaken, so disorganized by his seizure that they had no room for suspicion of a stranger. But should she remain, or try to go her own way? The Zealot, with his desire for drama, had been formulating ridiculous plans for the better part of half a day. The remainder sat around discussing the details of the rabbi's capture, endlessly reviewing an event they could not change. They reminded her of a beheaded hen, although without the bird's frantic energy.

"We could not win against five hundred," a gray-haired man named Peter pointed out. "Besides, the rabbi would not approve of violence."

"He can hardly approve of being executed," Simon snapped, "while we sit here and do nothing."

"Why should they execute him?" Miriam asked. In their extremity, the group had accepted her completely. They no longer even glanced curiously at Benjamin, who stood by her chair, slack-jawed, staring at the texture of a sheepskin rug beneath his feet.

"Why?" asked Simon rhetorically. "Because the Governor fears

130

him. He is the leader who will drive the Romans from our country."

"Hardly that," Judas protested quietly. "He never seemed to me to take the least interest in politics."

"The Governor does not fear him," Miriam said mildly. "The Governor hardly knows he exists."

"Who told you that?"

Miriam shrugged. "The Governor. I asked him recently about the rabbi, but it was obvious he had heard no more than public gossip—and believed little enough of that."

Judas turned toward her with an interested look. "You know Pilate?"

"Yes."

"Well?"

Miriam smiled inwardly, but only said, "Well enough."

"Even five hundred men should not deter—"

"Shut up, Simon," Judas said. He turned back to Miriam. "If you know Pilate, do you know why he has taken the rabbi?"

"No," she admitted, "but I doubt it is for execution. I can see no reason why he should bother." Remembering Pilate, she found she had less antagonism toward him than toward most of her clients. He had been both generous and relaxed, two qualities she admired, even in men. And while he seemed foolish in some things, she did not consider him a fool. The difference was subtle, but real. Above all, she had sensed little real cruelty in him, an odd find in a world where men were cruel by their very nature. Which was not to say that Pilate would not execute the rabbi should some necessity arise—he had enough strength for that, if she judged him correctly. But she could not imagine him ordering an execution without good reason. Did good reason exist? Simon was determined to see the rabbi as a Zealot. Judas obviously thought of him as something different. Of the two, her instinct was to trust the judgment of Judas, who seemed altogether more reliable and sober.

"Neither can I," Judas agreed. "But then I can see no reason why he was arrested in the first place."

Miriam lowered her voice to exclude the other men. "Did he speak against Rome?"

"Not in my hearing," Judas said. "As a matter of fact, I once heard him tell a group of men they should continue to pay taxes to Caesar. It wasn't a very popular remark."

"Perhaps the Governor was worried about his Zealot following?" Miriam suggested.

Judas shrugged. "There's only Simon really. I can't imagine anyone taking *him* too seriously." He smiled slightly. "Can you imagine how long he would last against five hundred Roman legionnaires?"

It was a puzzle. When she had asked Pilate of the rabbi and his ability to cast out demons, it had soon become apparent that the Governor knew considerably less about the man than Longinus. The name had been familiar by repute and that was almost as far as it went. Pilate had been interested, of course, especially when he sensed Miriam's own concern, but he had asked more questions than he answered.

After a moment, Judas asked, "Do you think he might simply release him?"

She considered the possibility. "I suppose he might." It was difficult to judge Pilate's actions when she did not know Pilate's motives.

"I should like to know why he was arrested," Judas murmured, echoing her thought. He glanced quickly at Miriam. "Would you go to the Governor and find out?"

"I?"

"It is in your own interests," Judas said. "I understand you have an illness only the rabbi can cure."

She stared at him, thoughts tumbling. Beside her, Benjamin moved uneasily, as if sensing threat. "Who told you this, Judas?"

"Why, Simon, of course. Is it not true?"

"Did he tell you the nature of my illness?" Here, surrounded by these strangers, she felt the old, familiar shameful sensations beginning to arise.

"No, he made a mystery of it as he makes a mystery of everything. Is it important?" A look of genuine concern flickered through his eyes. "You must not worry if you are ill—the rabbi Joshua is a remarkable healer. I'm sure he will be able to help you."

Miriam glanced gratefully toward the Zealot, still arguing his case for violence with the gray-haired Peter. Was Judas right? Could the rabbi free her from a demon? Aloud, she said, "It is of no importance. But you are right. It is in my interests to find out what has happened to your rabbi."

"You will go to Pilate then?"

Could she go to Pilate? Suddenly it occurred to her what troubled her about this man Judas. He was an innocent. Not an obvious innocent, for the characteristic was well hidden by his urbane air and obvious intelligence. But he had not troubled to press Simon for the real reason for her visit, despite the fact he mistrusted Simon's judgment in most things. Knowing next to nothing, he had gone to meet her, guided her to this house. He had answered her questions freely and openly. He had accepted at face value her claim to know the Governor, without wishing to find out in what circumstances she had met him. For all he knew, she might be a Roman informer, sent to seek out evidence against Joshua. Now he proposed to trust her on a mission of obvious importance to them all. Astonishing innocence. Dangerous innocence. In her experience, innocence was *always* dangerous. It bred misunderstanding. Misunderstanding led to dislike, sometimes even hatred. In such circumstances, the innocent had no protection. They suffered greatly, even perished, never recognizing that the fault lay in themselves.

But to her vast surprise she found she felt protective toward Judas. Something in him made her wish to spare him suffering. An odd emotion for Miriam the Harlot, hater of men. To cover it, she said coldly, "And what shall I say to him? 'Why have you made a prisoner of the rabbi? His followers demand to know.'"

He seemed surprised and a little pained by her tone. "I should have thought subtlety . . ." He shrugged. "I suppose it depends how well you know him."

Was it possible he was not even aware of her profession? She realized no hint of awareness had entered any aspect of his conversation, which meant, to her, that he was either a saint or simply ignorant. A man's response to a known prostitute was always predictable: scorn and fascination. The proportions varied, man to man, but the base ingredients were invariably the same. Judas had shown neither, which must mean he did not know. Should she tell him?

The question threw her into confusion.

What was wrong with her? She looked at the man squatted on

the cushions near her. Soft eyes, a pleasant, bearded face, cleaner robes than those of Simon and a preference for the darker, Bedouin colors. He would be somewhere in his thirties, perhaps? Certainly no more than forty. A civil servant of Rome who had somehow been caught up in the little religious movement generated by the rabbi Joshua. An ordinary man. Not rich, not poor, not short, nor overly tall, not especially handsome. Why did she hesitate to tell him she was . . . what she was? She had only met him the night before. He meant nothing to her. No man meant anything to her!

He felt warm. The warmth generated from those soft, brown eyes. She thought about it and realized they reminded her of Benjamin's soft eyes, without, of course, the underlying blankness.

She stood up abruptly. "Come outside with me, away from the others."

He looked surprised, but nonetheless rose to follow her. Benjamin moved between them, whether by accident or as a gesture of protection she could not guess. They moved out, all three, from the villa into the pleasant greenery of the gardens.

Miriam stopped and turned to him. "I am Miriam," she said.

He nodded, puzzled. "Simon told me your name."

"Miriam of Magdala."

"A pleasant village. I was sent there once with the census takers. The lake must be delightful in summer."

"You have not heard of me?"

The same puzzled look. "Heard of you?"

"I am a harlot!" Miriam hissed.

"Yes, I know."

She could not believe she had heard him correctly. Her eyes never left his face, searching for the hint of scorn and fascination. There was neither there. "I sleep with Romans," Miriam said, "for the sake of their gold."

The look of bewilderment was overlaid with a sudden smile. "Rather like me in your own way," he said. "I haven't slept with any yet, but I can't imagine it would be any more boring than the work I do for them."

"You don't mind?" The question was forced from her, uncharacteristic, inexplicable. She was behaving like a child. She could not stop behaving like a child.

The soft eyes blinked. "No, I don't mind. I can see why you ask.

134

There was a time when something like that would have upset me. I used to be terribly pompous about how other people should behave. I was like Simon, I suppose, thought I knew what was best for them better than they did."

A sudden intuition flowered. "The rabbi changed you?"

But Judas was shaking his head. "Not really—he can be fairly intolerant himself about some things. I suppose I just grew out of it. Life is very short, you know, and I always feel it is difficult enough to find yourself without taking on the responsibility of other people." He found a stone bench and sat down. "Was Pilate one of your clients?"

Without hesitation, Miriam broke the prime rule of a lifetime. "Yes."

"Then I can see your difficulty," Judas said. "The thing is, if you don't go to Pilate, which of us can? We need to know what is happening to the rabbi. We need to take action. That is really why they are listening to Simon in there. They are no more fools than you are, but they feel helpless. Threatened too, of course. When men feel helpless and threatened they need action—even the stupid sort of thing Simon is suggesting."

In his childlike way, Benjamin reached out and took the sleeve of Judas's robe, fingering the material. Judas smiled vaguely at him.

"I shall go to Pilate," Miriam said.

22

"A visitor for you, Excellency," said Corax formally. His face remained immobile, but there was the softest glint of malice in his eyes as he added, "The High Priest Caiaphas."

"Oh gods," Pontius exclaimed, "not now of all times!" He had retired to the privacy of the residency orchard to consider his talk with the rabbi. The man was amazing—truly amazing. Pontius had to give Corax full credit for his insight. Appearances were deceptive. But he needed time to ponder and consider. Trust Corax to hunt him out, especially with bad news like Caiaphas. "Can't you send him away?"

"Excellency, this is the High Priest. An important man in Jerusalem."

"What does he want?" Pontius asked irritably. "Surely he said all he had to say at the last audience?"

Corax pursed his lips, creating something as close to an expression as his features were ever likely to achieve. "I believe he may wish to discuss the rabbi with you. News of the arrest seems to have reached him rather quickly." He hesitated, an actor's trick, since natural hesitation was as foreign to Corax as the Gallic tongue. "Which reminds me, dear Pontius, you have not told me your own conclusions about our reluctant guest."

"No, I haven't, have I?" Nor had he the slightest intention of telling Corax anything. Not yet. Not until he had time to think, to consider the implications. Rome! He could smell it. He could taste it. He could feel its warm, sweet evening air across his brow. By the gods, but Rome was close now. Evenings spent with friends who spoke Latin without Hebrew accents. Decent wine, free-flowing, full-bodied, purple and dry, not the cloying, sickly-sweet vinegar these Israelites preferred. Intelligent conversations. Women with short noses. The glorious sensation of moving once again at the very center of the world. And tickets to the Games. Gods, how he missed the Games. But he would return to them in triumph, thanks to this wonder-working rabbi. "Corax," he said, intoxicated by his thoughts, forgetful of his resolve, "have you seen my leg?"

"Which one?" Corax asked without batting an eyelid.

"This one!" Pontius said excitedly, hitching up his toga. He waited.

Corax bent forward to stare at his leg. He turned his head slowly to look up at Pontius. "A shapely limb, dear boy," he murmured.

"I'm not asking you for compliments," Pontius snapped. "I want you to examine it."

"What am I looking for?"

"Do you see a blemish, Corax?"

"No, dear boy."

"Any cut? Any sore? Any discoloration of the skin?"

"None, Pontius. I have known courtesans who would be proud to own a leg like that." He straightened up. "Why do you ask?"

"Corax," Pontius said excitedly, "when I was still in Rome an ulcer developed on that leg. At first I thought nothing of it—a small enough irritation; one picks up these infections in the baths from time to time. But it would not go away. I tried creams and salves and herbal ointments, but nothing worked. I even ate a portion of that bitter resin bees use to gum up their hives—a physician assured me it would cure anything. But it did not cure my ulcer. That ulcer itched, Corax, the day I gambled on the dwarf. I think it may have affected my good judgment, but no matter. It itched while Sejanus pleaded my case with Caesar. It itched on the boat to this godforsaken country. It itched through my inauguration as Governor. It has itched, on and off, through every hour of every day I have been here. Look again at my leg, Corax. What do you see?"

Corax looked. "No ulcer," he said.

Pontius gripped his arm. "The rabbi cured it! With a touch! He stroked it and the itching stopped at once. Within an hour the skin was closing over. Within two my leg was as you see it now—no sign of a wound, no irritation whatsoever. Corax, my dear friend, the rabbi has the healing magic. There is no doubt about it!"

Corax said, "Are you sure?"

Pontius released his arm to glare at him in annoyance. "What's the matter with you, Corax? A few hours ago you were trying to persuade me the man might be the greatest sorcerer the world has ever known. Now you ask me am I sure. Of course I'm sure. My leg is the proof."

Corax turned away and began to toy with the leaf of an olive tree. "Ah yes, he may be able to heal. But can he kill? That was your own point, if you recall."

"Surely he can reverse the spell!" Pontius shouted. "You said so yourself!"

"Did you question him on that point?"

"No, not directly, but—"

"Then there is still room for doubt. I am a rational man, Pontius, as you know."

"Rational!" Pontius screamed. "The rabbi is a wizard. We can take him to Rome and enter him in the Games exactly as we planned. It will be the sensation of the century!"

"I am disturbed by his hump," Corax said.

"What hump?"

"It did not concern me at first, but then I thought deeply on what you said, and, you know, it is perfectly correct. If he is such a great healer, why does he not rid himself of that hump?"

Pontius gripped his arm again, more in anger than excitement this time. "He doesn't have a hump," he hissed. "A slight curve of the spine, that's all. Close up it's hardly noticeable. His posture was distorted by the angle at which we first saw him. Standing beside him you notice nothing. Well, almost nothing. A slight curve of the spine, hardly even that."

"Well, why does he not rid himself of the slight curve of the spine?" Corax persisted.

"How should I know?" Pontius asked. "I didn't question him about it—that would have been an appalling breach of manners. Perhaps he hasn't had time to cure it. Perhaps he doesn't care about it."

"Wouldn't you care about it if you had it? Which, gods forbid, you ever should."

"I am a Roman," Pontius snorted. "These Hebrews are different from you and me. Different priorities altogether. Look at the man, Corax. Poor as a dormouse. That robe of his has seven patches. Seven! If I could cure ulcers the way he does, I'd be on the next ship for Rome and make my fortune in a month."

"Not everyone has ulcers," Corax pointed out. Then, obviously recalling a chronic complaint of his own, he added, "Now if it was piles. . . ."

"Ulcers—piles—what's the difference? If you can cure one you can cure the other. That man could cure anything. Did you see his eyes?"

"No," Corax admitted. "Does he squint?"

"Of course he doesn't squint! By Mars and Jove, if you had seen his eyes you wouldn't joke about them. I don't mind admitting they terrified me. A sorcerer's eyes."

"Then," said Corax, "now you are convinced he is a sorcerer?"

"Yes, I am," Pontius said with conviction. But he was not, not anymore. A tiny mouse of doubt was gnawing at his certainty, bred by Corax's questions. Could the man never leave well enough alone? It was his idea to take the rabbi to Rome. His idea to enter him in the Games. His idea to recoup everything Pontius had lost—and more—in one dramatic gambling coup. He was the one who insisted the rabbi was a wizard. He was the one who argued

138

that the healing magic might be reversed. And now, out of sheer perversity, he was questioning every word of it. Pontius glared at Corax and said sourly, "We had better talk to that old fool Caiaphas."

The High Priest rose as they entered the audience room, baring his horse's teeth in an ingratiatingly oily smile. "Honored Excellency," he said, "how good of you to see me."

"Your Holiness," Pontius acknowledged shortly. He took his official chair and sat down rigidly. He had had enough of trying to treat this idiot informally. All the man did was take advantage of it, calling every second day without so much as the courtesy of a prior appointment. They were all the same, these religious Hebrews, suffering from delusions of their own importance. Exactly the sort of thing you would expect from a race without the imagination to believe in more than one god. Oh for the life in Rome where the citizens had a sensible religion and the priests knew their place. But Rome seemed further away than ever now.

"I came to congratulate you, honored sir," Caiaphas said, still smiling his herb-stained smile. He seemed uncommonly pleased with himself about something, an observation which made Pontius immediately wary.

"Congratulate me?"

"Why, on your move against the rabbi, honored sir. Prompt, decisive, and well timed, if I may say so."

By Jove, but news traveled fast. Of course, Caiaphas had his own ax to grind about the Joshua fellow, so perhaps it was not too surprising. But what did he want now? In Pontius's experience, no one ever made an official visit merely to offer congratulations, especially scheming priests. "Thank you," he said cautiously.

"Frankly, Excellency, I was surprised. I had not thought you fully appreciated the seriousness of the situation at our last meeting. If I may say so without giving offense, it did not seem to me you realized the danger of this man. But I was wrong. I am delighted to see I was wrong."

Pontius reached beside him for an orange and found the bowl empty. He would have the slave's head for that! How could anyone endure this man without something to eat? Out of the corner of his eye he noticed Corax biting on a pear. He had made damned sure his own fruit bowl was filled. To Caiaphas, Pontius said carefully, "It is generous of you to say so, Holiness."

139

"Hardly that, sir. Hardly that. Your good judgment is legendary in this land. It was merely that I misinterpreted your response in my anxiety to see this matter dealt with." He hesitated and a sly look crossed his features. "You have him well guarded, of course?"

"Of course," Pontius confirmed.

"*Well* guarded," Caiaphas emphasized. "He has a considerable following—as you know, of course," he added hurriedly. "It is not beyond the bounds of possibility that his men might try to free him."

"He is held here in this house, protected by my personal guard. A tribe of Huns could not free him."

"Delighted," Caiaphas said. "Delighted to hear of it, Excellency, honored sir." He did indeed look delighted. He leaned forward, smiling, "And the execution, Excellency—when is it planned?"

"Execution?" Pontius asked blankly.

"The crucifixion," Caiaphas said. "I feel crucifixion would be the best course, rather than hanging or anything of that sort. As a warning, you appreciate."

"Warning?"

"To his followers. We don't want any more nonsense once we've rid ourselves of this rabbi, do we?"

Pontius took a deep breath. "I was not planning an execution, Holiness."

"Not . . . not planning an execution?" A look of panic entered the eyes of Caiaphas. "Excellency, the man is dangerous. Very dangerous indeed. There must be an execution. For the sake of the state and all our peace of mind."

Corax was right. The rabbi did frighten this man. Could there really be something in his prattle about a native rebellion? Pontius doubted it. The rabbi had been taken without a fight. There were no demonstrations on the streets. It gave every indication that his following was small. Yet Caiaphas claimed that he was a threat to the state. Why?

"Caiaphas," he said soberly, "why do you feel this man is dangerous?"

"He preaches sedition against Rome," Caiaphas said promptly.

Pontius shrugged. "Sedition against Rome is talked in every tavern in the city. It is only natural in an administration of this type."

"His followers claim him as the Messiah, Excellency."

"A poor-looking Messiah," Corax put in mildly. "Do your prophets claim the Messiah will be born with a hump?"

Caiaphas frowned. "A hump? The rabbi Joshua has no hump."

Pontius cast a triumphant glance toward Corax, then said to Caiaphas, "My secretary has an obsession about humps. But you must surely agree on one thing, Holiness. The man we are discussing is not an imposing figure. A Messiah surely would be cast in a more heroic mold."

"I am not claiming this man to be the true Messiah," Caiaphas said hurriedly. "Not at all. Not in the least degree. I am merely saying his followers believe him to be such."

"And I appreciate your point," Pontius said patiently. Were there no slaves nearby to send for fruit? "But it does not negate my own. When people look for a hero, they naturally look for someone who looks like a hero." The phrase was inelegant, but the meaning clear enough, even to someone like Caiaphas. "Is this not so?"

"Indeed it is, Excellency."

"And as Corax has suggested, this rabbi scarcely looks like a hero. Is this not so as well?"

"That too, Excellency. His appearance reflects his low origins."

"Then may it not be that you overestimate the power he holds over his followers?"

Caiaphas leaned forward earnestly. "His power is not founded on physical appearance, honored sir. It is based on sorcery!"

"Sorcery?" Pontius exclaimed with every indication of astonishment. "Surely you jest, Holiness." He resisted the temptation to throw Corax another look of triumph.

"I assure you I do not, Excellency. I do not expect a layman to appreciate these matters, but Anninaias has investigated the situation thoroughly."

"Who is Anninaias?" Pontius asked.

"My Temple deputy, Excellency. He is a man with a profound knowledge of these magical abominations. He has devoted a lifetime to their study—the better to combat them, of course. He assures me the rabbi uses the very blackest of occult lore to influence his followers."

Better and better! The very blackest of occult lore was exactly what a gladiator needed. This rabbi was a better wager even than the dwarf. If Caiaphas was right, he could decimate a battle royal with a glance. "How dreadful!" Pontius exclaimed, wide-eyed. He leaned forward. "You trust the judgment of your deputy in this matter?"

"Implicitly, Excellency. He has studied the *Zohar*."

Pontius stopped himself from asking about the *Zohar* just in time. The last thing he needed was another lecture. Instead he said, "Very well, Holiness, your concern is noted and the information you have given me is appreciated."

Caiaphas smiled. "Then I take it, honored sir, that you will be setting a date for the execution?"

"I shall certainly consider what you have said most carefully," Pontius told him diplomatically. He watched the smile fade abruptly, then stood up to denote that the audience was at an end.

When the man had gone, he turned thoughtfully to Corax. "What do you know about this, Anninaias?"

∫23

Miriam entered the barracks flanked by two armed guards. The escort amused her, with their armor, swords, heavy muscles, and grim faces. Was one woman alone such a threat to the security of the residency? They had even separated her from Benjamin, who had, oddly enough, gone with them without a hint of an objection, as if, somehow, he knew no real threat was posed to the welfare of his mistress.

The barracks themselves had a familiar look. Although she had never before visited within the walls of the Governor's estate, the soldiers' quarters in the main garrison were familiar to her from the distant days when her demon had driven her to entertain the common legionnaires, and Roman barracks were Roman barracks wherever they happened to be located. There was always a starkness about them, a contradictory quality of dinginess and scrubbed wood, which was like nowhere else on earth. The men, she remembered, slept on rough wood bunks, twenty-five and fifty to a room. Even here there was little in the way of personal

142

ornament, as if the Romans feared losing their masculinity through any deviation from the utterly necessary.

They marched her along an empty corridor, armor clinking, sandals slapping fiercely on the floorboards, and showed her into the Commander's office, another spartan affair with one small table, several wooden chairs, and a cabinet near the solitary window, possibly containing writing materials and files. A bust of Tiberius, poorly executed in plaster, stood on a pillar near the door. Otherwise the office was empty, empty too of the Commander.

They withdrew, leaving her alone, although presumably they now stood guard outside the door. She walked to the window and looked out. It overlooked the barracks square, where a small detachment of men were wheeling in endless precision circles at the command of a noncommissioned officer. How strange that men should learn to fight this way, yet learn they did, and learn well. This was the real pillar of Rome, beyond mistake or argument. Not her gold, for Egypt probably had more gold than Rome. Not her emperors, for the line had degenerated since the name of Julius Caesar extended and inspired an empire. But the iron discipline of Roman fighting men remained. And so long as it remained, the empire was intact.

Tiring of the endless repetition, she turned, intending to sit down. But as she did so, the Commander entered. Miriam tilted back her head and faced him, enjoying the look of obvious discomfiture on his heavy, handsome features. After a moment, she said, "Good day to you, Longinus."

"They told me it was you. I scarcely believed them." He walked past her to stand behind the table as if he felt safer with a barrier between them.

"Because I came here? I wished to congratulate you on your new appointment. Commander of the Governor's Guard is a substantial post."

"It scarcely required a personal call."

Miriam glanced around her coolly. He was embarrassed, as she knew he would be. It took noble breeding to carry off a meeting of this nature, and Longinus, despite his high position and perfectly correct, clipped accent, did not have it. "You are not pleased to see me?"

Though lacking breeding, he did not lack backbone—never that.

143

"My pleasure or otherwise is not the point. This is a military barracks and I am its commander. I do not believe this to be the place for any woman."

"And especially not . . . ?" She left the words unsaid, but they hung between them in the air. Longinus was ambitious. Longinus had done well for himself. He could not afford the scandal of entertaining a woman in his quarters. Especially not a harlot.

He turned away from her, glancing out the window as she had done earlier. "What do you want, Miriam?"

"Well," she said, "you are direct at any rate. But then you have always been direct with me, as I recall from other circumstances."

He swung round abruptly. "I cannot believe you intend to do me harm."

"Do you harm, sir? The leader of the Governor's guard? A citizen of Rome? What harm could a Hebrew woman carry for such a one as you, Longinus?"

"You say I am direct. So be it. I shall be direct with you now. Although I have seen you in your professional capacity—"

"Professional capacity?" Miriam smiled, mocking him. "How delicate you are, Longinus."

He ignored the interruption. "Yet I still have felt there was some friendship between us. Now I wonder. In my . . . direct way, I wonder if you have not heard about my appointment as Commander and have thought that an opportunity to put a price on your silence about the fact I have visited you."

This time her smile was completely genuine. "Longinus, dear Longinus, I could buy and sell the tunic off your back, Commander's salary or not. When I wish to have your gold, I shall earn it as I always have. And what a fool you are, Longinus. Do you suppose for an instant anyone cares that you have visited Miriam of Magdala? I assure you you are in excellent company on that score. Who could point the finger at you? Name me your military superior and I'll wager I have entertained his superior in turn. Besides, it is expected for a soldier to take a woman. People worry about him if he does not."

He did not look altogether reassured. Nonetheless he said, "What is it you want then, Miriam?"

Miriam caught his eye and held it. "I want to see Pilate."

Longinus blinked. "The Governor? You wish to see the Governor?"

144

"Exactly. No more, no less, no gold, no threats. A simple audience with the Governor. In private."

"But why come to me? One applies for an audience with the Governor through normal channels."

"And waits for months," Miriam shrugged. "If, that is, his civil service would permit a woman of my profession to visit him at all." It was a genuine concern. She had no means of reaching Pontius Pilate directly with a message. Written communications were read and reread by a score of undersecretaries who made decisions on the Governor's behalf. Only the politically powerful could circumvent the system. Pilate might never hear she wished to see him. Nor—she was forced to admit it—was she certain he would see her even if he did hear. He struck her as a man of different kidney from this oddly prudish Sicilian. He would not have the same fear of scandal. Which meant, of course, that he might easily decide to see her, would welcome her with open arms. But it might equally well mean he would not. It was a risk she dared not take. She shook her head. "No, Longinus, I cannot apply through normal channels. My business with Pilate is urgent. I wish you to take me to him."

"Impossible. Out of the question."

"And you talk of something more between us than professional pleasures? I too had thought you something of a friend."

He ran his fingers through his hair, a sure sign of nervousness. Soon he would toy with the pommel of his sword. "What do you want with the Governor? Perhaps someone else . . ."

"No one else, Longinus. My business with the Governor is private."

"What you ask is impossible. I cannot arrange it."

"You can arrange it, Longinus," Miriam told him coldly. "And you will."

As she predicted, he began to toy with the pommel of his sword. "Be reasonable, woman. Can I go to the Governor and tell him a woman he does not know wishes to see him on business she will not discuss? He would laugh at me."

"He would indeed. Fortunately I do not require you to take that approach." She knew, of course, she had him. Her power over Longinus had always been a tangible thing, only partly based on the arousal she could call up in him almost anytime she chose. Another part, the greater part, drew strength from something in their characters, a curious interaction which made Miriam the mistress and Longinus the slave. It had showed within the bedroom. Despite her race and her profession, Longinus still thought of her as a lady. It was apparent in his every reaction. He could not see behind her accent and her bearing, nor control his reactions to her manner. He accepted her body gratefully, with passion, as he might have accepted the body of a noble Roman matron. For Longinus, the Longinus now hidden by veneers of success and sophistication, was still a peasant. He might have removed his body by a thousand miles from Sicily, but he had not yet completely removed his mind. He commanded the guard and accepted salutes, but beneath the military self-assurance, he was strangely lost in it all. He suspected he did not quite belong here, and the suspicion made him vulnerable.

Miriam leaned forward. "All I require is that you escort me safely to the Governor's residence and physically make sure I may reach him. You will have no need to announce me, or involve yourself further in any other way. I shall not tell Pilate how I reached him or who assisted me—you have my word on that. And you have my word that Pilate will be pleased to see me." Was it true, she wondered? She did not imagine in any case he would be particularly displeased.

"How will you leave?" Longinus asked.

Miriam smiled. "I expect the Governor will escort me when our business is completed."

"Are you . . . Do you intend to . . . ?"

"As I said, that is not your business. But as it happens, I do not intend to . . ." She let the sentence trail mockingly.

Longinus shook his head. "I don't know."

"Come now, Commander of the Guard, what risk do you take? You are required to protect the Governor. Am I a threat to him?"

"I cannot take you in daylight," Longinus said firmly.

Miriam considered. There were perhaps two hours till sunset. Say an hour beyond that before Longinus would agree to go. Could the rabbi come to harm in three short hours? It seemed unlikely. And besides, there was strength in Longinus's voice. She did not feel she might easily move him on this point. She nodded briefly. "I agree. We shall go after dark when there is less chance of being discovered."

"You had a man with you when you came to the barracks," Longinus said.

146

"My servant, Benjamin."

"He stays here."

"Agreed." She would have liked Benjamin with her for the reassurance he always gave, but it was not important in these circumstances. She was under no threat while Longinus was with her, and as she was an experienced judge of men she did not think for an instant that Pilate would harm her.

"And I must search you. I cannot permit anyone to enter the Governor's presence who might be carrying a concealed weapon."

She stared at him coldly, wondering whether to make an issue of the point. But she could see the fear in him. She reached for the fastening of her grown, let it slip to the ground. He flushed crimson.

Miriam stood naked. "Search me, Longinus," she told him icily. It did not matter to her. He would do exactly as she said now. In three hours she would see the Governor. In three hours she would find out what might happen to the rabbi Joshua.

24

The flames of the little oil lamps fluttered wildly, throwing dancing shadows across the Governor's study. It was a surprisingly small room for the residency. Three of the walls were honeycombed in wood to house a minor library of scrolls. Most of them were records of Judaean affairs and Roman histories, but there was one section near the paneled door which presumably reflected the embracing interest of that lively old libertine, Junius. In this section, Pontius had discovered, every scroll was pornographic in its content.

By day, the room was intimate and warm. On nights like this, however, it was difficult enough to keep the oil lamps lit. The problem was the central heating, which the civil service staff insisted should be lit on cool Judaean evenings. In the study, the hot-air ducts had been badly angled, so that wherever the lamps were set they flickered and sometimes blew out altogether. Since Pontius was no student and seldom used the study after dark, the problem had never seemed a pressing one. But now he found himself wondering what might be done to cure it. Anninaias, he found, was a sinister figure. Their conversation was a sinister conversation. Under the circumstances, the flicker of the flame and the dancing shadows made Pontius nervous.

"There was," Anninaias was saying, "one certain instance of necromancy, Your Excellency. It concerned a man named Lazarus, who died from a fever. The corpse was actually prepared for burial when this Joshua undertook to revive it."

"Did he succeed?" Pontius asked, suppressing a shiver.

"It is reported that he did."

"Does this sort of thing happen often in Judaea?" A mad question, but it was a night for mad questions. Pontius had seldom met a human being quite so disturbing as this priest. He had the coldness of the grave about him, especially in the eyes.

"There have always been sorcerers who pretended to raise the dead," Anninaias told him, "although the process is expressly forbidden by our Law since the days when King Saul required the Witch of Endor to perform such an operation. Today, of course, those who claim the power are mostly charlatans. It is possible to administer certain poisons which bring about the appearance of death, then to dispense an antidote which revives the victim. The credulous are suitably impressed."

"Do you think this happened in the case of—what was his name?—Lazarus?"

"In this case, no," said Anninaias. "For the burial preparations to be complete, Lazarus must have been dead for at least three days. Even if he had been poisoned, an antidote would not have proved effective after so long a delay."

"Then how did he do it?"

"Probably by means of a forbidden ritual from the *Sepher Shelomoh*, the Book of Solomon."

"I see," breathed Pontius, who had not the slightest idea what the man was talking about. He decided to move to the heart of the matter. Anninaias had certainly proved far less of a bore than his ecclesiastical superior Caiaphas, but Pontius had no intention of spending the night discussing corpses which stood up and walked.

148

He slipped his hands into the folds of his toga to warm them. "This rabbi, this Joshua, has a reputation as a healer."

"Shaitan will always heal bodies in order to capture souls," Anninaias said coldly.

"Shaitan?" The name was familiar, although he could not quite place it. Then it came to him. "Oh yes, the evil demon. Caiaphas mentioned him."

"No mere demon," Anninaias said. "The Lord of All the Demons. The Ultimate Adversary."

"You think," Pontius said, "the rabbi might be in league with this entity?"

"If not actually possessed."

"Possessed? You mean Shaitan may be acting through him?"

"It is possible. Possession is rare, but by no means unknown."

"If Shaitan acts through the rabbi," Pontius said carefully, "that would suggest the rabbi must wield the powers of Shaitan."

"Undoubtedly he does."

Pontius licked his lips nervously. "Powers of destruction?"

"Of course. The Adversary is destructive beyond men's imagining."

Excellent news indeed. Pontius had a mental picture of the Circus arena. On one side was a giant, larger even than Trajan. On the other was the rabbi. They approached and circled one another warily. The rabbi raised a hand and destructive power beyond men's imagining struck down the giant. The vision was immediately replaced by a more subtle scene. Once again the rabbi stood in the arena, but this time he faced the Emperor's dwarf. What a contest that would make—magic against magic, power against power. He could see them weaving spells in the air as thunderbolts clashed overhead. What a spectacle! What a thrill for the crowd! What an opportunity to put one over on Tiberius. Pontius could almost feel the Emperor's gold in his hands—assuming, of course, this priest was right about the rabbi.

"Let me make sure I understand what you are saying," Pontius said slowly. "You suggest the rabbi Joshua may be possessed by Shaitan, Lord of All the Demons?"

Anninaias nodded. "Yes."

"But you are not certain?"

"As certain as a man may be," Anninaias said.

"Why?" asked Pontius bluntly.

There was no change at all in the priest's expression. "Your Excellency, I have studied occult lore for many years. There are signs."

"What sort of signs?"

Anninaias shrugged. "This rabbi claims to be the son of the One God Whose Name May Not Be Spoken. Such a claim is blasphemy. Shaitan is the Father of Blasphemy. This man preaches sedition against Rome, the overthrow of the established order. Shaitan is the Lord of Chaos. This man practices necromancy with the corpses of the dead. Shaitan is Keeper of Sheol, the Land of the Dead. This man tends to lepers. Shaitan is the Giver of Leprosy and All Unclean Illness. This man—"

"Enough," Pontius said. It was an impressive list, and the priest certainly seemed to know what he was talking about. He leaned forward. "Now tell me, Anninaias, when this Shaitan takes possession of a human body, does he retain all his demonic powers?"

"Alas no, Your Excellency. In his primeval state, Shaitan is virtually limitless, boundless. His power is universal. But when he enters a human form, his abilities are limited to the potential of the mind and body he inhabits. Naturally, he still exhibits great powers, but they are not limitless."

"He may be overcome?"

"In a sense. The body he inhabits may be destroyed. As my Lord Caiaphas has told you, this is precisely what we of the Temple suggest must happen in the present case."

"If I execute the rabbi, this will destroy Shaitan?"

"No, Your Excellency, it will not. Shaitan himself is far beyond the reach of human action. But execution will destroy the vehicle through which he operates and rid the world of one of his manifestations. This is as much as we may hope for."

Pontius said, "Let me return to this question of Shaitan's limits, while still in possession of a body, that is. Suppose someone possessed by Shaitan—this rabbi, for example—suppose such a one was required to use his powers in a destructive manner, would he be able to do so?"

Anninaias nodded. "Of course, Excellency."

"He would be able to kill?" Pontius asked.

"Yes."

"Even someone bigger than himself?"

"Physical size is no protection against the powers of Shaitan."

"Even someone armed?"

"A sword is useless against sorcery," Anninaias said.

Pontius sat back. "Let me put a hypothetical case to you—an extreme, exaggerated circumstance. You know, of course, that we Romans often celebrate those festivals called the Ludi?"

To his surprise, Anninaias smiled. "Your Games. Ah yes, I have heard interesting reports of them."

"Suppose," Pontius said, "this rabbi was entered in the Games against a trained gladiator, a man skilled in the martial arts, the best gladiator in Rome, let us say. Would Shaitan protect him?"

"Assuredly. Shaitan takes care of his own."

"In the contest, would the rabbi win?"

Anninaias nodded. "By using sorcery, he would win."

"Suppose," Pontius said, thinking of the dwarf, "he was forced to face another sorcerer. What then?"

"Another sorcerer, Your Excellency? I had not thought you entered sorcerers in your Games."

Neither had I, Pontius thought sourly. Aloud he said, "I was speaking hypothetically. But in such a hypothetical circumstance, what would be the outcome?"

Anninaias stared at him, as if trying to read something in his face. Eventually he said, "In a battle of sorcery, the wizard with the greater power must always win."

"Yes," said Pontius, "but how can one judge which has the greater power?"

"In sorcery, there is no power greater than the power of Shaitan."

"So the rabbi would win?"

"Unless his opponent was also possessed of Shaitan," Anninaias nodded.

The Cathay dwarf would scarcely believe in a Hebrew demon, so the chances of his being possessed by Shaitan were minimal. Which meant the rabbi would have the edge. A decisive edge, according to this expert. Pontius sighed happily. It was all he needed to know, really. He decided to draw the conversation to a close. "Well, now, Anninaias, you have been a great help to me. A very great help. And I shall certainly see that Caiaphas hears how useful your advice has been." He made to stand.

"A word with you, Excellency," Anninaias said coolly.

Pontius sat down again. There was a price to everything in this world, even occult advice.

"The Lord Caiaphas has told me you may not execute this man," Anninaias said bluntly.

It was a topic Pontius had hoped to avoid. Still hoping to avoid it, he said, "I have not yet made up my mind. Execution has grave implications."

"Especially for the victim," Anninaias told him shortly. He had a thin face with all its planes clearly defined. His eyes, which had always been cold, now grew hard. "I have told you of the danger of this man. Are you still undecided?"

"Yes," Pontius admitted uncomfortably. For the first time he wished he had invited Corax to this little meeting. Everything about the man made him unaccountably nervous. Perhaps it was his knowledge of sorcery. There was no trusting men who had such knowledge, even priests. Especially priests. Briefly he wondered if Anninaias had ever been tempted to practice as well as study.

"It will not go well if you remain so," Anninaias said.

"I beg your pardon?"

"The Temple will formally demand his death."

Had he heard the man correctly? It was the sort of remark he would not accept from the High Priest himself, let alone his deputy. To put him in his place, Pontius said, "Demand? The Temple is in no position to demand of Rome."

"The people will demand his death," Anninaias went on relentlessly. He appeared not one whit overawed by the power of Rome.

"The people?" Pontius echoed again. "Are you speaking of the few who follow him or the multitude who have never heard of him?"

"The multitude have heard of him, all right, Pontius Pilate. You must not judge the interests of the multitude by what filters through the residency walls. You may rest assured the rabbi is known." He paused, staring at Pontius. "And hated."

It was intolerable—the man's tone as much as his words. Pontius felt the anger flaring in his stomach. He seldom stood on ceremony, and never really thought of himself as anything more than the Emperor's ape, but all the same, this upstart of a priest

152

would treat him as the Governor of Judaea. He narrowed his eyes threateningly. "What is the Hebrew rabble to Rome, priest? The decision is mine and I shall make it without reference to anyone. And especially without reference to the Temple or the mob."

Anninaias held his eye. "You are Governor, Pontius Pilate, by the Emperor's pleasure. The Temple has friends in Rome."

"Are you threatening me?" Pontius could hardly believe his ears.

"I am telling you to execute the rabbi!" Anninaias snapped. "I am telling you that if you do not, there will be pestilence and bloodshed on this land. I am telling you that the people—the mob, as you choose to call them—will rise in arms and stage a bloody revolution that will lead the Emperor to recall you as an inept ruler who cannot keep order in a loyal province. This is what I am telling you, and you would do well to listen to me." He stood up and bowed. "I bid you leave, sir."

He was gone before Pontius thought to close his open mouth.

25

Something was wrong. Miriam could feel it in her bones so strongly that she stopped, here in the middle of a moonlit fairyland Longinus had told her was the Governor's private garden.

"What's the matter?" He was nervous as a kitten, one of those strong men who could face physical danger without a tremor, but remained terrified of offending his superiors. In other circumstances she might have felt sorry for him. He was, after all, risking the wrath of the Governor himself, who, to Longinus, stood next only to the Emperor and Jove. But pity, in the present circumstances, was a luxury she could ill afford.

She waved him silent and stood listening. The garden was almost breathtakingly beautiful. Too beautiful for Pontius, surely. Yet she could not imagine it the work of the obsessive Junius either. Perhaps one or the other of them had simply commissioned a landscape designer of superlative taste. Whatever the answer, the result was certainly a masterpiece, one she would dearly have loved to see in daylight. Nearby, she heard the tinkling of a tiny stream. More distantly, a night bird hooted. What then was wrong?

It was a stirring, soft as a whisper.

"Can you hear something?" she asked Longinus.

He listened. "No." Then, with the nervousness replaced by something close to fear, "Is someone coming?"

"No one," Miriam said shortly. It was not the sound of movement, not the sound of footfalls, not a sound at all, perhaps, but something on the edges of her own imagination. She turned on him, her unease translating into anger. "Why do you behave like an old woman, Longinus? If someone should come, you have merely to send them away again. You are, after all, the Guard Commander."

"But what if it is the Governor? Or one of his aides?"

"If it is the Governor, you may safely leave matters in my hands," Miriam told him sharply. "If one of his aides, then he will undoubtedly assume we have come here to make love and tactfully withdraw. In either case, you have nothing to worry about." She moved off ahead of him, treading the winding path through a heady scent of herbs. Nothing to worry about indeed, yet why then was she so uneasy? She strained her senses, but this time there was nothing save the rustle of her gown and the sound of Longinus breathing.

They reached a small gate in a low stone wall. Miriam waited while Longinus opened it and waved her through. They emerged into a paved courtyard, with a wing of the residency rising sharply from its farthest edge.

"Follow me closely and do not speak now," Longinus whispered. "I left instructions for one door to remain unguarded. Once we are inside we shall be comparatively safe. The Governor prefers few guards within the building and most of the civil servants will be asleep at this hour."

"And Pilate himself?" Miriam asked. "Are we to burst into his bedroom?" The thought amused her. She could imagine herself telling Pontius that since he had been gracious enough to inspect her boudoir, she had decided to return the compliment.

154

"The Governor is having talks with Anninaias. He should not yet have retired."

"Anninaias?"

"A priest of the Temple, deputy to Caiaphas. We had instructions to bring him here earlier this evening."

Miriam turned to him in rising annoyance. "I cannot speak with Pilate while he prattles to some priest."

"Please keep your voice down!" Longinus glanced fearfully around him. He reached out and took her arm firmly. "Anninaias will be leaving about now—that is why I would not take you earlier."

"How do you know?" Miriam asked suspiciously.

"He has nightly duties at the Temple. He must leave now in order to perform them."

"Even if the Governor requires him to remain?"

"The Governor will not require him to remain," Longinus hissed. "The priest is a guest, not a prisoner."

"I see," Miriam said. She followed him across the courtyard to a door that was indeed unguarded, and, when she tried it, unlocked. She turned to Longinus. "Where does Pilate entertain this priest?"

"In his study. It is an informal audience."

"And where is his study from here?"

"Up the stairs and right to the end of this corridor. Not far. That is why I chose this door."

Miriam placed one hand on his breastplate. "Then you need escort me no further, brave Commander. I shall find my own way from here."

He started to protest. "But—"

"No argument, Longinus," Miriam said firmly. "You have told me where to find him and I shall follow your directions."

"But the priest Anninaias—"

"I shall not interrupt His Excellency's discussions, have no fear. Is there a room nearby that is certain to be empty at this hour?"

"The library is next door. No one goes there after sunset."

"Then I shall wait there, with the door a little ajar, until the priest leaves. From what you tell me, I should not have to wait long. I promised that you should come to no harm from this adventure and I intend to keep that promise. You have risked enough in taking me this far. I can continue alone, and should I be discovered, you have my word that I shall not reveal your part in this affair." She pushed firmly, so that he fell back a step, and slowly closed the door.

The feeling of wrongness was stronger in the house.

Miriam leaned against the door, staring up the corridor. Torches flickered at regular intervals along the gray stone wall. The floor was flagged in stone and felt cold beneath her feet. Why was she so uneasy? Pilate, she knew, would never harm her. It was doubtful that he would even wish to send her away. At the very worst, he might try to take his pleasure of her—a small enough price for news of the rabbi. The corridor itself was empty and there was no sound. What troubled her then?

She began to walk. Her legs felt heavy, as though the floor beneath her feet had melted and gone sticky. Was she ill? The air around her felt oppressive, dank. Her heart was pounding.

She forced herself to walk, one foot before the other. What was wrong? What was wrong? There was fear in her, dreadful fear. But of what? Of nothing! She found the staircase and began to ascend, moving slowly, like a tired old woman. She had never felt such fear before. She wanted to turn and run, to cry out, to scream. Instead she forced her legs forward.

After an eternity she reached the top. As she looked round for the study door, she heard the distant singing.

Miriam chilled. Not here! Not now! Lord God Jehovah, let it not take me now! Adonai preserve me, let it not come near! She clutched the ornamental balustrade and held it, shivering. The thing was there, nearby, on the outermost edges of her mind, singing its clear, still, tuneless song. She heard raised voices from behind a door, presumably the study Longinus had mentioned, but she could not move.

The moon was full! She remembered the moonlight in the garden. A full moon, or near to it. But the thing only took her in the dark of the moon. Never at any other time. Never, since the first black night it possessed her. For years now she had arranged her life around that single fact. It was the one thing that had enabled her to survive, the one thing that kept her from insanity or suicide. Never at any time but the dark of the moon, and tonight the moon was full.

Yet still she heard the singing.

156

The study door burst open and a slender figure in priest's black emerged. The singing flared to fill her mind, to drown her ears, to swamp her soul. She stared at the thing in priest's robes and knew it instantly for what it was. Miriam screamed her hatred and launched herself toward it, hands outstretched like claws. It could not take her now, for it was locked in human form. She could tear and rend and strangle and destroy. In human form the thing could die. She would be free!

The priest caught her wrists. He was immensely strong for one so slender. He held her immobile while she screamed and raved. He stared into her eyes and smiled a slow, triumphant smile of recognition. His own eyes writhed like serpents, and the serpents slithered out to strike toward her. She tried to pull away, but could not move.

Then, the darkness of a tomb engulfed her.

26

She awoke to sunlight and a soft bed in a strange room. There was no hint of the singing, no oppressive feeling in the air. She sat up. The room itself was opulent, furnished in the Roman style with considerable emphasis on drapes and curtaining. Whoever slept here liked the color blue, it was featured everywhere. There was a marble fireplace with a wood fire burning in the grate—unusual by day in this climate. On the mantelshelf, near a small shrine to the household gods, was a comic terra-cotta of an ugly Oriental in the process of being devoured by a lion. Near the door was the inevitable bust of Caesar. No, not Caesar, when she looked again, but a Roman she did not recognize.

There was someone with her in the bed!

Miriam spun round to find herself staring into the blue-gray eyes of Pontius Pilate. "Good morning," he said. "Your condition seems somewhat improved." As he sat up, she could see he was completely naked. He glanced down at himself and grinned apologetically. "You were extremely cold, so I thought it best to warm you. I had the servants light a fire also." He slipped from the bed, pulled on an undertunic, and began to wind his toga. "Are you hungry? Shall I have us sent something to eat?"

She found her voice at last. "Thank you."

As she recalled, he was no trencherman, and when the food arrived, her recollection was confirmed, for he took only a little fruit. To her own surprise, Miriam discovered she was famished. He watched her silently while she consumed an interesting mixture of grains and nuts, several orange segments, a pear, some figs, and a little steamed fish. When she had finished he remarked admiringly, "At least your experience did not affect your appetite."

"What happened to me?" Miriam asked him.

Pontius walked to the window and drew the curtains back a little further. Framed in sunlight, he was, she thought, almost a striking figure—not overly tall, perhaps, but handsome in the Roman way; and he had the patrician stance. She could imagine him sporting himself liberally with the matrons of Rome. In a moment of sudden insight it occurred to her he could not be very happy in Judaea, isolated from his own kind.

"What happened to you?" he echoed. "To be frank, Miriam of Magdala, I am not sure. One of your Temple priests—a man named Anninaias—was with me in my study for discussions on . . . certain political affairs. As he was leaving, I heard a scream. Naturally I rushed out, and there you were, lying unconscious in the doorway. Anninaias had gone," he added. "I expect screaming women unnerve him."

Memory of the horror flooded back. Miriam felt her eyes widen involuntarily as she sank back on the pillows. "There is a demon in him," she whispered. "A foul thing that has rotted his soul."

Pontius looked keenly at her, then came to sit on the edge of the bed. "So you know about that, do you? I thought it might be a trifle exaggerated—you know how these priests go on—but Anninaias assured me the rabbi was possessed by Shaitan himself."

"The rabbi?"

"The rabbi Joshua. You were speaking of the rabbi, were you not?"

Miriam stared at him in bewilderment. "Not the rabbi— Anninaias! He is an abomination!" Like me, she thought, but at least I fight. I fight it every time. In Anninaias she sensed

158

something very different. She sensed a man who had coldly welcomed the corruption for the power it brought him.

"I can't say I took to the fellow myself," Pontius remarked, "but isn't that putting it a little strongly?"

"No!" Miriam said urgently. "There is a demon in him! A foulness! It has eaten his soul and now animates the shell."

Pontius frowned. "This country seems to be overrun with demons. First the rabbi, now, you tell me, this priest. We really have nothing like it in Rome."

She sat up, allowing the bedclothes to slip down from her body in her agitation. "Pontius Pilate," she said, "you must understand—"

There was a small knock on the door, which opened instantly as Corax entered. "Dear boy," he exclaimed, "they tell me you had that Anninaias fellow here last—" He stopped, catching sight of Miriam seated naked in the bed. "Oh, do forgive me, Your Excellency, I had no idea you were entertaining a guest."

Pontius sighed heavily and waved him to come in. "You remember my secretary, Corax, of course."

Miriam tugged the bedclothes up as this tall, stooping man with the perpetually paralyzed expression walked across and gravely kissed her hand. "How very nice of you to pay a call on us," he said. "His Excellency has talked of nothing else since the evening he visited you." He hesitated. "I don't suppose you've brought that little black girl with you?"

Despite herself, Miriam smiled. "I'm afraid this is neither a social nor even a professional call, noble Corax, whatever the appearances." She glanced at Pontius and decided now was as good a time as any to broach the purpose of her visit. "I hoped His Excellency the Governor might be prevailed upon to tell me what he plans to do with the rabbi Joshua."

To her surprise, Pontius groaned. "Not someone else who wants me to execute the rabbi! What is wrong with these people, Corax?"

"I do not want you to execute the rabbi!" Miriam protested. "If anything, I hoped you might release him."

"Ah, now that may be difficult . . ." Pontius murmured.

"His Excellency has many things to consider in relation to the case," Corax put in pompously. "The man has implications beyond the obvious."

She thought she caught a warning look pass from Pontius to

him, but the Governor only said, mildly enough, "What is your interest in the man, Miriam of Magdala? Are you one of his followers?"

"I have friends among them." She was surprised to find that it was at least partially true. She felt a warmth toward Judas that she could not remember ever feeling for any other man.

"But you yourself . . . ?"

"No, I have never met the rabbi, but I have a disease which they tell me he can cure."

Although Corax's face remained immobile, he still contrived to look both startled and concerned. "A disease? Dear lady, not . . . ?" He glanced toward Pontius. "His Excellency . . ."

"Rest assured it is not a socially communicable disease," Miriam told him coldly. But she felt, if anything, amused. There was something about Corax that put him almost beyond the reach of anger.

Pontius Pilate himself seemed less concerned. "He is certainly a healer. I can vouch for that personally." He began to tug the hem of his toga, then seemed to think better of it. "I had a long-standing leg ulcer which he appears to have banished completely."

"Do you plan to release him?" Miriam asked.

He hesitated. "Not at the moment. Not for a little while at least. But you may rest assured he will not be executed. You may rest completely assured of that."

"The man is too valuable," Corax said. "In the opinion of His Excellency."

"In the opinion of His Excellency and of Caiaphas and of Anninaias," Pontius said heatedly. He turned to Miriam. "What happened between you and Anninaias last night?"

"I tried to kill him," Miriam said without thought of consequences.

"Good gods!" Corax exclaimed.

But Pontius only said, "He had much the same effect on my own temper at one point. You say he is possessed by a demon?"

"The priest?" Corax asked. "Possessed?"

"He is rotted," Miriam said. "There is nothing inside him save the thing."

"How on earth can you tell?" Pontius said curiously. "He seemed a trifle sinister to me, I must admit, but I would not have put it beyond that. Are you an expert in these matters?"

160

"I know something of them," she admitted. Could she ask to see the rabbi? The fact that he was in no danger of execution might be good news to his followers, but the fact that he might be imprisoned here at the Governor's pleasure was not good news to her. The full moon would wane, and when the crescent passed out of the sky, the thing would come for her again. Somehow the prospect now seemed utterly unbearable. If she could reach the rabbi, talk to him, he might perform the necessary magic.

The problem, of course, was how to persuade Pontius Pilate to permit it. It came to her abruptly that she did not know how to handle this man. She might stir him, of course, arouse his sexuality. She might move him to anger, even to violence, for that was her practiced art. But to persuade him to take this course of action—that was another matter. For that one needed to stir his friendship. Did this man feel friendship toward Miriam the harlot? It was not a question she had ever been curious about before and she did not know the answer.

"I'm sorry?" she said. He had been speaking and she had not heard.

"I was wondering," Pontius repeated, "if you might like to meet the rabbi—since you say you have not actually done so." He gave her a curiously unreadable glance. "There's something I should like your opinion on."

27

Caiaphas stared at his deputy in astonishment. "You have talked with the Governor?"

"Yes."

I gave you no leave to do so, sir!"

Anninaias shrugged. "When the supreme authority orders, one has no option but to obey."

"The supreme authority," Caiaphas said angrily, "is the Lord God!"

"Ah yes." Anninaias smiled slightly.

"You had no right to neglect your Temple duties, Governor or no Governor."

"Scarcely neglected," Anninaias told him coldly. "A few minutes late, and even that was not occasioned by Pilate but by—" he seemed to hesitate "—an unimportant incident as I was leaving."

"See it does not happen again, Anninaias," Caiaphas snapped. The occurrence disturbed him even more profoundly than he dared show. Anninaias was the archetypal schemer. Heaven alone knew what he might do, closeted alone with a man like Pilate. Caiaphas stared at him with ill-concealed mistrust. A high priest who permitted his ambitious deputy to engage in private political discussions with the Roman Governor was unlikely to remain High Priest for long. Anninaias had always been far too willing to speak on behalf of the Temple, negotiate on behalf of the Temple, and without reference to his superior in any way.

Anninaias shrugged again. "There should be no necessity," he said. The cold eyes locked on Caiaphas's own. "You were correct in your evaluation, Holiness. The Governor has no intention whatsoever of executing the rabbi."

"I know," Caiaphas said irritably. They were seated in the throne room of the Temple palace, but even so, even on his home ground, Caiaphas felt uncomfortable with this man. The problem was that he remained ultimately uncontrollable.

"I supported your own contention that the Temple favored execution."

There it was again! The assumption that he could speak on behalf of the Temple. But the man was cunning—there was no way to question his basic premise. The Temple did not approve of upstart preachers. They were a danger to the established ecclesiastical authority. Caiaphas swallowed gall and nodded. "Thank you."

"Unfortunately, the wishes of the Temple have no influence on him."

"Are you surprised?" Caiaphas asked. "The man is a heathen. He worships pagan gods. Do you expect him to listen to the Lord's Anointed?"

The cold eyes looked thoughtful. "For political reasons, perhaps. In any case he did not. I suggested the populace would not favor the release of the rabbi."

162

"You did? What gave you that idea?"

"The populace will listen to the Temple even if the Governor does not."

"I see. You have decided what line the Temple must take with the people?"

"Not at all, Holiness," Anninaias said smoothly. "That decision was already taken by yourself. I merely echoed it."

It was true. The damnable thing was it was true. The man was slippery as a serpent. Caiaphas said, "So you feel we should incite a mob, do you? Demonstrations in the streets, calling for the rabbi's execution? Threaten bloody revolution, perhaps?"

"I have already mentioned that possibility," Anninaias told him calmly. "The Governor was not impressed."

"Of course he was not impressed! You know how Rome deals with revolutions. The Legions would put down any major insurrection in half a day. And if it was ever discovered we had been involved, the Temple would be razed to the ground. Did you even think of that?" He subsided. "Besides, the rabbi is not important enough for such a dangerous course."

"I disagree," Anninaias said promptly. "The rabbi's following increases daily. It would be a gross mistake to underestimate his potential influence." His eyes wandered thoughtfully toward a window. "However, you are perfectly correct in your estimate of Roman reaction to mob violence. It is one thing to threaten, quite another to attempt to carry out the threat."

"Then what do you propose we do?" Caiaphas asked sarcastically. "What plan of action do you have to influence this noble Roman?"

Anninaias looked at him soberly. "Since Pilate has no ears for the moral authority of the Temple, and no mind to listen to the wishes of the populace, then we must approach the matter more obliquely." He paused, eyes hard. "Through Herod."

"Herod?" Caiaphas echoed.

Anninaias nodded. "Herod has highly placed friends in Rome itself. Pilate will listen. That, Holiness, is the reality of political power."

§28

The head server set down a turkey which had been stuffed with a goose which in turn encased a chicken, a pheasant, a pigeon, and a lark, the whole garnished with larks' tongues and soused in a thick, rich gravy. Serving maids bore haunches of mutton, steaming platters of asparagus, vegetable macédoine, yams imported from Africa, three loaves hot from the oven, a calf's head, cooked complete with eyes and brains, a tureen of soup, several baskets of fruit, and a gallon jug of rich, dark wine.

"Won't you join me?" Herod invited munificently. "There should be enough for two."

Anninaias bowed his recognition of the honor, but said quietly, "Thank you, no, Tetrarch. I have already eaten."

"Pity," said Herod without rancor. His mood had been sunny since the report of the risen Baptist's arrest, and remained sunny now, even when forced to give audience during a meal—a circumstance normally guaranteed to produce a condition close to apoplexy. But then again his visitor was a Temple priest and one had to show some respect for the cloth. He waved the man into a chair. "Some wine at least. An excellent brew—the resin gives it a delightful tang."

"Thank you, Tetrarch," Anninaias said. Slim fingers curled around the goblet stem as a slave-girl poured the wine.

"Well, Anninaias," Herod said bluffly, "how goes it with the Temple?" He generally felt uncomfortable with priests, and this one, the High Priest's deputy, made him more uncomfortable than most. The man was too thin, for one thing. He never seemed to eat. You could never trust a thin man, not entirely. But if thin men were bad, thin priests were worse. You never knew what to talk to them about. No point in talking to them about sex since they didn't have any. And they claimed that serving the Lord put them above politics. This one wasn't even interested in food. The only topic left was the Temple.

"It goes well with the Temple," Anninaias said.

Which seemed to exhaust that subject. Herod reached out for some mutton.

164

"And yet," said Anninaias, "it may be that the Temple needs your help."

He knew it! He knew it! He'd known from the moment this black crow had requested an urgent audience. A priest of the Temple never came anywhere without his hand out. Herod swallowed a mouthful of mutton and said, "I'm afraid I can't manage very much at the moment, Deputy High Priest. The treasury was greatly depleted by the cost of my poor brother's funeral."

Anninaias interrupted him smoothly. "Not money, Tetrarch. Not a donation. Your generosity toward the Temple is little short of an embarrassment to us."

"It is?" Herod blinked, surprised.

"In this instance," Anninaias said, "we seek only your support."

Support? Herod disliked the sound of the word. Support? A request for support could be even more troublesome than a request for a donation. "Support?" he asked, wishing he did not have to ask. The level of his annoyance was rising, spoiling his appetite.

Anninaias, who had only sipped his wine, not quaffed it like any sensible man, set the goblet down. "Is the Tetrarch aware that some of his more superstitious subjects are following a new teacher?"

"Are they?" Herod asked innocently. He had long since learned that when dealing with Temple priests, one gave away nothing. Nothing at all.

"A little hunchback named Joshua ben Joseph."

"Joshua?" Herod murmured thoughtfully. "Joshua ben Joseph. . . ."

"No doubt you will recall him presently," Anninaias remarked coldly, "since I understand men of this type have caused the Tetrarch considerable inconvenience in the past."

"Men of this type?" Herod asked, frowning.

"The Baptist, for example," Anninaias said.

"Ah yes!" Herod sighed. "The Baptist. Yes. Yes, indeed. Inconvenience." He tore a leg from the turkey and took up his own goblet with his free hand.

"The Temple is anxious that no such inconvenience to the Tetrarch should recur."

"You think it might?" asked Herod promptly. "You think this Joshua may prove troublesome?"

Anninaias shrugged. "Perhaps. Who can say? But it is obviously important to nip potential trouble in the bud. Would you not agree, Tetrarch?"

Herod decided to show something of his hand, if only to cut matters short. "This new rabbi won't be giving anybody any trouble. The Governor has arrested him."

"For the present," Anninaias said.

Herod glanced across at him suspiciously. "What do you mean by that?"

"He will trouble no one for the present. As you say, the noble Pilate has arrested him. But when he is freed . . ."

"Freed?" Herod gasped. The thought that the rabbi might be freed had never occurred to him. It came of judging others by his own standards. When the Tetrarch's men arrested someone, he stayed arrested. They threw him in a cell and left him to rot. Which was only as it should be, of course. When people did anything bad enough to get themselves arrested, they deserved to rot. But he had forgotten that Roman customs were different. Now that he came to think of it, the Romans were always arresting people and letting them go again—some perverted notion of justice. He felt fear rising in his stomach and tore off the second turkey leg to still it. Could Pilate be so stupid as to let the man go?

"Indeed, freed, Tetrarch. Sooner or later he must be, under Roman law."

"But they can't let him go!" Herod exploded. "It would be madness." His mind had begun to work at fever pitch. Could he send the man's head round in a parcel to his cell? Perhaps with a short note of apology, regret at the inconvenience, that sort of thing? But Salome would never let him have the head back now, not after the way he had treated her. She'd taken that very badly, very badly indeed. *Sheol* had no fury like a woman scorned. None. None at all. Of course, he might *force* her to give up the head. It would be pleasant to flog the brat until she agreed, perhaps take her afterward to seal the bargain. But then he would have her mother to face. No chance of flogging Herodias, of course. She had her own men, loyal guards inherited from her husband. Start flogging Herodias and he could have a palace revolution on his hands before the third stroke of the lash. What could he do? What could he do?

"I agree," said Anninaias easily.

"You agree with what?"

166

"That it would be madness," Anninaias said, surprised.

"Madness? Of course it would be madness! The man is a rabble-rouser! A Zealot. An enemy of the state. You wouldn't believe the problems he caused me with all his ranting about incest. Herodias could hardly sleep at night, she was so worried."

"Incest?" Anninaias asked. "But was that not John who spoke of incest?"

"Yes. Yes, of course, John. I was momentarily confused," Herod said. "But this new one is just as bad, just as bad. They're both the same, you know. By which I mean to say they're both the same *type*. It's the sun. They sit out in the desert and get too much of the sun. It addles them. Then they march back and upset normal people."

"He is calling himself King of the Jews," Anninaias said.

"He's calling himself *what*?"

"King of the Jews," Anninaias repeated blandly.

"But *I* am King of the Jews around here!" Herod shouted. "This is treason! Wouldn't you say so, Deputy High Priest?"

Anninaias smiled coldly. "Without a shade of doubt I should say this is treason. And the Tetrarch knows the penalty for treason."

Herod rose abruptly from the table and began to stride around in agitation. His meal was ruined now beyond retrieval. "Death!" he screamed. "The penalty is death!" It was the obvious answer. It solved all the problems. No more worry about that damned head. Have him crucified to stop his nonsense. And stake him when he was buried to make sure he didn't pop up again a second time. That would do for John! That would finish the damn Baptist! That would put Herodias and Salome firmly in their places! "Death!" he screamed, a fleck or two of foam forming round his mouth in his excitement. "Death! Death! Death!"

"May I respectfully suggest, Tetrarch," said Anninaias quickly, "that you seek immediate audience with the Roman Governor?"

167

29

It was comforting to have Benjamin at her side again; strange how so much of her self-confidence relied upon his presence. Pilate had granted her wish without a moment's hesitation. He seemed anxious to please her, although why, she could not fathom. He only said he wished to talk with her —possibly at some length—after she had seen the rabbi. With all her experience of Romans, the Roman mind was still difficult to understand.

Miriam walked along a residency corridor, her sandals slapping on the tiles. It was reassuring at least to realize the rabbi was being held in the residency itself, and not the barracks. That fact alone suggested Pilate valued him. As did the fact that he would not permit her to see the rabbi alone. Miriam had fought hard on that point, but the Governor remained adamant. Corax would accompany her, and with Corax would be two armed members of the residency guard. They flanked her now, rigidly upright, as if she herself were a dangerous prisoner. Did Longinus know, she wondered? Did nerves still eat his stomach lest she mention how he had helped her enter the building? It was odd that Pilate had shown no curiosity about how she reached him. She had imagined a governor's first thought must be to question how his security had been breached. But he had asked no questions at all, as if other concerns so preoccupied him that there was room for nothing else in his mind.

"Almost there," Corax remarked cheerfully. "A room in the west wing."

She found herself becoming nervous and uncertain. Was she placing too much hope on this rabbi? He had a reputation as a healer, but her affliction was not medical. Her body and her mind were sound. It was her very soul which had become infected. Had any physician power to heal the soul? Simon the Zealot seemed to think the rabbi could help her. And Judas thought his teacher had talked with God in faraway Bengal. But all the same, Miriam had seen self-delusion in many, many men. She had watched it twist their thoughts and their behavior. And she did not think herself

168

immune. Could the rabbi help her, or was she chasing fantasies? What sort of man was he really? Corax said he was a hunchback. Pilate denied it vehemently. Simon thought him the Messiah. Judas doubted it. She was not even sure of his blood. Some said he was a purebred Jew. Others claimed he was a Roman's bastard. What was the truth of this man?

The wing was much like any other, except that one door was guarded. The soldiers stepped aside at a gesture from Corax. One of their own escort moved forward to open the door. They were inside before Miriam had further time to think.

It was not a single room, but a suite—the man was important to Pilate indeed! She glanced around and despite her nervousness could not suppress a smile. There had obviously been orders given to make the Jew feel at home. As a result, the rooms had been furnished in the Roman idea of Hebrew taste. Gone was the understated elegance, the Roman starkness with the passing hint of luxury which characterized the remainder of the residency. In its place were rugs of sheepskin, hanging mats which appeared to have been woven by desert tribesmen, brazen urns and decorations, furniture ornately carved in darkwood, no fewer than five *menorahs*—one in silver which looked both ancient and extremely valuable—a brassbound scroll chest (for the rabbi's library?), a gong, and a filigree screen. The overall impression was bizarre.

As if catching her thought, Corax murmured, "A little overdone, in my opinion, but the Governor insisted on it. We tried to get a representation of Moses for the household shrine, but alas there was none to be had in the market."

Before she could decide if he was joking, the door closed and a small, robed figure moved out from behind that ludicrous screen to face them from the center of the room.

"My dear sir," said Corax grandly, "you have an important visitor. This beautiful creature is Miriam of Magdala. She brings you good wishes from your followers."

Miriam stared, aware suddenly of the pounding of her heart. She turned to Corax. "May I speak with him alone?"

Although his forehead remained unfurrowed, Corax moved his eyebrows in what might have been a frown. "The Governor's orders, my dear. . . ."

"Do you always follow Pilate's orders, noble Corax?"

"Well no, but—"

"He will do me no harm. That is obvious to look at him. And besides, my servant Benjamin may stay."

"I doubt if Pontius was in the least worried about his harming you," Corax whispered. "Rather the reverse."

She glanced at him in genuine surprise. "Why should I wish to endanger the rabbi? And what could a woman do in any case? Do you see a sword about my waist?"

"No," Corax admitted, "but your servant could tear him limb from limb." He glanced at Benjamin. "He looks the type, if you will forgive my saying so. No, it is out of the—" He stopped, as if a thought had struck him. "But if he is what Pontius thinks he is, an attack could scarcely harm him," he murmured. "And if he is not, then it will not matter if the brute strangles him." He turned to Miriam and gave one of his rare smiles.

"You could remain just outside the door with the guards," Miriam said urgently, not understanding his words, but sensing a change in his mood. "If anything was to happen, you could reach us in moments."

"Indeed we could," Corax agreed. "May I assume you will neglect to mention this to Pontius?"

"My word on it, before the Lord God Adonai."

"Who could resist such a noble oath from such delightful lips," said Corax gallantly. He gestured to the guards and all three of them withdrew.

Miriam turned to find Benjamin moving with a sleepwalker's slowness toward the rabbi. "Benjamin!" she called sharply. "Stay by me!" But he ignored her. She stared in paralyzed panic as he reached out one broad hand toward the rabbi's throat. "Benjamin!" she whispered. The hand moved up to stroke the long, black hair.

"Don't be alarmed," the rabbi said to Miriam. He grinned at Benjamin without a hint of fear. "I think my hair reminds him of a goat he tended. He was a goatherd once, was he not?"

Miriam nodded, wondering how on earth the man had known. She was bewildered by Benjamin's behavior. He seldom did anything unusual of his own volition and had never, so long as she had known him, approached a stranger without a direct command. And why this stranger in particular? She was forced to admit that she was mildly disappointed in the rabbi. He was a small, young man, hardly more than thirty, very dark-skinned and black-bearded. In build he reminded her of the foul priest Anninaias: slender and light-boned. But there the similarity ended. Anninaias had a city gloss about him. This man had the wiry dryness of the desert about him, and the wildness of the desert in particular in his eyes. She had seen such men before. They wandered from time to time into Jerusalem, usually in the wake of a nomad caravan, mystics intoxicated by the desert and by God, sorcerers, full of weird thoughts, preachers living in a world that was not real. She could smell the desert madness he exuded, see the sandstorms reflected in the deep, dark eyes. Was this the man for whom the Governor had set aside a suite of rooms? Old Junius would have been less impressed. He had longer experience of the lunacies bred in Israel.

But did this desert madman know the spells to banish demons?

"Will you sit with me, Miriam of Magdala?" the rabbi asked. "I have a childhood injury which still troubles me from time to time." As he turned, she noticed the slight twisting of the spine—was this what Corax meant by a hump?—which tilted his left shoulder downward. A fall, perhaps? If he came from a poor background, there would be no physicians to cure the results of a childhood fall. And so, she wondered, when the boy became a man did he study the healing arts because of it?

He squatted in the manner of desert men. Miriam chose a chair near him. Benjamin stood by her shoulder, relapsed once more into his familiar immobility. "Why have they arrested you, rabbi?" Miriam asked him quietly.

"I do not know. The soldiers came and took me. I was held for a night in their barracks, then moved here." He glanced around and added with wry humor, "The Governor builds odd jails."

"He does not plan to harm you," Miriam said. "He may keep you here a little while longer, but he has personally assured me you will not be harmed."

He took the news with no great show of interest. "The Roman said you had news of my friends."

"They sent me to find out how you were, how you were being treated. I can now tell them you are in no danger."

"Does Simon threaten to raze Rome to free me?"

Miriam smiled. "Something like that."

"It will come to nothing. The Lord ordains these circumstances."

"The Lord *Pilate* ordains these circumstances," Miriam said, "and I have his word you will not be harmed." Odd how disinterested he seemed.

The rabbi said, "What is your servant called?"

"Benjamin."

"He looks very strong."

"I have him to protect me." Why was she talking of Benjamin? She needed to ask him about the demon spell. She *only* needed to ask him about the demon spell.

"He can do that well, for he walks within the minds of men."

Miriam blinked, not understanding. But now she needed to know about his spells. Corax might return with the guards and end the audience any time. "Rabbi Joshua," she said. "I have been told you have the healing magic."

"Who told you?"

"The Governor himself. And Simon. And Judas."

"It is true."

Miriam leaned forward. "Rabbi, is it also true you have the power to banish demons?"

"Only the Lord God has that power."

There was a hint of evasiveness in his tone. "Judas says you talked with God in India."

He looked toward her thoughtfully. "Many odd things happened to me in India. I walked there, you know, searching for enlightenment."

"Yes, Judas told me."

"My spine was badly deformed. It is still a little twisted, you may have noticed. I met healers in Bengal who worked to straighten it. But they did not entirely succeed, as you see."

What had this to do with demons? What had this to do with God? Was the rabbi even madder than he looked? He sounded far older than his appearance showed, an old man whose thoughts rambled through strange pathways. A heavy disappointment gripped her stomach. This was another desert prophet like the rest. Men believed in him because they needed to believe. Despite her disappointment, she said kindly, "It does not show greatly. It is a small injury now."

But he scarcely seemed to hear her. "As they worked on my spine, they did me a great service. They caused energy to flow along it and infuse my brain. When this happened I saw visions of

172

the worlds beyond the universe." He nodded. "God spoke to me."

So he was not rambling after all! "Did He give you powers?" Miriam asked eagerly.

"All men have powers. Some merely do not recognize them." The evasion again. It showed in his voice and his eyes. Did he mistrust her? She had entered the room in company with Romans, by permission of his jailers. Was there any reason why he should trust her?

Miriam took a deep breath and made the ultimate admission. "Rabbi, I am possessed of a demon."

She waited, almost breathless, not knowing what to expect. He stared at her and as he stared the desert tempests raged and swirled. Eventually he said, "I see no demon in you."

She shivered. "It enters me by night, at the dark of the moon."

He looked away. "Then it must be banished at the dark of the moon."

"Can you work the spell, rabbi?" she asked him desperately. "Can you work the spell if I come to you at the dark of the moon?"

But he did not answer her directly. Instead, he said, "These Romans know little of our customs." He looked around at the ludicrous room. "They brought me here and gave me all this." He smiled. "They gave me water and oil, but no cloth to wash my feet."

His feet? He was thinking of his feet? Had he not heard her? Did he not care? She was infested. The foulness in her was a living thing. She sought his help and all he talked about was feet! Did he wish her to grovel, this desert man? Did he wish her to kneel and plead with him? Miriam sighed inwardly as an ancient coldness reemerged to take possession of her soul. Roman or Jew, rabbi or fool, they were all the same, these men. They saw a woman such as she and wished only her subjection.

"Where is the water and the oil?" she asked.

He gestured only vaguely, but when she searched she found a water jug and bowl, a jar of unguent, smelling of musk and spices. A Roman choice, but all there was. She went to kneel before him, filling the bowl.

"There is no cloth," he said. Nor could she provide one. It did not matter that her robe was finely made, expensive, for there were many more at home and clothes had little value for her. Yet it was too tight about her body to tear easily without first removing it completely. And while she had stood naked before many men, there was something in this man which gave her pause, engendering a small uneasiness. And so the ultimate humiliation. She dipped her long hair in the bowl. "I wash your feet, rabbi," she said softly.

She removed one of his sandals, then the other, and used her hair to wipe away the road dust from his feet. She took the oil and poured it in the hollow of her palms, then began to rub it gently into his skin.

"Dear lady, what on earth are you doing?"

She swung round, startled, at the voice of noble Corax, standing in the doorway now, flanked by his wooden guardsmen. The face was as immobile as ever, but the eyes glittered in amusement.

Miriam realized abruptly she was kneeling before the rabbi, hair dripping on the Oriental rug, her hands caressing his bare feet. She flushed and stood up swiftly. "His feet—" she stammered. "I—"

"Ah yes," Corax nodded. "His feet." He pursed his lips. "But I think I have bent the rules quite far enough. You must come away now."

"A moment more, noble Corax," Miriam pleaded. Her heart, she found, was racing.

"Not even a moment," he said kindly enough. "For one moment leads to another. And one thing leads to another, as even I have discovered from time to time. Bring your servant and we shall go."

He took her arm gently and led her through the door, ignoring her protests. She looked back once and saw the rabbi watching her, smiling a little, warmth and pleasure in his eyes.

And as the door closed, on the outermost edges of perception she heard the cool, clear singing.

But it was not the demon's song.

30

Pontius stormed through the residency, scattering administrators, slaves, and servants like a warship in a fishing fleet. He discovered Corax at last, eating fruit in the long gallery. "Where have you been?"

Corax looked up with a pained expression in his eyes. "Dear boy, you required me to escort the woman Miriam to see our rabbi," he said mildly.

"Oh, yes. Yes, I did." Pontius glanced around. "Where is she now?"

"She has left, noble Pontius. She seemed upset."

"Left? You let her leave?"

Corax spread his hands helplessly. "She was your guest, my dear fellow. I could hardly treat her as a prisoner."

"Dear gods," Pontius moaned, "I wanted her opinion of the rabbi! What is wrong in this place? Why does nobody listen to me?" He rounded on Corax. "Do you know who has been here?"

"Indeed not. My duties as your—"

"Herod!" Pontius interrupted.

Corax's eyebrows climbed a fraction of an inch. "King Herod?"

"What other Herod is there? Arrived two hours ago with his entire entourage. No formal application for an audience. No polite appointment. Unbearable, Corax. These people suffer from delusions of grandeur."

"They believe their god has chosen them," Corax said reasonably. "I expect that is where the trouble starts. All the same, he is a king in his own right."

"He is a king by sufferance of Rome! And I am Rome's representative, gods help me! Am I to be treated like some tradesman, to be called on at all hours?" He began to pace the gallery in agitation. "He waddled into the reception room—Jove, but that man is fat. A mountain of flesh. I've seen thinner hogs in Pompeii. He waddled in, wearing his full regalia. No guards, of course—that isn't permitted, as you know—but a full entourage of slaves and servants. And far too many handsome young Jewish boys among them for my liking. I am no prude, Corax, but the thought of that blubber mountain corrupting fine young men completely turns my stomach."

"Perhaps his belly does not permit him to couple with a woman," Corax suggested.

"His belly will not grow less the way he eats," Pontius told him sourly. "He demanded food. Demanded! Did you know that? Sat himself on a pile of cushions—none of the chairs fit him, of course—and literally demanded food. Said the journey had exhausted him. Four miles from his palace to the residency and he was carried all the way! And not just fruit or a light snack either. Cooked meat. Lamb, to be exact. And insisted his own cooks prepare it!"

"Surely he did not think he would be poisoned in the Governor's residence?"

Pontius waved his hand irritably. "Not poison, you fool—their damned food laws. Naturally I had to permit it. We're not supposed to interfere with their religion unless we have to. Then I had to sit and watch him stuff his stupid face for half an hour before he deigned—deigned!—to say a word about the purpose of his visit!"

"What was the purpose of his visit?" Corax asked curiously.

Pontius's shoulders sagged abruptly and he came to seat himself beside Corax on the bench. "He wants the rabbi crucified."

"Oh," Corax said.

"Do you think that old fool Caiaphas has had a word with him?"

"More than likely," Corax agreed. "These Hebrews listen—even kings—to their priests. Did he say why? Why he wants an execution?"

"Oh, he prattled on about subversion, danger to the state, blasphemy, that sort of thing. I wasn't really listening."

"You should have been, dear boy. He has influential friends in Rome."

"I know," Pontius nodded. "That's what worries me."

"Can you resist a request of this nature?" Corax asked.

"He made it officially."

"Yes, but can you resist it? I mean, you are the Governor—he's only the King."

Pontius turned to stare out through the window. The residency grounds were truly beautiful, lush, well-watered, as expertly tended as any garden of a Roman villa. It would be pleasant, he

176

thought, to become a gardener and spend the remainder of his life persuading plants to grow. The only drawback was that they would have to be Judaean plants. He turned back to Corax. "I could refuse. Certainly I could refuse. As Governor I have that right, in theory. But it really only postpones the matter. If Herod wants to insist, all he has to do is send a message back to Rome. He's been bribing senators on and off for years. Even Tiberius owes him a few favors. Who's going to back me in those circumstances? It isn't even as if he wants to slaughter a Roman citizen—this is one of his own. I'd have a directive for his execution back on the next ship out."

"So it's serious," Corax said.

"Very," Pontius agreed.

"What did you tell him?"

"That I would consider his request. What else could I tell him?"

"Was he satisfied with that?"

"No, of course he wasn't satisfied. He wants a definite answer. I stalled him for a few days, but I'm going to have to make up my mind soon."

Corax stood up. "I don't suppose he would be satisfied to have the rabbi banished?"

"Banished?" Pontius echoed. "What good is that to me? I want him for the Games."

"I was thinking of banishing him to Rome."

Despite himself, Pontius smiled. "You have a devious mind, Corax. But I doubt if it would do. Herod has his heart set on crucifixion."

Somehow Corax managed to look thoughtful without moving a muscle of his face. "Perhaps we can give him what he wants."

"And waste the rabbi? Corax, however much you doubt it now, I am convinced that man is a sorcerer—and better at it than the Chinese dwarf. Caiaphas thinks so. Anninaias thinks so. They should know, shouldn't they? They're priests and religion is the closest thing to sorcery. If I execute the rabbi, I'll never get a chance like this again. It's Rome, Corax," he said heatedly. "Our chance to get back to Rome!"

But Corax waved one hand vaguely. "I would never dream of wasting him, dear boy. I was thinking of stage-managing a crucifixion."

"I don't follow you."

Corax shrugged. "Faking the whole thing. What do peasants like Herod know of modern execution techniques? These people are still at the stage of strangling babies at birth. They're quite uncivilized under the veneer. I doubt Herod, Caiaphas, or Anninaias could tell a real crucifixion from a fake if they helped nail the victim up themselves. All we have to do is satisfy them you've complied with their request, then spirit the rabbi quietly off to Rome and enter him in the Games under a different name. No one would be any the wiser."

"You mean execute him in private?" Pontius asked. "Or pretend to?"

Corax shook his head. "I doubt they would agree to that. Kings and priests always suffer from chronic suspiciousness—it's quite difficult to hold the posts without it. And, of course, traditionally executions have always been public. We would have to have a very good excuse for holding this one in private, and even then I can't think how we could possibly keep the three of them away as privileged observers."

"The priests want him crucified as an example to his followers," Pontius murmured. "Herod didn't mention it, but I expect he will as soon as they remind him."

Corax nodded. "So it must be a public spectacle. Cleverly faked."

"How do you fake a crucifixion?" Pontius asked curiously.

Corax sat down again on the bench, close by Pontius, his voice persuasive with enthusiasm. "Do you know how crucifixion works, dear boy?"

"You nail them up and they die. Eventually," Pontius said. He had never really thought about it.

"No, the precise detail," Corax said. "Do you know why they die?"

Pontius frowned. "Starvation?" he hazarded. Some criminals stayed on their crosses for a week or more. Since they were usually imprisoned without much food for a time before that, he thought starvation, combined with pain and weakness, was probably the answer.

"Not starvation, dear boy—not at all," Corax told him. "I once made a profound study of execution methods—one has to amuse oneself somehow—and I may be something of an expert. The real cause of death is suffocation."

178

"Suffocation?"

"It isn't something you'd think of immediately, is it? All the blood tends to take one's mind off it. But if you talk to an executioner, he'll tell you the secret of a good crucifixion is the angle of the arms."

"Have you talked to executioners?" Pontius asked in creeping distaste.

"Frequently," Corax said enthusiastically. "Utterly charming fellows for the most part. The thing is, when the angle of the arms is just so and the body hangs with the arms at full stretch, it locks the rib cage. The poor man is unable to breathe."

"Then why doesn't he die immediately?" Pontius asked. "How long can you hold your breath? Three minutes? Four at the most?"

"Ah," Corax told him, "but the arms are not at full stretch all the time! You forget the legs are bent before the feet are nailed. In this way, your hardy criminal can push up against the nails to relieve the tightness of his chest. Until his feet get too sore to support him and he sinks down again."

"So that's why they keep bobbing up and down on their crosses," Pontius mused. "I've often wondered."

"And that," said Corax, "is why we break the legs to kill them. Once the support goes, they suffocate in three or four minutes, as you say."

"It hardly seems an easy process to fake," Pontius remarked.

"Oh, but it is!" Corax told him. "You will forgive my saying so, but most people are as ludicrously ignorant of these things as you are. And Hebrews more than most since it is not their own form of execution to begin with—although gods know they enjoy it well enough since we introduced them to it. Now, if I can tell you my plan in detail: the first thing is to nail him through the palms rather than the wrists. The executioner will tell you it has to be the wrists, otherwise he can pull himself free—flesh tears, but a nail through the bone has you firmly fixed. But in this case, of course, we want him to be able to pull free when the time comes—I'm assuming, of course, that the rabbi will be in on our little scheme."

"Naturally," Pontius murmured, fascinated.

"And we will have to treat the feet in a similar fashion. No question of nailing through the ankles as would usually be done. Cross the feet and drive the spike through the instep so that it misses the little bones and once again he will be able to pull free easily when the time comes."

"When the time comes," Pontius said. "You keep saying 'when the time comes.' When is he supposed to get down with all those people watching him?"

To his astonishment, Corax smiled broadly, his eyes actually crinkling in delight. Then his face froze back to immobility. "Ah, this is the most ingenious detail. If you agree to crucify the rabbi, Herod can scarcely object to your setting your own date for the execution."

"No . . ." Pontius said uncertainly, not seeing what Corax was driving at.

"Set it for a Friday!" Corax said.

Pontius stared at him in dawning delight. "The day before their Sabbath! Of course, Corax, of course! They'll all go home at sunset!"

"Leaving us to take him down and spirit him away," Corax concluded triumphantly.

Pontius could not stop grinning. "By the gods, Corax," he breathed, "I think you may have something there!"

THREE

31

"So it's going to happen?"

"The date is set," Judas told her. "An official pronouncement posted this morning."

"Pilate lied to me," Miriam said. "When the rumors started, I did not believe them. He swore to me there would be no execution." She wondered why she felt so disappointed. She had never trusted men before, why now should she have trusted the Roman Governor? Yet she had, and her trust had been betrayed.

They were walking together in the Garden of Gethsemane, a vast public parkland much favored by young lovers, as much on account of its winding pathways and secluded bowers as for the beauty of its plants. The early spring had coaxed flowers and scents almost as profusely as a summer's day. They had walked through flowering juniper, past a rhododendron bank, admired acacia, and scented the sharp citrus tang of verbena. And everywhere the rose of sharon, no less lovely for the fact it was so commonplace. Here, in this place, she could almost forget. She and Judas might be lovers, opened to the beauty of the garden by the flowering of their own emotions. What a strange thought for Miriam of Magdala, to be looking at a man and thinking of him as a lover. They were not lovers yet, but they had grown so close in the past weeks that sharing their bodies was no more than an easy incident that would come when it would come. What a strange thought for Miriam of

Magdala, who had stirred so many men with a single word, a single glance—and despised them every one.

So much had changed. She closed her eyes and listened to the rabbi's song. In her mind, she could still hear it, cool and clear as mountain wine. It soothed her soul like balm.

She was wearing blue, a short robe of light linen. Blue was Pilate's favorite color, judging by his bedroom. Could he not hear the rabbi's song? And if he heard, could he still plan an execution? Would even Romans execute a God? Despite her betrayal, she could not believe Pilate an evil man. Weak in some things, strong in others, cruel certainly, in many ways. But it was a thoughtless cruelty bred of his time and his culture, and a far cry from evil. She had met evil and she knew its smell. None of that foul scent clung to Judaea's Governor.

There was, she knew, a great deal she did not understand. There were things beyond her comprehension, as the loathsome thing which once invaded her had been beyond her comprehension. She shuddered at the memory, even though it no longer touched her now. The dark of the moon had come and gone without so much as a hint of that foul singing. Banished. Gone from her completely, without rituals or spells. Driven from her by the rabbi's presence in the moments of their single meeting. Yet he had told her the thing could only be exorcised at the dark moon. Did he not realize the extent of his own powers? The man who talked to God had still retained his pristine innocence.

She felt clean. For the first time in years she felt really clean. She had always bathed her body after each encounter with a client and twice a day besides, but not all her oils and unguents had ever washed away the putrid slime the thing left in her soul. Not until now. She felt light-headed, free.

She also felt afraid. "Will his followers do anything?" She was thinking of Simon, with his mad plans of attack and rescue. Not so mad now, perhaps. No risks were too great to save the rabbi.

Judas shrugged lightly. "The group has broken up. The Temple priests have been very active since Joshua was taken, and I suppose they grew afraid." He stopped, glanced up thoughtfully into an olive tree. "He used to call Peter his rock because he was so secure and reliable. Even the Rock has crumbled now." He turned to her. "They have gone into hiding, most of them—I could hardly guess where to find them."

184

"Even Simon?"

"Even Simon. For all his bluster he is out of his depth." He sighed in genuine sorrow. "It will destroy him. He has lived his life pretending to be a man of action. Now when action is needed, he finds it was all a game."

"Are we really the only ones left, Judas?"

"Left loyal? The only ones."

She loved this man with the brown eyes and the pleasant face. That was something else the rabbi had given her, the ability to admit to love. The warmth in her toward him was so strange she hugged it to herself in the night like a child's toy. Why Judas? She did not know. Even now, they had only been together a few weeks. She had known more handsome men, had certainly known men far more rich and powerful. Yet Judas was the one who touched her. She loved his company, adored his voice, trusted his opinions and his intuitions. Perhaps it was his hands. He had beautiful hands, strong and finely formed. There were soothsayers who claimed to tell a person's character from their hands. Looking at the hands of Judas she could well believe it.

"Judas, do you believe he is the Messiah?"

He shook his head. "No, not the Messiah. Never the Messiah. The prophets say the Messiah will come to lead the Children of Israel out of bondage as Moses led us out of Egypt. He will be a soldier of the House of David, a great military commander. Those will be the days when Israel is strong, strong in the way that Rome is strong. It may take a thousand or two thousand years. Sometimes when I dream at night, I see Israelites fighting, and they are great fighters. In my dreams they fight with fire and chariots of steel. Not even Pharaoh's children can stand against them. The Messiah may come to us in those days, but he is not among us now."

"Then what is the rabbi?"

Judas took her hand and they sat together on a grassy bank. His eyes had darkened, not in anger but in introspection. "The rabbi," he said, "the rabbi is a strangeness. Not something prophets could predict. I don't know what the rabbi is. I met John the Baptist once and thought him completely mad, but Joshua admired him. I cannot understand a man like that."

"But you can love him?" Miriam asked quietly.

"Oh yes. Understanding is not necessary for love, otherwise we could never love at all." He lay back, turning his face upward to the sun, the brown eyes closed. "Do you think a civil servant might be a philosopher, Miriam? Long ago it came to me that the world is very different from the way it seems. It's easy to understand the world, you know, because men make the world and men are simple. They have simple desires and simple motivations. They look for food and shelter, wealth and power, with many children as security for old age. By understanding men, you understand nations, for nations are no more than large collections of men. And yet, when you understand all this, you still do not understand events, for it seems to me there are forces outside the world which reach in to complicate the picture."

"In all your talk you have not mentioned women," Miriam reminded him.

"Nor have I, for it is men who hold the power."

"But every man is born of a woman."

"And trained by her from birth," Judas agreed. "Perhaps that is how the things outside reach in. Women are more in tune with them. They see more easily beyond appearances."

"And the rabbi?" she prompted gently.

"The rabbi comes to us from beyond this world, I think." He sat up suddenly. "Oh, he was born here sure enough. A very mundane birth by all accounts. His mother was in a stable, of all places, when she reached her time. He once told me he could still half remember the smell of manure. But that was only the appearance. Something has reached into that man—perhaps here, perhaps in India, it does not matter—and is using him." He groped for words. "It is as if there were creatures greater than ourselves who play games with events on Earth. They see patterns we do not see. They see the whole when we can only see the part. Most of the time they leave us to our own devices, since however hard we try we cannot really break the pattern. The fastest stream may still run only in its bed. But there may be times which are important to the pattern, times when the thread might break and the work be destroyed. At times like that, those Great Ones from beyond the world must step onto the stage. So they disguise themselves in human bodies and begin to play a part." He smiled suddenly. "Judas the Philosopher."

But Miriam said, "You are right, Judas. It may sound unlikely, but you are right. My demon came from beyond the world." She

186

had told him freely of her demon. It was the first time he had embraced her, protective and gentle as a father to a lonely child. "Sometimes when it was in me, I could see through its mind a little. Its real home was far away—too far even for us to imagine. It existed in the chill black night between the stars. There was no warmth in it, no love, no light. Just ageless putrefaction. That creature was not bred on Earth. Yet it found a way here. It used me, and it is using others now. It has an interest in events on Earth." She looked at him soberly. "It has an interest in the rabbi."

"Strange forces are afoot," Judas remarked. He stared into the sky, as if to discern them there.

"I was foolish," Miriam admitted. "Even knowing what I knew, I did not see it in the rabbi. Not straightaway, at least."

He smiled again. "It is well hidden. You do not expect a great power to reach into a man like that. He's too young and too small and comes from Galilee. What good thing ever came out of Galilee?" He shrugged. "But then you would not expect to find a demon acting through the body of a beautiful woman."

"Or a priest," Miriam said.

He had started to rise, to continue their walk. He stared down at her. "A priest?"

"Anninaias," Miriam told him.

"The Temple deputy?"

She nodded. "The thing corrupts him to the bone."

His startled look was fading, replaced by an expression of dawning comprehension. "They say Anninaias is the real force behind the moves to have the rabbi killed. They say he went to Herod, who insisted Pilate must agree to crucify him. He is the real power in the Temple, you know. Caiaphas is the figurehead, but Anninaias has the power."

"I once met Anninaias in the residency," Miriam said. "He did not expect to see me, so he was unprepared. He was angry with Pilate and had let slip much of his disguise. I could see the demon in his eyes. I could smell it from his body. I could hear its song encircling his mind. God knows, it was all familiar enough to me then, so there was no possibility of a mistake. But I was blind. I did not understand what this meant. I did not even ask to find out why Anninaias called on Pilate. I know now it was to persuade him to execute the rabbi."

"Yes," Judas murmured.

"If I had," Miriam said, "I might have realized at once there was more to Joshua than met the eye. I thought at first he might be mad, as you thought John the Baptist mad. Then I thought him weak. He reminded me of an old man, lost in an old man's dreams. Why should the demon wish to destroy a sorry creature like that? Except that he was not a sorry creature underneath. He was not even closed to me. If I had only had the eyes to see it. But I had not. It was only when the Romans led me out that I heard the singing. It was so lovely I thought my soul would split with joy." She looked at him, wondering if he understood.

"Come walk with me," he said.

That section of the garden was planted on a hillside. They chose a pathway back down into the valley. As they walked, Judas said, "My father was a very holy man. When I was young, he used to tell me tales of war in Heaven. He said that the Lord God strove with Shaitan and Shaitan strove with the Lord. My father said that as long as the war remained in Heaven, the Lord God always won. But sometimes, when the Lord's attention was distracted, Shaitan would creep down to Earth and start the war up again there. When that happened, the Lord was forced to come to Earth as well in order to stop the total corruption of mankind." He smiled at the childhood memory. "I thought it was all a fairy tale."

"And now you're not so sure?"

"Not sure at all. This thing that took you, this thing that controls Anninaias, might be what my father and the priests call Shaitan."

"And the force in the rabbi?" Miriam asked.

Judas shrugged. "Who knows? It seems almost blasphemous to think about it."

"What will you do if Pilate executes the rabbi?" Miriam asked.

"I think once I might have killed myself," he told her frankly. "I spent a long time drifting before I met him. There's nothing like the civil service for drying out your soul. You're secure and comfortable and you have enough to eat, but you can never quite understand why life is so sterile. I used to lie awake at night and wonder if there shouldn't be more to life than this. That was when I started to wonder about forces reaching into the world from outside. But I don't think I really believed it. It was just something to ease away the boredom. Then I met Joshua and it was like a dash of cold water. I started to feel alive again, as if I was doing something with meaning, as if I was involved in something important. Not that I quite understood what, of course, but the feeling was all that mattered. If someone had asked me that question in the first few months, I should have told them I could not live without the rabbi. He was the meaning of my life and I could not face returning to the old ways." He turned to her. "But that was before I met you."

Miriam reached out to take his hand. They walked together in silence into the valley. Behind them somewhere, out of sight, but always within earshot, was Benjamin, perhaps following, perhaps immobile, perhaps staring at a bee or flower. He never left her, but Judas, dear Judas, did not seem to mind. Sometimes he talked for hours to Benjamin, unconcerned by the lack of answers. Just three of them against the awesome power of Shaitan: a gentle civil servant, a former harlot, and a blank-eyed imbecile. She had tried to avoid the thought for days now, but there it was, fully formed. They were caught up in a cosmic drama that took no account whatsoever of their own wishes. They had joined the war in Heaven that was being played out now here on Earth. Behind appearances, the Lord controlled them, like pieces in a convoluted game. Strange to think, but there seemed no escaping it. And yet, what could they do, these three poor powerless souls?

There was still the rabbi. While the rabbi lived, the Lord's song might still be heard on Earth.

"We have to try to stop it, Judas," she said softly.

"The rabbi's execution?" He nodded slowly. "Yes, I know."

32

"I would prefer to stop this altogether," Pontius said. Even from the elevated vantage point of horseback, it looked a foul place for an execution. *Gol-Gotha*, the Place of the Skull, in Hebrew. He could see why at a glance. The hill itself looked stone-dead, a rocky, sterile slope crouched brooding just outside the city walls. The place was riddled with caves and caverns, tunnels, clefts and niches, and the caves and caverns, tunnels, clefts and niches were stuffed full of bleached bones and rotting corpses. Jerusalem had buried her dead here for centuries. The natural rock holes saved the trouble of having graves dug. And what a delightful refinement to execute the criminal classes right here on the hilltop. It gave them the opportunity to reflect on their limited future as they climbed, and the hilltop was a short, downhill journey for the body afterward. A Hebrew refinement, he reminded himself. They had used this place for execution with pious practicality generations before the first Roman soldier set foot across the border. What a race! God's chosen people? God's chosen clowns!

"Indeed, who would not?" Corax agreed. "The problem, dear Pontius, is how to do so."

They had ridden ahead of the entourage and now watched the official line struggle up the hill on foot. Even the residency guard looked depressed by their surroundings. He could see Longinus at their head and even though Longinus had never struck him as a particularly imaginative man, distaste for the burial place was clearly written all across his features. Pontius sighed. Corax was right, of course. All his efforts to stop the farce had failed so far, and now there was so very little time left—the rabbi's execution was set for tomorrow. Inspection of the site was theoretically the Governor's last official involvement. He twisted in his saddle. "Do you think I should go to Herod?"

"Oh, hardly, Excellency. Far below your dignity. Bad enough to have to crawl to a king, but to crawl to a king pig is unthinkable."

"Hardly crawling," Pontius said, piqued. "He's the key to this whole damned business. If I could persuade him to step aside, I could handle the priests, all right. Don't you imagine I could handle the priests?"

"Assuredly, dear boy," Corax said blankly. "They are friends only with the Creator of the Universe. They have no influence in Rome."

"That was my reading of the situation," Pontius mused. "Supposing I ordered Herod to come to me—that would be in keeping with the protocol, would it not?"

"As I recall," Corax said, "you already suggested Herod might care to pay you an informal visit. He seems capable of procrastinating his reply forever."

190

"He doesn't want to see me," Pontius shrugged. "But if I put a little teeth into the invitation . . . an escort of Roman guards, for example?"

"Hardly the best way to put him in good humor," Corax said mildly. "The object, after all, is to persuade him to your cause."

"I wasn't entirely thinking of persuasion," Pontius said. "The man seems beyond rational argument. I was thinking of bribery."

Corax, who was possibly the most ludicrous figure ever to climb up on a horse's back, tugged a linen kerchief from his tunic sleeve and wiped his brow. They were both sweating profusely. The sun here seared in a way it never did in Rome. "Bribery?" Corax asked. "The man is fabulously wealthy."

"Yes," Pontius murmured, "that's the problem." In his palace, which Pontius had taken considerable care never to visit, Herod was reputed to dine (if that was the word) from golden platters.

"The art of bribery," Corax said, "is to seek out that one thing which your victim lusts for most in all the world, then offer it to him."

"And what does Herod lust for in all the world?" Pontius asked.

"I don't know," Corax admitted. He was obviously in one of his more irritating moods.

"Perhaps not Herod," Pontius suggested. "Perhaps the Temple." His horse began to wheel of its own accord, made nervous by the smell of death. What a foul place for an execution. If men must be killed, he had always believed, let them be killed cleanly, in decent surroundings. Here was doubly bad since he had no desire at all to have the rabbi killed, only to make sure he came to no harm. Who could guarantee freedom from harm in a place like this? His horse completed a nervous full-circle, presenting him with a panoramic view of the entire vile neighborhood. If the rabbi had the slightest sensitivity, he would be dead before his cross went up. The horse's revolution had brought him back facing Corax. "The Temple is always anxious for more wealth. The Lord provides, but not abundantly, to judge by the poor mouths of the priests."

"You're not suggesting offering funds to the Temple, noble Pontius?" Corax asked, a shocked note creeping into his voice.

"Yes," Pontius said aggressively. "Yes, I am. The rabbi is a vital investment. It's worth a little gold to me to keep him."

"We will not lose him," Corax said reassuringly.

Pontius snorted. "No, but he may be damaged. I've little faith in your scheme except as a last resort."

"All the same, isn't it going a little far to offer gold to this Hebrew god? That's what you would be doing, you know. Give to the priests in the Temple and this Adonai fellow gets the benefit. Better altars, bigger offerings, richer drapes, more of that disgusting oil. I cannot imagine our own gods would look favorably on it, fair-minded Roman deities though they might be."

It was a point Pontius had not frankly considered. He frowned. "What do you think they would do?"

"Thunderbolts," said Corax seriously.

"Are you sure?"

"I should think so."

Pontius frowned again. "You don't hear of them hurling thunderbolts much nowadays, do you? I haven't heard of it."

"You don't often hear of Roman nobles paying tribute to the Hebrew god either," Corax said. "I can't see them turning a blind eye to that."

"I suppose not." Pontius chewed his lower lip. It was all becoming very difficult indeed.

Although the remainder of their party was still straggling up the rocky hillside well out of earshot, Corax pulled his horse in close and dropped his voice. "I don't see why you're so worried, Pontius. My scheme will work. There's no doubt about it. I have gone over every detail personally with Longinus. He is a most reliable man. Most reliable."

"Who else is in on this?" Pontius asked. The trouble with Corax was that he had no discretion whatsoever. He was quite liable to hire heralds to broadcast the Governor's wishes. Let it be known this rabbi shall merely pretend to die; and this on the Governor's instruction!

"Longinus and one other. A reliable man too—Longinus has vouched for him. One of the guard party."

"Why two, for gods' sake?" Pontius asked. "Isn't it enough to tell Longinus? Damn it, the man is Guard Commander. Surely he could arrange things on his own?"

"It's for afterward," Corax said, "when they take the rabbi down. Longinus needs someone to help him and he does not want the soldier starting to ask questions if he finds the man is still alive."

192

"If?" Pontius asked coldly.

"When, dear boy—I meant to say when. You really are terribly touchy about this whole affair." He coughed. "And the executioner, of course."

"What about the executioner?" Pontius asked sharply.

"Well, naturally," Corax said, "I had to tell him."

Pontius groaned. "Is there anyone in the whole of Judaea who does not know about this, Corax?"

"You exaggerate," Corax said. "How could we avoid telling the executioner? We have to make sure the arms are wrongly angled to leave as little pressure on the ribs as possible. We have to make sure the nails are placed in palms and feet where they do least damage. You can't do that without the executioner's cooperation. As a matter of fact," he went on confidentially, "the man made some very useful suggestions. I did mention before that I've frequently found these executioners quite capital fellows. He really entered into the spirit of the thing. He suggested we use brand-new, freshly polished spikes. Less risk of infection, he says. And since they are perfectly sharp, they may cause a little less pain going in."

"Do you realize what we're talking about?" Pontius asked. "Or have you lost sight of the reality of this situation? We are going to take the rabbi tomorrow and nail him—*nail him!*—hands and feet to a cross of wood. He will have to carry the damn thing up this mountain, because if we try to avoid that it will look suspicious, so he will be fairly well exhausted to begin with. Then we nail him, and whether the spikes go through the wrists or hands, whether they are polished and sharp or old, rusty, and blunt, they *are* going to hurt, probably unbearably. He's going to bleed, Corax—bleed like a stuck pig. Then we're going to let him hang here, in this infernal sun, hour after hour until the Jews go home and Longinus can dismiss the guard—except for this other guardsman you've brought in—and bring him down. He's only a small man, Corax. If that doesn't actually kill him, it should go a long way toward maiming him for life. It could be years before he's fit enough to enter the arena."

"Just why I have been feeding him like a fighting cock. Prime beef, imported wine, oranges. He is strong as a horse now. He will not go up on that cross until tomorrow mid-afternoon. What hour is sunset at this time of year? Around seven. The Jews will start to leave an hour before that. Give the stragglers a short while to clear,

193

then allow Longinus a further interval to bring him down. At very most—at *very* most, dear boy—he will be on the cross for less than three and a half hours. You could survive that length of time yourself, Pontius, and you are not even a sorcerer!"

It was a point. "Do you think his magic will aid him?"

"I have not discussed the question with him—he is rather a taciturn individual, as you may have gathered—but logically one would assume so. What's the point of being a sorcerer if you can't control a little pain? That's all it is, you know, noble Pontius. No organic damage, the arms carefully positioned to allow him to breathe. All he has to endure is a little pain. For less than three and a half hours. How long did your leg ulcer trouble you?"

"Nearly a year," Pontius said automatically.

"There you are then."

The frozen-faced imbecile thought he had proven something. All the same, as he explained it, the possibility of the rabbi's survival did not seem so outlandish. It might be a time before he could walk without a limp, but beyond that . . . And if he turned the healing magic on himself, then even the nail wounds might go in a day or so. "After he is taken down," he said to Corax, "what then? What is the plan then?"

"I told you that, dear boy."

"Tell me again."

Corax sighed ostentatiously. "Only two witnesses will be present, Longinus and his colleague. Or possibly three if the executioner remains to watch. They take down the rabbi and stanch the blood flow from his wounds, possibly give him a little wine to refresh him and dull the pain. Then they wrap him in a woman's cloak—this is very important as a means of disguise —and take him directly to the residency. It is highly unlikely that he will be seen, but if he is—I say *if*—it will naturally be assumed this is just another of your Hebrew women."

"My Hebrew women!" Pontius exploded.

"Calm yourself, noble Pontius, the rest are almost within earshot. We will take him to a private room in the residency, where the Greek physician will tend to his wounds and general health."

"You've told the Greek physician?"

"Naturally," Corax said. "If he is to tend to the rabbi, he needed to know in order to prepare his unguents. Have no fear. I have

194

sworn him to secrecy by Zeus Olympus and told him he will be executed if any word of our little scheme leaks out. Once the rabbi is fully recovered, we shall smuggle him on board ship, possibly in woman's guise again, and hence to Rome and your triumph at the Games."

Something Corax had said reminded Pontius of a loose thread in the plan, one he had meant to query long ago. "There is a point. Won't they be suspicious when they return after the Sabbath and find no body?"

"Won't who be suspicious?"

"His family. His friends. His followers. Herod. Caiaphas. That other one who looks like an upright bat—the Temple deputy."

"Why should they be suspicious?" Corax asked. "Longinus will be prepared to swear the rabbi's legs were broken and he died on the Sabbath morning. He will claim we buried him. He can even show them the tomb. The rabbi's uncle donated it. It's not much more than a large cave, really, but the Hebrews will be impressed. Even caves are quite difficult to come by on this hill now—so many of them already used, you appreciate."

"And what," asked Pontius carefully, "if someone wants to see the body? What if someone wants to open the cave and see the body?"

"We can show it to them," Corax said blandly. "One body looks much like any other, especially in a gloomy cave."

For a moment the implications did not sink in. Then Pontius said, "You've procured another body?" Even for Corax it was incredible.

"You surely did not expect me to leave that loophole open? You owe me three *sestertii* for the gravedigger, incidentally."

"I don't suppose you let him know what the body was for, did you?"

"No," Corax said.

Pontius leaned forward on his horse. On the other side of the hill from the official party, he could see two black-robed figures climbing the hill. It was too far away to make out the features clearly, but the taller of the two had the walk of Caiaphas. So they too were making the grisly inspection. How he hated these black-robed priests. On impulse he turned to Corax. "Why did you come here, Corax?"

The frown showed in the voice if not the face. "Because you practically ordered me to accompany you on the official tour of inspection."

"Not here, to this place," Pontius said irritably. "Here to this demon-ridden country. Why did you come to Judaea? You had no reason to. You were well enough liked in Rome. You owed very little money. You are of good birth, so you had a position of sorts. Your seat was reserved for the Games. You had no wife to trouble you. We'd known one another for a good few years, but not so closely that it would have cost you more than a passing thought to wave me good-bye when the ship pulled out of harbor. Why did you request the post as secretary and follow me here into exile?"

Corax stared past him blankly in the direction of the two priests climbing up the hillside. "I was bored with Rome," he said.

33

Caiaphas paused, winded. It was all very well for these younger priests, but it was difficult for a man his age to retain dignity while climbing ground of this type. Boulders everywhere, and the ground that wasn't boulders crumbled underfoot. The entire hillside was honeycombed in caves, many of them dangerously near the surface, and he had a horror of breaking through, plummeting downward into a cavern beneath. But there was no avoiding it. Tradition insisted the High Priest reconsecrate the ground anew each year before the Pesach executions. It was ceremonies of this nature that religion was all about. He glanced up. "Isn't that Pilate on the horse?"

"I believe so, Holiness," Anninaias murmured. He was not even breathing heavily, hardly appeared to be sweating at all despite the heavy raiment. Sometimes the man didn't seem entirely human!

"What is he doing here?"

"Inspecting the site, I should imagine," Anninaias told him. "It is the custom for the Governor to do so before any execution in which he is personally involved."

"Inspecting alone?" Had the man no sense of his position?

"I doubt if he is alone, Holiness. I expect the remainder of his party is hidden from us on the other side of the hill."

"Oh, yes. Yes, of course." He took a deep breath and moved onward several steps before a fierce stitch in his side persuaded him to sit down for a moment on a stone. "We shall remain here and contemplate for a time," he told Anninaias, who bowed his head briefly in acknowledgment.

They remained in silence while the worst pain of the stitch died down. Then he heard the cold voice of Anninaias. "Are you satisfied with the arrangements for the execution, Holiness?"

"Satisfied? Of course I'm satisfied. The Romans know what they're about in this sort of thing if nothing else."

"The Governor Pilate was not anxious to see the rabbi put to death."

"No, he wasn't, was he? But a word in Herod's ear soon sorted that out."

"Perhaps," Anninaias said.

Caiaphas rounded on him with a sudden, flaring suspicion. The man's mind never ceased scheming and plotting, plotting and scheming. "Perhaps?" Caiaphas echoed. "What do you mean by that, Anninaias?"

"Holiness, did you not stop to wonder why the execution date was set for the afternoon of the day before the Sabbath?"

"No," Caiaphas said honestly. "So long as he avoids the Sabbath itself, one day is as good as any other."

"Indeed so," Anninaias agreed. "But is the rabbi's crucifixion not to be a lesson to his followers? Are they not to come and watch their so-called Messiah squirm?"

"I might not have put it in those terms, but you are broadly correct, Anninaias."

The cold eyes swung toward him. "A brief enough lesson, do you not consider, Holiness?"

Under the chill of those eyes, Caiaphas suddenly realized what the man was getting at. "Oh, I see. You mean they'll have to break his legs at sunset?"

"If our reluctant Governor permits the legs to be broken."

197

"But he must. We can't have the rabbi dying on the Sabbath itself. It would be most unpleasing to the Lord."

"Of course," Anninaias said.

They lapsed again into silence. For some reason Caiaphas felt uneasy. Why did Anninaias have this perpetual effect on him?

After a time, Anninaias said softly, "The executioner is Roman."

"Yes, of course he's Roman. The Romans are the experts in crucifixion." He scowled. "Besides, we are not allowed to do it."

"We are not permitted to *order* it," Anninaias corrected him. "There is nothing in Roman Law to say a Jew should not assist at a crucifixion."

"The Romans are better at it, more experienced," Caiaphas said.

Anninaias nodded. "Just so." He paused again, far more briefly this time, before he said, "The Governor's chief secretary has ordered the physician Aristophanes to hold himself in readiness on the day of the execution."

"How on earth did you learn that?" Caiaphas asked in considerable agitation. Anninaias seemed to know far too much about everything for everybody's good. Had he spies in the residency itself?

"Is that important?" Anninaias asked. "You may take it the information is accurate. I thought Your Holiness might assist me in explaining it."

"Well," Caiaphas groped, "I suppose he wants to make sure the man is really dead. A medical opinion."

"Is it not unusual to require a medical opinion, Holiness? One would have thought that after crucifixion there would be little enough room for doubt."

"I'm sure I don't know. I don't attend these things every day."

"Perhaps you are correct, Your Holiness," Anninaias said. "Perhaps it is safe to trust Pilate with this matter."

"Safe to trust—? Of course it's—" He hesitated. Suddenly he felt very old. Should he retire from office, take the Temple pension, and sit back to observe the passing of events as a respected Elder? It was a considerable temptation. He would no longer have to climb this ghastly hill before an execution. He would no longer have to bow and scrape to Governors, no longer have to worry when the next madman would set himself up as a Messiah. He could rest and contemplate the beauty of the Scriptures, read the Torah and the Talmud daily, till the Lord decided on the time to call him home. He took a deep breath. "Look here, Anninaias, what exactly are you driving at?"

Anninaias raised his cold, dark eyes to the figure of the horseman on the hilltop. "Why, nothing, Holiness," he said. "Nothing at all."

§ 34

The house seemed curiously empty without her maids, although the servants proper remained. She still employed a housekeeper, a cook, two footmen, guards, a serving girl, and Benjamin, of course. But the servants were discreet, while the maids had never been, so that their absence was felt. At least by Miriam.

"An impressive establishment," Judas said. He walked over to a small, heroic wall frieze which delicately depicted the Sabine rape, and bent to examine the artist's signature. "Is this genuine?"

"Oh yes," Miriam said.

"I thought he never left Rome, whatever the inducement."

She smiled and took his hand. "I am a very wealthy woman. The wages of sin."

"The rabbi used to say the wages of sin were death. I could never understand that myself."

"I can," Miriam said. "It's very easy to get caught up in this world. After a time you start believing that is all there is. Before you know it, your spirit begins to wither—like your experience in the civil service."

She led him from the hallway to the main reception room. How many men had she entertained here within these four walls? How many cold and violent couplings had begun in these luxurious surroundings? But the demon had left her now, taking with it the bitterness, the chilling arrogance, the blanket hatred of mankind. Only memories remained, and tonight, perhaps, those memories too would be exorcised.

"This is better and better," Judas said admiringly. "Your tastes are Roman."

"Most of my clients were Roman," Miriam told him. She had almost ceased to watch for hints of a reaction, and he gave none now.

"I'll say this for the Romans, they know how to be comfortable without clutter. Is that from Germany?"

"Yes."

"There seems to be a fashion for things Germanic in Rome nowadays. You would imagine they would despise the styles of a captive nation."

"Hardly captive," Miriam said. "The Huns cause them more trouble than any other nation in the empire."

"Even Israel?" he grinned.

"We give them no trouble at all." She sank down on a divan. "I imagine that is why the Hebrew style has never been a Roman vogue."

He came and sat beside her. "Do you think they will ever leave?"

"The Romans? Someday. Not soon. But everything changes. Even Rome cannot possibly endure forever. I suppose someday we shall have the land to ourselves."

"Do you think it will make any difference?"

Miriam glanced at him, not understanding.

"Men like Simon think Rome is the root of all our ills," Judas said. "They think that if we could only somehow throw the Romans out, we would be left with paradise. I used to half believe that too, you know. I suppose all of us were fed nationalism to some degree throughout our childhood. It seemed such a simple solution, very clean and clear-cut. Then, as I got older, I began to doubt. The Romans don't interfere a great deal at a day-to-day level. Whole tribes of Israelites have never even seen a Roman. Did you know that?"

"I had never seen one until the age of twelve," Miriam remarked. "I was brought up in the country."

"There you are," Judas said. "But even in the cities, even in Jerusalem, life goes on much as it would if the Romans were not here. The rabbi always says if you are unhappy, you should look for the cause in yourself, not in other people."

It all came back to the rabbi. He was interwoven in their lives. After a moment Judas said, "Are you nervous?"

"About tomorrow? Yes. Yes, I am."

"So am I," he admitted. "In fact, I'm downright frightened. I have never been much of a man for action. Do you think we can really save him?"

"I am sure of it," Miriam said with far more confidence than she actually felt. But they had to save the rabbi because the rabbi had to be saved. Anything else was utterly unthinkable. She stroked the back of his beautiful hand. "Would it make you easier if we went over what we have to do again?"

"Not really," Judas said. "We've been over it a hundred times."

"And you don't mind my part? With Longinus?"

"No, of course not."

"There will be no feeling to it," Miriam told him, not entirely reassured.

"I know."

"If there was any other way—"

He took her hand and squeezed it fondly. "Miriam, dear Miriam, what's past is past. Let it lie. If I have any real worries, it's Benjamin."

The words surprised her momentarily. Then she realized he could not see Benjamin the way she did. "He is very strong and obedient and utterly loyal. He will play his part, you'll see."

Judas nodded. "I am just afraid he may not understand what is needed from him."

"There is more behind that blankness than you might imagine," Miriam said. And in fact it was true. The mind of Benjamin was a total mystery, but she had ceased to make the mistake of underestimating it. However low his intelligence, he still somehow managed to be where he was needed, to act when he was needed. He obeyed clear orders blindly, like a faithful dog, and sometimes —quite often, in fact—anticipated orders before they were given. In many ways she was happier to have Benjamin to help them in their plan than she would have been with a normal man. At least she had no worries that he might try to follow his own devices. But Judas, with all his sympathy, had not known Benjamin long enough to realize his strengths. She looked into his soft brown eyes and saw the worry there. The rabbi meant more to him even than he had admitted. To divert him, she stood up suddenly. "Would you like a bath before your meal? A proper Roman bath?"

"Have you one here? Have you really?"

"Of course," Miriam said, smiling. "Did I not tell you I was a very wealthy woman?"

"I've never had a proper Roman bath," Judas admitted.

"Then you shall have one now," Miriam told him grandly, "in the proper Roman style."

She had one of the footmen escort him to the *tepidarium* while she changed into a short, white bath tunic of fine linen. When she joined him, he was seated naked on the bench, a towel wrapped around his loins. The steam had made his beard and hair lank and she smiled with pleasure at the sight of him. "It isn't quite so hot as I imagined," he told her.

"This is the cool room. It permits your body to adjust."

"I think mine may have adjusted now."

"Good," Miriam said, "then we will move on to somewhere warmer."

"Will you be all right?"

She smiled. "I am accustomed to it. I seldom bother with this room now."

They walked together through another door. The damp steam heat struck them like a wall. Miriam caught sight of the attendant slipping through the second exit. His job was only to prepare the room, and he had strict orders to leave when they entered. This, Miriam had decided, was to be their night—Judas's and hers. Tomorrow was a different day. Tomorrow belonged to the rabbi. But tonight was theirs, and she would share it with no one, not even her servants.

The attendant had done his job well. The furnace roared fiercely beneath the vast heap of porous stones against one wall. Miriam walked across and ladled on more water from the drum so that steam rose around her like an aureole. "A little warmer now?" she asked Judas.

"It's incredible," he breathed.

"We shall not remain too long the first time," she told him. "I have seen strong men faint clean away from overdoing things the first time."

"I could well believe it." He sat down on the bench, already sweating profusely. The steam blurred the outlines of his body, but she noticed well enough that the muscle tone was firm, the stomach flat. The sight of him produced a pleasurable stirring. An unusually pleasurable stirring.

"How long would a Roman stay in this heat?" he asked.

"Hours sometimes. Half the business of the Senate is conducted in the baths and that can go on for a day at a time."

"Amazing!" Judas said.

"Do you wish to leave? Is it too hot for you?"

"Not just yet," he told her. "It's a remarkable feeling—as if I had never been really clean before."

"Yes, you have that feeling even if you wash before you come in." She came to sit beside him. How strange that she could not seem to get enough of this man, his closeness, his warmth, the faint spice aroma of his body.

As if he sensed her mood, he asked, eyes twinkling, "Do Roman ladies take their baths with Roman gentlemen?"

"In certain circles," Miriam told him blandly.

Judas frowned. "But surely," he said seriously, "the ladies cannot feel much benefit while they retain their tunics?"

Miriam raised a mocking eyebrow. "It would be most improper for a lady to remove her tunic if she bathed with someone other than her husband."

"I should have thought bathing with anyone other than her husband would have been fairly improper to begin with." He sighed. "I am loath to say it, but I doubt I can stand much more of this heat. Is this the finish?"

"Not at all," said Miriam. "The best is yet to come." She took him to an anteroom and wrapped him in a toweled robe, then led him out into the marble hall with its gigantic, sunken tub. "The water is heated," she told him, "but it will feel pleasantly cool after the steam." She waited. When he did nothing, she said, "Come on, Judas—off with your robe."

"I left the towel behind."

"You mean," said Miriam in mock astonishment, "you are naked now underneath that robe?" She began to laugh and tugged the robe playfully until it slipped from his shoulders. He made a single, despairing attempt to cover himself, then jumped into the pool.

When they had both dried off and dressed again, she took him to the little dining hall where—until now—she had always eaten only when she was alone. It was one of the few parts of the house which did not reflect the latest Roman style. Instead, in some unconscious recollection of her childhood, it was intimate and almost rustic. She caught sight of his face as he entered, then asked uncertainly, "Don't you like it?"

"It's beautiful," Judas breathed. "I could tell this was your taste."

"Could you?" she asked delightedly. "Could you really?"

The meal was a success as well. It was so long since she had entertained a member of her own race that she had almost forgotten the food laws. But she had drawn from the memories of her peasant childhood to help the cook create a minor masterpiece of fowl garnished and stuffed with vine leaves, grapes, and sage. The wine was rich and sweet and red, not to her taste at all, but Judas obviously enjoyed it. They broke bread together afterward and ate a little honeyed fruit as a dessert.

"Do you always eat as well as this?" he asked her.

"I scarcely eat at all," she told him truthfully. "I have never had much appetite for food. Some days I make do with just a little fruit, although there are other times when I become quite ravenous for no apparent reason and I consume anything that's put before me. I was hungry tonight."

He was hungry too, although not in the same way. She could see it in his eyes, released by the warmth of the wine, an open longing that reached out to bathe her in a glow of love. "Judas," she said softly.

"Yes, Miriam?" His eyes would not leave her.

"I want it to be tonight."

He nodded. "Yes."

"I want it to be here. Here in this house. Can you understand why?"

"I think so."

She was wearing white, a Grecian gown that flowed in soft folds to her ankles. She stood and led him to the bedroom, her own room where she slept alone and had never entertained a client. Like the private dining room, it was an oddity in this Roman-mannered house, full of the warmth and softness so stylishly denied elsewhere. She stood before him and removed her gown.

And when he took her, it was devoid of all violence, without a single hint of conquest.

35

It was a vile day for an execution, sultry, overcast, and threatening rain. Pontius woke with a headache, as if there might be thunder in the air, although the other possibility was a hangover. He had consumed much wine the night before to dull the nagging worry that something, somehow, would assuredly go wrong. If there was any consolation in the morning, it was that Corax had matched him drink for drink and must thus be suffering at least equally now.

He stood by the window, as naked and uncaring as he had dragged himself from his bed, and stared out gloomily across the residency lawns. Nothing stirred as far as the eye could see, but he could imagine beyond the estate, beyond the guarded walls, Jews by the hundreds pouring into Jerusalem for their idiotic Feast of Passover. He had not yet personally witnessed Pesach, as they called it, but Junius had once described it to him in some detail and it sounded truly dreadful.

Jerusalem was an overcrowded city at the best of times. At this time of year, however, residents welcomed relatives, who poured in from the surrounding countryside on foot, on horse, on donkey, in carts and caravans and even an occasional litter. Since Hebrews could not bear to leave their valuables, they brought them too, clanking bundles of gods knew what, and strings of farm animals, mainly reeking, flea-infested goats. These animals—and a good percentage of the ruder visitors—fouled the streets beyond description. Adding to the odor were the itinerant merchants, who clung to the inflowing crowds like leeches, offering pressed meats, bread, slaughtered carcasses, pots, pans, execrable wine in resinous sacks, and spices. They knew their market well, said Junius, for food was really what the Passover was all about. When the religious observances were completed (or possibly as part of them—the old Governor had not been completely sure) every Hebrew household ate and ate as though they feared starvation might knock on their doors tomorrow. In the main they ate spring lamb, even the poorest among them. Somehow the wholesale slaughter of these inoffensive little creatures had significance before their Lord.

205

The purpose of the whole affair, well hidden in its actuality, was commemoration. At one time in their ludicrous history, the Jews had fallen foul of the Egyptians, who had incautiously decided to make them slaves. Even on his own relatively short acquaintance with the Children of Israel, Pontius could have told the ancient Pharaoh that was a mistake. But after a time he found it out for himself. Pestilence, pollution, and bedbugs followed the Jews into Egypt. On the advice, presumably, of his sanitation department, the Pharaoh turned them loose again.

And the Jews celebrated the event to this very day!

This, thought Pontius, was the problem with a race devoid of history. Rome had her great wars, her battles won, her vassal countries conquered. What had these Israelites to console them? They had won nothing, conquered nothing, achieved nothing. They had come out of a desert and might as well have stayed there. Their god—the only one, apparently, who would have anything to do with them—was so dissatisfied with their behavior that he sat upon a mountain and gloomily dictated childish rules, which the Jews naturally broke at every opportunity. God's chosen clowns, Pontius thought, as he had thought often enough before. Fitting subjects for the Emperor's ape.

He turned away from the window, weighed down with depression, as Corax entered. Would the man never learn to knock and wait for a reply?

"Dear boy," said Corax cheerfully, "what a fine body you have, and no mistake. That penis of yours must be the envy of every Roman husband—and the delight of a good few of their wives. Would that my own poor equipment only halfway measured up."

Pontius waved him to silence and reached listlessly for his undertunic. Somewhere in the night he had totally lost faith that he would ever again pay tribute to Venus between a Roman matron's thighs. "Have you a headache, Corax?" he asked.

"Me? Why no. Seldom felt better in my life. Which is as well, is it not? A busy day ahead of us—and an exciting one. I trust the morning finds you in equally good spirits?"

"The morning," Pontius said, "finds me sick of life, sick of Judaea, sick of rabbis, sick of sorcery, and sick, Corax, of you." He pulled the tunic over his head, blinked twice, and opened the chest which held his official toga. He began to wind it listlessly.

"You will feel better after breakfast," Corax said decisively. "Shall I have them send you up some orange segments?"

"Yes," Pontius said. "Some orange segments." Odd to think that on that fateful day at the Games he could scarcely afford an orange in his own right. Now the residency staff would carry them by the ton if he ordered. And on trays which, if they were not precisely silver, were at least a passable imitation. It was progress of a sort, surely? Yet it did not feel like progress.

But he did, in fact, feel better after eating. The sharp tang of the oranges cut through his thirst and stopped his mouth from feeling like the inside of a sewer. But it did little for the headache, since as he ate, the old recollection surfaced. He found himself reliving, as men do in their minds, an earlier conversation.

"Now tell me," he had said to Anninaias, "when this Shaitan takes possession of a human body, does he retain all his demonic powers?"

And Anninaias had replied, "Alas no, Your Excellency."

Alas no. Not "Fortunately no" or "Thank the Lord no," but "Alas no," as if he were actually sorry this demon Lord of his could not work more evil while in human form.

Alas no. What an odd thing for a Temple priest to say.

36

"He wants to die!" Judas screamed.

He sat up in the bed, eyes wide open and as blank as Benjamin's. Miriam was reaching for him even before she was properly awake. "There, my love," she whispered. "There . . . there. . . ."

"It's part of the plan," Judas said excitedly, staring into worlds she could not see. "He knew they would take him. He usually goes to sleep early, but that night he stayed awake. None of us wanted to stay in the villa, but he was waiting for the Roman soldiers."

"Wake up, Judas," Miriam said quietly. "You must wake up. It's all right, my darling. It's all right."

"Simon wanted to fight them, and so did Peter. Yet he would not let them fight. He went with the soldiers like a lamb. But he knew they were going to kill him. He could see it. *You could see it, couldn't you?*" His head turned as if he were talking to another person, someone standing in the room beside the door. The impression of a presence was so strong that Miriam followed his gaze. There was no one there.

"Judas. . . ."

"You knew the priests would make the Governor kill you. You knew it and you wanted it! You have to die, don't you? It's important to you that you die. . . ." His voice trailed off and life began to return to his eyes.

"It's only a dream, my darling," Miriam said gently. "Only a dream. It cannot hurt you."

His body was trembling and there was perspiration on his forehead, but the breathing was slowing, the wild look dying.

"Only a dream," Miriam repeated. "Only a dream, my Judas."

He turned eventually to look at her. "Miriam?" he said puzzled.

"I'm here, my darling."

"I thought the rabbi was here." He glanced around the bedroom.

"You were dreaming, my love. A nightmare. It's over now."

He sank down on the pillows, half his mind still fascinated by the dream. "He told me he wanted to die." He shook his head. "No, that's not it—he told me he needed to die. What a strange thing to dream."

"You're worried about what we have to do," Miriam said. "But it will be all right. You'll see, it will be all right. We'll save him and we'll take him to a place where Pilate and the priests will never find him."

"He told me it was terribly important that he should die. It was horrible. I saw him crucified. He was all bloody, hanging on a cross, and he was dead." Judas shuddered. "But he was smiling. Even though he was dead and I knew he was dead, he was smiling."

"He won't die," Miriam said soberly. "We'll make sure of that. You and I and Benjamin."

Judas reached for her and they lay close together for a long time without speaking.

208

Then Judas said, "When you met the rabbi, did you talk of India?"

Miriam nodded her head."Yes."

"He once told me of a story he had heard in India. The people there are like the Romans. They believe in many gods. But they venerate one god in particular. The story was that the Earth Spirit asked this god to help her get rid of a plague of demons. So the god decided to be born on Earth as a man named Krishna. Krishna's mother was a virgin, so the Indians are convinced he must have been a god. The story is quite long and I don't remember all the details, but it seems Krishna moved about the country performing all sorts of wonders, so that people came to think of him as a great religious teacher. He spent a lot of his time with ordinary people—the Bengalis told the rabbi he was very fond of milk-maids. He also fought against the demons and killed large numbers of them, but the odd thing was he could not kill the demon king unless he himself died."

"Why not?" Miriam asked.

Judas shook his head. "I don't know."

"And did he die?"

"Yes. That's why I remembered the story. I think the rabbi said his followers nailed him to a tree."

"Oh," Miriam said.

"I was wondering," said Judas thoughtfully, "if the rabbi believes he has to die the same way."

Miriam slid from the bed and went to find her clothing. "The rabbi will not die today," she said decisively. "Not while you and I and Benjamin are here to help him. You can forget your bad dreams and your tales of India, Judas. Tonight we will dine with Joshua."

But beneath her show of confidence, she felt far less certain.

§37

On fine days, which were most days in Judaea, the Roman courts were held outdoors. Pontius sat upright in the Judgment Seat, a chair of such striking discomfort that he often wondered how many accused criminals were condemned for no better reason than pains in the Governor's backside. The noonday sun hung overhead, a relentless orb of brass that showed in hazy outline through the thickening cloud. He could smell the moisture in the air, which made his headache throb even more abominably. There would be a storm soon—in a few hours at most. In the meantime he was forced to suffer a sore head and a sore backside. Such was the fate of the Emperor's ape. Beside him, two boy slaves kept huge leaf fans in constant motion, but the air itself moved sluggishly and though it was less than an hour since he had emerged from a refreshing bath, he now felt sticky and too hot.

Corax emerged from the residency building and picked his way between the rigid lines of guards like some ridiculous, gigantic bird. He bowed formally toward the Governor, then took his seat one level lower than, and a little to the right of, the Judgment Seat. Pontius noticed that he had brought a cushion.

They waited.

The formalities of Roman courts in occupied territories were designed as much to impress the natives as to administer the Law. Before the Judgment Seat and its several subsidiary chairs was a fine, paved courtyard, framed on two sides by an open colonnade. The soldiers, handpicked legionnaires as well as members of the Governor's own guard, formed an immobile military avenue. (How did they bear the heat in armor?) Scribes, heralds, and advocates—although few enough of the latter—also held to their places in the courtyard. They were like stately, dignified splashes of white, since the formal toga was obligatory here.

As they waited, the Temple contingent approached along the military avenue, like a flight of huge slow bats. Ludicrous to wear black in a climate like this, but then Hebrew priests were especially ludicrous. Caiaphas, thought Pontius with some faint surprise, had suddenly begun to look his age. There was more gray in the hair, and much of the snap had gone out of his walk. By contrast,

210

his deputy Anninaias seemed to have grown taller. And more menacing. What was it about the man? A Hebrew without political power, a young man—at least in comparison with Caiaphas—not even at the peak of his religious profession, a nonentity really. Yet menacing. Some men had that inherent quality, of course, irrespective of their social or political position. But Pontius had never seen it quite so strongly marked as it was in Anninaias. And the strange thing was that it seemed to have grown more marked since the last time they met. Then, Anninaias had been a slim, sinister figure. Now, though he was not at all changed physically, the quality of menace hung about him like a cloud.

Behind the High Priest and his deputy were the lesser members of the Sanhedrin. All had a curious standing in the court. Their rights were more a matter of tradition and expediency than of any written canon of Roman Law. Strictly speaking, since they had refused to a man the benefits of Roman citizenship, they should not attend a Roman court of law at all. But within Judaea, the priests had their own courts, the part-civil, part-ecclesiastical legal structures of their own tradition. These courts were administered by Herod—when he could be dragged away from the table—or were so administered in theory, for in practice, except for special occasions and politically important cases, the priests did more or less as they liked. It was the ecclesiastical aspects of these courts which posed the problem, for Rome had a strict policy of noninterference in the religious rites of any native province under her protection. What then was to be done?

It had never been Pontius's problem, thank the gods. The procedure had been long established by the time the Emperor appointed him Chief Ape of all Judaea. For the most part, Rome did nothing. The priestly courts continued as before, meting out whatever punishments they saw fit—including death—the accused in each case was a Hebrew. Purebred Romans could not be tried. Those Hebrews who had accepted Roman citizenship had the option of trial in the Roman court, although most of them, to be fair, accepted the jurisdiction of their own kind. But Rome did not step aside completely. Roman or Jew, citizen or not, there were certain instances in which Rome reserved the exclusive right to act. The Hebrew courts might, for example, behead one of their own kind. But they could not crucify him under any circumstances. That was the sole prerogative of the Roman court.

But since Rome did not wish to appear dictatorial, the ecclesiastical court was permitted to refer an accused to Roman justice, hence exposing him to any penalty the Roman court might care to inflict. And if the Roman court, of its own accord, decided to try a case in which the priests were interested, they had the right of representation at any and all hearings. Furthermore, they were entitled to enter a prosecution case, with any of their number permitted to argue like a Roman advocate. It was a convoluted system and it made Pilate's head ache more severely just to think about it.

Behind the priests trailed their attendants, a motley crowd, thankfully small. They were all freemen since the Hebrew god permitted no slave to a priest. Free or not, none of them was actually paid, but each had the right to certain dues levied on the Temple faithful. These must amount to a substantial sum, judging by their clothing, which was gaudy to the extreme. Pontius considered barring them as unfitting to the dignity of the court, but he knew he would do nothing. The sitting was a mere formality, mercifully short, and he wanted nothing to prolong it.

"Hail to Pilatus, Praefector Supremus of Judaea and the Roman Court therein," a herald called on the High Priest's behalf. A typically slippery Jewish move this: the High Priest avoided public obeisance on account of some obscure Talmudic precept that he was permitted to raise his voice only before the Lord. Pontius gave him the benefit of a stern nod, befitting his present role. Close up, the man looked not merely old, but positively decrepit. Had he taken suddenly to drink or lechery? Pontius could think of nothing else that would produce such dramatic degeneration.

"Advance the prisoner!" the herald called. He was a beefy man with a pronounced Sicilian accent who looked as though the strength had drained from his brains into his throat. Normally Pontius scarcely noticed him. Today every shouted word reverberated through the aching cavern of his skull.

He watched the prisoner approach, dark and wiry, wild-eyed still, but at least somewhat cleaner now than when he was first taken into custody. Pontius noted that Corax had given him a new robe—nothing ostentatious, of course, simply well-laundered linen. The man walked slowly, as if in a dream.

"Advance Joshua ben Joseph of the district of Galilee," that idiotic herald roared.

Corax tilted his head back to whisper loudly, "See how well fed he is? He has gained nearly five and a half pounds. Strong as a horse."

If he had gained nearly five and a half pounds, Pontius could not see where he carried it. But he supposed Corax knew what he was talking about. Not that very much could be done at this late stage in any case. In a moment, Pontius would formally confirm the sentence. By midafternoon, the rabbi would be taking his chances on the summit of Golgotha Hill. If he could stand the pain and loss of blood for a few hours, then he should be up and about again in a matter of weeks—assuming nothing went wrong.

And if something did go wrong? Pontius tried not to think of that. Bad enough if the man weakened and died. In that case Pontius could say good-bye to any real chance of ever getting home. But worse if he survived and the plot was subsequently discovered. Now, there was the real danger. The priests would go screaming to Herod and Herod would go screaming to his bought senators and the senators would go screaming to Tiberius, who had little love for Pilate to begin with. By the time that wheel turned full circle, Pontius could easily imagine himself Governor of a goat herd in Syria or trying to administer some half–mad German tribe. If he kept his head at all! Dear gods, how did he let Corax talk him into these wild schemes? The man's only motivation was relief of his own boredom.

Best get it over with. Too late to stop the process now. "Bring the prisoner to me," Pontius ordered.

"Advance the prisoner to His Excellency," the herald shrieked.

From out of the corner of his eye, Pontius suddenly noticed Anninaias. The priest was staring at the prisoner with such intensity that his dark eyes had grown large and luminous. And he was smiling! His features were contorted into a grimacing mask of glee and malice unlike anything Pontius had ever witnessed before. What was the matter with the man? If one knew no better, one might easily imagine he had a personal ax to grind.

The guards marched the prisoner smartly to the large flagstone beneath the Judgment Seat, then stepped back in a precision movement that left him abruptly isolated. Pontius glanced at him once, then looked away. He disliked holding the man's eye, since something there disturbed him even more profoundly than the aura around Anninaias. To get it over with, he said quickly, "Read the charges."

213

A lector stepped forward, unrolling a scroll. He had one of those plummy, resonant voices that Pontius associated with the undertaking profession. "You, Joshua ben Joseph, late of Galilee in the Province of Judaea, are here accused that you did *unus*—preach and advocate sedition against the established rule of Rome, her Emperor Tiberius Caesar, and his lawfully appointed praefector, Pontius Pilate, Governor of Judaea; *duo*—style yourself Jewish King, or King of the Jews in contradiction to the rights and privileges of Herod Antipas, by grace of Rome and hereditary right, ruler of this province under the appointed praefector, Pontius Pilate, *tres*—blasphemously claim communion with Adonai, the Lord God of the said Hebrew nation; *quattuor*—"

Pontius stopped listening. The charges were formalities, drawn up by Herod (where was that fat pig anyway?) in consultation with Caiaphas and gods alone knew who else, but certainly Anninaias by the looks of him. Whether they were true or not made not the slightest difference. The Temple wanted him dead and could have produced a hundred witnesses prepared to swear he had pissed in their precious Ark had the necessity arisen. It was all formality now, wrapped up and agreed upon.

After a while, the pressing silence told Pontius the lector had stopped. He coughed. "Have you anything to say before I pass sentence on you?" he asked the prisoner. In asking he was forced to look at him. The man looked fevered. Had he caught something? Was he ill? It would be consistent with the recent luck of Pontius if the rabbi survived the ordeal of the next few hours and then keeled over from the plague.

The rabbi stared at him silently.

"In that case," Pontius said, relieved that things were moving speedily at least, "it is my decision that you be taken this day to the execution ground at Golgotha and there crucified in accordance with the Law of Rome until you be dead." *Or until my mad friend Corax prizes out the nails.* He stood up to signify that the proceedings were at an end.

"He must be flogged," a voice said.

Pontius stopped, then turned. The voice had been that of Anninaias, but it was that doddering old fool Caiaphas who had struggled to his feet. "Excellency," he whined, "the point is well made. In charges of this nature, the Canon Law states flogging must precede the execution."

Pontius sat down again, then leaned forward to whisper to Corax. "Is this true?"

"I suppose theoretically, dear—" He remembered the occasion "—your Excellency. But who would have thought they would have pressed for it when they're having him slaughtered in an hour or two?"

"So you haven't made any provisions for this?"

"Not as such," Corax admitted.

"What am I supposed to do now?" Pontius hissed. "Flog him now and he'll hardly be able to stand by midday meal time, let alone survive an afternoon nailed to a beam!"

"I'm sure you exaggerate," Corax whispered. "He's much stronger than he looks."

"If this sort of thing can go wrong now, what's going to go wrong this afternoon?" Pontius asked furiously. "I have a good mind to wash my hands of the whole affair."

"Nothing will go wrong this afternoon," Corax reassured him. "It's all arranged."

"But what am I going to do about the flogging?"

Corax shrugged without turning his head. "You'll have to order it, I'm afraid. It will look too suspicious if you don't."

Pontius straightened. Anninaias was glaring at him—there was no other word for that look. Caiaphas was staring at him, as were the horde of black-robed Temple priests. He felt suddenly as if he had been caught up in something ultimately outside of his control. The sensation was one of an unharnessed chariot which has slipped its blocks, and begins, ever so gently, to roll downhill.

"Flog him!" Anninaias said, his voice holding all the force of a direct order.

"He should be flogged," Caiaphas whined.

The rabbi, at least, ignored them. His eyes were still filmed with a feverish glaze, as if he were drunk or had been chewing some narcotic herb. He seemed unconcerned by what was going on, as if he listened to other voices.

Could any man survive a crucifixion—even an arranged crucifixion—on top of a flogging? The flails had tiny metal beads fixed to their leather thongs. Every stroke dug out little craters of flesh.

"Flog him!" Anninaias repeated. The black-robed priests took up the words like a chant. It grew louder and louder in the sultry air.

It was all getting completely out of control. The chariot was rolling faster now. "Very well!" Pontius shouted. "Flog him if you like!" As he strode past the prisoner he paused to whisper, "You may use your sorcery to dull the pain."

But he doubted somehow if the rabbi even heard him.

⚮38

Only at Pesach was Jerusalem like this.

The crowds seethed in the streets by the thousands. She watched them from the window, Judas by her side. Pilgrims, priests, food merchants, perfume sellers, children, soldiers, farmers, scribes. They mingled and jostled and flowed, noisy as a market square. Animals added to the confusion. The bleating of sheep and goats, the raucous bray of donkeys, the sharp staccato sounding of horses' hooves. Carts rumbled, baggage clanked. Within the confusion, a steady stream moved purposefully in one direction, toward the south gate of the city which led out to Golgotha. A public holiday in search of a gruesome public entertainment.

"There are many of his followers down there," Judas said.

"They go to see him executed," Miriam remarked. She was fascinated, horrified, by the faces. They were excited, happy, alive. Mouths smiled and joked and laughed. If he had followers down there as Judas said, they were followers devoid of sorrow, followers on holiday. Are we so much better than the Romans? she thought sadly. The Romans at least made no pretense. They held their Games expressly for the joy of shedding blood, and called it sport with no more noble claim. The devout Hebrews, commemorating their deliverance, sought their sport too, but pretended it was something else—the sober implementation of the Law, the punishment of theft or blasphemy. Did the judges, Roman and Jew, take account of public needs? There were always crucifixions at

Passover, as long as she could remember. Had they all been strictly necessary, or had the judges merely remembered Pesach, remembered the need for a little public entertainment? In all the years, how many victims had been butchered to make a Hebrew holiday?

"I am afraid," Judas said.

"We will free him—you will see."

"I am afraid of our plan," Judas told her.

She could not blame him. It was a fearsome plan, born of desperation. It would work. In her heart she knew it must work. Yet she feared it too. She dared not let him see her fear, for he was far closer to the rabbi than she would ever be. And if she appeared to weaken, even slightly, the love that Judas bore for Joshua would persuade him to abandon the plan completely. Then the rabbi would die.

There was no alternative. She knew this beyond a shadow of a doubt. If his followers had not deserted him—if his followers were not down there now delighted by the prospect of his blood!—there might have been another way. A score of them perhaps might have created a sufficient diversion for the rabbi to be snatched away. A fast horse waiting could have helped make good his escape. How Simon Zealotes would have loved it! Risky, no doubt. Uncertain, certainly. Yet so clean and direct and full of drama.

But in all Jerusalem she could not find a score of men prepared to risk their lives for Joshua. His followers had fled, all but Judas. Judas, Benjamin, and herself. Just three against the treacherous Pilate, the scheming priests, the Roman Legions, and the screaming crowd. That left no room for direct action of any sort. Only subtlety remained.

Appalling subtlety. No wonder it frightened Judas.

"What do you fear in our plan?" she asked him, knowing well the answer.

"That we may kill him," Judas said.

Was it fair to go on pretending? Miriam recognized her own resilience and her strength. If the demon had done nothing else for her, it had at least made her hard, allowed her to do what had to be done, without reservation, when no alternative remained. But Judas was a free soul too. He had the right to make up his own mind without influence. His love for the rabbi had earned him that, surely. Miriam turned away from the window. Benjamin was squatting by one corner, watching them with blank, brown eyes. "We may kill him," she told Judas softly. "But if we watch and do nothing, that will kill him too."

"You have the—?" He could not bring himself to complete the question.

Miriam nodded, "I have it. I have had it since that day we discussed what to do, in the garden of Gethsemane."

"It didn't seem real then."

"No," Miriam agreed. "But it was real. Then and now."

He was obviously in torment. "Is there no other way?"

If there was another way, her mind could not find it. She said nothing.

"But what if it's too strong?" Judas asked desperately. "Have you ever done anything like this before?"

For an instant she was tempted to lie, but only for an instant. "Judas," she said, "do you remember once telling me how the rabbi raised his friend Lazarus from the dead?"

He nodded. "Yes."

"I did not believe you. That was before I met him, of course, but even if I had known him then, I do not think I should have believed you. It is one thing to heal—there have always been healers, there have even been men who walked and talked with God. But to raise the dead? Is this not a miracle beyond belief?" She hesitated, watching him. "Besides, I knew how it was done."

Judas blinked. "You—I don't understand."

Miriam sighed deeply. "I knew many men in the course of my profession. It's true that most of them were Roman officers, nobles, diplomats. But not all. The only real key to my door was wealth, and certain men grow wealthy in strange pursuits. There was a Roman soothsayer who had amassed a fortune through the accuracy of his predictions and was banished from Rome because of other, less respectable activities. He pretended to work magic. He was a trickster, not a sorcerer. But a very good trickster, and it was he who taught me how to raise the dead." She knew how much this was upsetting him, but she could not stop now. If he was to choose, he had to know it all. "The secret—and you know this secret, Judas—is a very special poison, compounded from hellebore, aconite, and monkshood and several other ingredients I won't pretend to know. Once administered, this compound begins to act on the system within moments. The victim

218

weakens, grows dizzy, faints. In a short time, a very short time, he appears to be dead. There is no trace of a heartbeat, no sign of breathing, and the body grows cold. In an hour—two hours at most—he *will* die. But before that time, despite appearances, he lives. If the proper antidote is administered within this time, he will recover. Poison and counterpoison—this is how my Roman trickster pretended to raise the dead. Judas, you asked me if I had ever used this poison. I have not. You might have asked me if I had ever seen it used. I have not. But I obtained it from my Roman trickster, and I believe this man knows his trade."

Judas came away from the window. His eyes were sunken and his face drawn, as if he had slept little, or had been exhausted by his violent dreams. Yet behind his concern, behind his uncertainty, she sensed a strength in him. Pray God it would carry him through. For the plan was dangerous, so dangerous she sometimes wondered how she had come to conceive it in the first place.

Miriam took his hand. "Judas, if I can reach Joshua before they crucify him and administer the poison, he will appear to die before they have time to nail him on that cross. If we claim the body at once, we have two hours to provide him with the antidote."

"You bought the compound from your Roman?"

She nodded. "Five gold pieces for the poison. A further four for the antidote."

"You trust him?"

God in heaven, how could she answer that? He was a rogue, a banished Roman, a lecher, and probably a good deal more besides. Had he sold her the real poison, or some substitute? Would his antidote counter the effects as he claimed? How often had she taken out the phials and asked herself these questions! And there was no answer, none at all. She could not test the poison, for he had given her a measured quantity, based on her estimation of the rabbi's weight. If her estimate was incorrect by more than five pounds either way, there might be problems. Nothing too dramatic, the man had assured her, but it might affect the timing of the poison. So she worried about her estimate, and she worried about the poison, and she worried about the antidote. Could she trust the Roman? She had trusted Pilate and her trust had been betrayed. Was another Roman likely to be any better? She did not know. But what was worse? Had he sold her harmless fluids which would have no effect at all? In that case they would watch helplessly while the rabbi died in agony on his cross. Had he sold her some other poison which could not be reversed? Then the rabbi would die sooner, that was all. One poison, one antidote. Two fragile vials. How could she know what they contained? "We have to trust him," she said simply.

"Yes, I suppose we do," Judas nodded. But the nagging doubts remained, for he asked almost at once, "If it is too large a dose . . . ?"

"I have the exact dose for a man the rabbi's size"—if she had estimated his weight correctly.

"We have no alternative?" Judas said uncertainly.

Miriam swung to him in sudden, flaring anger. "You tell me if we have an alternative, Judas. Don't leave it all to me. Don't leave me the responsibility. I don't want to bear it alone. I don't want to wonder if I am about to murder him with poison. I don't want to wonder if the antidote is real. Tell me another way, Judas. Give me another plan!"

"I'm sorry," Judas said.

Miriam took a deep breath to regain some semblance of control. "It is almost time," she said. "We should be leaving now."

39

They were like animals. They smelled like animals. They sounded like animals. They behaved like animals. Most of them, Pontius thought sourly, looked like animals. What a race they were, these Jews. God's chosen people acting out their destiny in this Middle Eastern backwater.

Why was one nation so different from another? According to the last census figures, there were almost as many Jews in the world as there were Romans. Both laid claim to history—the Jews actually traced their lineage back to the creation of the world. A Jew had two arms, two legs, two hands, one head. A Roman had the same.

Why was it then that Romans ruled the world and Jews did not? Watching them now, as they milled around the market square, Pontius saw no mystery in the situation whatsoever.

He could not look at the rabbi. The man half hung between two guards, his robe bloody and tattered, his back like raw meat. A vicious flogging. He looked three-quarters dead already. What sort of sorcerer was this who could not even protect himself from a single Roman whip? How long would this carcass last in the arena? One minute? Five, if he had strength to run? There was no magic here, no sorcery. Just one of their god's chosen clowns come out of the desert to upset the other chosen clowns. They had turned on him like wolves and were now in the process of tearing him to pieces. No magic here. If the man had ever been a sorcerer, he was not a sorcerer in the market square.

Strangely, Pontius realized, he no longer cared. Perhaps he had never cared, had never quite believed in the triumphant return to Rome. When all was said and done, the real Games were those men played out in their own heads, like Pontius with his game of the magical gladiator and the winning bet. All fantasy and moonbeams. The reality was here in the market square: a young madman with a twisted spine, exhausted by a Roman whip. He would never stand in the arena, this demented rabbi. He would never hurl thunderbolts at the Emperor's dwarf. He was a crude bone die in games played out by others. The return-to-Rome game played by Pontius. The relief-of-boredom game played by Corax. The stay-in-power game played by Caiaphas. The climb-to-power game played by Anninaias. All games that seemed so serious. But one player at least had set the game aside now and discovered there was real blood on the sand of the arena. Poor Joshua, thought Pontius, what have we done to you with all our games? But at least I can try to save you. Not for your sorcery. Not for the arena. But because—and only because—you should be saved. Call it a gesture to the gods, even a gesture to your gloomy, graybeard god.

The High Priest Caiaphas was on the rostrum, preaching morality to the crowd. His voice rustled like dry leaves. He was visibly dying of old age as if some bat were clinging to him, sucking out the lifeblood from his veins. What had aged the man? What a tragedy the man was. Bad enough to be a bore. To be an old, ecclesiastical bore was ten times worse.

221

"Tell the old fool I wish to address the crowd," Pontius told the ever-present Corax.

"Really, dear boy? What do you plan to say to them?"

"Mind your own business, Corax," Pontius said bluntly.

He mounted the rostrum with a feeling of relief, as if he were taking charge of the situation for the first time. It seemed to him in that instant as if he had not so much been playing a game as that a game had been playing him. Were men played by their games? It did not matter. The play was finished now. Perhaps it was not too late to make amends.

He looked out on the sea of faces. A Roman crowd would have been clean-shaven. These Hebrews were all bearded, even the young men. Black beards, black eyes, long noses, curly hair, and the all-pervading stench of goat. For Pontius at that moment, it summed up all of Israel.

How could he put it to them? There was only one way. He would put it to them bluntly.

"Today," he said as the crowd fell silent, "you celebrate your Passover." He used their own term, Pesach, intermingled with the Latin so that they gave him a ragged cheer. When the noise died down, he raised his voice to make sure of being heard throughout the crowd. "It is customary at this time of year to give you the life of a condemned man. To give him his freedom as your Lord gave your ancestors freedom from the land of Egypt." He paused. "I give you Joshua ben Joseph!"

"The Passover pardon?" Corax asked. He sounded vaguely disappointed.

It was the ending of the game. The rabbi's followers were in the crowd. They could take him and rub salve upon his bleeding back. In a week at most he could be riding for his native Galilee. Rome had tried him and convicted him, and Rome had pardoned him. He might, of course, be tried again. But if he kept his mouth shut, he could live forever.

"Barabbas!"

The name rumbled like a single roll of thunder, a noise that had no right to come from any human throat. Pontius glanced down, startled to discover it was Anninaias who had spoken. Like Caiaphas, the man had changed out of all recognition, even since that morning. His features had coarsened somehow, his mouth widened, his body thickened. But most amazing of all was the change in his voice, for it had dropped now to a raucous bass. But there was no denying its raw power.

"Barabbas!" Anninaias said again, repeating the name of a thief who was also scheduled for Passover execution.

"We want Barabbas!" someone shouted from the middle of the crowd.

"I give you Joshua!" screamed Pontius. He stared at Anninaias with an open loathing, half believing Miriam's theory that this man had a demon in him.

"Barabbas!" Anninaias growled again.

And the name echoed, bouncing to and fro until it was chanted by the crowd.

"Barabbas!" they told him. "Give us Barabbas!"

§40

"I want that man," Pontius said quietly. He felt calm inside and icy cold. They had moved away from the official party and were standing apart in private isolation, protected by Pontius's position as Governor and the impromptu cordon formed by the alert residency guard.

"Want what man?" Corax asked, staring around him blankly.

"The priest," Pontius said. "Anninaias. I want his head." He felt as if something had snapped painlessly inside him. The sensation was peculiar, as if for months he had let all the real decisions fall to other men, but was now quite suddenly prepared to make his own. His emotions were clearly defined. There was a hatred in him for Anninaias stronger than anything he had ever felt before. The man was like carrion, dangerous, troublemaking carrion. Twice he had set himself against Pilate—once by insisting on the flogging, once by blocking the release of Joshua. And that, thought Pontius simply, was twice too much. The time had come to extract payment.

"Are you serious, dear boy?" Corax glanced at his face, then added, "I see you are."

"Have him arrested," Pontius snapped.

"On what charge, noble Pontius?"

"Does there need to be a charge? I am Governor, damn it!"

But Corax said, "I'm afraid there does. The man may be a nasty troublemaker, but he is still second in command at the Temple. If we were to take him now without reason—without good legal reason, that is—the ripples would reach all the way to Rome."

"In that case," Pontius shrugged, "have him quietly assassinated. You can arrange that, surely?"

"Dear boy, this is most unlike you."

Pontius turned to stare at him levelly. "Unlike me, Corax? Yes, perhaps it is. But I have had enough. I never wished to be made Governor of this dungheap. But I *am* Governor, and it looks as though I may have to stay Governor for a long time to come. Since that is so, I plan to make the best of it. I plan to live like a Governor, act like a Governor, and enjoy the privileges of being a Governor. And none of that includes being pushed by a slimy upstart of a Hebrew priest. The man has ambitions beyond his station. He has interfered twice in this business with the rabbi, and I wouldn't be at all surprised to learn he was the one who whispered in Herod's ear to begin with. Caiaphas may be technically the High Priest, but he's a weakling and a fool. What's more, he's getting old. Anninaias is the real trouble. He is the real trouble now and if Caiaphas retires and Anninaias becomes High Priest he will be bigger trouble in the future. Let me put it to you bluntly, Corax. I want him eliminated while the job is relatively easy."

"Assassinated?" Corax said needlessly.

Pontius nodded. "Assassinated."

"It will not be easy to arrange, dear boy."

"Doubtless you are right," said Pontius, "especially since it must be done discreetly. But I have every confidence in your abilities, my friend." He moved off a little way, then stopped. "One more thing, Corax. I want this done quickly. Very quickly."

41

Blood was spurting from the wrists and feet. Three burly Roman soldiers hefted the cross upright, sliding its base into the waiting hole and tamping earth back in with practiced movements of their feet. The man slumped forward, shrieking, but the sound was cut off almost instantly. His head jerked back and even at a distance it seemed as if his lips were turning blue. Then he pushed down on his bloody feet and managed, agonizingly, to straighten his legs. His chest heaved and he screamed again. Someone giggled in the crowd.

Miriam watched, her stomach churning. Was this what they planned to do to a man whose only crime was that he had been touched by God? What sort of world was this that permitted such horror? She was glad Judas was not here to see it. As he watched the crucifixion of the thief, he would have seen only his beloved rabbi on the cross. Even for Miriam the thought was almost too much to bear. For Judas it would have been impossible. But Judas would not see it, would not see the second criminal prepared for execution. Judas waited in the tomb beyond the hill, preparing salves and unguents. Only when he heard the shout of the crowd announcing the arrival of the rabbi would he make his way to the head of the hill and prepare to play his part.

Where was the rabbi?

The execution should have begun. The crowd was here to see it. Two executions were even now taking place. But no sign of the third victim. No sign of Pilate. No sign of Caiaphas or his repulsive, demon-ridden deputy. No sign of Longinus, who had charge of the execution detail. It was already well past the middle of the afternoon, although probably not quite as late as she imagined. The sky had grown dark as if sunset were approaching, but the darkness really came from the thickening cloud. There was going to be a storm. She could feel it in the air, a hot, oppressive weight that squatted on the hill and waited for release in rain.

"Souvenir, lady?"

The peddler was an emaciated, rat-faced man with a country accent, one of the nomad merchants who attached themselves to the crowds of Passover pilgrims. He was festooned in his wares—

225

sacks hanging from his back and wrist, strings of clanking wood and brassware dangling from his shoulders.

"Very cheap, lady," he urged her. "Souvenir of the occasion."

He was holding something out to her, clasped in his grubby hand, pushing it within inches of her face. She stared at him blankly for a moment, then her eyes focused on the thing in his hand. It was a poorly executed carving of a cross, and hanging from it, face distorted, was a tiny wooden figure.

"No," Miriam said.

"Come on, lady," urged the peddler. "You can well afford it. Show people you've been here."

"No," Miriam said again, sickened.

Benjamin stepped between them, his jaw slack. He placed one broad hand on the peddler's chest and pushed. It did not seem a violent movement, but the man reeled backward, tripped, and fell. His wares—ornaments and figurines and carved wooden crosses with their little hanging men—cascaded on the ground. "Here—" he protested in alarm. Benjamin moved forward and kicked him, barefooted, in the ribs. "Come on, lady, I didn't mean offense!" He scrambled to his feet, more frightened than hurt, and ran.

"Thank you, Benjamin," Miriam said. He stared blankly after the peddler for a while, then bent and picked up one of the little crosses the man had left behind. He held it close to his face as he examined it in fascination.

Where was the rabbi? What were they doing to the rabbi?

She had a sudden panic that they might have changed the place of execution. But then she told herself that could not be. Golgotha was the official execution site. Tradition allowed no deviation. Yet it was growing very late. Even allowing for the thickening clouds, the sun was surely dropping toward the horizon. And when the sun set, the Sabbath began. A man might not be executed on the Sabbath. That was the Law. Here, in Judaea, that was even Roman Law.

She glanced around, aware of a certain restlessness among the crowd. It seemed she was not the only one worried about the lateness of the hour. Already one or two were preparing to leave, people who lived a good distance away, and were forced to forego some of their holiday pleasures in order to reach home before the Sabbath began at nightfall. Those who lived closer could afford to

226

stay awhile. But even so, they must be wondering, as she was, about the lateness of the hour. She wished she could see the sun to judge the time more accurately. But the dark clouds were unbroken now, unbroken and ominous.

Miriam was frightened, and becoming more so. Mentally she reviewed her plan again, wondering if she would even have the opportunity to attempt it. The twin phials—such innocent little ceramic bottles by all outward appearances—rested in the pocket of her summer cloak. She herself stood near the foot of the hill, away from the main press of the crowd. Behind her was the south gate of the city, out of which the rabbi and his escort must emerge. Beside the gate, unattended, was the wooden cross they would be using for the execution. He would be forced to carry that cross the whole way up the hill, along the winding execution path that would take him within a yard or so of where she stood.

Except for Benjamin, she was virtually alone now. Apart from a few stragglers, the bulk of the crowd was positioned higher up for a better view of the hanging men. But she had to assume that when the rabbi came, some of them at least would run back down to see him. Then the soldiers would link arms along the path to keep it clear.

For her plan to work, it was important that she reach the rabbi as he began his journey upward. If she administered the compound to him early, he might collapse too soon and be swept away before Judas could play his part. If she left it too late, then he might easily be nailed up before the poison took effect, and once on that cross, his fate was in God's hands, not in hers. So the timing was crucial. If the rabbi collapsed at the summit of the hill, Judas would be there to claim the body, along with members of the rabbi's family, whom he knew well. They did not know about the plan, of course, but she had no doubt Judas could persuade them to take the rabbi at once to his tomb. Where, if all went well, Miriam would be waiting with the second phial.

For so vital a sequence of events, she needed to be certain she could reach the rabbi at the bottom of the path. She needed to be certain the soldiers would let her through. And for that she needed the authority of Longinus. And Longinus was still not here.

"Miriam? Miriam of Magdala?"

She turned, half expecting that the peddler had come back. But it was not the peddler. For a moment she hardly recognized who it was at all. Then he pushed back the hood of his desert cloak and she saw his face.

"Simon Zealotes!"

"Keep your voice down!" he hissed. He glanced around, fearful that anyone had heard her. "The Romans are hunting for us," he said. "They're after anyone who had ever had anything to do with the rabbi. Even you. When I saw you here, I thought I had better warn you."

She turned away from him coldly, in no mood for his games of intrigue. "I thank you, but I am not in danger."

"We're all in danger!" Simon hissed. "When the execution was announced, we went into hiding to make our plans."

Plans? Miriam chilled. "Are you planning a rescue?" This idiot could ruin everything. A half-baked attempt at violence was all that was needed to prevent her from reaching the rabbi.

But he was shaking his head impatiently. "No, not a rescue. That's impossible. Plans for afterward. After the execution!"

Stupidly she repeated, "After the execution?"

"Don't you see?" Simon asked excitedly. "Don't you see what those Roman fools are going to do?"

Bewildered, Miriam said, "They are going to crucify him."

"They are going to martyr him!" Simon corrected her. "It's exactly what the Movement needs! Once he's martyred, if we play things right, half of Israel will flock to our cause. What a sorry day for Rome. There will be Hebrew fighting men on every corner. We have a symbol, a fish, the sign of the new age of freedom. It will fly on our banners as tribute to the martyred rabbi. When they nail him to the cross, this day will mark the beginning of a glorious—"

"Kill him!" Miriam hissed to Benjamin.

"Now just a minute—" Simon protested, his eyes suddenly wary.

"You bastard!" Miriam spat. "All you care about is your infernal Movement! Not the rabbi. Not people. Not anything but your death-and-glory games. You are—"

Simon began to back away as Benjamin advanced. "They're all with me," he protested. "All of them except Judas, who ran away somewhere. We honor the rabbi. He's our martyred Messiah. We call ourselves Joshuans in his memory."

"His memory? The man is still alive!"

228

"We will carry his banner across the whole of Israel and sweep the Romans into the sea. We have support now. They're all with me, all of them the rabbi chose, except Judas, and he'll join when we find him."

"Judas join you?" Miriam sneered. "Judas has been with me, Zealot, and he would not join you if you paid him off in silver."

Despite Benjamin's looming bulk, a sly expression crossed Simon's face. "With you, has he? I've been wondering about Judas. What's he been doing with a Roman's whore then? Maybe it's best if he didn't join us. How long can you trust a man who's been sleeping with a Roman's whore?"

"Kill him!" Miriam hissed again. "Break his back, Benjamin!" She was beyond rational thought, gripped by a fury that swelled through her like an ocean tide.

Simon broke and ran. And as he ran, he called back, "We'll get you for this, whore! You and that traitor Judas! We'll get you!"

Benjamin stopped, uncertain what to do. Miriam shrieked at him again to kill the fleeing man. But her words were drowned by sudden cheering from the mob. She swung round in time to see the execution party emerging from the south gate of Jerusalem. Her eyes locked upon the rabbi. There was blood across his forehead, streaming down his cheeks and into his eyes. His robe was torn and streaked in blood. There was blood on his hands and on his legs. He moved weakly, like a dying man.

42

"He will not survive," said Pontius soberly. Since the flogging, the rabbi's condition had degenerated alarmingly. Already, more than once on the walk, he had reached out to his captors for support.

"He does not look at all well, I admit," Corax agreed. He was as wooden-faced as ever, but his eyes had taken on an expression of genuine concern. "But at least we have delayed things thus far, so he will have even less time than we estimated to endure his ordeal." He glanced at the glowering sky. "I estimate no more than an hour to sunset, possibly less."

"In his condition, I doubt he can survive the shock of nailing. He should never have been whipped." His hands tightened until the knuckles showed white. "That bastard Anninaias!"

"It may be some consolation, noble Pontius, for you to learn that little matter is now in hand."

Pontius glanced at him in surprise. "Already?"

"Already," Corax nodded. "It occurred to me after our discussion that I knew just the man for the job. He has his instructions now and will complete the contract as circumstances permit."

Pontius smiled thinly. He could see the black-robed horror standing near the summit of the hillside. Death could not come too soon to a thing like that. The smile faded as he turned his attention back to the scene at hand. The rabbi was standing alone now, a lost, solitary figure oozing blood. The crowd had seen him and was running cheering down the hill. Two members of the military escort had moved off to one side to drag the huge cross over to the path.

Pontius frowned suddenly. "He won't be required to carry that thing, will he?"

"I believe it may be customary," Corax said.

"Didn't you arrange with Longinus to have somebody carry it for him?"

Corax looked uncomfortable. "I fear, noble Pontius, that with so many other details on my mind, that one may have slipped it."

"He can hardly stand as it is!" Pontius snapped. "Better get across there and tell Longinus to have one of the soldiers carry it."

"Not a Roman soldier—think of appearances."

"Anyone he can find then," Pontius said irritably. "Just as long as the rabbi isn't weakened any further."

Corax bowed formally. "Rely on me to do whatever I can, dear boy."

43

"Longinus," Miriam called gently.

He turned at the sound of his name, staring blankly in her direction. The guards had linked arms along the pathway so that she was half-hidden by their bulk, one face among many in a pressing crowd.

"Longinus," she called again.

His face was lined with strain and his eyes had that haunted look a man gets when his resources have been pressed to the limit. Longinus obviously did not approve of this execution. He saw her at last, and tensed.

"Longinus," Miriam said coolly, "order your men to let me through—I must speak for a moment to the rabbi." She employed her most aristocratic tone and manner and noticed with satisfaction that those around her in the crowd fell back a little.

But Longinus himself turned away!

Miriam fought the sudden, flowering panic. She had come too far to give up now. Always in the past she had been able to control this man. Lord, let her control him now. But in the past, a soft voice whispered, she had controlled him through that snake between his legs. And she had planned to use it again. For her first idea had been to draw Longinus aside, to stir him, to spend a little time with him, making sure beyond all possibility of doubt that he would permit her through. But Longinus had not been at the hill when she arrived. Now he was here with the rabbi, but the execution was about to begin. She no longer had time to stir him, no longer had time to do anything but plead.

Something warned her she must not plead.

"Longinus!" she snapped, her voice like ice.

He turned again, scowling. "No one may come through," he called. "Governor's orders."

"You know full well, sir, that the Governor's orders do not apply to me."

"I don't know that. I don't know anything of the sort."

Two soldiers had dropped the wooden cross beside the path and were dusting their hands together like workmen finishing a job. A small, official group had clustered round the rabbi. In a moment they would force him to begin his walk. If she did not reach him before that happened, his fate was surely sealed.

"Perhaps," Miriam suggested loudly, "you would prefer me to take this up with the Governor himself?"

But to her surprise, Longinus only shrugged. "Take it up with whomever you like. I have my orders."

They had placed the cross across the rabbi's back. Incredibly he remained standing, even took two halting steps. Then he staggered and fell to one knee, half-pinned by the heavy beam. A bored-looking soldier stepped forward to help him back onto his feet. It was going to be too late!

"Ah, Longinus, my dear fellow, so this is where you're hiding." Miriam swung her head at the unmistakable voice. It was Corax, a stork in a toga, yet as welcome as salvation. "The Governor is a trifle concerned about the prisoner's condition, Commander Longinus," Corax said. "Do you thing you could be a good fellow and find somebody to carry that thing for him? Not a soldier, I think—humanitarian considerations must stop somewhere—but if you can find a civilian volunteer . . ."

"Noble Corax!" Miriam shouted. "My servant will carry the cross!"

That ludicrously blank face swung toward her. "Why, Mistress Miriam of Magdala, how delightful to see you. Did I hear you say you could help us?"

"My servant Benjamin," Miriam repeated. "He will carry the rabbi's cross."

"Is that the ugly brute with the shoulders?" Corax asked. "Oh, yes, he should be strong enough." He poked Longinus on his armor-plated chest. "Well come on, man, let the lady and her servant through."

As the soldiers opened up a way, Miriam reached into the pocket of her cloak and separated the two phials. That with the poison was a rounder bottle, little larger than the top joint of her thumb. She curled her hand around it and began, very carefully, very gently, to loosen the cork.

Benjamin moved ahead of her almost eagerly. He seemed to have taken to the rabbi the first time they met and she felt some memory of it might be in him now. Sure enough, he stopped to touch the rabbi's hair, then stared at his own hand curiously when it came away stained in blood. He glanced around at Miriam

232

silently, then moved forward and took the cross, swinging it over one shoulder as easily as if it had been made from balsa. The rabbi's dark, wild eyes swung around toward him. "Thank you, Benjamin."

But if Benjamin heard, he gave no sign. Without having to be told, he started up the winding path. The end of the heavy wooden cross dragged a noticeable furrow behind him in the ground.

She was close enough to touch the rabbi now, her heart pounding. Everything depended on the next few seconds. "Rabbi Joshua . . ."

All his movements—even the simple turning of the head—were painfully slow. But his voice was surprisingly strong when he spoke. "There is a remarkable strength in Benjamin."

Corax was bearing down toward them, and behind him Longinus. Could she do what must be done? Could she do it swiftly, secretly? In her pocket, the cork came free and she stoppered the bottle with her thumb.

"Rabbi Joshua," she repeated loudly, "let me wipe the blood from your face." Without giving him a chance to answer, she pulled a cloth from her cloak, hiding the little poison bottle within its folds. She reached toward him, praying that he might understand, or if not understand, at least trust her. "Drink this, rabbi," she whispered urgently and pressed the bottle to his lips.

∫44

"Wasn't that Miriam of Magdala?" Pontius asked curiously as Corax returned to his side.

"You have the eye of an eagle, dear boy. That's her servant carrying the cross—you remember the odd one who couldn't decide whether to let us in?"

"The sullen brute with strangler's hands? Yes, I remember." How long ago that all seemed now. Long ago and in a different world. He was struck by a sensation of savage unreality, as if he

233

were taking part in some bizarre Greek play. Why had Miriam come here? Why was the rabbi here? Why, for that matter, was Pontius Pilate here? For an instant it seemed to him that no one retained control of his destiny. They had all become actors, playing their parts, unable to deviate from their allotted lines.

"That should help the rabbi conserve his strength, at any rate," Corax remarked with some satisfaction.

But as he spoke, the rabbi stumbled, reeled, and fell.

The crowd pressed forward, roaring. Was it pity? Was it anger? One crowd noise was much like another. Joshua, they might call, and one might hear it as Barabbas. With the huge cross upon his back, Benjamin plodded up the pathway without once looking back.

"Ah good—he's on his feet again," Corax said.

Pontius looked away. "I don't want to watch this," he remarked. What in the world was happening to him? He had seen men bleed and die at every Circus festival. He had cheered with the best of them at Roman triumphs which brought back the severed heads of Huns. Philosophically, he believed suffering was necessary for the development of character—as long as it was someone else's suffering, of course. And he hated these Jews. He hated their looks and their smell and their religion and their customs. He hated their priests. How he hated their priests. Much cruelty, much hate—all rolled together in the soul of Pontius Pilate. But he did not want to watch the suffering of this little madman with the twisted spine.

He turned and signaled to his retinue, then walked without another word to where his carriage waited just inside the city gate.

45

It was working, Miriam thought wildly. Alone beside the execution path, she carefully examined the phial. Empty. He had trusted her. He had taken it.

The crowd, what was left of it, followed the rabbi's progress up the hill. A scene from a nightmare. Benjamin was close to the summit now, carrying that massive cross of wood as easily as if it were a sack of corn. But the rabbi was far behind, walking, staggering alone. Even his guards had drawn away from him, for it was obvious escape was far beyond his power. The back of his robe was brown with blood. There was fresh blood on his face and forehead. He moved like a sleepwalker, like a swimmer underwater. Behind the line of soldiers, the crowd moved with him, oddly silent.

It was growing very dark.

The rabbi fell, but rose again at once. Did he even realize where he was? He started back along the path, but downhill now, going the wrong way. A soldier stepped out to turn him, almost gently. He stumbled on a stone. There were many stones along the execution path.

Would the poison take effect? Every moment brought him closer to the appearance of death, but she could not be certain whether this was the result of the soothsayer's compound, or simple exhaustion. Pilate, brutal, treacherous Pilate, had obviously ordered him flogged. It was the only explanation for the caked blood on his robe. And someone had further lacerated him about the head, exactly how she could not guess. Could any man stand up to such ill-treatment?

He fell again and took a long time to get up. Yet somehow he managed.

Benjamin had reached the top. He placed the upright of the cross into its waiting trench and bodily pushed it erect, a feat that normally required at least two burly soldiers. As the rabbi said, there was remarkable strength in Benjamin.

But there was no strength in the rabbi. He was stumbling almost at every second step. She noticed that he clutched his stomach and realized that the poison must be working in his system.

The crowd had surged ahead. They were waiting for him at the summit now: the silent Jews on holiday, a black-robed figure who could only be a priest, Longinus and his Roman soldiers. Benjamin stood proudly by the towering cross. And though she could not see him, somewhere in that crowd was Judas, the only one who cared, waiting, as only a lover can wait, for the outcome of their desperate gamble.

Somewhere overhead there was the faintest growl of thunder.

235

Two soldiers moved toward the upright cross and made to take it down again. They would need the beams along the ground to nail him on, of course. For a moment she thought Benjamin might try to stop them, but they seemed to be talking to him and he stepped peacefully aside. Once he no longer held it, the cross began to topple since it was not properly supported in its trench. The soldiers grabbed it hurriedly and lowered it gently. Gentle with an artifact of wood, so savage with a thing of flesh and blood.

The rabbi fell again, a few yards from the summit, and this time did not rise. It began to rain, large, warm drops about the size of drachmas, which momentarily marked the ground, but then were swallowed without trace into the dryness of the earth.

For a long time, no one moved. The rabbi had fallen so often that they simply waited for him to rise. But he remained motionless, surrounded by a deathly stillness.

Eventually a Roman soldier moved to prod him cautiously with one foot. Then he knelt and fumbled with the rabbi's robe. His commander, Longinus, began to run toward him. A murmur like a swarm of bees rose up from the crowd. Then suddenly Longinus was shouting orders and more of the soldiers were running down toward the body. The black-robed priest moved forward and stood in silhouette against the skyline. Another thunder roll and the rain began to fall in torrents, scattering the crowd.

At the foot of the path of execution, Miriam of Magdala wrapped her summer cloak around her, then moved quickly off in the direction of the waiting tomb. The rest was up to Judas now. Pray God he moved with speed.

46

The first sharp fury of the rain eased into a steady downpour, trickling over rocks and turning earth to mud. More and more of the crowd broke away to run back down the hill to shelter, but some remained, unmindful of the rain and the nearness of the Sabbath sunset, determined to be there when whatever was to happen happened.

The kneeling soldier turned around to look up at Longinus. "He's dead, sir."

"Dead? Are you sure?"

"No heartbeat, sir. And he isn't breathing."

Longinus knelt and slid one broad hand under the folds of the rabbi's robe at the breast. His face set into hard, rigid lines. As the rabbi lay, his face pressed into a small channel of rainwater which turned red from the caked blood as it flowed. Longinus stood and called back, "Carry him up to the flat ground!" Three of his men ran to obey.

"Is he dead?" someone in the crowd asked.

Longinus said nothing, but the soldier who had touched the body growled sourly, "He's dead all right, as a coffin nail."

"He's dead," the questioner repeated to his neighbor. The word began to pass through the remainder of the sodden crowd.

They carried him the last few yards to the summit and laid him on a flat-topped rock above the encroaching mud. Incredibly, a soldier removed his cloak and draped it respectfully across the body.

"Is there a doctor here?" Longinus called loudly.

In the crowd, a woman began to wail, a high, shrill keening that was abruptly lost in another roll of thunder.

"It's an undertaker he needs now," someone remarked and laughed sharply.

Anninaias stepped forward, his black robes slick with rain. "I have some medical skills, Commander," he said smoothly.

"Have a look at him then," Longinus snapped. He glanced around him almost angrily.

The priest bent to examine the body. In the crowd, the wailing woman suddenly collapsed. "It's his mother!" someone said excitedly. Figures gathered round her and in a moment she was being supported as she half stumbled down the hill.

Anninaias turned, his face impassive. "Joshua ben Joseph is dead."

In the confusion, the Roman military had broken ranks. Judas pushed toward a gap, heart pounding. The rabbi had been so weak, so very weak. How long could he survive the poison in his system? Every second without the antidote brought him closer still to real death now.

Longinus nodded briefly toward Anninaias and mumbled something to himself. He looked at a loss about what to do.

"He's cheated that, at any rate," a soldier remarked cheerfully, glancing up toward the groaning figures of the two crucified thieves.

Judas reached the edge of the crowd. Could he carry it through? Could he persuade them to let him have the body? Could he persuade them quickly?

"Well," said Longinus aloud, "that's put paid to any execution."

Judas felt a hand on his arm.

"Just a moment now, Commander," Anninaias said to Longinus.

"Traitor!" a voice hissed in Judas's ear.

Yet others of the crowd moved away now. It was wet and there would be no execution.

"This man was sentenced as an example to his followers," Anninaias said. "Alive or dead, he should be nailed up on the cross."

Judas jerked his arm. "Let go of me!" he snarled at Simon Zealotes.

"Crucify a corpse?" asked Longinus. He stared with loathing at the Temple priest.

"Do you deny it was the Governor's order?" Anninaias asked him smoothly.

"You betrayed him!" Simon screamed above the thunder roll. "You and that whore bitch Miriam!"

Longinus glanced round. The Governor's party was no longer at the bottom of the hill.

"Crucify him!" Anninaias ordered.

"For God's sake, Simon, let me go! You don't know what you're doing!"

"Crucify him!" Anninaias said again. He was standing close to Longinus. His eyes were large and in them serpents writhed.

"Let . . . go . . . of . . . me!" Judas shouted.

Longinus turned and said something to a soldier. A thunderclap drowned out his words.

"I'm sorry, sir?" the soldier asked.

"Nail him up," said Longinus. "It doesn't matter now."

Judas struck Simon fully in the mouth and jerked his arm free as the man fell back. He whirled and pushed between two Roman guards, then stopped.

The rabbi's arms were stretched out on the cross. The spikes protruding from the wrists were polished and brand-new.

47

Something was wrong. Something was very, very wrong.

Miriam sat on a rock in the gloomy recesses of the cavern and fought a silent battle with herself. She knew she dared not interfere. The job that Judas had to do was delicate beyond comparison even with her own task of reaching Joshua with the poison. He had to take possession of the rabbi's body. He had to convince the Romans that as a follower he was entitled to it. He had to insist, with full authority, that the corpse be carried quickly to its tomb, and carried by Benjamin alone. If he was questioned, he could only play a massive game of bluff. Yet the bluff had to work, for the rabbi's life depended on it.

She looked around the cavern, a deep natural fissure in the rock so dark that even in the daylight she was forced to light a lamp to see. Strange to think of this as a rich man's tomb. And yet it was, despite appearances. They said the burial hill of Golgotha was riddled by a hundred thousand caves and caverns. But the dead of centuries lay in them, so that empty caverns were as rare as marble tombs. A devout Jew might wish to rest with his ancestors in Golgotha, but only a rich Jew could afford the price. Even death bowed before the economics of supply and demand. The rabbi's uncle must have paid a fortune for this family tomb.

It had been readied for the burial, a necessity lest Pilate's men chanced to inspect it. Near the cave mouth lay the burial shroud and wrappings, the funeral jars of oils and preserving balms. But here to the back, on a high ledge that even torchlight would not easily illuminate, were healing salves for the rabbi's wounds, bandages to stanch the blood, and one small ceramic bottle filled with a green fluid which, she prayed, would stop the poison in his system.

Could he possibly survive? She remembered the horror in her stomach when she had first caught sight of him at the bottom of the execution path. The bleeding head and back, the glazing of the eyes. So broken and full of pain. And she had fed him poison in the hope that it might save his life.

It was too long. Judas was taking far too long.

So difficult to judge time here, with nothing more to do but wait within the timeless fissure in the rock. Could the dead sense this stillness? When she was young and still went with her parents to the Temple, the priests sometimes talked of eternity, the state beyond time. Was this stillness a little like eternity? It was so difficult to judge time here. Each minute seemed like centuries. Could she really be certain something had gone wrong?

Fears crawled through her mind like soldier ants. Eventually, despite the danger that she might be seen, she went to the mouth of the cave. The rain had almost stopped and it was dark outside. Then she knew for sure. Something was very, very wrong. She left the cave and began to stumble wildly up the hill.

48

The storm was passing and the rain had eased, but the sun had set and it was almost dark now. Nothing remained of the Jewish crowd. Even the most tenacious of the stragglers had gone to their homes for the ritual feast of lamb. The ranks of Roman soldiers were gone too, probably to less devout pursuits. There was only Longinus and two of his burly legionnaires left of the execution detail. And three corpses on three crosses, two with broken legs, all three hanging still.

The legionnaires were playing dice. Longinus sat apart on a

rock, his head buried in his hands. Judas walked wearily toward him.

"Centurion . . ." he said.

Longinus glanced up.

"May he be taken down now?" Judas asked.

"Are you a Jew?"

"Yes."

"I thought you people had to be indoors by sunset."

Judas shrugged. There was no importance to the Sabbath now. The Lord's authority had passed away from Israel. "May we take him down now?" Judas asked again.

Longinus strained his eyes against the gloom. "Who's that with you?"

"A friend," Judas said.

"Is it the Magdalene's servant? The one who carried the cross?"

"Yes, Benjamin."

"Are you a friend of hers?" Longinus asked.

"Yes," Judas said. He felt weary beyond description. The plan had come so close to working. So very, very close. But though they thought him dead, they still continued with the crucifixion. Once on that cross, poisoned, unconscious, unable to move a single muscle of his legs, he must have died in minutes. But if they had not saved him, at least he had been spared the pain of suffocation.

"She is a very strange woman," Longinus said. "I never thought to see her here. Is she a follower? Has she sent you for the body?"

"Yes," Judas said again, too weary to explain.

"Take the rabbi down," called Longinus tiredly. The soldiers left their dice game and moved to uproot the cross. "Sit down," Longinus said to Judas, gesturing toward a rock. "It's a messy business. They're used to it, but you wouldn't want to see."

Judas sat. No, he thought, he would not want to see. He wanted living memories of Joshua ben Joseph, not the picture of a bloody, broken corpse.

"This is the oddest business I've ever been involved in," Longinus sighed. "Is Miriam a follower?"

"I suppose she is," said Judas. How could he ever tell her that he had failed?

"An odd business," Longinus said again. "Even Pilate didn't want to see him dead."

241

Surprised despite himself, Judas said, "But Pilate was the one who condemned him."

"To please those bloody priests and Herod," Longinus shrugged. "But he never meant him to die. I had my orders to take him down the minute the crowds left."

A sudden chill had taken hold of Judas's heart. "What do you mean?"

Longinus smiled wanly. "Hard to believe, isn't it? Condemn a man and then arrange to save him. But that's the way it was. That's why he arrived so late for execution. We were supposed to nail him up wrong, to give him a chance to last out until the sun was set. Then when the Jews all left, we were supposed to take him down again. It might have worked too, if he hadn't been so weak. Poor sod up and died on us before we had a chance to help him. And then that Temple butcher insisted he be nailed up anyway —properly done through the wrists and ankles, not that it made any difference then." He paused, staring thoughtfully at his feet. "There he was, properly crucified, almost as if it was somehow meant to happen."

Oh God, Judas thought. Oh God, oh God!

One of the soldiers marched up to Longinus and saluted smartly. "All done, sir. We've laid him out on that rock." He pointed.

"Did you cover the face?"

"Yes sir."

"You can go back to barracks now," Longinus said.

"Beg pardon, sir, but what about those two?" He gestured toward the bodies of the thieves still hanging.

Longinus shrugged. "Nobody's interested in them now. You can leave them until morning."

"Yes, sir. Thank you, sir."

Longinus turned back to Judas as the soldiers left. "All ready for you, on the rock. Is there a grave prepared?"

"A tomb," said Judas woodenly. "Quite near here. Benjamin can carry him." He was beyond tears, beyond all sorrow, but not, he found, beyond the all-embracing reach of guilt. The sheer enormity of it almost overwhelmed him. They had killed the rabbi. Between them, he and Miriam had killed him. Without the poison, Joshua would have been crucified. But only for a time. The Romans would have taken him and nursed him when the crowds had gone. He might have lived. He might have lived!

"What's that?" asked Longinus.

Judas realized he had spoken the words aloud. "He might have lived."

"If he hadn't collapsed just then you mean? I suppose he might. But he was very weak. The flogging cost him a lot of blood." He stood up and began to collect his weapons—sword belt, javelin, and shield.

There was sound near the rock where the soldiers had laid out the rabbi's corpse.

"Someone else with you?" Longinus asked sharply.

"No," Judas said uncertainly.

"There's somebody about there," Longinus hissed. The tiredness had fallen away from him and he stood like a hunting dog with every sense alert. "The rabbi had Zealots among his followers, hadn't he?"

"Yes," Judas said. Was it Simon?

"Those bastards are always up to something. Slaughtered a dozen of my best men in an ambush less than a month ago." His hand tightened on the shaft of his spear.

Something was moving on the hillside. But whoever moved had not yet seen them, for there was no attempt at stealth.

"He's over there, by the body," Longinus whispered. "You'd better stay back—this could be dangerous."

Judas fell back almost involuntarily. He could make out nothing in the gloom, but Longinus was poised, his soldier's body straining like a bowstring. Whatever he saw, he did not like. Judas followed the direction of his gaze. Nothing. The flat shape of the rock, the bundle that had once been the living body of the rabbi Joshua. Nothing more. But the sounds were clear enough: small stones moved by someone's feet.

Then he saw it. A slim figure silhouetted against the skyline, bending over the rabbi's body with one hand upraised.

Miriam! It was Miriam! She must have come up from the cave and—

"No!" Judas shrieked.

Longinus hurled his spear.

Judas was running even before he heard the strangled scream. Not Miriam! Not Miriam as well as Joshua!

But it was not Miriam. As Judas reached the rock, he found the black-robed figure of the Temple priest Anninaias slumped across the rabbi's body. His eyes were open, but he was clearly dead. The spear of Longinus had pierced his side.

§ 49

Miriam heard the scream, somewhere to her right. She veered, moving as quickly as she was able. The rain had stopped and the sky seemed to be clearing from the west, but there was no moon and the terrain was rough. She scrambled over a rocky outcrop and suddenly saw the crosses silhouetted against the night sky. Two crosses. Just two crosses!

But if they had not crucified the rabbi, where was he now? And where was Judas?

"Judas!" Miriam called wildly.

"Miriam!"

She spun round. He was close by, but she still could not see him.

"Over here, Miriam!" And suddenly he was beside her, his arms about her. But even in her relief she noticed his body was trembling.

"What happened, Judas? Where is the rabbi?"

She could see his face now, a rigid mask of sorrow. "Miriam, he's dead. The rabbi's dead. Simon—I couldn't—I couldn't stop—" He wept then, huge convulsive sobs that wracked his body.

"What happened, Judas? You must tell me!"

A tall figure was striding toward them through the gloom. "Who is it? Who's there?"

"It's all right, Longinus. It's Miriam of Magdala," Judas called. The appearance of the newcomer seemed to lend him a measure of control.

"What's happened?" Miriam asked again. How could the rabbi be dead? Their plan had worked! Their plan had to have worked!

The rabbi was touched by God and God would not allow their plan to fail.

"They killed him," Judas said. "He fell and they . . . they thought he was dead, but they still nailed him to the cross. I . . . I couldn't stop them."

"It was the priest Anninaias. The priest insisted."

Anninaias! The foul demon-ridden Anninaias! The cold corruption in his soul could not endure the living rabbi. How Anninaias must have hated. To crucify a corpse!

"Anninaias," Miriam whispered. "Spawn of Shaitan."

Longinus reached them. "Miriam? Is it you?"

"It is I, Longinus. Have you crucified the rabbi?"

"He died, lady. The Temple Priest wanted him hung on the cross as an example."

"He could not live," Judas whispered, half to himself. "He could not use his legs to free his lungs. He died there, on the cross."

"Anninaias!" Miriam hissed again. Her oldest enemy. The living vehicle of her demon. Foulness in a human form.

"He won't trouble you again," Longinus remarked.

Miriam looked from one man to the other. "What has happened?"

"Longinus has killed him," Judas said.

"Anninaias?"

"A moment ago. Only a moment ago."

"My spear pierced his lung and his heart," said Longinus with just a hint of pride.

"Why did you kill him?" In her hatred she was actually disappointed. She would have liked Anninaias for herself.

Longinus shrugged, came close to a tight smile. "I thought he was a Zealot planning ambush. It is no matter—the Governor wished him dead."

"Pilate?" This from Judas.

"Pilate planned with him to kill the rabbi," Miriam said.

Longinus half turned away. "I have spoken too freely already."

Something troubled Miriam, some factor she could not quite place. Then it struck her. "The sun has set!"

Judas looked at her. "What is it, Miriam?"

"The Sabbath has begun. A priest would not walk abroad on the Sabbath." But Anninaias was no priest, her mind reminded her: he was Lucifer and Shaitan, Astoroth, Asmodeas, Beelzebub, Lord of the Flies.

"That one would never mind his priestly vows," Longinus remarked, echoing her thought in more prosaic terms.

"But what was he doing here?" Miriam persisted. "Was there no comment when he did not leave at sunset?"

"He left all right," Longinus told her. "He has only just come back."

Priest or demon, why would he come back? The rabbi was dead, the body crucified. Why would he come back? "What was he doing when you speared him?"

"He was by the rabbi," Judas said. "The rabbi's body."

"What was he doing?" Miriam asked again. Then the implications of the words of Judas reached her mind. "The rabbi's body is still here?"

"By the rock, lady. My men laid him out."

"What was he doing to the rabbi's body?" Even though the time to fear had gone, she felt afraid. Beneath the fear, so strange, so deep she could not face it, was excitement.

"Miriam—" Judas began.

"I want to see the body."

"Better not to, lady. It is not pretty."

"I want to see the body," Miriam insisted. She suppressed a rising hysteria to add coldly, "I want to see what Anninaias was doing to the body."

"It's not important," Judas said gently. "The rabbi is dead, beyond harm."

She jerked away from them, tired of argument. A hint of her old sharpness returned. Men were always fools, especially at a time like this. By the time they realized what was happening, she had reached the rock. She pulled back the cloak and looked down on the rabbi's face.

It was peaceful, clear of blood, washed clean by the pouring rain. She could see the cuts for the first time, a band of lacerations round the forehead. But the face was peaceful.

The crumpled blackness that was Anninaias lay beside her feet. Longinus had retrieved his spear, for there was no sign of the weapon. Curiously, Anninaias's face looked peaceful too, as if he had achieved some sort of liberation in the act of dying. She stared at the marble features and found herself thinking he was almost handsome.

Then she saw the stake.

Judas reached her. "Come away, Miriam. I'll call Benjamin and we shall take him to the tomb."

"He brought a stake," Miriam said.

"Stake?" Judas frowned.

She rounded on him excitedly. "Judas, Anninaias brought a stake! See? It's still there by his hand." She stooped and picked it up.

"Miriam—" said Judas.

She gripped his arm. "Don't you understand? Anninaias did not think the rabbi dead! He brought the stake to kill him—to keep him in the grave. It is the Temple way with witches."

"He is dead, my darling. You must try to understand that."

"The antidote!" said Miriam. "We must try the antidote!" She fumbled in the pocket of her cloak, then remembered she had left the phial back there in the tomb. "Judas, we must take him to the cave at once and give him the antidote."

"They crucified him," Judas told her gently. "He hung there on the cross for hours. He could not live."

There was no time for discussion, no time for anything but action. "Benjamin!" Pray God he was near. Pray God this man who never left her should be near now when she had most need of him.

Benjamin appeared, stepping from behind a rock.

"Take him and follow me," called Miriam. She shook off Judas's restraining hand and started down toward the tomb. Behind her Benjamin swept up the rabbi and followed her, surefooted as a mountain goat.

"Miriam!" Judas called out after her.

Longinus had reached the rock. "What is happening, in the names of all the gods?"

She ignored them both as she began to run. Benjamin, she knew, would follow at a steady pace. She stumbled in her haste and grazed her leg, though not seriously. She was seized by a sense of dreadful urgency. She must move quickly. She must find the bottle and administer the antidote. The demon that had looked out from Anninaias's eyes would not make a mistake about the fact of death, for death above all was the demon's province. But it had seen life in the rabbi! Against all reason and all odds, it had seen life. And it had sent its servant, Anninaias, back up the Hill of Golgotha to extinguish that last spark of life with the final, deadly magic of a witch's stake. She must find the antidote and bring it to the rabbi. God would not permit the plan to fail.

She reached the cave and found that the oil lamp had gone out. She wasted precious fumbling moments finding it, wasted more with flint and tinder getting it alight. Shadows danced across the cave wall and a single bat swooped down from somewhere high up near the ceiling. She ran and scrambled to the ledge. A noise behind her. She glanced round and saw that Benjamin had reached the cave. He set the rabbi gently on the waiting shroud, then stepped back and squatted down, staring at him blankly.

She had to hurry. Dear God she had to hurry!

Miriam felt along the ledge. Her fumbling fingers met the jars of salve. But the small ceramic bottle was not there! It was not there! She took a deep breath, forcing herself to be calm. It was where she had left it. She felt again and found it.

As her fingers closed, she heard the demon's song.

⟨ 50

It was slime. It was ordure. It was cesspits of putrefaction. It was the barren emptiness between the stars. It took her like a lover, clinging to her with the stench of rotting meat. Her nerveless fingers dropped the phial and it shattered on the stone floor of the cave.

Miriam screamed in terror, but the scream did not reach her lips. The thing crawled up her spine and stretched out, bloated, pulsing, in her skull.

Miriam ran. She ran through caverns of her mind, along dark corridors, hiding, cringing from that awful foulness. In the moment of her panic, it seemed as if she ran beyond her body, so that she saw herself possessed like Anninaias, saw the thing that walked the world now in the form of Miriam the Magdalene.

She watched and felt her body move.

It controlled her, every nerve and fiber. Infestation had never before been so complete. She crouched quivering in horror as the thing caressed her, decaying tendrils feeding on the wild fear in her soul. In some new way she was linked to it as she had never been before. She could even sense its thoughts, like bubbles oozing from a swamp.

It hated. It was all hate. Hatred for mankind, for love, for life itself. It was denial of the sunshine on a summer's day. It was insects feeding on a corpse. It was the Lord's negation. It was Shaitan.

In the body of the Magdalene, Shaitan laughed.

She saw him then in all his awesome majesty. And he had beauty. Such dark beauty that her heart stood still. He came to her in man's form, tall and upright in his ebony perfection. His eyes were still and cold and cruel, yet so beautiful. He touched her hand and ice-fire flowed within her veins.

"Come with me, Miriam," the Dark Lord said. "Together we have work to do."

Miriam was back inside the cave. She saw the fragments of the phial on the floor and smiled a little. Poisons? Antidotes? What pathetic plans these humans made. They could not see beyond the first skin of reality. They could not sense the drama and the form. They acted in the void of their stupidity, weak fumbling little interferences that made no difference to the cosmic dance. Poison? Antidote? She laughed.

She saw the stake where she had dropped it, lying on the cavern floor. The stake that Anninaias had tried to use, stout wood sharpened to a vicious point. Strange that she could not recall how she had brought it here, yet how inevitable, how destined, that she had. She bent to pick it up.

With stake in hand, she walked toward the rabbi. How feeble he looked now. How weak, how helpless, lying on his shroud. Had he ever really been a danger? This little twisted Jew beset by fears and doubts who dared to interfere with the Principalities and Powers? This creature who dared challenge what he could not understand?

So helpless now. . . .

Miriam slowly knelt beside him, staring down into his face. The grave had claimed him as the grave claimed all men. How easily that one fact was forgotten. All his power was locked now, immobile, rigid as this very corpse. The Earth had washed his face and feet with her soft rain, but could do no more. The Power was powerless.

She saw the wounds along his forehead. The fools had crowned him with a wreath of thorns. How easy it had been to reach them, these bags of offal with their mutilated foreskins. Some thought him God and worshipped him. Some thought him the Messiah and followed him. Some forced the thorns into his skin and jeered that he was now the Jewish King. What imbeciles! What twisting, feebleminded morons! What bloated flies! What worms!

It was the time of the dark moon and his power was strong. This woman was a better vehicle even than the Temple priest Anninaias. She had much beauty and men could seldom see beyond that. She had intelligence and presence and the power of command. How she had fought him all these years! Each time he entered her she fought. But she was his now, his alone. If there had been an error, it lay in his desire to control Anninaias and infest Miriam at one and the same time. A simple matter normally, but at this Time and Age when Forces moved abroad, he had been temporarily distracted. But now, with Anninaias gone, he could afford to give her his entire attention. What a jewel! What a plaything! What a snare for souls this Miriam would make!

She smiled again and clasped the stake in both her hands, raising it above her head to strike.

Her servant Benjamin, squatting immobile, slack-jawed, near the corpse, suddenly looked up. And touched her mind!

Miriam reeled back as if she had been dealt a blow. "Benjamin!" she screamed. But the liquid brown eyes locked on hers and would not let her go. Her body froze, the stake still poised. There was pressure in the air around her, pushing her back and back within her skull.

"Benjamin!" she screamed again.

She was in a strange, familiar place of hills and valleys, corridors and caves, a paradox of moonlight, sunshine, shadow, darkness, blinding light. And Benjamin was with her, face expressive, eyes alert.

"Fight him!" Benjamin commanded.

She saw the awesome Dark Lord reclining as a giant on a hill. She saw the oozing slime of putrefaction swelling out toward her

250

like a tidal wave. No human could fight this! No human could fight this and hope to win!

"Fight him!" Benjamin commanded.

"No!" shrieked Miriam.

A globule of green luminosity detached itself and floated out toward them. Benjamin swatted it with one broad hand as a man might swat a fly. It exploded in a silent burst of corrupt light.

"Fight him!" Benjamin commanded. "The rabbi will give you strength."

"The rabbi is dead!" screamed Miriam.

"The rabbi does not die," said Benjamin, now armored like a warrior of ancient Israel, a David and Goliath all in one, a prince, a king, a Solomon. The slack-jawed imbecile was gone.

"He walks within the minds of men," the rabbi whispered in her ear.

She turned and saw his face. It too had changed.

"He walks within your mind now," the rabbi said. "To help you fight the demon."

"You cannot fight me," Shaitan called, majestic on his hill.

But Benjamin embraced her, filling her with power and love. "Look," he said. "See, Judas has come here to help you."

And she saw Judas, gentle Judas, carrying a sword.

"The demon chose you," whispered Benjamin, "so only you can fight him. But the rabbi gives you strength."

"Who is the rabbi?" Miriam whimpered.

"You know the essence of the rabbi," Judas told her, "for you have seen his face."

"Fight, Miriam!" urged Benjamin.

She took a step, one hesitant step forward.

The universe cracked open. She was on a broad and fertile plain. The Dark Lord stood before her, more beautiful than any creature she had ever seen. He smiled at her and stretched out both his hands. "Fight me, Miriam? Why should we fight? We might be lovers, you and I."

She stared at him, unspeaking.

"Come, Miriam," he told her softly. "You might be Queen of Heaven. With your rare beauty and my power, we might together storm the battlements and rule the universe forever."

"Foul creature!" Miriam spat out. Her body shook with loathing.

The Dark Lord changed into that putrefying thing, that bloated horror of primeval slime. "Fight me then!" it roared. "For I have taken you before, bitch of the human kind, and I will suck you dry again."

It was the ultimate destruction, pestilence and war, rotting corpses from a million graves. It was terror and it oozed toward her like a mountain.

"It is nothing," the rabbi murmured. "It is empty in itself."

But she could not believe it nothing. She could see it, smell it, hear the sucking slime. And yet she did not run. For the first time she saw the thing approach and moved, in horror and reluctance, out to meet it.

The singing enveloped her.

The universe was bursting with the demon's song. Discord and chaos, the pure, shrill call of harmonic evil. It swept her out beyond the plain and into everlasting darkness.

The darkness writhed.

She was alone. There was no Benjamin, no Judas. There was no rabbi with his promises of strength and power. There was only Miriam, frightened, helpless Miriam, alone and isolated in that pulsing darkness.

She was a child again, an infant at her mother's knee. With child's eyes she saw the world's corruption. She saw cruelty and death, meannness, pettiness, and strife. There was no battle, for the Dark Lord had already won. The world was a shell, a golden pomegranate that had rotted at the core. She could not fight a war already lost.

Floating further, deeper, she still fought the darkness.

It was like nothing she had ever experienced before. It was utter evil, the slime demon magnified a thousand, thousand times. It raged around her like a tempest. It clawed at her and strangled her and pressed on her and crushed her to a point no larger than a pin.

The darkness was a Presence, vast as Time. Here was ancient evil, stalking the primeval forest, slithering through grass and swamp. Here was the spirit god of insects, poison plants, and crawling things. Here was the one great Enemy of life on Earth. And it enfolded her.

It is nothing. It is empty in itself.

As the words of the rabbi Joshua reached out from memory, the darkness changed, became a Void. Cold, black laughter echoed through her mind. *See, I am nothing,* it said laughing, *I am empty in myself.* But the Void was drawing her, drawing her in and in and in. It laid her bare, then peeled away layers of her soul. It burned like acid, froze like ice. It peeled her, layer upon layer, until nothing else remained. Skins of serpents, drifting shells, the body and blood and mind of Miriam, floating through this awesome Void. What else remained?

Miriam remained.

She felt fear. The fear crawled through her soul like lice. Fear of obliteration. Fear of pain. Fear of madness.

Madness gibbered at the edges of her mind, gnawing like rats in a cellar. Her thoughts became distorted, blurred. She watched convoluted patterns whirl in space, heard the night sounds and the bats' cry and the wail of sorrow.

She must hold on.

So easy to give in.

She must hold on.

The demon showed her visions of the future and she knew them to be true. She saw the children tortured in the rabbi's name. She saw divine power called down in a blessing on the great machines of war. She saw suffering and death, terror, horror, blood, twisted bodies, deformed babies. She saw the world itself catch fire.

The rabbi's gift, the Darkness said.

If she released her hold, she would find peace. The whirling, writhing pressures would depart to let her rest.

She wanted rest, but she endured.

The shrieking, gibbering, singing maelstrom swirled about her, swept within her, washed her, bathed her, took her and infested her. Yet somewhere deep within her soul, alone and helpless, isolated in the outermost reaches of this hellish cosmos, Miriam endured.

And suddenly it stopped. . . .

She was in the cave, the rabbi's tomb. She felt weak. Her body ached and trembled. Sounds seemed distorted, far away. Her eyes could not quite focus. Yet she was clean. She felt the sweet, pure balm in every fiber. The demon had departed. The thing of slime and foulness was no more. She had fought it in her terror and her weakness. She had challenged it to take the innermost kernel of her soul. She had endured against the awesome power of Shaitan. She had won!

"Miriam."

The voice of Judas. She felt so weak and yet she smiled. The loving, warming voice of Judas. But she did not turn toward him. She looked instead toward the rabbi and heard the gentle sweetness of the Lord's song.

Her arms fell and she dropped the stake. All was becoming clearer now. The outlines of the cavern, the crouching bulk of Benjamin, the flickering lamplight that picked out the still form on the winding sheet. No breath, no warmth, no movement, yet . . .

She looked again at Benjamin. "The rabbi," she asked gently. "Is he truly dead?"

ϚEPILOGUE

The pretty little slave reached out to dab an errant orange pip away from the Governor's chin. Pontius stared thoughtfully toward the closing door. "What do you make of that now, Corax?"

Corax turned toward him blankly. "A predictable enough development, in my opinion, noble Pontius. Religious movements are like fungi—they tend to flourish best in the most disgusting environments. And all they need to start is a single, tiny spore."

Pontius shook his head. "I should not have thought the rabbi would have generated such a following. I don't believe he even knew much sorcery, you know."

"Ah," Corax said, "but he is no longer a simple rabbi, or even a simple sorcerer. When we killed him—as the mob believes—we transformed him into a much more potent personage altogether. We made him a martyr. People will always follow martyrs. It is so much more preferable to becoming one themselves."

Pontius sat silent, thinking of the report he had just heard delivered. There seemed to be so many reports of the rabbi's followers these days. It was beginning to look as if they might soon outshine the Zealots. Fortunately they had not the Zealots' habit of ambushing Roman soldiers.

Eventually he asked, "What do you make of the rumors that he has risen from the dead?"

Corax reached out for his second bunch of grapes. "Dear boy," he said, "these Jews would tell you anything."

255